The Mi Series

Book 1

Either Side of
Midnight

Tori de Clare

Dedicated to those I love most. You know who you are. Everything I do is for you, including the writing of this book.

You provide all the inspiration I've ever needed.

In memory of my dad who died when I was 18. He aspired to having a book published. This book is a tribute to him, and to my mum who taught me to play the piano.

Acknowledgements

Authors give birth to their books. An idea is conceived, then nurtured and developed with care and imagination over many months. It is an intense labour of love. Sleep-disturbing, painful, joyful. Compulsive. Successful completion (at least for me) depends upon the support and encouragement of family and good friends. I'm blessed with both. To those who read this work in its adolescence, thanks so much. Your feedback was invaluable. Without you, this story might have sat idle on my computer for ever. To Deb, my author friend, my partner in hot chocolate and chat, and not crime – your insight and help has always made all the difference. Your creativity never fails to stimulate me.

No part of this work may be reproduced, electronically transmitted or photocopied in any way or by any means without the express permission of the author and publisher

Either Side of Midnight

Tori de Clare

1

Just another Saturday evening close to the end of September and a young woman, eyes smarting with soap, stepped out of a shower on the second floor of a generic hotel situated a mile and a half from Manchester Airport. The shower continued to dribble long after it had been shut off. The water pressure, ever shifting, had flashed hot then cold, an unforgiving cycle that had scalded and chilled her in equal measures, forcing an early exit while soap suds slid down her skin.

She twisted her hair inside a towel, turban style, half dried herself, then, body still damp, wrestled her way into some flimsy white underwear that she'd bought but never tried on. Anxious to see herself, she stood in front of the mirror only to discover a screen of mist. She lunged at it with her left hand, swiping at the steam, aware of the weight of the new ring on her fourth finger. Her engagement ring was stacked on top of it. A miniature tower of platinum with a diamond turret. Her finger felt constricted inside the metal, squeezed, the flesh being asked to assume an unnatural shape.

When she stepped back and studied what she saw, a stranger glared back at her, hazy vapours circling her head. A stranger with searching eyes, slender legs and the toned body of a late teenager who'd never had to concern herself with calories or gyms. A 19-year-old who'd been home-schooled, cajoled, pushed and protected, and highly trained in one specific field. Music. One of those rare super-smart types, too busy filling expectations to give a crap about Instagram or Snapchat.

She really wasn't sure about the transparent underwear she had on. Over the top? Maybe. She knew more about *sonata form* than silk. But curiosity was igniting fizzy fireworks inside her belly and a path of exploration and discovery lay just beyond the bathroom door. Still, they stood, Naomi and this stranger in the mirror, unmoving, regarding each other warily. Naomi Hamilton had woken up as a girl that morning, but the stranger scrutinising her was called Naomi Stone now, which might mean that she was looking at a woman. She wasn't ready to be a woman, not at nineteen. So weird to wake up as a girl, a Hamilton, and go to bed as, and with, someone else.

These thoughts pinned her to the bath mat beneath her feet. Just about everything she'd done today had been a first for her so the entire day had held a surreal quality. Colours had appeared more vivid, sounds more penetrating and distinct. It was the newness and novelty of it all that seemed to transform even familiar things. She'd never worn a blue garter before today. Never had flowers woven into her hair or had her arms pattern with goose bumps at the sound of an organ. She'd never worn a veil over her face or spoken at the front of a church. She'd never missed her twin as much as she did today. A twin, yes. Annabel. Nonidentical in the extreme. Her twin's not dead. She's spending a gap year in Japan, that's all. Naomi understands Annabel's reasons for dodging the wedding, but it hasn't prevented the stabs of disappointment that have knifed her randomly throughout the day.

The twins were born either side of midnight, so they've never even shared a birthday. They don't look like sisters and have few interests in common. Their lives are polar opposites. None of that matters to them. They have a bond that only twins can understand and Naomi wished more than anything that Annabel had made it home today.

She reclaimed herself from the pull of the girl-woman in the mirror and lifted her black travel bag, dumping it gracelessly on the edge of the bath. She lifted out a white silk robe which was thigh-length and, like the underwear, new and unworn. Arms inside the sleeves, she tied the belt and watched herself again, all the while sensing Nathan's impatience through the stillness. She'd been too long. Adrenaline was prodding her to exit the bathroom and join him now, but she was stalling for some ghostly reason that was shifting round the edges of her consciousness.

She ripped the turban from her head and shook her hair until it fell in dark snakelike strips, waist length. She was buying time. Only when she fingered her throat vacantly did she finally realise what was troubling her. Her necklace. So obvious now it had come to her. It was a gift from Lorie on her twelfth birthday and, until this morning, she'd never taken it off. It was a slim gold chain with a cross that she never intended to take off, even today. But she'd had to swallow and then stomach a nauseating truth: that weddings come with obligations to please other people. Who? Didn't matter who – just people! She'd assumed, stupidly, that it was *her* day. Well, no! Long story short, she'd ended up swapping her treasured necklace for a row of pearls and diamonds – some family heirloom that was arguably ugly. She'd never asked her mum to dig the thing out of the loft and impart some speech about her grandmother, but that's what happened. Lorie's eyes urged Naomi to take it, so she took it and wore it. Old, new, borrowed, blue. Two ticks from that list in one necklace. As if Naomi cared. It was her mother who lived by lists, not Naomi.

Time was sliding. She told herself to move, to locate the necklace and put it on so she could begin to feel like *her* again. It was in a floral bag with a string-pull top beside a bottle of perfume and the bag wasn't anywhere in sight. No hiding places in here. She'd brought it in the black travel bag, but . . .

. . . Troubled now, she returned to the bag. Laid carefully in the bottom was an outfit for the morning and clean underwear, nothing else. Confused, she scanned the room. The floor was clear but for one shampoo sachet and scraps of confetti. Her wedding dress filled the door. She heaved it roughly to one side, past caring if it fell. It didn't, but the floral bag wasn't underneath.

It was missing. *Missing*. The word burned into her head and froze her limbs. Only her mind was in motion now, drawing a linear account of the day. Much of it was a blur, but she found she could sketch the previous hour easily enough.

There'd been a small gathering in front of the restaurant as they drove away, Nathan at the wheel. Her mum, unsmiling, managed a stilted wave of her hand as they left. The black bag, half unzipped, was pushed up against Naomi's feet, passenger side. The floral bag was slouched lazily on top.

During the short drive, Nathan chatted, touched her legs, played with the fingers of her right hand. When he finally used both hands to steer the car through the hotel car park and nose the bonnet against a row of bushes, Naomi released her belt and sifted through her bag for a polythene sleeve that held the hotel and flight booking information and their passports. So there were only two possibilities: either the floral bag had tipped onto the car floor or had been dropped in the hotel grounds. The second scenario was unsettling. And unlikely. Large bottle of perfume. She was certain she'd have heard the drop.

What happened next? Oh, Nathan appeared at the passenger door and opened it. His grin was ear-to-ear. He grabbed her coat and bag, and then his from the back seat, just the few items they'd need for the hours before the flight. Nathan hoisted one bag over each shoulder then pulled Naomi out of the car, taking care not to catch her dress. He held her hand, found a gap between the bushes and led her along the path that skirted the building. They checked in, took the lift to the second floor and stepped onto the corridor where the silence was somehow heavy and seductive. Despite the bags, Nathan lifted her into his arms and walked, without speaking, to room 209.

The door opened onto a dark room washed in shadows. Nathan closed the door with one foot and set Naomi down. A tall featureless shape in the gloom, he pressed her to the nearest wall. His scent was familiar and inviting, hands hot around her neck, breaths shallow, pulse alive, stubble a little rough against her face. He kissed her, tenderly then urgently. It wasn't the time for talking, she knew that. But her plans had included a shower, a squirt of perfume, the new underwear she'd bought especially. And, of course, her necklace. She needed that. Just didn't feel ready for what he was doing. The speed of things. So when his lips lowered to her neck, she spilled her thoughts and begged a little time. Nathan sighed, closed his eyes, said fine, whatever, please be quick. Except it was all going wrong. Her floral bag had vanished and the thought had disturbed a fleet of butterflies inside her chest.

A light patter on the bathroom door reminded her that she had a husband. *A husband!* Without words it also said time was up.

'Just coming,' Naomi called. So now she'd better go. Ready or not.

Nathan didn't reply, but she knew he'd crossed the room when the bed groaned beneath his weight. The temperature sharply dropped as she left the bathroom in her flimsy bra and pants beneath her white gown. Without her necklace, she just felt naked. Within a few silent strides she was looking at the room for the first time, and at Nathan lying on the bed wearing only the dark trousers of his wedding suit. With a vertically arranged pillow behind him, he was half sitting up, ankles crossed, one arm jammed behind his head.

'Whoa!'

His eyes roamed over her. He wet his lips and extended a hand. Naomi padded forward and placed a palm in his.

'What took so long?' He pulled at the belt on her gown until it loosened and the gown gaped open. He paused to appreciate the view. 'Wow. I mean, worth it, but . . . are you OK?'

He wasn't looking at her eyes or he might have spotted the worry in them. He was weighing her scanty underwear. Her legs. She stood, enjoying the way he was examining her. The look on his face. It induced weakness, excitement, anticipation, a cocktail of feelings all at once. When she didn't speak, his eyes returned to hers.

'You're not nervous?'

'No.' A pause. 'Maybe a bit. But it isn't that.'

'What's wrong?'

'I've lost my necklace.'

He focussed on her eyes. 'Which one?'

'*The* necklace. My cross.' His answering nod said, Oh, *the* necklace! 'I had it in the car. It was definitely in my bag, but now it's gone.'

'Things don't just vanish. Hey,' he squeezed her hand, 'don't worry, we'll find it. It's weird seeing you without it.' He smiled. She knew he wasn't understanding her attachment to it. How sick she was feeling at the thought of not see it again. The way her imagination was running away. 'Are you going to stand there all night?'

'Shall I turn the light off?'

He laughed. 'No way! I'm not about to imagine you in the dark.' He tugged on her hand. 'Come here.'

Naomi sat carefully down and lowered herself until the back of her head was resting against Nathan's stomach. She twisted her neck to look at him, at his hair, mid-brown, short and teased into shape, his blue-grey eyes and strong bone structure, the slight cleft in his chin. While he plunged his fingers inside her hair and massaged her scalp, Naomi reached for her necklace through habit and found bare skin.

'Today's been surreal,' she said. Nathan nodded in agreement. 'Like watching everything from a distance. A bit like a dream.'

Nathan leant forward which hardened his stomach, forcing Naomi to sit up too. He wanted to be closer. To touch her face.

'Agreed.' His eyelids were folding. He pulled her so close that he slipped out of focus. Naomi's eyes were closing too. 'But in my favourite dreams, we're not in a cold church chanting vows.' He cupped her neck in one hand, making gentle contact with her lips. It was the sort of kiss that was going nowhere and she knew that there was something. Nathan pulled back to look at her.

'You haven't noticed the bed?' Frankly, she was struggling to notice anything with her necklace gone.

'What about it?'

'Hard as hell,' he said. 'And it creaks. I swear the pillows are orthopaedic.'

Naomi chuckled. 'You haven't tried the shower!'

He rolled his eyes. 'I'm seriously regretting staying here tonight.'

OK, granted, the room was a bog-standard double. Very average. They were off to the Caribbean to stay in a luxurious beach villa for a week, and then cruising the islands for another week. It was all they'd thought about, talked about for months. Nathan had never talked about sleeping. Not tonight.

'Why didn't we book something better for tonight? Bit short-sighted, wasn't it?' Nathan said.

'We'll be out of here in hours.'

'Exactly. By tomorrow night we'll be in an exotic pad with a four-poster bed and our own patch of private beach.'

'I can't wait.'

He secured her in his arms. 'While you took an age in that bathroom, my brain started working again. Look, no promises, but I reckon I can wait one more night if you want me to.' He pulled back to gauge her reaction, his jawline twitching with tension.

Naomi collapsed into a smile. 'No way!'

'I wanted this to be special for you and we've got planes roaring past the window and the sodding bed's made of rock.' Nathan leant forward and kissed her forehead. She tucked her face beneath his chin and inhaled the fragrance on his neck, a subtle mixture of aftershave and a scent that was uniquely his. The tremor of a pulse in his neck, quivered against her cheek. The only sound was the whisper of silk as his hand brushed up and down her back. 'I'm serious. If you want to wait . . .'

She'd tell him to get real soon. The thought of spending the night waiting, resisting . . . no! Too much of that already. At the same time it was as though her necklace had a voice that was more insistent than Nathan's.

'So?' Nathan pressed. She'd forgotten there was a question. In that moment she reached a snap decision. She had to act.

'Course I don't want to wait.'

He panted in relief and his face brightened up. 'Sure?'

'Nathan, I'm looking forward to this as much as you are.'

He moved to kiss her again. 'Impossible.'

She blocked him, pressed her fingers to his lips. 'I have to do something . . .'

Naomi unravelled herself from Nathan and hurried to the chair beside the bed. Her short raincoat was draped over the arm of the chair. It felt heavy when she lifted it. Nathan slowly sat up to watch her as she slid out of the robe and into her coat. She roughly folded it across her chest and tied the belt at the waist. Nathan looked intrigued.

'Is this a game, like dressing up or something?'

She was about to disappoint him. 'No game. Look, I have to find my necklace.'

His forehead creased. 'What, now? I thought you wanted to –'

'Sorry. I can't concentrate. It's priceless to me and I'm scared we might have dropped it on the way up here. Give me a couple of minutes, would you? Then you'll have my full attention. I promise I'll be quick.'

Her wedding shoes were tucked beneath the chair. She pressed her feet inside them.

On the bed, Nathan was twitching with disbelief. Naomi felt a flush of guilt, but she was just about ready to leave. 'Slow down would you? If you want it that badly, I'll get it for you. Let me cool off a minute and find a top. My shoes are –'

'By the time you've found them I can be back.'

'No, Naims.' Nathan's eyes scanned the room. 'I've got a T-shirt in my bag.' He swung his legs onto the floor.

'Don't be so macho,' she said, collecting the keys from the dressing table. 'Besides, I prefer you without your top.' Naomi scurried to the bed, dropped a kiss on his head and shook free of his hand when he tried to take hold of it. She bolted for the door. 'You're adorable when you're frustrated. Keep the bed warm.'

Nathan started to say something that was stolen by the closing door. Naomi trotted along the empty hotel corridor towards a door that was half wood, half glass. A weight was bashing against her right leg which turned out to be her phone. She withdrew it just as Nathan shouted from behind.

'Naims!'

She turned. The naked top half of him was curled around the doorframe. She laughed, held up her phone, signalled for him to stop shouting.

'Call me,' she mouthed, and Nathan vanished inside the room.

Beyond the heavy door was a staircase and a lift. The stairs were tempting. She wanted to keep on the move, but she was determined to retrace her steps. She summoned the lift. The doors opened immediately and she darted inside. Empty. She pressed for the ground floor and it touched down seconds later. As the doors slipped open, her phone vibrated in her hand.

'Missing me already?'

'What do *you* think? I'm coming with you.'

'No need.'

'No arguments.'

'You'll have to catch me up,' she said, playfully.

'I will. I've found my top and I'm just putting my shoes on. Where are you now?'

Near the reception desk. She gave him a running commentary, glancing, as she did, at her new wedding band. She'd soon get used to the feel and weight of it.

'I'm almost out of the building.'

'I'm just leaving the room,' Nathan shot into her right ear.

She crossed in front of a mahogany reception desk and switched the phone to her other ear.

'You're fussing like my mother, Nathan,' she said, enjoying the game far more than her frustrated voice implied. 'I'm a big girl now.'

'So I've just seen.'

Naomi giggled into her phone while Nathan chuckled in her ear.

An ash-blonde receptionist caught her eye from behind the desk. Naomi radiated some warmth in her direction because she was gushing with it, but hassled and busy, the receptionist didn't reciprocate. Naomi really didn't care. The magic of tonight meant blocking everyone else out of it, with absolute relish.

'You're stalking me,' she continued, forgetting the frosty blonde.

'Too right, Mrs Stone. I'm trying to drag you back to bed.'

'Drag me hey? I might not resist.' She had no problem slipping into a quiet throaty voice. She felt like an actress, absorbed in her role.

'I like the sound of that.'

The carpet gave way to a strip of black tiles leading to the glass front doors. The doors slid open and cool air hit bare legs and penetrated her thin coat in seconds. The September sky was fully black and the moon was half-hidden behind spectral grey cloud that brought images of her wedding veil. Colours from the sunset were dissolving in the west.

'You're panting, Nathan.'

'Because I'm charging down the stairs after a mad woman who prefers necklaces to sex.'

'You sound unfit. I'm wondering if you have enough stamina for the next fortnight.'

'After months of deprivation? Only question is, will you keep up with me?'

'I like my chances.'

Her heels clomped loudly against the stone path. She was hurrying along, liberated, almost skipping in the shadows, the hotel wall to her left. She was keenly scanning the ground for her floral bag now and seeing no trace of it. The car floor was the best hope. If the search yielded nothing, plan B was to ask Frosty Receptionist if it'd been handed it in at the desk.

Naomi could see the car roof now. She raised the keys and the lights flashed to disable the car lock. The hotel wall turned the corner, but she ploughed on straight ahead. The car was just beyond a narrow path behind a row of severely clipped bushes.

'OK, I'm virtually there –'

A figure darted from the bushes. Someone big. Dark clothes. Balaclava. He lunged at her before she could react or yell. Shock had snatched her voice. She dropped the keys and meant to scream, but it stuck in her throat. Her legs turned to water, so now she was lame as well as mute. Her phone was torn from her fingers. It clattered and skidded across the concrete. Something fluffy smothered her head. One hand gripped her from behind and something sharp dug into her side. All happened at lightning speed. Nathan's voice was on the ground, pouring from her phone, wherever it was. He was repeating her name over and over and her voice had gone.

'Don't scream.' The voice was deep.

She didn't because she couldn't, but she gasped and tried to pull away from the blade. He held her tight. Her heart had become a wild animal that was leaping around inside her chest. She was forced to keep moving. Her legs trembled with the weight of her. The point of the blade cut through her coat. It was against her bare skin, scratching then tearing. A gush of warm fluid slipped down her side. She expected a rush of pain which didn't arrive. She was forced to stumble along, blind, listening to her own breathing beneath what she guessed was a small blanket. Her brain was fighting to keep up. She had to unscramble it and think. A car door opened and the knife withdrew. Naomi's wrists were slammed behind her back and bound with something sticky, and effective.

Nathan was yelling desperately now. Not through the phone – his actual voice, calling out to her in the distance, getting closer. *Think, think.* Her head was pushed down. Reason had abandoned her. She saw shadows across the car park floor. The light was poor, but she caught sight of a white trainer behind her. It was a no-brainer, which was just as well when her brain had ceased to work. She raised her right heel and stabbed down hard.

He shouted out and, suddenly, she was free. She darted forward. Freedom lasted four steps. Strong hands snatched her arms, flipped her around, lifted her off her feet and flung her over a broad shoulder. The blanket tumbled down his back and was trapped between them. She could see Nathan sprinting along the path. She kicked wildly and found her voice. Arms constricted like a python around her legs, securing her more tightly.

'If you want to live, don't struggle.'

She struggled harder. Nathan yelled, hysteria in his voice. 'Naomi.'

'Nathan. Help. Help me.' Her voice was disappointingly weak, panic strangling the sound as she hung upside down. Her stomach wretched and her diaphragm heaved out one final word. 'Nathan!' A guttural, desperate plea, the last-ditch attempt to reach him. He was yelling too, but she knew he wouldn't reach her in time.

All her muscles squirmed for freedom. Biting him occurred to her too late. Naomi was thrown down. Her head crashed against something solid. She thought her arms might snap. The screaming of her name grew louder before the door slammed shut, compressing her into darkness.

A delay, and then the pain hit like a falling axe – an explosion in her head and a searing current down both arms. She lay still, chanting Nathan's name over and over. The sound wasn't carrying. She'd been hurled into a vacuum. An engine ignited. The faint smell of petrol and stiff carpets registered somewhere. She heard Nathan shouting and thrashed around, clawing to sit up. Space was too tight.

They'd left Nathan's voice behind. The car was moving now, screeching around sharp corners, jerking her with it, bouncing her whole weight onto her arms with her right wrist jammed into her lower back. Another car was close behind. Nathan? How? She dropped the keys, she remembered now. This sparked an ember of hope.

Without the use of her arms, it was an effort not to bash her head. Her cramped legs pushed against the solid mass in front of her and she stiffened, concentrating on protecting her head. Nathan was still pursuing. Naomi was panting, which was sending her lightheaded. Only when it dawned on her that she was in the boot of a car did she feel herself slipping from consciousness. She clung on, afraid to let go. The claustrophobic darkness felt tangible. It was pressing on every part of her like she was cocooned in a womb. The moisture evaporated from her mouth until she couldn't swallow.

She shuffled onto her side and scrambled for breath, but the harder she inhaled, the more the blackness squeezed tight. *If you want to live, don't struggle. If you want to live, don't struggle.* The words ran through her mind in *his* voice until her head finally caught up.

She recognised the voice.

The realisation was a violent blow that made her dizzy. Her fight slunk away, leaving her in the grip of nausea – great menacing fingers that reached down her throat and raked over her stomach, before her brain, mercifully, shut down.

2

She came round, didn't know where she was, but knew she was afraid to move. Her body was juddering with constant movement. Her arms ached and her head hurt. Something scratchy was grazing her cheek on one side. She opened her eyes, closed them, opened them again, wide. The darkness was as dense either way and she was blind. Naomi frantically blinked her eyelids up and down. Made no difference. The blackness was without layers or texture and didn't improve with time.

So she lay still, resisting a full-on panic, listening to her breathing, feeling the warmth of her own snatched breaths against her face. The stale air had nowhere to go. Her stomach was off, rotten, a toxic mixture of car sickness and terror. The hum of the car engine was constant. Her brain raced to make sense of things and her memory tossed up a tussle with a stranger and a knife. She tried to sit up, a reflex action. Soon realised that she couldn't. Out of options, she quit struggling and focussed instead on breathing and not vomiting.

Her legs were free, so she groped about with her feet, connecting with her small parameters, confirming all over again that she was trapped and definitely not dreaming.

The car moved swiftly and smoothly for an eternity. She daren't imagine the fresh air outside because the next stop could be Scotland for all she knew. And it was the not knowing! It was impossible to tell how fast they were travelling and if Nathan was still following. Her senses were heightened. She knew this even though she was blind. She was super aware of every sound and feeling in her body. The seconds were crawling and seemed to have divided into micro moments. Each one was dragging like she'd never known. She was measuring time in milliseconds now. Her music training, this. Counting time was what she did. Music was like this – not only divided into beats per bar, but half beats, quarter beats, eighths, sixteenths and smaller. A sound track flooded her mind. Some messed-up Stravinsky, no comfort at all. She wished she could switch if off and clear her head in order to concentrate. To work out how the hell to escape.

She was lying curled up on her side. As she started to shift around, she realised that her body was yelling at her. Her arms and wrists wanted freedom. Her legs needed room to stretch. Her head was screaming for painkillers. Her stomach was begging her to be still. Her lungs were demanding air. Close to panic, she knew the key was to stay calm and focus on breathing, one ragged breath at a time.

Her mouth watered and she was forced to swallow her spit. *Don't vomit. Please, no.* She closed her eyes pointlessly until the loathsome feeling subsided, then slowly sloped away. Now she moved her attention to the car and to what was happening outside. They'd slowed and were trundling along in no rush, no urgency at all. Sounded as though they were in a steady traffic flow. The car was working down the gears then speeding up again. He was driving normally to deflect attention. This could only mean they'd lost Nathan. A bubble of panic rose and expanded in her chest until her lungs couldn't fill with air.

Calming herself took time. *Think, Naomi.* She couldn't have been out for long. Nathan must be trailing somewhere close. There was shouting outside, then laughter, inducing another droplet of hope. A possibility, however unlikely. Naomi squeezed her brain, imagining the scene she couldn't see outside: regular street, traffic lights, shops or houses, pubs, people ambling along dressed up for a Saturday night. What time was it? Maybe nine? Nine-thirty? Instinctively, she raised her legs and pounded hard against the lid. The volume was encouraging. She gave it all she had and he responded with an explosion of sound. The throbbing pulse of dance music, the Ibiza nightclub type, was thumping at the tempo of her heartbeat.

Above it, a siren was growing. Naomi stopped kicking and listened. The music dropped but didn't stop. The siren was drawing closer, the sound swelling every second. There was more than one siren. Snatching her chance, she resumed her kicking campaign, adding her voice, yelling for help. The sirens closed in until she couldn't hear herself anymore. A cacophony of noise, but it was as soothing as a symphony right now. She could almost taste fresh air and freedom. The car wasn't fleeing, it was slowing down. Even blind, she was picturing Nathan with the police, or maybe following in his car. They pulled over and stopped. Her muscles slackened. She drew a couple of shallow breaths as the wailing sirens caught up. Time held still. She found she was holding her breath. Bad idea. She inhaled again and realised in that moment that the sirens had screeched past. She wasn't the focus of the emergency. They weren't stopping.

'No,' she screamed, panting. 'Nooooooo.' The defeat was crushing. She fought back with her legs. The final hope was only a thread – strangers outside. The music pumped up again to counter her efforts. She adjusted her position and stiffened to brace her head, jabbing upwards, her legs working to stab the prison roof.

This is what it must feel like to be buried alive.

The car moved off, slowly at first. Picked up speed until it was cruising along a straight road. The worry of injuring her head was replaced by the dread of the car not stopping again. The thought of heading out of the city towards quieter roads injected her legs with more strength. If only she could pierce the lid and create some air holes.

The car stopped only once more. Traffic lights, she guessed. After a few minutes of driving non-stop and no sign of life outside, she gave up and lay motionless, breathless, beaten. They were still on a straight course following an endless road without bends that was taking her further from Nathan every hampered breath. Maybe death lay at the end of it. Death. A little word, loaded with menace. *Don't go there.* She shuffled onto her side again and wriggled, trying to shake the word away and loosen the tightness around her wrists. The aching in her arms has progressed to pain. Relaxing might help. Yeah right!

How the hell did I land up here?

Naomi visualised Nathan, frantic, searching the roads. She thought about her parents too, oblivious, making their way home from the reception, her mum flooding Henry with a tide of complaints. And Henry, patient at the wheel in his driving gloves, absorbing the words, consoling himself that at least he had a Rolls-Royce.

The car turned and slowed to normal street speed. Naomi sensed no life outside, no people or cars. Instead she pictured a hushed unlit lane lined with colourless swaying trees and open fields beyond them, beneath the gaze of a drowsy moon. And animals scurrying around, hunting, dicing with their lives to cross a narrow road. The unlucky one in a hundred would be splattered then pecked to nothing. The food chain would go on. Maybe she'd become part of it, mutilated, dumped, a banquet to whatever roamed the English countryside after dark.

'Stop it,' she muttered, clearing her head, realising that the person driving the car was more of a threat than anything outside. 'Think.'

She couldn't think! Couldn't move past the painful division of her life in a heartbeat. Why hadn't she listen to Nathan? Or waited for him? Why had she left the hotel at all? *Because I'm stupid, that's why. Stupid, stupid. And superstitious.* Weird to think that she could actually suffer death by supreme stupidity. She even had the time to think about that right now, to consider what she'd done. No second chances. She could cry, like really howl, but what was the use? Childhood had hammered into her that tears change nothing.

The car slowed, swung into a left, and then another. It was rattling along a road with loose stones which were spraying the underneath of the car. Naomi sensed the end of the journey and started to fantasise about breathing freely. Outside was deathly quiet. She guessed that kicking would be futile now. *Save energy.* Her eyes were open wide. She saw only blackness and breathed in the dense air that felt low in oxygen – levels at critical. Like being at the bottom of an ocean with a near-empty oxygen tank. Naomi was afraid of deep water. Couldn't swim, so the comparison didn't help. The car slowed again and the air only seemed to thin. The promise of breathing fresh air was all she could think about now, overriding the thought of facing whoever was at the wheel.

The car stopped. The engine coughed, then died. Silence. *Fresh air. Let me breathe.* Suddenly her dying wish was to inhale some air. Just that. Nothing moved. Seconds slithered by, became a minute, then two. Still counting. Compressed into darkness, she felt each beat and all the subdivisions. Nothing stirred and she felt close to meltdown.

Each breath was more difficult than the last. Speaking would cost too much energy, but she was losing control. Desperation does that.

'Let me out. Please. Let me out.' She paused to inhale the silence and snatch what oxygen there was. 'Let. Me. Out.' The sound was diminishing with each word, panic taking hold again. Maybe God wasn't so deaf.

'Dear God, please help me. Get me out of here and I promise –'

The boot opened. She hadn't heard the approach. She promptly stopped speaking. Her eyes squinted a bit then focussed on the figure in front of her in the dull light. Chilly air rushed in. She drank it in frantic gulps.

The figure, still wearing a balaclava, reached forward and grasped her arms. Even in a semi-lucid state, she knew she should take in what she could. Her instincts booted up. She scribbled some mental notes. He was tall and slim. And strong. Maybe six-one, six-two, long fingers, clean nails, nothing rough. He was wearing jeans and a dark top behind a black jacket, not fastened. The top had some words she couldn't make sense of and he mustn't catch her staring. He hauled her out. She was light-headed. This had better not be a toilet stop because she couldn't face that boot . . .

'On your feet.'

The familiarity of the voice was there again. She couldn't place it. She noticed the white trainer that should have white laces. The dark smear must be blood. He followed her eyes.

'Don't try that again. And don't scream or I will use this,' he said, matter-of-factly. He dragged his jacket to one side A gun was wedged down his jeans, just like Hollywood. The sight of it was a relief, oddly! Shot, or raped and brutally murdered? She'd take the bullet every time, goad him to use the gun if necessary.

By now she was standing, her eyes scanning anything worth noting, freezing the scene in her head, hideously conscious that her coat had fallen open. It was torn and stained heavily down one side. Come to think of it, her waist stung on the same side. The belt was impotent. She had no hands to cover herself and he was watching her through the two narrow slits. With no hope of deciphering the colour of his eyes, the blanket was flung over her head again. Naomi recovered her mental notes, snatched urgently in passing. They consisted only of a dim, deserted lane, no houses, a single parked car about twenty metres away, and two huge wrought iron gates in the opposite direction attached to a high stone wall either side. There were trees too. Yes, lots of trees just as she'd imagined. Crispy leaves rustled in a cool breeze. The air smelt smoky, but it was air all the same. She continued to inhale it greedily.

She couldn't see anything without looking at the ground. The blanket was short, but hung to thigh-length. It partly covered her at least, shielding her from the wind. Her right arm was seized above her elbow and she was towed along in the opposite direction to the gates. Exposed as she was, she tried to lag a pace behind. They were walking along a stony path until he switched course and crossed a strip of earth where it became too dark to see at all. The anticipation weighed on her and the fear seeped in.

'Don't hurt me,' Naomi begged, loathing her choice of words, her tone of voice. Cliched. Weak. Pathetic. 'I got married today. Please. My parents have money. You can call them.'

Apart from growling, 'Save it,' the reaction was about zero. So she stopped babbling and allowed herself to be dragged along in heels, balance compromised from losing the use of her arms.

He stopped and pulled her in front of a low stone wall that she could see beneath the blanket. He ripped the blanket away and at eye-level was a broken railing, and beyond this, bushes.

'After you,' he said, hoisting her off the ground, instructing her to go feet first. Without the use of her arms she couldn't have managed alone. He stopped assisting when he'd steered her into a sitting position inside the bars. 'Slide down,' he said, nudging her back. He seemed to have firm purpose here in this place and Naomi sensed he was in a hurry.

She could do nothing but obey. The wall was less than a metre, she reckoned. She slid down, grazing her back, landing on broken twigs. There was no way of glimpsing through the dense bushes in front. He was through the bars in one movement and the blanket was back over Naomi's head and he was steering her sideways, to the right, until they emerged into better light and onto a path.

'Take your shoes off,' was the next command.

She hesitated then stepped out of them. A hand scooped them up. He was wearing a silver wristwatch which told her the time. Almost ten o'clock. They continued on, small stones digging into Naomi's feet. Mercifully there weren't many. The path was long and cold and straight. If they'd been heading for a house they'd have reached one by now.

'Where are we going?'

'Don't speak,' was his comfortless answer, said with no emotion, tone almost robotic.

There was nothing left to say. The machine by her side was programmed and couldn't be swayed. She sensed it as instinctively as she suspected that something dreadful was about to happen. Out of options, it was pointless to object. She was powerless and compliant. Didn't know what else to do. They continued the silent trek and her legs were shaking. The fear had invaded her so physically, she was struggling to coordinate movement. Her bladder could leak at any time.

Glimpsing snatches of the shadowy path Naomi stumbled on until he tugged her into a sharp left. Grass underfoot, suddenly. They were weaving between . . . what? Naomi's heart stalled when she caught sight of a stone slab rising from the grass. Comprehension took its time, then its toll. A headstone. A cemetery? Her legs failed. He yanked her to her feet and shoved her forward. She was shivering, her teeth bashing together. The need to speak overcame her again.

'Please. What's happening? Don't do this.'

'I said don't speak.'

Something sharp jabbed into her right arm near the top. Her first thought: *he's punched me*, until she realised she'd been injected. Clouds filled her mind and the cool air was losing its bite. Walking was becoming a chore. Her feet dragged. Her head was floating, reality becoming less clear. His voice pulled her back.

'Keep moving.' He was clawing her arm, roughly shaking her.

Naomi carried on with help, but she couldn't hold the weight of her head. Her chin rocked around on her chest. Her legs were becoming warm, numb. They stopped walking and the blanket was torn away. Her eyes adjusted. She forced herself to focus hard, lift her head a little. They'd stopped beside a graveside, loose piles of earth on each side. A huge arrangement of flowers sprawled out near my feet. The top half of a man was holding a spade, looking up at them from inside the hole. A sobering sight. He climbed out and jabbed the spade into the ground. He didn't speak but he stared Naomi up and down like she was dinner. Her inhibitions were melting, but she was clinging to her mind, the one thing they couldn't access.

'No,' she muttered, 'no, no, no.' The objections carried on, but she wasn't sure she was making sound. She was aware of pressure on her arms, supporting her. The tape was being unravelled behind her back. Her arms were free, and sore. She couldn't use them. Either they'd gone to sleep or detached from her body. The discomfort told her they were still attached. Her left hand was grabbed, which sharpened her senses again. Her rings were being ripped from her finger and a hand was trawling up and down her thigh.

'No,' she objected, without real conviction. 'Please. Nathan. No.' Sentences wouldn't form.

'I think she wants a man,' said the one closest to her – the guy who climbed out of the ground. His breath was sour.

'No time,' said the other.

'Give me a break.'

'I said no time.'

'Just let me –'

'Put her in,' said the guy who stole her, insistent and commanding now. She was floating again, relieved to be free. Oblivion was calling, but a nagging voice in her head was warning her to hang on, to latch on to the men, the cemetery. What they were doing. Preservation, see. She wanted to live. She *had* to live. She had a husband now, a family . . .

Naomi must have drifted. Things had shunted forward. She was lying on a hard surface in a deep pit. It was as chilly as a fridge. Someone was looming over her. Behind him, the moon was a lopsided white ball with a misty halo. A few stars peeked out, barely daring to look. Her head wouldn't move, but her eyes rolled just enough to focus on the man in the mask and watch him withdraw his gun. He stepped down until his feet were touching her legs, and crouched.

'Check we're alone,' she heard.

She couldn't speak, couldn't object, couldn't move a muscle besides her eyes. It was an effort to keep them open. Her eyelids gave up and folded. She felt something hard and cold against her head close to her eye and heard the gun fire, a deafening sound that rattled her brain but couldn't rouse her muscles. She was paralysed. Another shot. Her face was wet. Something warm was slithering across her eye, down one cheek. A long pause. Fingers dug into her neck.

'That's it, she's dead. Check.'

No reply. Naomi had been pronounced dead by the man with the recognisable voice. She heard it, which could only mean one thing: she wasn't dead. She heard a zip then felt herself being constricted inside something as the zip stopped near her neck.

Through a mental fog, she clung on. She needed to scream, warn them she was conscious. *That's it, she's dead.* The words echoed in her head as if they were bouncing around an empty room. They couldn't get out. There was no door. They weren't true. She had to tell someone they weren't true. She wanted them to be true when she felt the weight of something heavy being hurled at her legs. Something was crushing her. She was losing her battle with consciousness. She loved Nathan, but that wasn't her final thought.

Buried alive.

Through closed eyes, she saw a blaze of white light. The zip roared past her face.

3

Alderley Edge, 2.

Miles, that is. Henry and Camilla Hamilton passed a sign. Henry's fingers were sore from gripping the wheel, but the sign confirmed that they'd soon be home. It'd been a delightful day, but Henry wouldn't voice it to Camilla. Couldn't. Her impressions of today would become the official line between them; her perspective, their joint experience. Fury was seeping from her pores and filling the car. All day she'd worn a mask and cloaked her feelings, in fairness. But Henry knew the truth. She was in the passenger seat beside him now, tossing thoughts, looking out of a window that was as black as her mood, clutching the little handbag on her knee, watching colourless trees as they zipped by.

'Hardly what we imagined for our daughter, Henry, is it?' She paused, panted a couple of noisy breaths. He did wonder how long before her thoughts erupted. A matter of when, not if. Like hot lava, they'd always spewed out.

'Mm,' he muttered. An attempt to remain invisible. A virtual minefield was ahead and he was keen to avoid it. His only safety was in silence. Camilla was barely aware of him anyway. Once the lava was flowing, it'd harden into certainty and eventually she'd burn out. Offering an opinion was to walk into that minefield. To disagree was to step onto a detonator. She wasn't looking for answers, or a discussion. She wanted only to talk, to assert her opinion and spin it into truth. Mounting a challenge was pointless and Henry knew it. Lesson learnt the hard way, multiple times.

'All that talent thrown away on that man.' She shook her head. 'What kind of a life will they have together? Nothing whatsoever in common.'

'Hmm.'

'He has no career path. No plans.' Camilla shook her head a second time and studied the view from the window. There was really nothing to see. 'Not a single person representing his family today. All wrong.'

She would speak like this, Camilla. It was the way she thought. In terms of absolutes. Right and wrong, black and white with no grey on the spectrum. Henry waited a moment in case there was more. 'Mm,' he growled.

'Did the best man look familiar to you, Henry?'

A benign question, at last. One he couldn't answer. He cleared his throat in preparation. 'Not in the least.'

'Dreadful speech. Crude and embarrassing,' she spat. 'And why Nathaniel didn't shave this morning . . . Must have been five days' growth on that smug face of his.'

Grasping the steering wheel was hurting Henry's hands. Thirty minutes was about his limit before griping pains would gnaw at his fingers. He'd been driving for thirty-five. He released the wheel one hand at a time and flexed his fingers inside his leather driving gloves. The movement caught Camilla's eye and she swung her head towards him. Henry suspected her eyes were emitting heat.

'Don't you think?'

Henry didn't understand the question. A teeny lapse of concentration and now she was testing him. Best and only policy, honesty. 'Sorry Camilla, my fingers have started to bother me. What was the question?'

'Your opinion on Nathaniel's facial hair,' she said slowly and deliberately as if he was a toddler. Her hands clapped loudly onto her thighs. 'You haven't been listening to a single thing I've said, have you?'

'Of course I have. No career, no family representation, no –'

'I hate it when you do that.'

'Do what?'

'List what I've just said.' Her tone was shrill. 'Only proves that you were hearing me, not that you were listening.'

'I can assure you I've been absorbing every word.'

She threw him a warning look which he collected out of his peripheral vision. She was upset. He got it. Sort of. Deep breaths and the storm might pass. Camilla shifted her gaze out of the window again.

Henry slowed, signalled to turn into the drive. The gates were open. He was pressing his palms against the steering wheel and wriggling his fingers constantly now.

'So,' Camilla said. She was having a stab at a calmer tone, but refusing to look his way, 'are we going to discuss the real problem, or not?'

He hesitated. 'Which is?'

'For goodness' sake!'

Henry could feel a knot of tension in his chest, but for his own reasons, he didn't retaliate. He was banking on an early night, not becoming tangled in a heated exchange that could lead to senseless hours of sleep deprivation. After wedding mania, life would resume tomorrow. With golf.

'I'm sorry, Camilla, I'm not with you.'

Camilla folded her arms and emptied her lungs. The air rode out without words, but nonetheless said, *Well, isn't that the truth*! Henry fed the steering wheel through his hands as they snaked down the tree-lined driveway. The house crept into view with the moon lying low and large right behind it. Apart from the dim glow of an outside light close to the front door, the house was lifeless, the windows blank. Camilla reached for the door handle and gripped her handbag.

'Read between the lines, would you. Apart from the fact that Naomi has just married beneath her, I'm disgusted that Annabel wasn't there.'

Here we go. 'That's understandable.' Henry stopped beside the front door.

'Yet you haven't mentioned her all day.' A direct accusation. 'Do I have to beg for information? Did she talk about coming, at any point?'

Henry lifted Camilla's hand and attempted a little squeeze. 'I didn't want to upset you by talking about her.'

She threw his hand back at him. 'Just yes or no?'

With some vague notion that eye contact might convey some sincerity, Henry finally turned his head and body towards Camilla. She was glaring at him, mouth in a tight line.

'Well no, she didn't intend to –'

'Right.' Camilla opened the door with one hand and plucked her key from her bag with the other.

She leapt from the car and viciously crashed the door shut. Henry winced, stroked the seat, watched Camilla's trim shape bob up the two steps and disappear inside the house. The car engine was purring, untroubled by Camilla's tone. He put her to bed in the garage, gently tucking her in with a dust sheet and the promise of a polish when he could. There was a light on in the en suite bathroom when he secured the garage door, in no tearing rush to get inside the house.

In the hall, he listened carefully, measuring his next move. Water was gushing from the shower. Henry was standing by the portrait that hung above the hall table. It could almost pass for a photograph. Naomi and Annabel smiled down in pretty dresses, aged twelve. Naomi was wearing her new necklace. Her hair and eyes were dark. Strange to think that she'd never call this place home again. Annabel had blonde hair, blue eyes. No twins had ever been less alike, but both girls were so beautiful in their way. Their eyes spoke of their friendship, their differences that didn't matter, their uncomplicated lives.

That was then.

***

On the green on a glorious morning, Henry was swiping the ground furiously with his golf club. Couldn't connect with the blasted ball and when he drifted to the surface and flicked his eyelids up and down, he realised with some relief why not.

Camilla's half of the bed was vacant. Henry rubbed the sleep from his eyes and listened to her movements beneath him in the kitchen. From the speed of the cupboard doors opening and closing, it was clear her mood hadn't brightened at all. When he'd climbed carefully into bed the previous night, feigning consideration, he was well aware that Camilla was awake. She was lying, stiff and still having lapsed into one of her silent periods that took her a hundred miles away and as many minutes to reach. He couldn't touch her. Even if he'd felt inclined to extend a reassuring arm her way, she wouldn't have had a bit of it. So he embraced the warmth and darkness that carried him away.

But, here's the thing now. This game of golf. Henry knew only too well that tact was required, that tricky manoeuvring would be needed in order to slither away under circumstances like this. He'd drawn up a hasty plan which amounted to listening to Camilla offload whatever was eating her, then offering to feed her.

Henry sat up and put on his Rolex watch, his parting gift for thirty-something years in an accountancy firm. Early retirement was an appalling mistake, until golf filled a hole.

It was now seven-fourteen plus a dozen seconds. The subject of Annabel would have to be raised. After last night, seemed unavoidable. With any luck, there'd be time to overcome hurdles and swing the conversation towards golf. With a delicate stroke, of course.

Henry meandered quietly down the stairs and into the kitchen to discover an assault-course of pots and pans. Camilla was on all fours at seven-sixteen in the morning, furiously scrubbing the inside of a cupboard. She pulled back to look at him.

'Why did they have to rush into things, Henry? She's just a child.'

He stood in silence.

Camilla consulted her watch. 'Is it too soon to call Naomi?'

'I would say so, yes, by about a week. They'll barely be out of Manchester. They're on honeymoon.'

She plunged her hands into a steaming plastic bowl and wrung out a cloth. The scent of disinfectant drifted Henry's way.

'Why not let Cynthia do that in the morning?' he suggested in his most sympathetic voice. It only brought a dark glance before Camilla disappeared inside the cupboard to resume scouring again.

'Don't mention that useless woman to me. Before we left for the wedding, I wrote her a note instructing her to leave the hall light on. She didn't. This morning, listen to this,' she reappeared and Henry made sure he was paying attention. 'I found the back door unlocked. I told her specifically to check that the doors were secured. I'm going to have to let her go.'

Henry was about to remind her that she'd waded through three cleaners in as many years, then reconsidered. The revised comment came out as, 'I'm sure you know what's best.'

After a slight pause, 'Of course, if you'd agree to move out of this huge and unnecessary house, I could manage without help.'

'We're happy here. It's our home.'

'We? We should never have left South Africa.'

Henry dried up and thankfully Camilla didn't pursue the topic. It was uncomfortable, watching her work. 'Cup of tea?'

She ignored this. 'Why couldn't he have allowed her to finish her degree at least?' Took him a moment to realise they were back with Nathan.

'She's every intention of finishing her degree, Camilla.'

To which, she refused to comment.

He was standing like a statue. A brittle silence was threatening to settle between them. Seemed an opportune moment for his planned line, so Henry fired it in a cheery tone while briskly rubbing his hands. 'Can I get you some breakfast?'

Camilla stopped working, turned, stared. 'What *is* the matter with you? Spit it out.'

Busted. 'Nothing. Just trying to cheer you up a bit, that's all.'

Camilla shook her head. Her tongue was still, but her eyes were saying plenty.

He continued, 'And as for Annabel –'

'I don't want to talk about her,' she cut in. 'It's a good job you're not an ambulance, Henry. Your response time is ten hours too late. The emergency, so to speak, has passed, and you slept through the whole of it. I wanted to discuss Annabel last night, but as usual I had to muddle through on my own, so now I don't want your input. Full stop.'

This stumped him, admittedly. 'I don't understand.'

'You never have.' Her voice faltered. She'd neither cry nor accept affection so he stood, waiting. He couldn't really say what for. 'Can't you go down to the golf course or something? I'm finding this whole conversation humiliating. I'd like to be alone.' Camilla drowned her cloth and fiercely squeezed.

Henry suppressed a grin. He daren't let it loose. 'But I don't like leaving you like this.'

She X-rayed him, one eyebrow slightly raised. 'I'm sure you'll cope.'

When she turned away, Henry wandered into the lounge pounds lighter, and sunk into the nearest sofa. A spot of sports news then he'd shower and change. As he reached for the remote control, the doorbell rang. At this time? It induced a flash of panic, the thought of anyone seeing him dressed like this.

'No, you stay there, I'll get it,' Camilla called from the hall, tone dripping with sarcasm. Her slippers clapped heavily against the wooden floor. The chance to dash upstairs had passed. Camilla had already opened the door and was exchanging words in hushed sentences. Henry strained to listen. It was a man she was talking to, he was sure. The voices were drawing closer.

Camilla appeared first, followed by a policeman carrying his hat. He was wearing a dark beard and round glasses and the kind of expression that prodded Henry with anxiety. Camilla's hair was the usual neat mushroom shape, faultlessly smooth. Her dark eyes were full of some emotion he couldn't place.

She was a different woman to the one who'd just clopped through the hall. She walked slowly past Henry and sat carefully by his side, taking one of his podgy hands into both of hers. Hers were lukewarm and damp and smelt of floral disinfectant. The clock marked out its slow march from the mantelpiece.

'This is PC Robert Hill. Something's happened. He needs to talk to us, Henry.'

***

A door opened. Naomi was alone in a bright room that was colourless and empty. If there was a door she couldn't find it, yet after a fruitless search, a door definitely closed. She heard it clearly. Her eyes opened to intense light. She closed them and reopened gradually. The empty room had disappeared and she found herself lying in a bed, comfortable and warm. She blinked a few times to adjust to brilliant sunlight. Her head hurt. Her limbs felt stiff and sluggish. As she grappled to understand what was happening, she heard footsteps running down some stairs.

Where am I?

'Nathan?' she called, voice weak. 'Nathan?' She was struggling to project the sound, so she opted to listen instead. No response. High-pitched sound was cutting through the silence though. She identified it as birdsong outside. There was a whole choir assembled somewhere, rehearsing frantically. Where was Nathan?

Naomi couldn't decide if she was awake or asleep. Her brain was fighting to unscramble, while her senses, dull and distant, lagged behind in her dream. The surroundings were unfamiliar. She was staring through a huge panelled window that ran floor to ceiling. Closer inspection confirmed that it was actually two doors with brass door handles. Full-length floral curtains were open and pinned behind brass holders.

She pulled her eyes away. Took effort. *What day is it?* She ran through the days of the week starting at Monday. Nothing made sense until Saturday. *Saturday?* Panic seized her for a moment. *I'm getting married.* That thought ushered in the memories: a long walk up a short aisle clutching red lilies with one hand and her Dad's arm with the other, and Lorie, her only bridesmaid, close behind. Nathan had looked over his shoulder, smiled, and extended his hand as she got close. She took it and handed her flowers to Lorie, just as they'd rehearsed.

Nathan locked his fingers into Naomi's and whispered into her hair, 'You look stunning.' He smelled of his favourite aftershave.

In the warmth of a cosy bed in direct sunlight, her memory threw up a scene in a misty bathroom where she was frantically searching for her necklace. She touched her neck to find it bare. The memories were clarifying. She recalled her shaky voice during the vows, the reception, the hotel room, Nathan holding her to his chest on the bed. She sat upright, gripped by the reality that Nathan was gone.

'Nathan!'

She remembered the claustrophobic darkness, relived the chill of *that* voice. The cemetery.

Am I dead? Naomi fixed her glare on the empty wall ahead, heart thumping. Surely her pulse wouldn't be so alive if she were dead. She twisted her head and scanned the breath-taking view through the doors that led to a wooden balcony outside. The sight beyond it made her gasp. If this was death, she could live with it. There was an assortment of tumbling hills stretching into the distance, speckled with sheep. The patchwork hillsides flowed through every shade of green. They were soaked in sunshine. The peaks were bald, a non-descript brownish colour crowned with an azure sky dabbed with a few brushstrokes of low white cloud. A single chimney peeped from a distant hill. Trees dotted the landscape, changing for autumn. She couldn't see any roads, but could pick out the slithering impression of a stream running away from the house.

Her heart-rate slowed and the panic subsided. Her eyes scanned the room. She was in a beautiful bedroom with plain walls, a wooden beamed ceiling, and a pale wooden floor. The bed had a cast iron black frame and an embroidered white duvet cover with a pale pink trim.

She rotated her head to complete her study of the room. To her left by the side of the bed close to the window was another door, ajar. Naomi could see a door trim and a couple of white tiles. A bathroom. Opposite the bed was a chest of drawers holding a single pink rose in a skinny glass vase. Beside it was a wicker chair with a cushion and a folded white towel. To the right in the far corner was the main door. It was closed and had a key hole, which meant it could be locked. Beside that was a long wardrobe with a slim mirror attached to one of two doors and she could see the bulge of her covered legs in the mirror. As she leant forward to find her face, it occurred to her for the first time that she was shackled to the bed.

Both wrists were secured by two metal rings covered in soft black leather. She followed the lines of two long chains attached to the bedframe behind her. The rings weren't tight around her wrists. No, the chains were coiled on the bed sheets and she could move freely. She found she was hurting all over. Not badly, but there was a general smattering of cuts and bruises; dull aches, sharp pains. One arm hurt more than the other. She investigated why and found a needle mark surrounded by puffy red skin.

Naomi lifted the duvet and discovered she was wearing a knee-length silk nightshirt buttoned all the way down. Her coat had gone. Someone had dressed her. Someone had looked at her in the underwear she chose for Nathan.

With a burst of energy, she kicked off the covers and checked herself carefully. She was still wearing the same underwear. She searched for other clues. Her legs were scratched and there was a bruise on her right shin. She frantically undid the nightshirt. Her side had been dressed with something square and padded, secured and crossed with two strips of surgical tape. Neatly done too. It confirmed again that someone had touched her, looked at her. There was no evidence of anything worse, but that proved nothing. Not knowing what had happened left her chasing scenarios and feeling nauseous. She hadn't saved herself for Nathan for some sick creep to snatch her and take advantage. She was pushing away the nagging thought that something could have happened already.

As Naomi flopped back against the pillow she had a flashback about a gun. *The creep owns a gun. Wait, he used it.* She had a memory of lying in a hole in the ground, seeing the stars behind a black figure that was holding a gun to her head. The memory was muddy. Either he used the gun or she dreamt he used it. What was clearest to her was the powerlessness she felt, the detachment from reality. The sound of gunfire was more-or-less the last thing she remembered. She pawed every inch of her head. It was tender on one side above her ear, but there was no dressing. She was leaning towards the probability that it was a dream until her fingers closed around matted hair on the same side. The white pillowcase behind her had smears of dried blood.

There was another fragment. She could remember pressure on her legs – something being thrown at her, and then a bright light. The memories were warped and unreliable. If she'd been covered in earth, there'd be signs.

Naomi sat up again and examined her nails, her legs and arms. There was the expected amount of bruises, no specks of dirt. But her rings . . . gone. She habitually reached for her necklace and was disappointed again. Trying to piece the night together had only left a half-finished puzzle. Nothing was clear after the walk through the headstones.

The soles of both feet were perfectly clean which meant the creep had washed her. Which creep? She shivered. There were two – one whose voice reached for distant memories, and a stranger. They could be downstairs right now deciding what to do with her, or *to* her. As beautiful as this place was, she had to get out.

She shifted her focus to long distance out of the window again and found the nearest neighbours – a cluster of five sheep at the bottom of a hillside. The closest house could be a mile away, even two. Smoke was curling from the chimney. Someone was home. *No one will hear me scream from here*. She was looking at a scene that could sell a thousand postcards and picturing whoever lived in the faraway house, sitting beside a log fire, horrified by the headlines. No clue that she was here, a smoke's-puff away.

Naomi yanked her gaze from the long window and directed it at the door. Drew breath, held it. She was lying, still as stone, sifting a sound that wasn't the birds. Her inner radar was on high alert. As soon as she realised that someone was steadily climbing the stairs, she fumbled with the buttons on her nightdress, fighting to fasten them before anyone walked in.

Her eyes were fixed on the door handle. Her fingers clenched the bedcovers. She was buried up to the neck in duvet when the clunking of a key turned in the door. It was loud and sinister and invasive. Her muscles locked when the handle started to move.

A tall figure appeared in dark clothes, carrying a tray. The balaclava he still wore took her right back to her first sight of him, when he'd leapt out and claimed her life, ripping from her everything that was comforting and familiar. He looked no less menacing here in daylight as he strode towards her with a red tray and what looked like a bowl of soup, a bread roll and a plastic cup.

Her pulse beat against her fists beneath the covers. His black jeans were ripped on the knees. Above them he wore a dark blue sweatshirt with Jack Wills in unsubtle white letters. The skin on his hands was smooth and clean – they were the type of hands that pushed a pen or computer keys. She was curious about the colour of his eyes behind the narrow slits, but the priority was to avoid eye contact. After an initial glance and the cramming in of as much information as possible, she buried her head in her knees.

He deposited the tray on the bedside table and the smell of fresh bread and chicken soup filled the space between them. Naomi was yelling inside her head. *Leave me alone. Don't touch me. Get out.* After hesitating for a few moments beside the bed, as if understanding her clearly, he left.

Naomi only let go of the tension when the key turned and the sound of his footsteps gradually diminished. She released her breath and wondered when he'd return and when she'd be forced to confront what he really wanted. Every part of her sensed the unfolding of a plan. The more she pieced together the events of the previous night, the more obvious it was that none of it had happened randomly. She wondered if he'd have waited all night to have snatched her in the way he had. If Nathan had been with her, would he have been taken too, or just dispensed of instantly?

The other guy from the cemetery didn't seem to be here at the house with them. Instinct told her that it was only two of them tucked away in this deserted place under open skies swirling with fluffy clouds and fresh country air and little evidence of human life.

Her palms were as clammy as the joints behind her knees. She wiped her hands and looked at them. They shook. The ghost of her engagement ring still haunted the fourth finger of her left hand.

With no appetite for the food, Naomi realised instead that she needed the bathroom. The feeling, all too familiar, was brought on by stress or panic. She'd experienced it every time she'd played the piano to a crowd or an examiner. Her piano tutor called it the fight or flight response. Labelling it didn't help. Performing was the only laxative she'd ever needed, until now.

Naomi kicked free of the covers and swung her legs over the bed in the direction of the bathroom. The bed was shoved up against the doorframe. She glanced anxiously over her shoulder at the chains and prayed they'd be long enough. The metal rings connected to the bed dragged noisily along the bedframe. On unsteady legs she made it to the bathroom and found a toilet on the outside wall, right behind the door. Better still, she could sit on it, just, but only with her arms outstretched. She rushed back to the bed and tugged at it frantically, only to discover that it was bolted to the floor.

'Crap,' she muttered, aptly, and returned to the toilet, accepting that sorting herself out would involve standing up and taking a couple of paces forward. At least she could sit down. The flush handle was on the right side. Plus, the sink, back to back with the bed, was within reach. Could be worse. It struck her suddenly and with chilling clarity how every detail had been meticulously measured. The luxurious corner bath and overhead shower behind the glass screen were hopelessly out of reach.

That done, Naomi dawdled to the bed and sat straight-backed on the edge, unsure what to do next. No options presented themselves until a door slammed and a car engine fired outside, igniting in her a spark of energy. She jumped up and strained against the unyielding metal chains to glean whatever she could. The car pulled away. She had no view of it. A hollow silence descended and brought a kind of aloneness she'd never experienced.

Now what?

Should she mourn the past or panic about the present? There seemed no point in either. For company, she tried to summon the faces of those she loved most, but her mind bubbled like a cauldron and was too dark and murky to conjure images. *I don't want to die. Dear God, please don't let me die here. Help me?*

She felt strangely incapable of ushering the words beyond the low beamed ceiling of the room. The future she'd expected had been torn away. So there was no future. There was only an empty green world beyond a long window, and bitter regret and unquenchable fear.

And chains.

4

(Twelve months earlier)

The Royal Northern College of Music, Oxford Road, Manchester: international magnet for seriously talented kids and producer of world-class concert soloists. The sight of it made Naomi feel small and spectacularly average compared to some of the musical gods who had strutted the corridors and filled the concert halls, defying the normal rules of human imperfection. How soon would people realise she was an imposter?

The large shiny lettering looked bigger and more polished than usual and carried more significance as they passed the building and followed it around the corner past the huge windows that only reflected the moving car and gave away few secrets of what lay inside.

Naomi already knew the college well. She'd been part of the Junior RNCM which had kept her busy every Saturday for the past few years and required thousands of hours of practise in between. This visit was different. This place was about to become home. The strangers bustling in and around the building were about to become her new friends and family. She could not imagine how.

The Sir Charles Groves Hall – residential hall to six-hundred and odd students – sitting right next door, announced itself in more bold aluminium lettering. They drove by in silence, circled the building and located the entrance.

It was all chaos and confusion at the reception desk. Naomi was queuing to get her room key. The parking area she'd just left had told the same story: a swarming hive of loaded cars and bewildered-looking parents led by teenagers who looked relieved that other kids had parents too. They could all begin the process of forgetting family and abandoning every lecture they'd been taught since the cradle, starting today. Some looked more ready than others.

Henry and Annabel were trying to park the car amid the madness. Camilla stood by Naomi's left shoulder unable to keep still in the short queue. She kept tapping her heels in frustration. Being in the role of helpless person in need of directions and instructions wasn't her thing.

'It needs more than one person to attend to all these students,' Camilla said, not gently, aiming her comments at the desk where one poor young lad was the solution to everyone's problems and was doing a great job of looking cheerful about it.

Camilla's gaze settled on a rep from the accommodation company who was handing out welcome packs.

'You get the key, I'll get the pack,' Camilla said, marching off.

'You do that,' Naomi muttered, relieved to be alone.

It didn't last. Annabel clawed Naomi's shoulders from behind and announced into her right ear that she'd already seen a deliciously hot guy carrying a double bass. She'd even heard someone call out his name. It was Will.

'Look out for him,' she told Naomi, who couldn't have been less interested.

Naomi found herself at the front of the queue. She collected her key card just as Henry arrived, arms full.

Naomi's room was on the top floor of a six-storey block. They stepped out of the lift and trudged along the corridor in search of the room that would house Naomi for the next academic year. Annabel was chattering senselessly the whole time.

'You've done well, Naomi,' Camilla said as they opened and held doors for each other. 'Every musician's fantasy this place. If I had my time over . . . '

The sentence needed no ending. Naomi, vaguely aware she was filling expectations and unrealised dreams, felt sick. Bravely heading the group, she'd now arrived at a dead-end that held two doors. One had a number that matched the label on her key.

Henry bent towards her ear. 'You can always come home at weekends if you're finding it hard.'

'Who'd want to come home?' Annabel said. 'This place is buzzing. Parties all this week.'

'She's here to focus, Henry,' Camilla chipped in, 'not to dip a tentative toe in.'

Naomi won her battle with the key card. The door opened and the room exhaled some odours which meant that it had been recently cleaned. Henry went in last, drowning in bags. 'I'm only saying that if –'

'Don't,' Camilla said. 'She's worked hard. What's the sense in diluting her opportunity? It's very competitive, music.'

'I'm not competing with anyone but myself, Mum,' Naomi said with a sinking feeling. Just hearing the C word filled her with dread.

Defeated, a silent Henry dropped the bags inside the doorway and cleared off to get the rest. Camilla disappeared inside the en-suite bathroom.

'This is awesome,' Annabel said, gazing out of the window, elbows on the narrow sill. Naomi joined her. The view was hardly pretty. The Halls of Residence branched into a square with a partly-paved, partly-grassed courtyard in the centre full of scurrying people with luggage. As Naomi looked into the rooms opposite, some of them occupied, she could only think how exposed she'd be unless she drew the curtains at night.

Annabel nudged her side. 'If Will's room is across there, I'm bringing some binoculars and moving in,' she whispered. 'Aren't you even excited? Manchester is crawling with students and you've finally escaped from home. You should be celebrating.'

Naomi glanced over her shoulder to check if Camilla was listening. She wasn't. She was pulling a duvet from a suitcase and flapping it up and down.

'I feel weird,' Naomi mouthed to Annabel. 'I'm not sure I'm cut out for all this.'

'What are you on about?' Annabel whispered fiercely. 'You're a fantastic pianist.'

'It's all relative, Annie. I'm just a little fish in a very big pond here.'

'Who told you that crap? Look, uni is as much about the experience and the social life as the study. This place must be full of geeks into ancient music like you. You can sit for hours talking about that guy who cut his ear off.'

Naomi rolled her eyes. 'I think you're confusing Van Gogh with Beethoven, who didn't cut his ear off, he went deaf.'

Annabel waved one hand dismissively. 'Whatever! Point is, loosen up a bit. It's time you did.'

'Annie, it's a music college, not Club 18-30.'

'You can still have fun. Check Will out for a start. I'm telling you he's hot.'

'Too hot?' Camilla said, suddenly. 'Shall I open a window?'

Naomi relaxed just long enough to share a conspiratorial giggle with Annabel, as Camilla barged between them and swung the window open as far as it would go.

***

Naomi lay on her bed that night staring vacantly at the smallish patch of ceiling that was all she could call her private space, aware of every unfamiliar lump and bump in her back from the narrow bed. The room was almost claustrophobic. She was conscious of her breathing, her pulse, the tension in her muscles, the noises outside which meant that people were out and about getting stuck in. The harsh centre light brightened the room too much, exaggerating its aloofness and its utter refusal to make her feel at home.

The welcome pack was ripped open by her bed, contents spilled. A miniature bottle of shower gel, a mini cereal packet, a sachet of Earl Grey tea. How was any of that meant to make her feel welcome? The accommodation company name was on the packet, *Liberty*. If lying here in a small room with nowhere to go and no one to talk to was liberty, she'd take the restrictions of home anytime.

Her clothes hung in the wardrobe. Her efforts to personalise the room amounted to a picture of herself and Annabel, a box of scented tissues, her record player and the pile of sheet music, CDs and old classical albums that sat neatly on the long desk to her left, the way Camilla had arranged and left them. They didn't start to fill the cavernous emptiness she felt inside.

She lay motionless, thinking about her family. Camilla, her overbearing mother, had also instilled in her a sense of belonging and security. It had taken this desolate moment for Naomi to realise how much she'd always counted on her. Absence had already managed to glaze over the cracks of general family problems and soften the shades of any differences they had. From now, Naomi had no one to rely on but herself. That burden fused her to the bed.

She closed her eyes and pictured Annabel with her ice-blue eyes, clear skin, infectious smile, long wavy hair naturally blonde – her unlikely twin. What drew crowds to Annabel was her sense of fun and her talent for mischief. To Annie, the world was only a huge adventure park made purely for her pleasure. She wanted to see it all, experience it all, grab life by the throat. It was too short to waste on boring stuff like museums, libraries and art galleries. Annabel couldn't bear the stifling silence of those places or the need to be quiet and well behaved.

Seeing the world through Annabel's eyes had opened Naomi's. She wanted to feel the same way, but couldn't. It wasn't that she wanted to hate classical music and poetry the way Annabel did, it was more that she envied the ease in which Annabel could negotiate life and the people in it and enjoy the journey. Accepting their differences had taken time for Naomi and been painful.

Separated at birth by fifteen minutes they were born either side of midnight, Predictably, Annabel was first. It was still the 22nd of October. It was the 23rd before Naomi found the same route. But there was one flaw in Annabel's character that Naomi didn't admire. It had caused problems in the past that Naomi was keen to forget right now.

She reached for her phone, needing to talk. She couldn't admit to family that she hadn't done any of the things they expected her to do, so she called Lorie, her best friend, who answered her phone with her mouth full.

'Lorie, it's me.'

'Hey, what's up? You sound upset.'

'I hate it here. I want to go home. Don't tell Mum I called.'

Lorie laughed, then apologised. 'Come on, you've only just got there. Give it a chance.'

'I'm lying in this little room on the top floor wondering what the hell I'm doing here.'

Lorie swallowed whatever she was chomping. 'You're following your dream, that's what.'

'*My* dream?'

Lorie was silent a beat. 'You love music.'

'That's not the point. Playing for myself is one thing, but knowing I'll have to perform in front of the other students is stressing me out. And pianists are always needed for accompanying and stuff. If anyone drops on me at short notice, I'll die.'

'You can always say no.'

Naomi twisted her hair around her forefinger. 'I know, but we'll be expected to . . .' She lapsed into a short silence.

Lorie filled it. 'Why aren't you out meeting people?'

'I've tried to go out, but I just can't.'

'How have you tried?'

'I've put my shoes on twice. I keep looking out of my window and seeing groups of people outside. Absolutely no one is by themselves except me.'

Lorie giggled into Naomi's ear, then her tone turned serious. 'Listen, there'll be loads of students sitting in their rooms right now just like you, wondering why they're the only ones on their own. You've got to get out and mingle. Put your shoes on again.'

Naomi sat up. 'My shoes?'

'Yes, put them on and go out. I'm not asking. You're not alone. I'm here, so you won't look like a saddo if you're chatting. Get a move on.'

After a few moments of hesitation, Naomi stood and walked to her wardrobe. She shoved on her Converse pumps and slid into a black jacket. Lorie waited without speaking.

'Done.'

'Good. Now open the door and go outside, simple as.'

Lorie kept Naomi talking as she locked the door, retraced her steps down the narrow corridor and took the empty lift to the ground floor.

'What's happening now?' Lorie asked her. Naomi walked through reception and outside onto the busy street. She stood still, watching weekend traffic chase by in both directions, filled with people who had a life and knew what to do with it. She clamped her phone between her ear and shoulder and zipped up her jacket.

'It's full of students out here. No one is on their own and everyone's laughing like they're having the best time ever and they've known each other for years. Now what?'

'Hungry?' a voice said behind her.

Naomi thought she'd said 'angry'. She turned round. She could hear Lorie telling her to keep walking in the direction of the shops as she dropped her arm.

Standing behind her was a short, plump girl with an invisible neck. It looked more like her head was balanced on top of her shoulders. Her hair was red and was as wide as it was long. It framed her face like a helmet and rested on her shoulders, spread out. Her eyes were milky blue and her expression, desperately serious. It was a change from seeing kids who looked afraid to be seen not laughing. The girl held up a box of takeaway pizza, announced the topping and asked if Naomi was interested in sharing. It took time to identify that the accent was Irish.

Naomi dissolved into a smile. The girl opposite didn't reciprocate. She reached for her non-existent neck and conjured a necklace from beneath her top, bearing a cross. Naomi noticed she had great nails. Long and white. Pianists couldn't grow nails.

'Ditto.'

Naomi's fingers automatically clasped her own necklace and a rush of relief washed over her. She could hear Lorie calling her name down the phone.

'Sure,' Naomi said.

The girl turned and started to walk towards the accommodation block. She was square all the way down. Her back was the same width as her hips and her bottom was flat. Pasty-coloured ankles showed beneath a long skirt. Naomi caught up and trotted alongside, brushing off the guilt pangs for the negative assessment. Focus on the nails. Great nails!

'Siobhan Dougherty,' she said, looking dead ahead.

'Naomi Hamilton.' She lifted the phone back to her ear. 'Lorie? Sorry. Can I call you back?'

5

The first week, though busy, only strolled by. Siobhan, her first friend, had featured in it loosely. Naomi could see Siobhan's room from her window. It was on the block to Naomi's left as she looked out and down a couple of floors. When the curtains were open, her only glimpse was the tip of Siobhan's navy pillowcase that housed a battered teddy bear named Snugpooh.

Was Siobhan a proper friend? Naomi had seen Siobhan for seven days and wasn't sure. If sharing a pizza over dull chat, having matching necklaces, arranging a joint trip to Asda and agreeing that Chopin's piano music was pretty amazing, then Naomi supposed that they were. They'd added each other on Facebook and swapped phone numbers.

She had mixed feelings about Siobhan. When she reviewed the week, she wasn't sure Siobhan had smiled even once. Whenever they met up, there was a kind of mouth twitch which went in the direction of a smile, but never got there. Siobhan never left Naomi with that cosy friendship feeling. And nothing improved or developed or got easier. Every time they met up it was like starting from scratch. Ask questions. Get the shortest possible answers. Then there were the stiff silences that could arrive suddenly between them that Naomi struggled through and that Siobhan didn't seem to mind or notice.

So Siobhan was Catholic, came from Dublin, was the oldest of five children, had seen Barry Manilow in concert three times with her mum, and played the flute. Her hobbies included meditation and tai chi. Boyfriend? No! Did she fancy anyone? No, but Daniel Craig (she decided after a long moment of staring at the floor) had nice eyes, she supposed.

Naomi shared a kitchen and cleaning rota with three other girls she'd seen most days. They were fine, no complaints. Two of them, Megan and Madeline – generally known by the end of the first week as M 'n' M – had paired off on the first day and hadn't been seen apart since. The other girl, Bridget, a singer, hardly left her room. If she wasn't blasting out some aria that rocked the walls, she was glued to her absent boyfriend over Facebook. Talking to Bridget meant only one thing: learning every tedious detail about Max Lloyd.

Being with new people every day was exhausting, maybe the hardest part of her new life, beating off the stiff competition of doing written and playing assessments to be put in suitable groups for this and that. Spare time was spent on the piano on well-established music repertoire she was sprucing up for her new tutor, a tiny softly-spoken Russian doll called Olga Kolesnikova, a 'legend' by all accounts. She was known for her volcanic passion for Romantic music that erupted regularly during her lessons, then cooled and settled in between.

Evenings meant catching up with Lorie and Annabel or wandering in some unmemorable bar with whoever she'd latched on to that day. Camilla had, as forewarned and promised, rung only once. It was part of a new regime to encourage independence or something. She'd ring every Friday evening at six. Whatever! Henry rang or texted more than that, but Naomi suspected he was breaking an agreement.

A week had been a long time. Naomi missed her room at home, her bed, her cat. Wearing her social face whenever she stepped out of her room was a drain, and tonight was the end-of-week Freshers' dinner, held at some posh city hotel. She had nothing to wear. She was meeting Siobhan outside the accommodation block at seven. It was now four-fifteen. She'd hunted through her wardrobe three times and found the same things hanging there each time. So she rang Annabel in a flap.

'Hotel dinner tonight and I haven't got an outfit.'

Annabel laughed. 'What are you like?'

'I've been busy. Plus, I only found out this afternoon that everyone's getting dressed up. I haven't really brought anything. What shall I do?'

'Stop talking and get yourself to the shops. They'll be closing soon.'

'They're not near, plus I'm no good at shopping – '

'Learn. Stop talking would you? Ring me from the Arndale Centre and I'll tell you which shops are cool. You look good in black. And get a picture of Will for me, I'm getting withdrawal.'

Annabel had gone. Naomi stood still, hands shaking, mind divided between rushing out to the shops and some other option which wouldn't come. Lorie. It was worth a try.

When Lorie's phone rang six times without a reply, Naomi's palms were starting to get clammy and she was trying to remember how to reach the shops. Then, suddenly, 'Naomi?'

'Lorie, I'm in a mess. I've got a dinner tonight and I haven't brought a thing to wear. I'm not used to –'

'OK, slow down. What time do you need to be out?'

'I'm meeting a . . . friend at seven.'

'That's loads of time. How about I bring some dresses over?'

Naomi backed up and dropped onto the bed. 'Really? I feel bad –'

'I've got no plans for tonight and I can be there in half an hour, OK?'

Naomi sighed, torn between guilt and relief. 'Are you sure?'

'Jump into the shower now and I'll text you when I get there. Give me forty minutes OK?'

Naomi lay back on the bed, closed her fingers around her necklace and shut her eyes. 'I owe you one.'

**

Lorie showed up exactly on time bringing a choice of six dresses and two pairs of shoes she hoped would fit (Naomi's feet were half a size smaller). She stayed until Naomi was zipped into the chosen black dress and was standing, shoes on, in front of the mirror. Lorie had applied Naomi's makeup, painted her nails and fixed her up with some swinging sparkly earrings.

'Why not take your necklace off this once. I've brought –'

'No I can't,' Naomi said.

'You're the boss.'

With twenty minutes to spare, they set about Naomi's dark hair. Lorie curled it using straighteners. After ten minutes it was parted in the centre and fell spectacularly into big curls at the bottom. Lorie backcombed it and set it with spray. A few jets of perfume later, Naomi was ready for the catwalk.

'You look incredible,' Lorie said as they stood side by side looking into the mirror. They were almost exactly the same height and shape, which, for clothes-swapping purposes had come in handy more times than Naomi could count. 'Go knock 'em dead.'

**

Luckily for Annabel, Will Barton was sitting on

Naomi's table that night. It turned out that he'd never touched a double bass in his life but was a cellist. He looked almost Spanish, everything dark right down to the neat hedge of thick black eyebrows, Mediterranean-coloured skin to match. He was kind of exotic in a way that impressed all the girls. He did nothing for Naomi. His army of followers flocked to hug him and yell too loudly and take pictures. Cameras and phones were busy while they waited for the main course, making it easy for Naomi to get Annabel's picture without Will even noticing. It was a good one too. Naomi grinned as she tucked her phone under the table and sent the picture to Annabel.

At her left side, all elbows and bare freckled arms, sat Siobhan. She'd dressed in a long black skirt and a black short-sleeved top with some sequins edging the neckline. Her only bit of colour was a row of pale blue beads that picked up the colour of her shoes. She was so stiff and still, it was as though she'd taken root in the chair. Naomi felt obliged to divide her time between trying to talk to Siobhan and having easy chats with Madeline on her other side. But Madeline was fast becoming too drunk for small talk. So Naomi focussed on Siobhan, finding that after a week of exhausting one another's bank of personal details, there was only the food left to talk about.

'So you like him?' she asked, rotating a wedding ring she wore on her right hand, which had been her grandmother's. It dug into her finger so fiercely it seemed miraculous she could turn it. Naomi was surprised, pleasantly. Siobhan didn't take the initiative with conversation very often.

'Like who?' Naomi asked.

She followed Siobhan's deathly gaze towards Will who was downing a whole glass of something blue without stopping. The empty glass brought a ripple of applause from his female fans, who handed him another one.

'Oh no, not me. My sister spotted him last week. The picture was for her.'

'He's probably going to drown tonight, so he is.'

Naomi laughed. Siobhan didn't.

'Do you like him?' Naomi asked, for something to say.

Siobhan closed her invisible eyelashes together and shook her head of bushy hair. 'No way. My mammy and daddy would kill me if I rolled home with that.'

Naomi laughed again. Siobhan turned to Naomi with confusion in her eyes. 'What's funny?'

'Nothing. No, I agree,' Naomi babbled, wondering how she'd managed to offend Siobhan. 'Seriously, my mum would do the same.'

'Right, OK.' Siobhan seemed satisfied. She pointed her gaze table-ward again and despite the party atmosphere, one of their awkward silences began, made worse by the general euphoria going on everywhere else.

Naomi stood, 'I think I'll nip to the bathroom.'

She smoothed her dress and cast her eyes around. Beyond the restaurant was a bar, dense with bodies.

'Toilets near the bar,' Siobhan said in a monotone in that heavy Irish accent of hers. Naomi was getting used to it and needed to interpret into English less and less.

'Thanks.'

Naomi gathered her phone and her small bag and set off, glad to be free of forced chat. A piano was being played somewhere, dinner-jazz style. She pictured a highly polished black or white grand and from the brightness of the tone, maybe a Yamaha. Above the drone of countless conversations, she picked out an impressive account of Gershwin's *Summertime*. Because improvising was at the opposite end of Naomi's musical experience of religiously obeying notes, time values and performance directions, it impressed her a lot.

She turned a corner. At one end of the bar on a tall chrome stool, a guy sat alone wearing dark trousers and a cream shirt. She couldn't not watch him as she walked towards him. The ladies' toilets were directly behind him. In front of him sat an empty slim glass with a rough chunk of ice and a slice of lemon.

He was nearly in profile as she approached. Naomi, with some fascination, watched his lips move as he spoke into his phone and stroked the glass with his free hand. She'd never been envious of a phone or a glass before that moment. He glanced up and caught her eye, looked down, did a double-take. He was staring intently at her now. It was fleeting. He half smiled, then dropped his eyes to his glass and carried on his conversation without further eye contact.

By the time Naomi had reached the toilet and closed the door, her legs wouldn't work properly. She replayed the double-take and the smile half a dozen times as she mindlessly used the toilet and stumbled to the row of gleaming sinks to wash her hands. Two giggling girls were applying makeup, faces buried in the mirror. Naomi was barely aware of them.

Did she smile back at him, she wondered? She couldn't be sure. She was certain about one thing: he was insanely gorgeous. He had short mid-brown hair, waxed, five o'clock shadow, perfectly proportioned features. She hoped he wasn't short. Did it matter, for Pete's sake?

She dried her hands and touched up her lip colour, anxious to get out of the toilets and also not ready to go. She hesitated, thinking things through. She didn't want to return to Siobhan while her heart was racing with the anticipation of some ridiculous hope centred around a guy she didn't know and who might not even be sitting where she'd last seen him, and might be single, or not. Should she walk past him as if he hadn't just thrown her off course? No. She couldn't open a conversation with him either, so she settled on getting a drink and not looking at him at all.

After a lingering sideways glance in the mirror, finding everything intact, she shook her fingers through her hair, picked up her bag and phone, took a deep breath and yanked open the door. There he was, close, peering over his shoulder at her. Her steps faltered with the shock. He returned his gaze to the bar. Naomi took two steps forward and felt the pull of his presence.

She made it to the bar and stood a couple of metres to his right, holding herself rigidly, ensuring her stomach was sucked flat in the black dress. She was aware of her breathing as she sensed the heat of his eyes. Her pulse was erratic, thoughts jumbled. Her phone was still loose in her hand. She put it down for something to do. Both girls behind the bar were busy. Naomi followed them closely as if her only reason for being there was to win their attention as soon as possible.

He stood up. She flicked him what she hoped was a neutral look. He was tall. And broad and slim and hotter than she'd remembered in the bathroom. *Keep calm, Naomi.* Weirdly devastated that he was leaving, she also knew she'd let him go. She didn't have the guts to take her all-to-nothing shot. Her legs had about frozen. He didn't leave. He moved to her side, placed an elbow on the bar and called to one of the girls who immediately darted over, smiling.

Naomi faced him, not sure she could speak.

'What can I get you?'

She cleared her throat and used the bar for support. 'Just orange juice, with ice . . . please.'

The bartender waited for the rest. 'Nothing for me,'

he said. She nodded and efficiently set about the job. 'Are you here with someone?' he asked her. Even his voice had an impact. Used to analysing texture and timbre, she weighed the tone quality and the way he'd emphasised with. His accent was unremarkable. Northern without any harsh edges. Nicely pronounced vowel sounds, not typical Mancunian, what Camilla would call well-spoken.

'Only my whole uni year,' Naomi said, face colouring. 'It's the end of Freshers' week. Everyone's off their heads already.'

He smiled. 'And you're hitting the orange juice?'

Her face was burning. She couldn't look directly at him. 'Must sound lame, but I don't drink.'

'Not at all?'

'Not if I can help it.'

'Any reason?'

'It tastes foul.'

He laughed. 'I hardly drink either. Different reasons.'

'Really?' It didn't occur to her until later to ask what they were.

He nodded. 'It's not lame, but it's rare. You must be the only one.'

'Actually, the friend I came with isn't really bothered either. The others have left us behind tonight. About every half hour they hit a new level. We must look excruciatingly boring, the pair of us sitting there, deadpan. It'd help if she had a sense of humour.'

Naomi felt an immediate tug of guilt, until another glance told her she'd drawn his smile again, and then it was impossible not to feel good.

'So I'm guessing you thought you'd escape for a bit?'

'Correct,' she laughed. 'I needed time out.' The bartender brought the drink and announced an extortionate price for it. By the time Naomi had fumbled about in her bag for her purse, he'd noiselessly paid up.

Embarrassed and flustered, she tried to look at him and found she couldn't. 'Thanks.'

'No worries. I remember being where you are now. First time away from home, meeting new people, having to learn new things, sink or swim. It's not easy.'

Finally, Naomi could feel the fire dying in her cheeks. She was managing to look him in the eye for longer periods. His eyes were grey-blue, she decided, a subtle mixture, hard to tell out of daylight. 'So you're a graduate then?'

'Have been for a few years now,' he said. 'I've never wanted a proper job though. I'm not ready to commit to it just yet. There are things I want to do first. You have to live a bit, don't you?'

Naomi had no experience of what he was hinting at or talking about, she only knew that being this close to this person was the most exhilarating feeling she'd ever had, and right now, she'd have considered trading an arm to keep him there. She couldn't stop herself from smiling warmly as she took her first sip. 'I suppose so.'

Her phone lit up on the bar, though the ringtone was swallowed by background noise. It was a text from Annabel. He looked down and saw the name.

'My sister,' Naomi explained unnecessarily, noting the thrill she got from spilling something personal. She hoped he'd do the same.

He nodded once. 'Look, I'd better get going. I'm meeting someone.' Her body deflated as she worked to hold her smile and her poise. 'He was supposed to meet me here, but apparently some blonde has detained him in a bar across town. I can't imagine she's nailed him down, can you?' He rolled his incredible eyes and licked his lips and finished with a smile. 'I'd better go and see if I can save him from himself. The guy's married.' He shook his head as if he despaired of whoever it was, put his phone in his trouser pocket. No wedding ring.

He. He said he, not she. She breathed more easily. 'OK then,' was all she could find. In the few silent moments that followed – that felt incomparably different from Siobhan's silences – he held her eyes. Should she say something? Maybe. Definitely. She couldn't speak. Or think.

'Enjoy your evening then . . .' he was saying, searching her eyes, asking her name.

'Naomi.' *Too eager.* She wanted to say it again differently. *Too late.*

He smiled again, allowing her time to note the row of neatly arranged teeth. He was astonishingly perfect. She was looking for flaws now just to convince herself he was real.

'Naomi,' he finished, voice low, absorbing the name. 'That's nice.' He had a slight cleft in his chin that only added to the face – this face she was now memorising and pinning onto a vacant wall in her mind for later. He hesitated again while she fought the impulse to grab hold of him and wrestle him to the ground. 'Nathan Stone. Lovely to meet you.'

'You too,' she said. *Don't leave.* He reached out and lightly touched the side of her arm. Her mind wiped clean. She could still feel the warmth of his hand against her skin long after he'd strode casually away without looking back.

Naomi picked up her phone, heart pounding, and opened the message. She stared at Annabel's three words and sighed, long and hard. *As HOT as!*

They were about the only words in her head too.

***

Naomi had won the lottery, but had lost her ticket. Well, not lost, just mislaid. She was certain she'd find it again. That's how she felt during the whole of the following week. *Nathan Stone. Lovely to meet you.* She'd have had a nice stash of cash if she'd banked a fiver every time those words had sung like a cathedral bell in her head. They'd come during conscious and unconscious moments. They'd echoed above the *fortissimo* sections of the Beethoven sonata she'd been practising for days. They'd intruded in her conversations, standing as a delicious barrier between her and whoever she was talking to, making her feel detached from them and connected with him, *Nathan Stone. Lovely to meet you.* It was an intensely pleasurable feeling. She held it closely, strangely invigorated, sharing it with no one. She'd lost the need to be a people-leech and scrounge acceptance and approval wherever she could.

Being alone in her room didn't induce panic anymore. It gave her quiet time to recall Nathan Stone's glorious face and recapture the sensation of his hand touching her skin, when he'd seared an imprint upon her that she could still feel.

And now she was trying so little, the relationships that week formed effortlessly. She found herself being invited to this and that room, and such and such a night out. She went to everything, taking Nathan Stone with her, her invisible companion who kept her smiling and laughing and oozing a new energy she didn't know she had, and very much preferred. Anticipating Nathan to be in every shop or bar, or coming towards her on every street, she dressed more carefully than usual and took loads of time over colours and contrasts and accessories. Deciding her wardrobe could use a facelift too, and with a sudden appetite for being out and about, she bought some new clothes.

Was she sending vibes of availability to all the guys? She didn't mean to. But it was the only explanation for the fact that on that same week, the compliments rolled and two guys asked her out. Flattered, but stumbling for words, she did what she normally tried not to do and lied. Sparing their feelings, she told them both she was already in a relationship. And it felt just like she was. Living with a person round the clock, hearing their voice, feeling their touch felt exactly like having a relationship. There was no room for anyone else while Nathan Stone was a constant presence.

***

Two weeks after the Freshers' dinner, with not a glimpse of Nathan despite a desperate search wherever she wandered, her sparkle was burning dim. Another week after that, with still nothing to fuel it but the embers of dying memories, she was feeling uncomfortably low. By now, she was relieved she hadn't mentioned Nathan to anyone.

Annabel hadn't noticed anything different. Lorie had noticed small changes and quizzed her. But Naomi sidestepped the questions, putting her mood swings down to her new environment, never mentioning the man who'd burned two minutes of her life and impacted it more forcefully than all the other things and people put together.

Truth was, she concluded in a dark moment on a dismal Friday afternoon three weeks after the event, there was nothing to tell. A man had bought a drink for a pathetic female years younger than himself who couldn't get served. *And?* She'd blushed like a kid. He'd been generous and polite and left her his name. *So?* Maybe Nathan Stone was one of those gifted people who could make whoever he spoke to, feel special. And he had made her feel special that night. *Hadn't he?* Maybe it was pity. He'd touched her arm. *Oh p-lease!* Maybe he'd touched four other arms on his way to the hotel door that night.

Naomi groaned out loud and covered her face as she lay on her bed. She was tired of going over the same questions that had no answers. Her head needed a clear-out. She rubbed her face and put her hands flat by her sides and opened her eyes to focus on a spider. For three days, it had made a home of the far corner of the ceiling and waited with endless patience for someone to call in. Naomi didn't have the heart to destroy its little web and chuck it out of the six storey window. She didn't know how it would find its next meal, but if it could stay put and be happy, she'd make room for a flatmate.

'I'll take the floor, you take the ceiling,' she muttered. 'Stick to your own half.'

She named it Sydney. So now it was male. And now, she decided, she was definitely crazy.

Naomi sat up and swung her legs onto the floor. She bowed her head and reluctantly decided it was time to move on from Nathan Stone. She clutched her necklace and uttered a few words, asking for strength to get on with it, move on. Fate had not granted a reunion with Nathan during the past three weeks despite pleading then bargaining, so that was that. Acceptance. Wasn't that the essence of faith? OK, so Nathan Stone was history. She stood up, trying to feel better. History or not, letting go hurt like hell.

Naomi looked at her phone and gasped. It was two minutes past three in the afternoon. How had time slid like that? She'd booked one of the music rooms for three and if she didn't get there by ten past, anyone needing a practise room could claim it. That was the system.

Practise rooms were hard enough to book without

skipping a session. Not enough to go around. In a burst of energy brought on by panic, she pushed into her shoes on the move, grabbed her music, her phone, her room key. She locked the door, ran to the lift, called it. It was five past three when she spilled onto the street to be met by a grey October sky spitting a soft drizzle she hadn't detected from inside. She tried to protect her music inside her cardigan. A stiff breeze caught a couple of loose sheets which escaped her fingers. They tossed around before landing. Naomi chased them and pinned them down on the pavement.

She half-trotted, half-walked the very short walk to the college and hurried through the doors head down, almost barging into Will Barton, who was burdened from behind with his polished red cello case. He dodged her with a broad smile, a loud 'Whoa' and two raised palms. Naomi apologised. Will grinned and carried on through the doors. Naomi, relieved to be dry, stopped to wipe her feet on the giant doormat and check her music was all there.

Ready to go again, she tightened her grip around her music and noticed it was eight minutes past three. *Crap!* She started running. From the reception desk, someone was moving towards her, slowing her flight. She focussed on him and stopped. The rest was surreal. Her lottery ticket – dressed in a pale blue top, dark jeans, black jacket and a warm smile – had just shown up and was wafting towards her in this state she was in. She looked a disaster. He looked divine and unblemished and unruffled, just as she remembered him. She held her breath. He caught up with her, uttering her name in a way that assured her that he'd found what he was looking for. She mumbled his in return, and examined those blue-grey eyes that had been the subject of her dreams for three eternal weeks.

She couldn't remember the sequence later, but somehow she found herself tightly bound in his arms right there in the middle of the busy reception area that dimmed, and the people with it. She closed her eyes and rested her head on his shoulder and shut out a world that meant nothing. There was only him. There was only this feeling. There was only now. And Nathan Stone continued to press her to him and wouldn't let go.

6

CAPTIVITY

With nothing to occupy her time but time itself, Naomi had drifted into sleep. It was an uneasy shallow place she sank to, infested with hellish images, dark shadows and high-pitched noises. She jolted awake and felt the relief of a bright, tranquil room. But one sweep of her eyes across it slammed her back into reality and had her anxiously finding her wrists, which were still wrapped in black leather and chains.

The chains were two individual lengths that ringed around the horizontal metal bar of the bed frame. They could noisily slide from side to side, and did, whenever she moved. There were four pillows. Naomi found that the most comfortable position was to lie on one side and bury the chains beneath the pillows, resting her arms out in front of her. Lying on her back was uncomfortable unless she was awake and could raise her arms above her head. Whichever way she did it, her arms had to be flat against the mattress so that the bed, and not her arms, bore the weight.

One cheek was wet with saliva. Naomi brushed it against her shoulder and lay still, concentrating on listening for a while. No noise at all. He'd gone out she remembered now, as despair washed over her in fresh, strengthening waves. The production of energy had packed up. She stared at the tray beside the bed. On it sat a red plastic cup of water, a bowl of cold soup, same plastic, same shade, plus a white bread roll lightly dusted with flour.

She had no clue what time it was. Morning? Afternoon? Late afternoon? She stood slowly and walked to the window, straining the chains as far as they'd allow. She wished she had Nathan's skill of glancing at the sky and assessing the time or finding north from the position of the sun. The sky held no clues for her. The sun was about to be swallowed by an ugly black cloud, which was being pursued by crowds more. Mind empty, she stood watching as the cloud eclipsed the sun and the others huddled in and the room dimmed and cooled quickly.

The constant suspense of waiting was inescapable. There was only waiting, watching, wondering, following a ring of doubt and fear that circled endlessly. Losing her necklace had meant losing something precious and personal. It had been her token with God, the private agreement they shared that she would wear it and remember Him, and He would protect her. At least, that was her take. The value in gold wasn't worth mentioning. What mattered was the deep-rooted symbolism that connected with a childhood she'd always remember and would rather forget. The necklace had been her companion during long spells spent alone. She took hold of it whenever she prayed. Maybe God was the real friend, but the necklace had become the link. She liked it that way.

She didn't know how long she stood there by the window untouched by stunning scenery, unaware of anything but the oppression of profound hopelessness. Her growling stomach brought her round. She felt no urge to fill it. She thought again of her parents coping with the news that something dreadful had happened, and couldn't imagine the pain and powerlessness. The thought that, with a phone she could assure them she was alive, caused a physical pain that made her legs drop into a crouching position. She stayed there until she ached all over.

She clambered back onto the bed and decided to drink at least. Not trusting what he might have added, she took the cup to the bathroom to refill. There was a new toothbrush in its pack, with toothpaste. She hadn't logged them until now. She drank two cups of water then awkwardly cleaned her teeth. There was a small window on the opposite wall fastened with a curly black wrought-iron handle. The whole thing would swing open. It was big enough for a body to squeeze through, probably. As she blotted her mouth with a nearby towel, a car was crunching towards the house again on loose stones.

Her legs weakened as she rushed to the bed and buried herself beneath the covers. As time passed, her breathing steadied. She listened carefully to the noises downstairs. Cupboard doors were opening and closing, bags rustling, drawers being pulled open, pushed shut. The kitchen must be directly beneath. She pictured him stocking up the cupboards for the long stay.

What was she doing here? Her mind threw up two recent cases where girls had been found after years of captivity. Both had been held by older men who'd cut them off from all life outside. Children had been born. One of the girls suffered Stockholm Syndrome and struggled to adapt to freedom.

Nauseous now, Naomi tried to clear her mind which was also being plagued by the other scenario, death. The only thinkable option was escape. Her mind latched on to it quickly, an attempt to push the vile stuff out. Concentrating on escaping as if it was a choice, was the secret to remaining sane.

A door closed beneath her, then the stairs were groaning again as steady footsteps drew closer. She froze. A key turned in the lock. Naomi, buried, didn't move. She felt him enter the room and walk towards her. He paused by the bed. Air felt in short supply under the covers. After an everlasting wait, he peeled the duvet back as far as her shoulders. She looked up and shuddered. The black balaclava was the first thing she saw hanging over her, pale blue eyes inside it. There was a small tattoo on his left arm, black ink, no colour. An animal? She looked away, too afraid to be caught staring. He spoke in his deep rich voice.

'Eat something.'

Naomi shook her head and closed her eyes. 'Let me go.'

A pause. 'Not going to happen.'

'I'm pleading with you, let me go. Please,' she whispered. Naomi opened her eyes and looked into his, taking what felt like a necessary risk. She didn't want to give him a reason to stay, but she meant for him to read the agony in her eyes.

'You're going nowhere. Get used to it.'

His voice was level, devoid of the kind of emotion that was strangling hers.

'I need my husband.'

Expecting a reply, Naomi refused to look away. Time passed in a brittle silence and her nerve faltered. She couldn't back down. His pale blue eyes calmly blinked and narrowed behind the mask. His hand stretched out towards her. She tried to withdraw, but there was nowhere to go. He firmly snatched her wrist. Naomi closed her eyes, shutting him out. Something soft was being pressed against her hand.

'No, no,' she said.

'Eat,' he ordered. Her eyes opened first, then her hand. He deposited the bread roll in her palm and let go. 'You'll never see him again.'

She breathed hard and fast while he strode unhurriedly towards the door.

'What have you done?'

He didn't look behind, didn't acknowledge her question. Rage got the better of her, replacing the fear long enough for her to sit up. 'What's happened to him?' she yelled.

Still he didn't look round. She pictured herself leaping up and circling the chains around his throat and squeezing full strength.

He opened the door and slipped quietly through it. Before he closed and locked it, he said, 'Save your energy. You're going to need it.'

***

Left alone for the remainder of that day, an everlasting night with only fits of sleep, and a long way into another day, Naomi was now slouching listlessly on the edge of the bed watching the sky, studying the spectrum of green shades that clothed the hillsides and ran flat to the house. She realised she hadn't eaten since the wedding reception. The soup was gathering dust. The rigid roll sat where she'd left it the day before when he'd tried to force-feed her. Her back ached from too much lying.

It was Monday. It was important to keep tabs on the days. She'd washed in the sink and brushed her teeth like she was getting ready for college. One tap wouldn't shut off properly. It didn't drip, but dribbled a thin stream of water. So now she sat alone waiting with her churned up feelings that were difficult to label. Fear was there in bucket loads. It had infected her mind and body, leaving fertile ground for other things to take root.

Left to stew and sit and sleep and rot and fume, boredom was becoming an issue too; frustration, a bigger one. Fury came and went and was surprisingly useful. It got her hunting for solutions and jumpstarted her brain into plotting an escape, until despair came round again and pinned her to the bed more effectively than the chains.

During the fury part of the cycle earlier that day, she'd paced the room as far as the chains would allow and discovered that the monster hadn't left her without clothes. In the wardrobe beside the bed, just within reach, she'd found two plain T-shirts, one white, one navy blue; a new pair of jeans her size, and a plain black fleecy zip-up jacket. These were hung side by side. Folded neatly and lying at the bottom of the wardrobe, was a spare nightshirt and new supermarket-style pack of 5 knickers in black, also her size. Beside them was a carrier bag with a hand-written label taped on which said, washing.

She'd stared for minutes in shock, then changed her knickers and put on the jeans beneath the nightshirt. She felt more secure in the jeans and was warmer. She put her wedding underwear in the washing bag, hoping he'd never take it. How the hell was she supposed to change tops with her arms in chains?

That done, she'd delved under the bed to investigate why it wouldn't move more than a centimetre. She found that the bed wasn't bolted to the floor, but that two brackets held the metal legs to the skirting board with screws. The screws were only slim. She had a go at loosening them with her fingers. Fat chance! In one of three dusty clusters beneath the bed, which had dodged a vacuum cleaner, she found a single brown hair grip. Uses, if any, had to be considered.

Naomi lay on top of the bed again and examined the hairgrip like she'd never seen one. She removed the small plastic tips. Even now with sharper edges, it was hardly a weapon unless she could jab him in the eye. She couldn't imagine him holding still while she aimed and fired, but she fantasised about it pointlessly.

So if it wasn't a weapon, was there any mileage in using it as a tool? Naomi got up and slid under the bed again until the chains tugged on her arms. She tried to loosen the screws with the curved end of the grip, but it wouldn't insert properly and wouldn't grip! She straightened it into a line and tried to insert one of the sharp ends, but it was a hopeless fit and there was nothing to hold on to. It had no grip. Any effort bent it.

Defeated, she threw herself on the bed again and her mood sunk. She put the hairgrip inside a pillowcase. So here she was now, slumped in a pit with no footholds in the darkest part of the cycle. She didn't know if the monster was in or out. She'd heard no car leaving, but then it was dead downstairs too. She couldn't sense his presence the way she had in the night when she'd lay tense and restless in the darkness, curtains partly open, wondering if Nathan was looking at the same moon, listening to the wind rifling through the trees, terrified of losing consciousness, her pulse impacted by every small noise and movement from the next room.

The voice. Whose voice? Where from? When had she heard it? Would her memory ever match it to a face? It was like seeing a vaguely familiar actor in a film without any clue which film he'd last been in. It was an itch she couldn't scratch. Thinking about it was like drinking salt water to quench thirst.

She dragged herself to her feet and padded barefoot to the window. A dot on a distant hill caught her eye. She watched it, vacantly. The sheep were white dots; the odd-figure-out was dark. A black sheep? It seemed at first to be static, but a patient study told her that the figure was moving as well as growing, which could only mean it was drawing closer. Over several minutes, the speck evolved into a line then a person with working limbs on a direct route towards the house. Not long later, she decided it was a man wearing a black hat, knitted, snugly fitted to his head. He skipped over the winding stream, something tucked under his arm, and headed for the house.

Plans to jump up and down and bash on the window, died. She knew who it was – the only person who already knew she was a prisoner here. Beneath low cloud, he climbed over a wooden fence and walked up the garden, emerging through a small wooden gate that sat between two bushes, carefully clipped. As Naomi willed him to look up so she could see his face, she wondered if her face was splashed across the front cover of the paper he carried. She also wondered which photograph would have been submitted, as if it mattered.

He didn't look up. Head hung down, wearing black canvas shoes, dark jeans and a blue and black striped hoodie, he strode out of view. A door opened downstairs, disturbing her peace, and suddenly Naomi didn't know what to do. She didn't want to see the monster, but she had questions. She had no appetite, but she needed strength. After a few minutes of noises from the kitchen, the stairs were carrying him to her again.

She'd already decided not to move, not this time. She guessed that if he'd wanted her dead, she wouldn't be alive with a stiff bread roll behind her. The key turned in the door. She sat, her back to it, chained, fingers knitted together. He walked in. She didn't look round. She heard the tray being moved from the bedside table. He didn't speak. She wanted to turn her head and look at him about as much as she didn't. She felt exposed out of bed.

He was leaving. So quickly? She'd braced for a confrontation he didn't want. Now she was panicking. She didn't want to be left for hours more with her fears and her unanswered questions. Without time to think, the words spluttered out.

'What do you want with me?' Naomi began in a small voice, pausing for an answer. She could hear him breathing now – short expulsions of air, long intakes. None of them carried any words.

'What's this about?' she pressed, eyes blurred into the greenery outside. 'Where am I and what am I doing here?'

Still nothing.

'What's happened to my husband? Why did you take me from him?' Tears pricked her eyes. The longer he stood in silence, the more questions flooded her head.

'What happened the night you brought me here? I remember lying in a grave. I was in a graveyard, wasn't I? You had a gun. You fired it. I saw a bright light.' She hesitated again. 'Then I woke up here, dressed, wound covered.' She paused again, reliving the confusion of those first thoughts. 'I've tried to piece that night together and I've wondered what you might have . . . done to me, what you might be planning to do. . .' Her voice tapered off. The tears came so that she could only carry on between sobs. 'I recognise your voice. Where do I know you from? Talk to me,' she said, voice rising now. 'Who are you and what do you want?'

Another silence rang out which caused a tightening inside Naomi's chest as she pictured him behind her, cowardly, face covered with his intimidating mask. A noise was developing outside. In the time it took to realise it was an approaching car, he'd flown in front of her to the window. For the first time his voice changed. He swore in an eruption of temper. His movements were quick and agitated. Naomi withdrew onto the bed and curled up by the headboard.

He flew to the bedside table, snatched the tray of fresh food and dumped it in the bathroom. Then he lunged at Naomi on the bed. She screamed. He clamped her mouth shut, leaned in to her nose-to-nose, and told her that if she screamed again it would be the last thing she ever did. He withdrew a tiny key from his pocket and unlocked her at the wrists. The chains, still attached to the bedframe, he buried with pillows, stacked up. Grabbing her right arm, he yanked her to her feet and bundled her into the bathroom.

There was a convincing knock at the front door, then a wait.

He tugged Naomi in front of him until she was inches from the black mask and in full view of his eyes again. He lowered his head to hers.

'You're going to sit quietly in here and not make a sound. Got it?'

There was nothing Naomi could do but agree. She nodded her head, wishing he'd let her arms go.

'If you value your life, do not move. Do not use the toilet or the taps. Clear?'

Naomi nodded again. Whoever was at the front door knocked again, less politely.

'Keep a cool head,' he warned, fixing his eyes on hers for a second before releasing his grip. 'Good girls get answers. You don't want to know what happens to bad girls.'

He pushed past her and shut the door, leaving Naomi panting and trembling. He thundered down the stairs. Naomi strained to listen. The front door opened to another male voice.

It marked the first opportunity, this. The possibilities ran riot in her head as she fought for calm and clear thought. It was hard to take in that she was free of the bed and that another person was in the house with them. Who was it? The risks occurred to her too. Should she yell and stamp her feet and beg for help? She looked longingly at the window, but had no plan.

While she scrambled for the right choice if there was one, two sets of footsteps were climbing the stairs; two voices exchanging words. She found her teeth chattering in the warm room. A decision had to be reached, and quickly. A discussion was going on outside the bedroom. She couldn't decipher words, she could only hear what sounded like a hammer bashing against concrete inside her left ear. Her eardrum was vibrating with the force of her pulse. By now, the voices had broken into the bedroom.

Naomi's mind had branched into two divisions, each had a cheer-leading team. One was urging her to scream, the other ordered her to be still and keep her word. Both made sense and neither made sense. Not used to taking risks, she was unprepared.

'You've moved the bed.' The stranger's voice.

'Oh yeah, I hope you don't mind,' the monster replied in a tone that sounded more-or-less normal. 'My girlfriend liked the view so much, she begged me to put the bed closer to the window.'

The stranger laughed. 'Perfectly understandable. So you've found the en-suite bathroom then?' A rhetorical question. 'The hot tap needs tightening up, so my wife informs me. I've brought a tool just to – '

'Slight problem,' the monster cut in, apologetically. 'My girlfriend is in the bath.'

Naomi's limbs stiffened. Her breathing sounded heavy. *Think.* So, the house was being rented, and the man standing right outside with the friendly voice would try to help her if she raised the alarm.

So what was she waiting for? There was a light rapping on the door, followed by, 'You still in there, babe? Everything alright?'

No! Help me. He's holding me here. Get me out. 'I'm fine,' she heard herself saying in Annabel's voice –

friendly, unconcerned. Why was she cooperating? She hated herself for it.

'Can I come back to fix it next week?'

The monster was more than reasonable. 'Yes, of course.'

'Well, I'll leave you to it,' came the stranger's voice, cheerful, not wanting to intrude a minute more. 'Any problems, give me a buzz. I'm away this week with my missus, but I'll stop by next weekend, OK?'

'Please do.'

She heard the footsteps move towards the door and small-talk start up. They were drifting away. 'Here's my mobile number in case of an emergency,' she caught. 'There's a newsagent just over the hill that way that has all the essentials.'

'Thanks.'

It was now or never. Naomi was shaking with the panic of knowing her chance was slipping. One thing stopped her from letting rip at the top of her lungs – the thought that the stranger might get killed if she dragged him into a problem that wasn't his. His 'missus' might never get him back. She pictured the monster ready with a weapon in case things turned ugly, and the man – defenceless apart from a spanner to fix the tap – falling prey. She couldn't do it. Panic gave way to nausea as her moment melted. She stood, listening to the footsteps of her only hope moving down the stairs and safely out of the front door.

Weak from hunger, she collapsed into a heap and broke down. She vaguely heard the car pulling away, taking the normal, pleasant-sounding man with it. She imagined him switching on the radio as the distance between the car and the house grew, leaving her trapped with an emotionless psycho.

The monster was soon back with her, hoisting her off the floor, balaclava back on, dragging her back to the bed. He secured the locks. Naomi had no strength to resist. He sat on the bed at a distance, watching her. It was a long wait before the tears dried up. Naomi quietened. She had nothing to say to him anymore. She wanted him to die a violent death right in front of her.

Turning her back on him, she curled herself in a ball and burrowed beneath the covers. The chains cut into her right arm at the top. She was so lost inside her head, it was a surprise when he eventually spoke.

'I'll answer one question.'

'Get out,' Naomi said, too softly. Appalled at how submissive she sounded, she flung back the bedding and sat up sharply, shouting full force, straining her empty stomach and not caring if she provoked him. 'Get. Out.'

The bed lightened as he stood up. He walked slowly to the door then hovered. His voice returned to its infuriatingly dead tone. 'Whatever you say.'

The key turned in the lock. Naomi threw the covers back over her head. Her breath was hot and bitter-tasting in the confinement of the duvet. Her head was throbbing painfully all over. She couldn't imagine what kind of a face hid behind that mask, but in an unguarded moment, she was going to find out.

'You'd better watch out,' she whispered very quietly, 'because I am going to kill you.'

7

LIBERTY

'I want to know everything about you,' Nathan said to Naomi from behind a glass of lime and soda, clogged with ice. He took a deep swig and returned it to the small table that stood between them. It had a crisp white table cloth and stiff linen serviettes that matched the colour of the carpet. They were sitting in a cosy English restaurant that boasted one Michelin star, a former Victorian cottage in a town called Prestwich, a few miles outside the city centre.

Naomi was still unable to believe that the previous day, Nathan had showed up at the college reception with only a name. Did they have a first year student by the name of Naomi – sorry, he didn't know the surname? The receptionist looked blank, until Nathan had turned to her and told her it didn't matter, that the girl he'd been failing to describe had just hurried through the door.

So here they were, Naomi pinching herself that Nathan Stone was opposite her, in the flesh, dressed in a pale grey shirt and black jeans with his dark-grey jacket hanging from the chair behind him. He'd fixed his eyes on hers as he'd told her about his relief of discovering her at the RNCM. He'd assumed she was a student at the University of Manchester and conducted a futile three week search of every department of the damned place.

'There isn't much to tell,' Naomi said, determined to lower his expectations from the start.

'Yeah there is. The first moment I saw you, you intrigued me, and it wasn't just the looks or the stunning dress. I'm betting on an interesting story or two. Tell me about your family and where you live. Siblings? Where did you go to school?'

'Well,' she began, 'I live in Alderley Edge.'

He frowned for a second and shrugged. 'Sounds familiar, never been.'

'It's not too shabby. A famous footballer lives up our road.'

'Who?'

'Can't remember his name.'

Nathan grinned. 'That famous?'

'And I have a cat called Tess. Once I'd named her, my sister named her cat Tickles. She still finds it hilarious when my mum shouts the cats one after the other.'

It took Nathan a second to work it out, then he laughed.

'Typical of my sister. We're twins.'

His eyebrows went up. 'Annabel?'

'How did you know?'

He lowered his voice. 'She texted you when I first met you, remember? It's the only thing I knew about you apart from your name. Are you identical?'

She'd been expecting this moment, but not so early in the evening. She reached inside her purse and gathered a small picture of Annabel, ready to gauge Nathan's response. It was an excellent photograph, perfectly capturing Annabel's energy and everything that was beautiful about her.

Sliding the picture across the table cloth, she watched Nathan lift it up. He laughed when he saw Annabel and handed the picture back quickly. Naomi, relieved he hadn't studied it for long, put it back in her purse.

'I'm glad,' he said.

'Why?'

'I can only imagine one of you.' Nathan reached for his drink again, his eyes never leaving hers as he drew a sip.

'We couldn't be more different.'

'Is she musical?'

'Not at all.'

Nathan undid his shirt sleeves and turned them over twice. 'So which uni is she at?'

'Didn't go,' Naomi answered. 'She's travelling for a year and starting uni next year. She sets off for Japan in two weeks, after our birthdays.'

'Which is what date?'

'Dates,' Naomi corrected and waited until Nathan frowned. 'We were born either side of midnight. Annie on the twenty-second of October and me the day after.'

'See, you're full of surprises.' Naomi was relieved when his next question left the topic of Annabel behind. 'Have you always lived in Alderley Edge?'

'I grew up in South Africa, actually.'

His eyebrows raised again. 'South Africa? I wondered why I couldn't place your accent.'

I felt good to surprise him like this. It made her feel mysterious and exciting when her perception of herself had always been the opposite.

'We lived in Johannesburg until I was eleven. We moved there from here when I was about four, but I don't really remember much before living in Jo'burg, except my gran's arms.'

'OK.'

Naomi laughed. 'She used to have these great big arms and she'd lie next to me on the bed and read to me at night. I don't remember my granddad. He must have been around at that time but he never said very much.'

Nathan put his drink down again. Naomi picked hers up and took a shallow sip.

'So what took you out there?'

'My dad's job. He's retired now, but he was a big director or whatever in an accountancy firm. They had offices in Manchester, London and, of all places, Johannesburg.'

Nathan rested his elbows on the table, put his fingers to his lips and moved closer still.

'I've never been to South Africa. What's it like?'

Naomi's eyes roamed the ceiling while she pictured the big detached, single-storey house they'd had there with open-plan rooms and the outdoor swimming pool, shallow end nearest the house. Naomi had only ever been in the shallow end. She panicked in water out of her depth.

She remembered the sunshine; the brightly-coloured gardens in the housing compound behind the tall barbed-wire fence; the honking of horns in the city; the chilly winter nights without carpets or central heating; the insects that dwarfed the English ones; the multi-coloured friends she'd had at school.

Her eyes returned to Nathan's. He was waiting patiently. 'Amazing,' she said. 'Probably my happiest time but . . . well, we had to move back here.'

'Did your dad lose his job?'

'No, nothing like that.' Naomi dropped her eyes to her glass and fingered a downwards stroke through the condensation on the outside of it. 'I was taken by a couple of men who hijacked the car.'

'You what?'

She looked up. His eyes were wide. She'd never felt so interesting. 'Mm,' she sighed, suddenly experiencing pangs of longing for Johannesburg. 'It's an incredible city, Jo'burg, but volatile. Poverty and wealth live side by side. It's in your face all the time, no escape. People are desperate enough to beg or steal. It's survival for some. Anyone nicely dressed with an expensive car will be a potential target.' Naomi paused as a waitress approached, pad in hand, ready to pen the order.

'I haven't even looked,' Naomi admitted, embarrassed that she'd been so lost in Nathan's eyes, the purpose of her being there hadn't even occurred to her. She swept her menu off the table and wildly started searching it for the main courses.

'I can come back,' the waitress offered.

Nathan held up his hand. 'One sec.' He turned to Naomi. 'You're not vegetarian are you?'

'No.'

'Can I recommend the lamb shoulder with madeira sauce?'

Naomi glanced down, found the lamb, scanned the description which included shallots and fennel among other things.

'Yes,' she agreed quickly. 'Sounds great.'

Spaghetti hoops on toast would have done. She was a new student having an unexpected dinner with Nathan Stone. Whatever he'd suggested would have been perfect because he was perfect. And hot and utterly gorgeous with his grey-blue eyes and his sexy smile that was all hers. The way he was looking at her made concentration on anything but him, impossible.

'Two of those please,' Nathan told the waitress.

She made a note, gathered the menus and left.

'You were saying,' he immediately said.

Naomi took another sip, conscious of his gaze closely following her. His eyes hadn't once strayed to the surrounding tables. It made her aware of every small move she made. With one hand, she smoothed her new black trousers under the table. 'My dad's into cars. Big time. So, I was eleven. We pulled up in a petrol station to fill up. Over there, attendants fill the car for you, offer to check the tyres etcetera. As long as you're tipping well, you can have any service you want.' Naomi suddenly became conscious of her hand gestures and that she was gabbling. She put her hands away and decided to slow down. 'Anyway, my mum got out of the car with Annabel, who was complaining there was something crawling on her leg. Two men sprung from nowhere and screeched off with me still in the back.'

Nathan's mouth fell open. 'Are you serious?'

'Uh-huh.'

'You must have been terrified.'

Naomi, dying to break into a big smile, resisted. 'Not as much as I should have been. I didn't know then what I know now. Living there was normal life. I didn't know much about apartheid. I suppose Mum shielded us. I didn't know anything about the British Empire or what political and racial axes people had to grind.'

Nathan nodded carefully. 'So what happened?'

'They only wanted the car. They told me not to worry, that they were only testing the car. I was naïve. I believed them. About half a mile down the road, they pulled over and told me to go back to my mum. So I did.'

Nathan shook his head. 'She must have been frantic.'

'She was. The police were there by the time I skipped into the petrol station wondering what all the fuss was about. My mum freaked out and told me what could have happened, then I freaked out too. I had nightmares about it for ages afterwards.'

'Did they catch them?'

'Nah. Did they even try? Who knows? We never saw the car again.'

'Quite an adventure for an eleven-year-old.'

'Hmm. Well, my mum was ready for coming back to

England virtually that night. I remember hearing the arguments from my room. I didn't want to leave. My dad eventually gave in like he usually does.' Naomi sighed. 'He got a transfer to the offices in Manchester and we got back to England in time to start secondary school that September.'

Nathan reached across the table and found her hand. Naomi had to cover the shock. He loosely locked fingers with hers and stroked her forefinger with his thumb. It was hard to keep cool and not close her eyes.

'The irony is,' Naomi finished, 'my mum wishes we'd never come back, but moved to a safer place in South Africa instead. Whenever she brings that up, my dad's eyes just roll.'

'I can imagine.' Nathan smiled. 'So how was school here after life in South Africa?'

'Horrible,' she said, acutely aware of their twined fingers and his capable hands and the mild scent of his aftershave that she caught between delicious food smells. 'I lasted about five months and left with my confidence in tatters.'

She dropped her eyes, gripped by the pain and the shame of that time, not wanting Nathan to read it.

'Hey,' he said, pulling gently on her hand until he'd reclaimed her eyes. His face was close. 'I'm sorry. We can change the sub – '

'No,' she said. 'It's OK.' She tried to smile, but it was a pathetic attempt. 'It's seven years ago. I'm over it now.'

'Are you?' he asked, searching her eyes.

She nodded, slowly, unconvincingly. 'It's just that my life switched course right then. One person changed everything. No one should have that kind of power, should they?'

'Which person?'

Naomi looked at the table, her drink, the salt and pepper pots. 'A girl called Sophie Wheatcroft.' Saying the name disturbed all kinds of feelings Naomi normally kept under control. Her memory still dug up images of the girl in dreams. Naomi could see her now: busty even at eleven, tall with blonde hair and feline green eyes that kept watch from an angular face. Nathan waited. 'She was in my form at my new school.'

'She bullied you?'

'She wouldn't have called it that,' Naomi replied, fidgeting with discomfort. 'It was more subtle – like psychological abuse. I was nervous. Shy, I suppose, which made me vulnerable. I just needed a friend.'

'A sitting duck for Sophie Wheatcroft?'

'Yep.' Naomi paused to clear her throat. 'I was a classical music geek, even back then.' Nathan scowled. 'It's true. Plus I was the weirdo with the strange accent who didn't know the netball or hockey rules. Basically, she made sure no one took me on as a friend. There's nothing more demoralising for a girl than being at a loose end.'

Nathan said, thoughtfully, 'Wasn't Annabel around?'

'She was,' Naomi nodded, 'but she wasn't in my form. She'd picked up the English accent in weeks and was like the celebrity of our school year. Her new friends thought she was really cool with her stories about huge rain spiders and parktown prawns – '

'Parktown what?'

'They're like giant crickets.' Naomi's stomach lurched as Nathan squeezed her fingers gently.

'Didn't Annabel include you?'

'She tried, but I didn't feel comfortable with her friends. I needed my own. I prefer one person at a time. Annie always has swarms of people, the more the better.'

'So it didn't work.'

'No.'

'Couldn't your parents afford a private school?'

'That was a private school.'

'Oh.'

There was a short pause. 'So to fill lunch breaks I'd go and play the piano. Things became unbearable when the boy Sophie Wheatcroft worshipped started to spend his lunchtimes with me. He used to sit at the piano in the school hall, sharing my stool. He played a bit himself, but he wasn't very good. He liked listening to me.' Nathan was unmoving, eyes fixed on her. Head bowed, Naomi flicked him the odd look. 'I really liked him, but being with him kind of sealed my fate and cut me off from any chance of friends. She made sure of that. She spread rumours that I slept with him. I was twelve, barely even knew what it meant.'

'You weren't the weirdo, Naomi, you were the talented newcomer who was threatening her territory. The only thing she could do was discredit you to make herself look better.'

'And she succeeded.'

'No, she didn't.'

'Well anyway, I confided in Annabel. She wanted to rip Sophie Wheatcroft to pieces, but I didn't want my twin fighting my battles for me. Maybe if she'd been my older sister . . . '

When Naomi went quiet again, Nathan asked how it ended up.

'Annabel told Mum.' Naomi sighed. 'She'd have found out anyway. I'd stopped eating, stopped playing the piano. It got worse once my mum started turning up at school and barging into the headmaster's office telling him how to run the place. I was mortified.'

Nathan's face was incredibly serious when Naomi eyed him again. She felt bad about dampening the mood.

Eventually, he said, 'Did things improve?'

'Only after I left school and was home-taught.'

'Couldn't you have tried another school?'

'I couldn't face it. For two years I was taught at home and looked after by a nanny. I was happier that way. I buried myself in music and my piano playing took off big time. That's when my mum sent me back to school – Chethams, a specialist music school in Manchester.'

'I know Chethams,' Nathan said. 'Isn't it a boarding school?'

'Yes.'

'Did you have your own room?'

'No. Dormitories. Only the oldest kids get single rooms. I stuck it out for another two years until I was sixteen. I learned loads about music and got my GCSEs, but I didn't like it there.'

'Why?'

'Chets is quite strict – a regime almost. The Practise Gestapo patrol the corridors to make sure you're on your instrument. It didn't suit me, working like that. I didn't stay for sixth form. I went back to home tutors and joined the Junior Royal Northern. I went there every Saturday until I got a place this year.'

'Sounds lonely.'

Naomi sighed, overwhelmed for a moment. 'It was, but my nanny I'd had from being twelve still worked at the house. She became my closest friend, still is. She's only seven years older than me. When I didn't need looking after anymore, she became my mum's PA really. The house is too big for my mum to manage by herself. The garden is huge and my mum grows fruit and veg and supplies a few local businesses. It's her hobby, her passion. She's always in the garden. Then we have one cleaner, Denise, who comes in for a few hours a week.'

'Sounds like a mansion.'

'It's pretty big. Two staircases, five bedrooms, four with en-suite.'

Nathan was impressed and shocked again. 'Five, with only two kids?'

'Well my ex-nanny used to live in, but she has her own flat now. She still has a room with us and stays sometimes. Thing is, my dad won't move. He doesn't like change and my mum can't really force the issue after dragging him back from Jo'burg, so the compromise is paying Lorie to help manage the place.'

'Lorie?'

Naomi managed a genuine smile as she thought of her. 'My ex-nanny and best friend, Lorie Taylor. She's virtually one of the family. Even my mum loves her.'

'Your mum sounds scary.'

The same waitress was standing by the table holding two square dinner plates. They'd been so deep in conversation, they hadn't seen her coming. The delicious smell of lamb made Naomi's mouth fill with juices. The meal wasn't huge, but it was artistically arranged. She studied it a moment.

'Enjoy your meal,' the waitress said.

'This looks amazing,' Naomi said, attempting to inject her voice with some enthusiasm, desperately hoping she wasn't scaring him off.

'Tuck in.' Nathan picked up his cutlery and gathered a forkful of food. Naomi did the same and got a burst of incredible flavours.

'That OK for you?'

'It's delicious.'

Nathan ate a mouthful too. 'So how many hours a day do you play the piano?'

Naomi, sure she must be boring him by now, was keen to change the subject. 'It varies. I suppose about four or five.'

'What?' Nathan came back quickly.

'It's not that much.' Naomi dropped her head again, overwhelmed by general feelings of failure that overtook her so easily. In an attempt to shake them off, she said, more upbeat, 'Your turn.'

Nathan continued to eat. He shook his head the way Naomi had as if he had nothing to tell. 'What do you want to know?'

She wanted to know everything, anything. Actually, there was something specific. 'You can start by telling why you talked to me in that bar three weeks ago, then didn't ask for my number.'

Her comment brought a half smile. 'However much of a cliché this sounds, I was incredibly attracted to you on first sight,' he said bluntly, emptying his mouth. Naomi, feeling an impulse to break into the *hallelujah chorus*, smothered a smile with a mouthful of food.

'Really?' she fished.

'Absolutely. And I didn't ask for your number for complex reasons, but mainly because of the age difference. I'm twenty-five. When I realised you were only eighteen I thought I'd better leave you to mix with people the same age.' Nathan paused to sip his drink and grind some pepper onto his meat. 'I know what it's like being a first-year student. It's important to bond with the others. I didn't want to intrude, plus I didn't know if you were attached.'

'But you came looking for me,' she said. The joy was definitely surging back in a rush.

'Couldn't stay away. You got inside my head that night and wouldn't leave. I admit I didn't do a very good job of trying to kick you out. Selfish or not, I had to see you again. I never expected to find you at the Royal Northern.' He paused to narrow his eyes. 'I want to hear you play.'

'I'm not that good.'

'Oh sure,' he said. 'I actually like some classical music you know.'

'Yeah?' Naomi chewed happily on a tender piece of lamb. *I want to hear you play* could only mean that Nathan intended to see her again. He already knew she hadn't stuck it out in a normal school and he wasn't running. He'd seen Annabel and he wasn't talking about her. He'd heard a bit about Camilla and he wasn't sweating. 'Like what?'

'Well it's got to be epic, like Beethoven or Mahler or Tchaikovsky. I can take or leave the soft soppy stuff. I hate Chopin – all those twiddly bits and fairy runs.'

Naomi laughed.

'I basically like to hear a full orchestra play on full throttle, not just one section of it while everyone else chills for ten minutes. That bores me.'

Naomi sipped her drink. 'I'm impressed.'

'Don't be. You're the impressive one,' he said right back. She looked at him, unable to fathom why. He must have read it in her expression. 'All that history of yours? Some would have crumbled, but you've had the guts to use your talents, focus on education and better yourself.'

'That's one way of looking at it.'

'It's the only way. I'm betting you've got a stack of A*s from school and loads of prizes for your music?'

She hesitated. He waited. 'How did you guess?'

'Anyone who spends five hours a day on an instrument isn't going to be a slacker with other work,' he said, and she smiled. He held her eyes for a long and happy moment. 'Why don't you know how amazing you are?'

***

It was getting on for eleven-thirty that night when Nathan pulled into the dead car park behind the college. He killed the engine and gave her a look loaded with promise, but he didn't make a move. He had hold of the steering wheel in one hand.

'I'll walk you to the door.'

Naomi was keenly aware of the quiet car, the darkness, the full moon that beamed without restraint in a clear sky spotted with stars, Nathan's closeness. 'OK,' she said, feeling giddy, almost lightheaded and weightless. She released her belt, collected her bag, stepped carefully out of the car.

Nathan was already on her side when she straightened up. There was no time for awkwardness. As soon as she'd closed the door, he took her neck in both of his hands and weaved his fingers into her hair and leaned in. His lips connected with hers, lightly brushing them at first, pulling away, returning. Her chin tilted up. His lips were cool, but his mouth was warm as their bodies shoved closer together, arms tightening around each other, the connection deepening.

It went on and on, and ended too quickly. They started strolling eventually, arm in arm, chatting between kisses, making slow progress. Near the reception door, he pressed her against the wall and kissed her again. She lost awareness of everything else.

Her eyes were still sealed when he leant his forehead against hers and announced that he was leaving. It brought her round. She could feel him breathing against her and was aware of his lean body, his smell, the pressure of his hands on her lower back. She felt her hair stirring from a mild wind and heard the passing traffic now and the students returning to their rooms in small noisy groups. She could have happily frozen that moment and savoured it for a very long time. She mustn't cling to him.

'OK.'

'How many boyfriends have you had?' he asked, still glued to her.

She opened her eyes and focussed on his. 'With my background? Are you kidding?'

He waited, expression serious. 'No.'

'Just one.'

'One,' he repeated. 'Where did you meet him?'

'Chets. He played the viola.'

'Viola?'

'A big violin.'

'Does it bother you that I'm not some gifted prodigy like everyone else you seem to know?'

Naomi grinned. 'Absolutely not. None of them are as easy to talk to as you. And some of them are pretty weird. Plus I do have other interests.'

'Do they include picking strange men up in bars?'

'They do now.'

The eye contact was close and intense and electrifying. She hoped he couldn't feel her pulse. 'I'm not good at sharing, Naomi, not when it comes to relationships.' He wasn't smiling anymore.

'Me neither.'

Now he smiled, or at least his eyes did. 'Good. Does this mean we're an item then? I'll be honest, I'm past loose relationships. If I'm with someone, then I'm with them. And I want to be with you.'

'I'm all yours.' It slipped out so effortlessly.

'I'm older than you. Are you sure you're ready for this?'

'Definitely,' she whispered.

His eyelids dropped and his head fell to one side. He kissed her again and the magic took over and possessed her. When he pulled back, the surroundings returned. 'I won't get in the way of friends or music, I promise.' His arm was leaning against the wall above her head. His other hand was holding her to him. 'So were you in love with this guy or what? What was his name?'

'Tom Butterworth.'

'Tom Butterworth,' he repeated, digesting it.

'And, no.'

'No?'

'I realise after tonight that I wasn't in love with him. Anyway, he let me down quite badly.'

His eyebrows sunk to a crease in the middle. 'How?'

She hesitated. 'I'd rather not talk about it.'

A short pause. 'Sounds like you're still hurt. Are you over him?'

'Oh definitely.'

'I'm confused,' Nathan said. 'Are we going to have secrets?'

She hesitated again. 'I'll tell you about him when I'm ready, OK?' He nodded carefully. 'I thought you were leaving,' she said, playfully, watching his mouth, hoping to invite him back to her lips to perform his tricks again.

He accepted and leant forward. 'Believe it or not,' he said against her lips, causing light vibrations. 'I am trying to.'

***

Naomi struggled to get into the building that night. Connecting her swipe card in a trembling hand with the narrow slot, took real effort. For the first time in a month, she took the stairs to burn some energy. On the way up, she found Lorie's number and dialled, hoping she wouldn't be in bed. She was desperate to tell someone and release some feelings. Annabel would be second choice.

Lorie was awake, just. 'What's up Naomi?' she said, sleepily. Naomi heard her TV volume turn down.

'Lorie, I've met someone.'

Lorie yelled down the phone. Naomi held it away from her ear and grinned like a clown.

'Where? Who? Why are you out of breath?'

'I'm climbing twelve flights of stairs to my room. He's just dropped me off now. I can't keep still.'

'Someone from college? Why haven't you mentioned him?'

'I'm sorry,' Naomi said, not sorry at all. 'I met him randomly in a bar three weeks ago. I never expected to see him again. He took me out for dinner.' She groaned. 'He's soooo gorgeous.'

Lorie screamed again. 'It's about time. Is he a student then?'

'No. He's twenty-five.'

'Twenty-five! Your mum would have a fit.'

'So don't tell her.'

'Obviously. What does he do?'

'I don't know.'

'Where does he live?'

'I never asked.'

'Naomi!' Lorie chided in an exaggerated voice, the way she did when she sometimes slipped into her *nanny* role. Naomi laughed into her phone. 'Did you actually find anything out?'

'He's called Nathan and he's got the sexiest lips on the planet. And he has to be the world's best kisser. What else is there to know?'

After they'd both laughed a while, Lorie said, 'I've met someone too.'

'Who?'

'His name is Simon Wilde.'

'Does he live up to his name?' Naomi giggled.

'Not really. He's an accountant. Your dad will love him,' Lorie said. 'But let's talk about him another time, it's your night. Naomi?'

'You've got your *nanny* voice on again.'

'I don't care, just listen to me. After everything you've been through, no one deserves this more than you. Don't let Tom Butterworth affect your confidence for ever, OK? Not all guys are like him. I don't want to hear any of this I-don't-deserve-to-be-happy rubbish. As long as this guy treats you well, you cling on to him, OK? I'm so pleased for you.'

8

Sydney the spider had gone walkabout when Naomi woke up the following morning to the sound of Madeline's clarinet next door. The constant sound of music echoed round the whole place and Naomi floated in it this morning. She lay, just listening. Madeline was playing the slow movement from Mozart's Concerto in A, and beautifully. Naomi hummed along, stretching like a cat.

She turned over in bed and scanned the room for Sydney. No sign. Her battered upright piano was cluttered with music and pencils and an old metronome that sat on top without its lid beside a can of hairspray. Her outfit from the night before hung over the chair that doubled as her piano stool. Shoes and books were scattered. The contents of her makeup bag littered the desk. A sack of dirty washing overflowed beneath it, covering her hair dryer.

None of it mattered. From head to toe, she tingled. As she yawned and smiled at the ceiling, details of the previous evening rushed back. It had taken her most of the night to find shallow sleep, and the remainder of it had only recaptured Nathan in vivid images.

Naomi imagined Camilla rigidly following her weekend routine at home, a place Naomi yearned for and thought about less and less. Camilla would not approve of her room here or the mess it had become. She'd wince at the toothpaste marks on the sink and the screwed-up towels on the bathroom floor surrounded by bare toilet roll tubes. And if she knew that *her* sensible, shy Naomi had spent an evening with a twenty-five-year-old man, she'd flip.

Naomi picked up her phone to check the time and noticed that Nathan had left a message. She opened it eagerly, wondering how she'd missed it. It had been sitting there since four-thirty, which was probably about the same time as she'd drifted towards him in sleep. It said: 'Can't think of anything but you. I intended to be cool about it but can't. I want to see you again. Ring me at whatever hour you get this. I'm free all Sunday.' He attached one kiss.

Without thinking, Naomi pressed the call button and Nathan answered after two rings.

'What took you so long?' he asked.

Naomi curled up on her side in bed and cradled the phone to her ear as if they were in a top-secret conversation. 'What time is it? I've just woken up.'

Nathan chuckled. She loved his laugh and her sense of achievement whenever she drew it. And now he wasn't opposite her, she could smile as freely as she wanted without the pressure of trying to look sophisticated. 'It's quarter to ten. How can you sleep after last night?'

'Exhaustion beat me. I've been awake for most of the night.'

'Are you busy today, Naomi?'

Resisting the impulse to yell, *For you? No, not busy at all,* she calmly replied, 'I'm always busy. On Sundays I do my washing and we usually clean up the kitchen so we actually have some pots and pans to use.'

Nathan tutted. 'You're not going to church then?'

'Church?'

'Don't think I haven't noticed your necklace. You wouldn't wear it so religiously if you weren't religious.'

So, he'd assessed little details. 'I do believe in God, and – don't laugh at me – I pray too. But I don't go to church. To me, it's all about how you feel inside. Don't you think?'

'I'll take your word for it. The last prayer I said was in a school assembly.'

Picturing Nathan as a small boy sitting crossed-legged in a school hall was impossible, but fun. 'Well, I've been on my own a lot, so praying helped me feel like I had company.'

'Yeah, but what d'you find to say?' Nathan said. 'No offence, but doesn't it feel a bit . . . weird?'

'No. I just talk like he's my friend.'

'He?'

'I think so. I tell him about my aspirations or what's bothering me. I ask for stuff, thank for stuff. Simple.' She paused, wondering whether or not to admit what was on her mind. Nathan cut in.

'I'm sure he's riveted. What was the last thing you asked for?'

He'd asked now, uncannily reading her thoughts. She drew a deep breath through her nose. 'That we'd find each other again,' she said, cringing beneath the duvet at how cheesy it sounded.

'Result. But how can you ever prove it wasn't a coincidence?'

'How can you ever prove it was?'

'I can't,' he laughed.

'Me neither,' she said, knowing she could never have admitted any of this if he hadn't been so upfront about his own feelings. 'But I did make a promise that if you came into my life . . .'

He waited. 'Go on.'

'No, I can't tell you unless I need to. It sounds crazy. Anyway, I'll have to keep the promise now.'

Nathan laughed. 'Is it going to be another one of those things that you tell me when you're ready?'

'Yep.'

'You're unique, Naomi Hamilton, you know that? If you can respect my deeply sincere atheist religion, then I'm sure I can make room for your determination to be a God-botherer. Deal?'

Naomi pushed her forefinger inside her hair and twisted. 'Deal.'

'So seeing as God hasn't got you tied up today, can your washing wait or not?'

Naomi glanced at the stuffed bag beneath her desk that was at least a week overdue already. It was a no-brainer. 'Without a doubt.'

'Good,' he said in a smouldering voice that made her want him right next to her, right then, with his full lips and his talent for using them. 'I'll take you for lunch. Be ready for twelve and make sure there's a piano available.'

***

By twelve, Naomi had cleaned up her room, helped sort the kitchen, had a shower, dressed and done her makeup. She was straightening her hair when Nathan rang to say he was parking the car. In an unruffled voice that intended to convince him she hadn't been flapping like a trapped bird all morning, she told him she'd come down and sign him in.

Her eyes looked over the room. She hadn't made the bed. She didn't know if Nathan would see her room or not, but she wanted it to be reasonable if he did. She hurriedly arranged the covers and plumped the pillows before she took a last look in the mirror and, deciding that she looked neither under nor overdressed in jeans and a plain white top, ran for the lift.

Nathan was wearing a black and grey checked shirt and dark jeans behind the glass door of the reception area. Her hand shook as she wrote his name and let him inside. He slid his arm around her waist as they walked through the paved area towards A Block. Violin music sang from an open window.

Nathan, arrested, paused to listen. 'Is that a CD?'

Naomi laughed. 'No, it's a guy called Sam Curtis, my year. He's practising the Sibelius Violin Concerto for the concerto competition.'

'He's insanely good. I'm already feeling inadequate and I've only been here two minutes.'

'Don't bother,' Naomi said, lowering her voice. 'Sam's amazing, but he's his own biggest fan. He plays with the window open every day. I've never heard him talk about anyone but himself.'

Nathan carried on walking. 'Am I going to get a guided tour?' he asked.

'You want to see my room?'

'Sure.'

Siobhan emerged from around the corner in a floor length skirt, carrying her flute and a tatty brown leather case that held her sheet music. The sight of her stony expression, big hair and milky-white skin reminded Naomi that she hadn't seen her in a while and filled her head with excuses. But Siobhan didn't stop to talk. She took one look at Nathan and nodded almost imperceptibly at Naomi. Nathan didn't notice her and Naomi didn't say anything, but found herself feeling guilty as Siobhan trudged heavily by, dragging her uncomfortable silence with her that was more condemning than words.

They took the lift to the top floor. Nathan looked over the banister down through the synchronized staircases with twisting black rails that tumbled to the ground, two per floor. They made their way to Naomi's door.

She drew a gulp of air. She was nervous. 'So this is

my room.'

He leant over and kissed her briefly as though he couldn't resist a second longer. 'OK, I promise to behave.'

Naomi fumbled with the door key, opened the door and was stupidly surprised at how organised the room looked. It hadn't been this tidy since she'd met Nathan at the Freshers' dinner and he'd injected her with enough energy to tidy the entire block. As the weeks had passed and the fizz inside her had flattened, the room had suffered too. Until today.

'Nice,' he commented. 'And you've got your own piano.'

'I'm not touching that thing for you,' Naomi warned as Nathan took her in his arms. 'It probably sounded great about fifty years ago. There are tons of Steinways and Yamahas in the college,' she said while he hugged her.

'Which do you prefer?'

'Steinway. Like asking if you'd prefer a Mercedes or a Ford.'

'Is the difference that obvious?' He kissed her lightly on the lips and withdrew a few centimetres.

She nodded. 'It is to me.'

'So Steinways are the Rolls-Royces of the piano world?'

'Pretty much. Yamahas are fine though. They're workhorses, built to last. I actually prefer my piano at home to any other. It's a Bosendorfer.'

He shrugged. 'Cheaper than a Rolls-Royce I hope?'

'It was forty-five thousand.'

'Forty-five k? That's mad,' he said, gently kissed her forehead. They walked to the window and looked down. Will Barton was passing by underneath. The black hair was striking against the polished red case. He was always shouting some greeting to someone or other as if there wasn't a living soul he didn't know or want to know. As Naomi thought of Annabel, Nathan pulled her into a sitting position on the bed.

'So,' he said, searching her eyes, 'Do you love it here?'

Nathan still had hold of her hand. Naomi sighed. 'Getting there.'

Nathan frowned. 'Meaning?'

'Meaning,' she paused to think, 'that it felt like the only option for me after everything that happened.'

'That doesn't sound good. It's never too late to switch direction you know.'

'It is.' She lowered her head.

'No, it isn't.' He lifted her chin 'You have to pursue what makes you happy.'

'I do love music,' she said as enthusiastically as possible. 'Besides, my mum is expecting great things of me here. I daren't disappoint.'

Nathan studied her for a long moment. 'Why would it disappoint her if you became what you wanted to become?'

'She wants me to become a musician.'

'You're already a musician. You must have spent half your life at your instrument to be good enough to get into this place.'

'I have,' she agreed.

He pulled her hand to his lips and deposited another gentle kiss. 'So why do I get the feeling you have reservations? What do *you* want?'

Silence. Her head was blank. 'I've never really wondered.'

'Sure you have,' Nathan responded seriously. 'We all know what we're passionate about, Naomi. It's what drives us.'

'It doesn't matter now,' Naomi said, eager to move on.

He shuffled round to look at her properly. 'Of course it matters.'

Nathan squeezed Naomi's hand while she persuaded herself to be honest with him. It was surprisingly difficult to form the words and release them out loud. 'I love books, but I have no time to read anymore,' she said. 'I used to write poetry. I always dreamed of becoming a writer. I think if things had turned out differently, I might have studied literature or creative writing.'

'Make things turn out differently.'

'No I can't. It's too late.'

She dropped her head again. He lifted her chin a second time. 'You're eighteen. What kind of an answer is that?'

She shrugged. 'I'll never be a concert pianist anyway.'

'Why not?'

'I'm nowhere near good enough. And if I was, I couldn't handle the pressure. Performing terrifies me. I'll probably just end up teaching or something. I have to be realistic.' She hesitated. 'Thing is, I don't want to be a teacher.'

Nathan seemed to be looking beyond her eyes and inside her mind. He put his arm around her and pulled her against his chest. Naomi found she had a lump in her throat that started to ache then hurt. She was surprised when the tears came. Nathan didn't speak. He just held her and kissed the top of her head.

'I'm sorry. I'm being ridiculous,' she said. 'Up to meeting you, I hadn't cried in ages. I feel really stupid.'

'Don't. Releasing emotion isn't a crime or a sign of weakness. I'm guessing your mum doesn't approve of tears.'

Naomi stiffened up and looked at him. 'How do you know?'

'Doesn't take a genius,' he said. 'I happen to think you're very strong and very considerate and far too accommodating.'

'Someone has to make up for Annabel.'

Nathan jerked his head back. 'Meaning?'

'Annie does what's best for her. Don't get me wrong, she's adorable, and funny and generous, but she gave up on all the opportunities my parents offered her: music, horse riding, gymnastics, swimming, tennis.' Naomi stopped to search the ceiling, sure there were more things. 'She prefers to party. She'd rather be with friends than us, any day.'

'She's eighteen, nearly nineteen,' Nathan said. 'I really don't see anything wrong with Annabel deciding what she wants out of life and going for it. Presumably she's passionate about more than just parties?'

Naomi stopped to picture Annabel. The thought that arrived first was watching her paragliding over the sea on some holiday which wouldn't come to mind. Naomi had stood watching, wishing she'd had the courage. 'She loves the outdoors and travelling. That's why she's delaying uni for a year and jet-setting. My mum isn't happy about it, but Annabel isn't bothered.'

'They don't get on?'

'No. Annabel will not conform.'

Nathan went quiet. 'Look, this is none of my business – '

'But I want to hear your opinion,' Naomi said.

He sucked a sharp intake of breath then let it out slowly. 'OK, why should Annabel conform, and why should you? You shouldn't be living your life trying to be what your parents want you to be and making up for your sister who's rejected their ideas. She knows what makes her happy and you should too. Even though you're studying music, you might find that your mum isn't satisfied with your career choice in the end. Then what?'

Naomi shrugged. Nathan wiped her tears with his thumbs. 'Your mum can only have as much control over you as you allow her to have, don't you see?' he asked.

'I've never really thought about it.'

'Well, maybe you should. You might discover a little more about yourself.'

'I sometimes wonder who I am. I sometimes look at Annie and resent that I'm the one who carries my mum's expectations.'

'You've allowed yourself to become that martyr without considering the impact on yourself. At least you've moved away from home. It's a start. Maybe it's time for some self-examination now.'

'Maybe I'm scared of what I'll find,' she said.

'I don't think there's any need,' he smiled. 'You're not on your own anymore. You've got me now and . . . ' He looked at her for a long moment. 'I'm crazy about you.' Naomi, stunned, couldn't speak. 'I know it's mad. We barely know each other, but no one has ever got under my skin like this. You don't have to say anything.'

'I feel the same,' she whispered. 'I don't know what's happened to me, but since we met it's been hard to concentrate on anything and keep control of myself.'

'Stop trying,' he said, leaning in to kiss her, properly this time. They slowly lay back entwined in each other's arms.

A sharp knock on the door yanked Naomi to her senses quickly. She jerked free and sat up, noticing that Nathan was unruffled.

'What's wrong?' he whispered.

Naomi froze, listening hard. There was another impatient knock. The knock, like a signature, was familiar.

'What if it's –'

Her very worst fear was confirmed. 'Naomi?' Camilla's voice was clear and commanding behind the door.

'My mum,' Naomi mouthed to Nathan, jumping up off the bed, smoothing herself down and checking herself in the mirror. While she flushed scarlet red, she wiped her smudged mascara. 'Coming,' she called. She could hear Annabel talking to her dad. The whole family had arrived. Nightmare. Naomi would never have wanted Nathan to meet Annabel so soon. And as for Camilla . . .

Nathan calmly rose to his feet, stretching to his full and impressive height. Why did he look so composed? With no time to collaborate a story, Naomi started for the door before any more time could elapse. Nathan caught hold of her arm.

'I'll handle things, don't panic,' he whispered noiselessly.

He released her and she hurried to open the door.

'Hi. Sorry, Mum, I was in the bathroom,' Naomi lied, feeling the need to offer an excuse. She was trying to remember to look pleased to see them at the same time. She couldn't imagine what her expression was really saying.

'An unpleasant girl with ginger hair signed us in downstairs,' Camilla said. Naomi was relieved the room was clean and tidy. 'She apparently recognised us from your Facebook photographs – ' Camilla stopped and looked over Naomi's shoulder at Nathan, then back at Naomi. Her tone tightened. 'You look flustered, Naomi. And upset.'

'No, I'm fine.'

'Three times I tried to call. No answer.'

'Really?' Naomi said, feigning innocence as she

remembered ignoring the calls. 'My phone's on silent.'

'I had no idea you were so busy.'

'I'm not busy,' Naomi said, cheeks burning. She turned to Nathan to hide them. 'Not doing anything are we? Nothing. Come in.' Naomi stood back and they filed past her.

'We've come to take you out for lunch to plan our birthday bash before I go,' Annabel piped up. Naomi's heart sank when she studied Annabel. She'd dressed up – no doubt for Will Barton's benefit – in skinny dark jeans, strappy wedge-heeled sandals and a small top that showed off her curves and the diamond in her belly button that Camilla never failed to complain about. A swinging necklace hung to waist length. Her long blonde hair was in freefall around her face, her lips were pale red and glossy. Naomi wasn't sure if she was more sickened about Annabel seeing Nathan, or him seeing her. Annabel's eyes lingered excessively on Nathan.

'I brought you a jumper,' Camilla said, ignoring Nathan, handing Naomi something black and soft that smelt of Camilla. 'It shrunk in the machine. I don't like things tight on me the way you girls do.'

'Why would Naomi want a second-hand middle-aged-woman's jumper?' Annabel asked.

'Classic shape and design. Perfect for Naomi,' Camilla said, eyeing Annabel. She snatched the jumper back, unfolded it and held it up against Naomi. 'See? Too good to throw away and excellent quality.' She folded it again.

Annabel muttered, 'Who gives a crap?'

Camilla glared at Annabel. Naomi, sure she was about to suffer death by mortification, found herself accepting the jumper and muttering that she'd try it on.

'I told you she'd like it,' Camilla said. Annabel rolled her eyes.

Naomi hoped Annabel would leave it there. Nathan saved the day by stepping forward and offering Henry his hand.

'Hi. I'm Nathan Stone, Naomi's friend. Good to meet you.'

Henry shook his hand enthusiastically. 'You too.'

Camilla, not giving him the chance to introduce himself, turned her back on Nathan and walked into the bathroom. She disappeared then returned and stood in the doorway and glared at Nathan.

'What are you doing in here? Doesn't the college have any rules about – '

'Camilla,' Henry said, intercepting the comment.

Inside, Naomi was curling up like a fallen autumn leaf. Annabel laughed openly. 'Mum this is the twenty-first century, not the days of the ark. Colleges don't babysit students. They're all adults, capable of adult behaviour.'

'Look,' Nathan said, face straight, 'Naomi was just showing me around the place. We came in here because she needed to get her coat and use the bathroom. We were about to go and grab some lunch.'

'The sink's dry,' Camilla said.

'Sorry?' Nathan said, voice light and polite.

'If Naomi had used the bathroom, the sink wouldn't be dry.'

'Camilla,' Henry said a second time.

'Mum,' Naomi said, 'I don't have to explain my reasons for using the bathroom,' which seemed just as well when she couldn't think of one. The heat in her cheeks fired up a notch. She was sure they were betraying her.

Annabel threw up her hands and let them clap loudly onto her thighs. 'You're being ridiculous, Mother. And you're embarrassing her. What Naomi does in her own room or her bathroom is up to her. What are you now, Inspector Morse? If she wants to have friends round, she can.'

All eyes were on Camilla. Hers were dark and ice-cold, and directed at Nathan. 'Well,' she said, delaying the answer with another tense silence, 'the immediate problem is, how are we going to take Naomi out to lunch when she has plans to eat with her friend here.' Accent on *friend*.

All eyes switched to Nathan except Annabel's which rolled again. Nathan's attention on Camilla didn't flinch. 'Why don't we go out together? I've heard lots about all of you. It'd be great to get to know you better.' No one answered. 'Problem solved,' he finished with a winning smile.

Camilla's eyes were as hard and unblinking as a pair of glass marbles.

9

It was two and a half hours before they were finally alone again, standing on Booth Street West, Central Manchester, backs to the accommodation block, waving off Camilla, Henry and Annabel. To save Henry's arthritic hands, Annabel had driven them in her sporty VW Golf – her eighteenth birthday present to match the money Camilla had splashed out on a beautiful black four-year-old Bosendorfer piano for Naomi. Or at least Annabel believed her fifteen-thousand-pound car matched the price of Naomi's piano. Only Annabel's ignorance had allowed for the price difference.

Naomi still felt bad about it. Camilla didn't. 'What she doesn't know won't hurt her. You have to have a decent instrument, Naomi. It's a gift for life and it's a necessity as well as an investment,' she'd insisted, 'unlike that heap of metal Annabel has chosen that will be worthless a couple of years from now.'

As the car headed to the traffic lights, indicator light flashing, Naomi was still thinking about Camilla's knowing look from the back window, a look that had said *friend, my foot.* She wondered when she'd be forced into a confession. Camilla wouldn't dutifully wait until her weekly phoning time of six on Friday. Not now the warning look had been doled out.

Henry was still waving as the car turned and merged into thick city traffic out of sight, at which point Nathan took Naomi's hand.

'I'm really sorry,' Naomi said, her muscles finally unlocking. She found her head ached. She realised she was breathing easily for the first time in hours. 'Obviously, if I'd known they were coming –'

Nathan threw his head back and laughed. 'Relax, would you.' he said. 'It's all good fun.'

'Fun? I can think of a few ways to describe my mum, but not fun.'

'Honestly, I enjoy a challenge,' he said. 'Did you see her face when she found out my age and that I work for a temp agency? She couldn't believe that someone with a first class degree in philosophy, of all useless things, would be willing to sell mobile phones to save up for travelling.'

Naomi relived the double blow she'd taken during lunch. She learned that Nathan planned to travel and realised it gave him something in common with Annabel. He'd leave when he had enough money. She'd been forced to react as if she already knew the details and didn't mind at all. Annabel, who'd made sure she was sitting directly opposite Nathan, had engaged him in minutes of conversation about her travelling plans, and his. Naomi had hated the way that, sitting by Nathan's right side, she'd had to sit through Annabel eating seductively and giving him the full force of her artistically made-up blue eyes. The fact that Nathan had ignored the outrageous flirting and had paid far more attention to Naomi and to trying to say something that was acceptable to Camilla, had been the only consolation.

Ordeal over, she turned to walk back to her room with Nathan, hero of the hour.

'Annabel seemed to like you, even if you weren't exactly a hit with my mum.' Naomi was attempting to sound casual, but she needed to fish.

'You think?'

'You don't carry a white stick.'

'I was being sarcastic,' Nathan laughed. 'Don't get me wrong, Annie's great, but she's definitely not my type.'

Naomi felt a stone lighter. 'Really?'

'Really. I hope I made that clear to Annabel. Her ego is strong enough to take it. To be honest, I thought it was obvious we were together, but she still wanted to steal the limelight, which I thought was a bit mean. Didn't you?'

The relief was indescribable. Naomi shrugged. 'I'm used to it. I always forgive her for those things,' she said, feeling suddenly generous.

'You're incredible, you know that?'

Naomi soaked up the compliment without finding a reply. She knew she'd review all the things Nathan had said, later on. She replayed the words to make sure she had them right, and stored them carefully.

When they arrived at the reception door, Naomi took her card from her pocket. 'You never told me you were planning to travel,' she said, unlocking the door, hoping her voice sounded light and enquiring.

'Come with me,' he said immediately. 'I mean it.'

Naomi hid the surprise. 'I can't. I'm committed to my course until next June.'

'I can wait until next June,' Nathan said, pressing the hand he was still holding. They walked through the reception and into the paved courtyard and strolled toward A Block. 'Let's go together. I'd much rather have company.'

'You're asking me to go away with you next summer and this is only our second date?'

Naomi found herself imagining announcing to Camilla that she was planning to go away with Nathan.

Nathan stopped walking and pulled her in front of him. Taking hold of her other hand as well as the one he already owned, he looked into her eyes. Music spewed from the open windows. 'Didn't you hear me?' he asked.

'Hear what? Sorry I was a bit distracted.'

'I said I'm sorry.'

'What for?'

'Scaring you off.'

Naomi studied his eyes, noticing the length of his dark eyelashes. 'You didn't. It's not that.'

He released her left hand to run his fingers through her hair, pushing it off her face. She fought not to shut her eyes. 'What then? Lack of money? Your mum?'

'The last one.' Nathan gathered her into a hug.

'In future, we'll deal with her together,' he said into her ear.

'So my mum didn't scare *you* off then?'

He pulled back to look at her. For a few seconds, the only communication was close eye contact. Naomi lowered her eyes to his lips, remembering how they felt and how they made her burn inside. Stunned by the urge to kiss him again, she didn't move.

'I suspect she's probably quite warm beneath all that ice,' Nathan said.

Naomi laughed. 'She is.'

Nathan's expression turned serious. 'Listen, I can invite you to come away with me after two dates because I know how I feel about you. And I've told you that when I commit, I commit. I'm in love with you. I can't help it. I don't say those things to every girl I meet, you know. I haven't had a girlfriend in a couple of years.'

Despite Nathan's comments, Naomi was still struggling to shake off Annabel's infectious laugh and the witty comments she'd made around the table that were still breaking into her thoughts along with the glossy lipstick. 'Have there been many?'

'Girls?' He hesitated. 'A couple.'

'A couple as in literally two, or a couple as in you've lost count?'

He managed a tight smile, but it was strained. At the same time, it started to rain. 'A couple as in literally two. That is, I've had two serious girlfriends, the second I was engaged to.'

'Really?' Naomi said, her heart feeling the effect, taking a noticeable dip that she hoped wasn't showing in her face. 'You were engaged at twenty-three?'

'Yeah, I was.' Nathan continued to look at her with his incredible eyes, but they lost focus while his mind was busy swimming with memories. Naomi waited patiently until he returned. The rain was getting heavier.

'Do you still love her?' she asked, realising too late she wasn't sure she wanted to know.

Nathan didn't answer the question. He glanced at the sky. 'Let's get back to your room. I really need to talk to you about someone and here's not the place.'

***

'Naomi's *friend*,' Camilla said from the back seat of the car, which was choked with magazines, scarves, jackets and empty McDonald cartons and lids pierced with straws. Camilla had spent the whole of the outgoing journey listing her complaints about the state of the car. 'Do I look like I was born yesterday, Henry?'

Henry didn't need to answer. Annabel would hijack the conversation and defend Naomi without him needing to get involved. October marked the fourth month of Annabel being at home fulltime after sitting A levels. With no plans to go university or get a job until she went away, and with Naomi having left, the bickering at home was almost constant. Only mornings were blissful, while Annabel slept.

'How do you know he isn't a friend?' Annabel asked, tilting her head, eyes searching for Camilla's in the mirror.

'I know.'

'And I'd know if Naomi had a boyfriend.'

'Loretta hasn't mentioned anything either,' Camilla said with the familiar wait-until-I see-her edge to her voice.

Annabel bounced straight back. 'Why would Lorie tell you? She's like that with Naomi.' Annabel crossed her third and fourth fingers and held them up.

'Seeing as I pay Loretta's wages, her loyalty should be to me. Isn't that right, Henry?'

Henry was only barely conscious. 'Mm.'

'You see?' Camilla told Annabel.

'Dad's half asleep. Anyway, I'm taking it that Nathan is available. And he's really hot – '

'That's enough.'

A big yawn overcame Henry. So many times he'd tried to referee the pair of them without success. They always seemed to be such a huge disappointment to each other.

Camilla returned a few moments of silence before landing a blow. 'It was embarrassing to watch you drool over him across the table, Annabel,' she said in her deliberate, quiet voice that meant that she was sure she had the upper hand.

Annabel turned shrill. 'What about when you marched into Naomi's room and asked what Nathan was doing there?'

'They deserved it. They'd been up to no good. It was written all over Naomi's face, didn't you see?'

'I saw her squirming because you gave her a minging old jumper.'

'He might have tried to take advantage if we hadn't

turned up when we did, might he Henry?'

'Mm.'

Annabel laughed. It roused Henry from a minor drift. 'Well he can *take advantage* of me, anytime.'

'That's enough,' Camilla snapped again, quieting Annabel. 'If you'd ever been more interested in your schoolwork than in boys, you might have got decent A level results, like Naomi.'

Ouch.

'I did get decent results,' Annabel yelled, glaring into the back seat through her mirror. Henry stayed on the sidelines, wondering when to intervene. 'What do you call an A, a B and a C?'

'Mediocre,' Camilla responded quietly as if it saddened her. 'We're off the subject,' she continued. 'It isn't the time for Naomi to be focussing on boyfriends. It's time for her music, without distractions.'

'Give her a break,' Annabel said, exasperated. 'It's time she had a boyfriend. It would be good for her. Who'd want to do classical music all day?'

'Naomi would.'

'Have you ever asked her?'

'It goes without saying.'

'No, it doesn't.' Annabel punched her brakes to stop at some lights and glared at Camilla in her mirror.

'I shall tell Naomi later, exactly what I think of her *friend*, Mr Stone,' Camilla said.

'Leave her alone,' Annabel snapped.

'Eyes on the road, petal,' Henry said, softly.

'She always listens to me,' Camilla said, with infuriating certainty.

A car horn beeped somewhere. 'That's the problem,' Annabel said, screeching away from the lights, convinced they must have turned green when they hadn't. Henry tensed and crunched invisible brakes and yelled out, but it came too late. A silver car caught the front side of the car from the right to the dreaded sound of crunching metal, jolting them violently against locked seatbelts.

***

'What's his name?' Naomi asked Nathan, who'd just announced as if it was top secret that he had a brother. With only two stiff chairs in the room, they'd slumped on the bed with the light off. The rumbling sky had dimmed the room. It was warm and cosy.

'Dan,' Nathan said, as if his brother had already passed away or something.

For a while it was as if Nathan couldn't find anything more to say about Dan. Naomi had been expecting to hear about an ex-girlfriend, but found herself waiting to find out something unpleasant about Dan.

'He's two years younger than me. Diagnosed with schizophrenia when he was seventeen.'

'I'm sorry,' was all Naomi could find to say. It didn't feel like the moment to admit she didn't know much about it.

Nathan looked into her eyes before lying down on his side, head resting on one hand. 'It's torn the family apart.'

'How?'

Nathan closed his eyes, held them, opened them. 'Long story. Loads of details,' he said, as though he barely possessed the energy to share them.

Naomi stretched out to mirror Nathan's position, head propped on one hand, elbow bent. They were face-to-face now. 'I'm a good listener.'

He hesitated. 'I'm sure you are.' He tried to smile. 'OK, here goes.'

Nathan spent the next hour close to tears, pouring out

Dan's problems to Naomi, about how he'd fallen in with the wrong crowd and gone from being a normal happy teenager (a really generous and good looking one, at that) to meddling in drugs and alcohol and turning into another person from the carefree kid Nathan had grown up with.

At sixteen, he'd scraped five average-graded GCSEs despite his academic abilities. Dan had left school with the hope of turning his life around within a year and returning to college. It never happened. He kicked the drugs and alcohol, and even the 'friends' into touch, but developed tell-tale signs of paranoia and delusional thinking.

His parents were desperate. GPs were consulted, but didn't help and Dan slumped into depression and hit a period where he never left his room for weeks. By now, he was convinced that the man with the black dog who passed the house twice a day at roughly the same times, was plotting to savagely kill him. "He always looks up at my window," he'd told Nathan with that wild tortured look in his eyes that chilled Nathan's blood. 'Dan,' Nathan had replied, 'the poor bloke's probably wondering why he's always being spied on walking his dog.' Dan couldn't see it. And he couldn't understand why Nathan couldn't see it. Even from the safety of his room, Dan was still convinced his life was under threat and that he could die at any moment. Someone with a loud voice kept telling him so. With his sleep patterns all over the place, he cowered under his bedcovers in constant fear.

His parents fought about how best to handle him. Their relationship was crumbling under the strain. Nathan, despite being in the final stages of his degree and living fifty miles away, headed home as often as possible. Determined to get help, he'd searched the internet and learned as much as he could. If doctors weren't prepared to take the time to properly assess him – anti-depressants had made things worse, if anything – and offer a diagnosis, Nathan was going to sort it before his whole family went into meltdown. He stumbled across schizophrenia. A light went on. Bingo. Nathan took Dan back to the doctors and suggested it, then demanded action. Things changed from there.

Naomi's position had given her a sore wrist, she realised when she moved it. She adjusted and lay flat on her side, arm as a pillow.

'Did things settle down?' she asked Nathan.

'Not really. He started taking anti-psychotic meds. He might have improved with the right kind of support, but my parents chucked him out when he was only eighteen.'

Naomi sat up and smoothed her hair. 'What! Why?'

'They said they couldn't cope. I was doing my finals, studying hard. It was hell. Never mind what was best for Dan or me, they put themselves first.'

'I can't believe that.'

'Neither could I, but they did it without consulting me.' He shook his head, the closest to tears he'd come so far. 'Just before I finished uni, they found him a one-bed flat about four miles away from where we live, furnished it and moved him in. That was almost five years ago.'

'How did they justify it?'

'It isn't justifiable is it?' he said. 'I think they were freaked out, couldn't handle it. Maybe they were ashamed, or afraid, who knows? Anyway, they said that they thought independence was best for Dan and that moving him out was best for their marriage.' He paused. 'Well, it might have saved their marriage, but it wrecked Dan. They make me sick.'

'Where's Dan now?'

'Stuck in his flat. He stumbles along, gets by. He's

still depressed and delusional, but he's been worse.'

'Do your parents see him?'

'At first they did. He's twenty-three now. They visit every month now whether he needs it or not. He survives off ready meals when he can be bothered to eat, and he's gone back to drinking.'

Nathan went quiet.

'That's awful,' Naomi eventually said.

'I've thought of bringing him here to live with me, but he doesn't respond well to change and I refuse to give my parents the excuse of opting out altogether.' He was quiet for a bit longer. 'So, there're three important things you need to know, Naomi. The first is that I don't have a relationship with my parents anymore. I moved here to Manchester from Bury once they cut Dan's visits down. I couldn't be around them. I had to make a stand.'

'Do they phone you?'

'Not much. I phone my mum on Mother's Day and her birthday. She phones me at Christmas unless there's something pressing in between. That's about it. They chose each other. I chose Dan. It feels like us versus them.'

'That's so sad.'

'What's sadder is that I tell most people I meet that my parents are dead. It's simpler than the truth. Imagine me explaining all this to the lads at work?'

'No.'

'Exactly. Second, I stay with Dan every other weekend and make sure he gets out to watch a game of footie or something. Big Man City fan. I take him to his counselling session. I cook for him and get a few decent meals inside him. I stock up his fridge and freezer. I sleep on his sofa for two nights, Friday and Saturday, so every other weekend I'm away and won't be able to see you. But I'll ring you, I promise.'

Naomi digested this information with mixed feelings. 'I could come with you,' she offered.

'That's the third thing,' Nathan said, finally sitting up. 'Much as I love Dan, he's done a few really bad things and I don't want you anywhere near him. I won't be telling him about you, sadly.' He took Naomi's hand and stroked it, looking at her carefully. 'The girl I was engaged to, Lucy, started coming to stay at Dan's with me until it all went wrong. Dan convinced himself that she was his girlfriend, not mine.' Nathan dropped his head. 'It wasn't his fault, but having Lucy around confused him. Obviously, Lucy was totally freaked out. The last time she came, he locked her in the bathroom with him and touched her up. He told her she might die if she left the house.'

In a sudden shift, the steady rain turned furious outside and thrashed noisily against the window. Naomi looked at the threatening grey sky that had descended and was breathing against the window. She returned her gaze to Nathan's troubled eyes. 'Is that why it didn't work out?'

'Yeah. Once she'd escaped his clutches, she told me we weren't visiting him anymore because he was dangerous. She never really understood that it was an illness and that he would never be a danger to me. She gave me an ultimatum, her or Dan. My parents had just about abandoned him. How could I do the same?'

Naomi thought about it. 'She shouldn't have expected you to.'

'Maybe. It wasn't easy for her either. Dan's a big part of my life. She wasn't prepared to share me with him, so we broke up. I haven't had a relationship since then.' He dropped his head, shook it. 'Do you know the really devastating part?'

'What?'

'Dan really missed her.' His eyes filled again. 'It was like she'd thrown him to one side too. He took it badly when I explained she wouldn't be coming anymore. I blame myself for taking her with me in the first place.'

'Was she really pretty?' Naomi asked inappropriately, overcome by curiosity. 'Sorry.'

'Don't be.' He paused. 'Yes, Lucy was very pretty and I loved her a lot.' He took her hand. 'But that part of my life is over and I've let it go. You're beautiful. Inside and out. However cheesy it might sound, you shine. I noticed it the first moment I saw you. But you need to know I'm not a neat, tidy package, Naomi. There's baggage. I knew it would take someone pretty special to tolerate me. So, I'm not presuming anything and I won't blame you if you want to duck out.' He drew a noisy breath. 'The point is, I have to give you the chance of opting out right from the start.'

He was playing with her fingers and lifting them one by one.

'I'm not going to bail on you. I want to be with you,' she said.

Nathan dissolved into a smile, the first for a while. 'Sure?'

'Of course I'm sure. It makes no difference.'

'Phew! I was hoping you'd say that.'

'But how are you going to leave him and go travelling?'

Nathan shifted position and they lay down side by side, hand in hand, fingers linked, eyes to the ceiling. 'I've agonised about that and I've talked to him. In the end, Dan suggested it to me. It will only be for a few weeks. He understands. My mother's going to have to take her turn properly while I'm away, isn't she?'

Naomi didn't answer. She was enjoying the heat of Nathan's hand and his body so close.

'So, I can finally answer your question now you know the background,' Nathan said. 'It took a long time, but I am over Lucy. That's the honest truth. I agree with you, that anyone who tells me to give my brother the flick is not right for me. I hope you can see now why I hesitated about getting your number in that bar, and why I can handle your mum. At least she's looking out for you. I can admire that. And I'm going to melt the ice with her, you'll see.'

Naomi laughed and squeezed his hand. 'Good luck with that.'

'We're being watched,' Nathan said, looking at a corner of the ceiling. Naomi followed his gaze.

'Meet Sydney,' she said.

'Sydney?'

'Yeah, he's been in here so long, it was rude not to give him a name.'

Nathan half sat up and looked down on Naomi. The pained expression he'd worn for an hour, had cleared. His face had brightened up. 'I'll tell you what was rude, your mum bursting in here earlier just when it was getting interesting.'

He closed the gap slowly. Naomi shut her eyes. Their lips had just made contact when Naomi's phone started ringing. Nathan groaned.

'That'll be my mum.'

'Are you going to get it?'

'I'll have to.' Naomi pulled her phone from her pocket and stared at the screen. 'Yep, as expected,' she said.

'The talk.' Nathan stood up and straightened himself out. 'OK, well I'd better get going before I don't want to leave.'

'I'm sorry.'

'I'm sorry I still haven't heard you play the piano.

Next time,' he said, pointing a finger at her. The phone nagged relentlessly. Nathan picked up the black jumper Camilla had brought in earlier. 'I'm going to dispose of this,' he said. 'Look at it as symbolic and don't take any nonsense, OK? Make sure she knows who's in charge of your life.'

Unable to ignore the phone any longer, Naomi answered it. 'Hi, Mum.' She stood and walked toward Nathan who was opening the door, ready to leave. He blew her a kiss just as Camilla sounded in her left ear.

'Naomi? Finally! Has that dreadful salesman gone, or were you just busy in the bathroom again?'

10

CAPTIVITY

Three everlasting days had passed since the landlord's visit. Naomi had held out in silence, determined to make the point that he could stuff his questions and answers for all she cared. She'd withdrawn inside herself to make her own plans.

His mask was coming in handy now she'd become desensitised to it. It robbed him of features and made him more of a thing than a person. Having tried at first to imagine the face behind it, she wasn't even curious now. She refused to look into his eyes when he visited. Appealing to him was pointless. She preferred to think of him as nobody's son, nobody's friend, nobody's concern.

She'd stopped trying to recall where she'd heard his voice. It didn't matter. Maybe only one of them would leave this place alive. Either way, a confrontation seemed inevitable. It was war and the rules of war applied. While there was a pact of silence between them and he was just a food-deliverer that might be wearing the mask because his features were twisted like the Phantom at the West End, it was easier to dehumanise him into a kind of machine that had never known a family and wouldn't be missed. So it was easier to construct a plan to destroy him.

It was Thursday now. Several times a day, Naomi reminded herself which day of the week it was, terrified of losing track. One day was the length of a week in her previous life. Time was getting the better of her and swallowing her up. She got lost in the folds and creases of endless days and nights now that every day was the same and every night was restless, and time had become meaningless and immeasurable.

All her life she'd taken the passing of time for granted. She'd never thought much about days and weeks and seasons and how each one was a slab of time that paved an easy and varied path through life. And yet each sunrise was evidence enough that the world was still following a cycle, however much the wheel of life appeared to have slowed. Each hour meant wading through pointless existence and dealing with emotions better buried. The pace of her former life was a mystery to her now.

Being a prisoner like this was a form of robbery and torture, and even murder. While he hadn't laid a finger on her so far, having ripped her from her life, he was slowly killing her. It was a painful death, made worse by the thought that the people she loved would be suffering too. Kill one person, you murder the whole family. If only she could tell them that she was still eating, still breathing, still hoping and praying she'd see them again. *Mustn't give up*.

***

Saturday. Another two days stretched then passed away without incident or words. Naomi had woken so early this particular morning that she'd watched the room take shape and the shadows slink away. She'd stood and walked to the window and carefully examined a dark sky stained with patches of deep violet and blue. Over the distant hill – only a black outline in the infant light – pinkish strips were breaking through the darkness, painting streaks of colour onto the horizon. A few birds had stuck around to celebrate the dawn. Morning hymns were being chirped worshipfully.

Naomi stood, listening, observing silently while the chains tugged against her wrists and the light strengthened outside and moved in, and the chorus swelled. Out of bed, her legs felt the chill of a clear September morning. She clambered into the jeans without turning her back on it. The moon was watching too, reluctant to bow out. A ghostly white mist smothered the fields between the house and the tallest hill, hiding the greenery. Still, the colours were compelling and beautiful. Delicate as they were, they had the power to move her to tears and fill her with a sense of awe.

The part of her that had started to rot through bitterness was cut away. It was bound to be temporary, but like an effective sedative it brought relief. She stood for a peaceful hour or so, feeling small beneath the gaze of nature, yet not insignificant. She had the clarity during that short time, to sense that she had not been forgotten. It was a feeling she couldn't explain. Simply put, she sensed that even in her isolation, God was aware of her. She collected the teardrops and felt the desperate urge to clean herself up. She'd swallow her pride when the monster visited, and ask to use the shower. She'd break her silence today.

He came in twice a day with food. Past the stage of suspecting him of poisoning it, logic told her that if he'd wanted her dead, she'd be buried already. For days now, she'd eaten everything he brought and drunk at least four cups of water a day. And seeing as she was willingly eating, he was readily providing food and found no reason to talk to her. It was a mutually acknowledged silence.

That Saturday, he came as usual mid-morning with

food. The smell of a full English breakfast had roused her taste buds for a while before he appeared with it. She could pick out the sausages and smoked bacon separately. Toast was on the menu too. As he walked towards her, bearing the usual array of red plastic, the sight of him stole the hope she'd felt that morning. The angelic glow burnt out. He'd robbed her once again.

The seeds of hatred took root quickly and germinated as he deposited the tray and lifted the contents onto the small table beside the bed. She depended on him to feed her like this and keep her alive. He could walk away at any time and leave her here to die. They both knew it. So was she grateful that he hadn't abandoned her so far? Hardly! She looked at him like a man from a hospital bed might look at a wheelchair after a serious accident where he'd just been told he might never walk again, and that he may as well get used to operating the chair.

Naomi sat up as he removed the final thing from the tray, a cup of orange juice. She'd decided in advance what she would say to him, but found that releasing the words into the quiet room and the atmosphere he always dragged in with him which lodged between them, more difficult than she'd anticipated. He collected the tray and started to make his exit. Only the sight of his back in a checked shirt and black jeans clicked her tongue into gear.

Say it, don't think. 'I need a shower.' Her voice sounded rusty after days of not speaking, but she'd carefully considered the wording and didn't regret the words as she heard them out loud. They sounded as assertive as she'd hoped. She'd decided upon 'need' not 'want', reasoning that the simpler the sentence, the more likely he'd be to respond. She wouldn't beg or bargain. The best thing, she thought, was just a straightforward, non-emotional request that would be easy for him to take in and therefore, more difficult to refuse. Robots could handle requests.

He turned, stood still, said nothing for a while. 'You can wash in the sink,' was his conclusion after some thought.

'I have been washing in the sink, but it isn't easy chained up. I can't wash my hair.' She held a section up. Her hair had lost its shine and now hung limply in ropey strips. 'It's dirty and I'm cold. I need to change out of this and put something warmer on.' Naomi grabbed her nightshirt and pulled it away from herself to get the message across. 'I can't change the top half while I'm fastened up.'

He turned quiet and still again, digesting the words. She could hear him breathing behind the mask and wondered if it felt claustrophobic.

'I'll think about it,' he said in his low snarl. Naomi, who'd braced herself for a refusal, didn't argue.

He left and locked the door. Naomi's pulse was pounding, but there was a sense of achievement – an unfamiliar feeling. She wanted a shower, but her priority was to plan an escape. She needed to examine the window and how far it would open and what lay beneath it. She would refuse to shower in front of him. Absolutely. So here she was, waiting again to see what he would offer.

He showered in a different bathroom and left the house in the car after breakfast and returned a long time later with more rustling bags. The hours passed more quickly than usual that day. She was surprised when she heard him clattering around in the kitchen preparing food again. She had no appetite. Her mind was too busy plotting; her thoughts were racing out of control.

Breakfast, she estimated, came between nine and ten o'clock every morning, and the second meal, between three and four. He only ever brought two meals a day, but the portions were generous enough to keep her going. It wasn't like she was using much energy except in thinking.

She suspected he wanted to visit her as little as possible, so two big meals were better than three small ones. It was like he'd brought her here only to keep her alive and avoid her. It was bizarre and unfathomable. It had to be part of a wider plan she was terrified of learning anything about. Asking him for something extra, the use of the shower, had presented him with a problem.

The meal took an age to prepare. She couldn't muster any interest in it while she was itching to be free. Naomi thought the clanging around in the kitchen would never end. Finally, the stairs creaked and he walked in with the fiery red tray, carrying what smelled like a roast dinner. It was. He deposited the contents onto the table beside the bed. Roast chicken and stuffing with a selection of veg. Cheesecake and cream. She was watching him. He didn't return her gaze, but busied himself collecting the empty plate and cup from the morning. The effort put into preparing the food was the strangest thing. The meals were never thrown together or bought pre-packed, but carefully constructed by hand. Maybe he was bored too.

He straightened up and looked at her with his black woolly face that had no slots for breathing, but a lookout for each eye. She could see the blueness of his eyes that she'd avoided for days. His pupils dilated.

'You can shower later. I got you a swimming costume.'

'A costume?' It could only mean one thing.

He didn't reply. The silence grew. She needed to be confident. She untied her tongue as quickly as she could. 'I refuse to shower in front of you,' she said, heart plunging, plans washing up on a deserted shore.

'Fine,' he said, heading for the door.

The panic fizzed inside her stomach. 'Wait. Can't we just talk about this?'

He stopped, turned. 'You want a shower. I've agreed on one condition. The terms are non-negotiable.'

He wasn't walking away. He was looking at her, waiting for a decision.

'Why are you doing this?' she asked. 'What's the point? How's it going to end?'

'Don't know yet.'

Don't know? She glared at him, confused. 'What don't you know? What you're doing, why, or how it will end?'

'All three.'

Naomi was aware that her feelings were being exposed all over her face as he looked steadily at her from behind his screen. She didn't know what to say, but she detected the impatience in his tone as he spoke again. 'Three seconds to decide.'

'OK, OK,' she said. 'Give me the swimming costume.'

'Later. Need to eat.'

He turned and left the room and locked it up. *Need to eat.* Naomi had never imagined him eating too. *So that's why he makes an effort.*

As she shuffled across the bed and lifted the red plate on top of her legs, for the first time she was aware of him eating simultaneously right beneath her somewhere. She didn't like to think of the monster in terms of needing food like normal people. She hadn't realised they shared mealtimes or ate the same things. The thought didn't sit comfortably.

Her head was preoccupied as she shovelled in the food and chewed and swallowed it mindlessly. She thought of him removing his mask and doing the same thing, and barely tasted any of it. She looked at the cheesecake and decided she didn't want it. Yet.

With thoughts of him returning, she turned restless. She crawled across the bed in the direction of the wardrobe and stood up. The wardrobe was within reach, just. She suspected, like the bed, it had been moved. She opened the wardrobe door and grabbed clean underwear and the fleece top. She sat stiffly on the bed clutching them to her, listening to the noises downstairs. He was running water, clearing up from the sound of things. Eventually, pots stopped rattling, cupboards stopped opening and closing, everything went quiet. He didn't come upstairs. She heard him speaking to someone on his phone and wondered what he was planning. She couldn't make out words.

A couple of hours trudged by, maybe more. The sun had begun a gradual descent. The room was dimming. Just when she thought he wasn't returning, he began climbing the stairs in no rush.

She tensed, couldn't stop herself. He entered the room bringing his atmosphere with him and a black swimming costume which he hurled onto the bed. In his hands he held two bottles, shampoo, conditioner. He pushed the door shut with his foot. She sat, clenching her jaw to prevent her teeth from chattering, though the room was warm. He walked past her and went into the bathroom. Her eyes fixed longingly on the door. The shower started up in a gush.

He returned and ordered her to stand. She obeyed. He removed a small key from the back pocket of his jeans, not much more than an inch or so in length. He took her wrists one by one and unlatched her. He deposited the costume in her hands. Her wrists felt bare and cold where the leather bands had gripped her for days. The thought of returning to them shortly was too much. He stood right in front of her now, tall and imposing, filling the room, blocking her route to the door.

He took her arm and guided her to the bathroom. At the door, he ushered her inside and only closed the door three quarters of the way. The room was becoming steamy. The light was on. Her eyes darted round and settled on the window.

'Two minutes to undress before I come in,' he said from behind the door.

Naomi stood, not wanting to take her things off like this. As her eyes returned to the door, she could see his shadow on the floor. 'Shut the door,' she called.

'One minute, fifty.'

'I want some privacy.'

'I've seen it all before,' he said in a monotone, as if it bored him.

Stunned, Naomi thought back to the first morning and of finding herself cleaned and changed. She shivered.

'One minute, thirty-five.'

Naomi stood, shaking, incensed. 'What did you do?'

There was a hesitation, which she didn't like. He cleared his throat.

'What did you do?' she tried again.

Naomi shuffled her feet and waited for an answer that wasn't coming.

'You're down to a minute.'

This was all going wrong. She'd planned to be locked in the bathroom alone with time to assess the window and the chances of getting out of it. Instead, she'd have been in earshot of his breathing if the shower wasn't spewing hot water into the bath. She looked down at the black swimming costume.

'Forty-five seconds.'

In a mad panic, Naomi undid the jeans and yanked everything off the bottom half of her. The top half she'd do separately. She stepped inside the costume and frantically pulled it up, eager to cover herself. She pulled the nightshirt over her head and fumbled with her bra before tugging it away from her and throwing it onto the floor. She pulled the costume up and shoved her arms inside the straps. Her chest wasn't covered at all. It was back to front.

'Ten seconds.'

No. She ripped it off. It was rolled up on the floor. Without a stitch on, she snatched it up, shook it straight, flipped it round, stepped inside and pulled it up with force. She'd covered the bottom bit when his shadow shifted as he stepped forward to come in. She spun away from the door and finished the job with the hideous sensation of his eyes on her back. She pushed her arms inside the straps and untwisted them on her shoulders. It was a tight fit, but she was covered at least.

Without looking back, she stepped inside the bath and hid behind the smoked-glass shower screen, burying herself in wondrous hot water. She couldn't see him now, but she could feel him there. His presence always changed the room. She closed her eyes anyway, and ran her fingers through her hair, head back. The shampoo and conditioner were nothing special. It wasn't like she needed to look good. Worried he'd pull her out before she'd finished, she washed and conditioned her hair first thing. After that she stood for a few pleasurable minutes, an avalanche of hot water pouring over her, warming her through. Being in a bathing costume reminded her of school swimming lessons in Johannesburg, where she'd hated the lesson, but enjoyed the hot shower at the end.

Time passed, the best all week. He didn't show himself, didn't speak, didn't move. After another ten minutes or so, she decided to get out before he forced the issue. She turned and found a round silver handle on the wall behind her. The water reduced until the handle stopped turning. The showerhead dripped a few times until silence returned. She stepped forward and saw him sitting on the toilet lid by the door. He stood, handed her a towel, told her she had two minutes to get dressed, went out, leaving the door open a little. This time, the only priority was to dress.

Hair dripping, she towelled herself until she was dry enough. Again, he counted down so she knew how the time was passing. She put on her underwear, her back to the door, and pulled up the jeans which stuck uncomfortably to her legs, letting her know she wasn't dry. With ten seconds to spare, she'd zipped up the fleece top and emerged from behind the door, determined to look calm. He stopped counting.

Naomi combed her hair with her fingers, pushing it back off her face. His dark hair was visible beneath his woolly mask. She looked him in the eye and fired her planned question. 'Where are we?'

'Lake district,' he said.

Her mouth opened with the surprise. She hadn't hoped of getting an answer. Encouraged, she went on. 'Which part?'

'A very pretty and very deserted part.'

She didn't press him for more, no point. He stuck out his hand, indicating for her to walk round the edge of the bed and back to the wardrobe side where the chains lay waiting on the bed. She slowly circled the bed, in no rush to put them back on. The door was closed, but as she edged closer to it, she was aware it was unlocked. She concentrated on the handle, hoping to open it with the power of her mind.

While that didn't happen, something equally as unlikely did. It seemed nothing short of a miracle and happened so fast, Naomi had no time to process it. She heard the high-pitched clink of a small key on the floor. She snatched a look behind. He'd dropped to his hands and knees in a flash and had an arm stretched under the bed. She saw an opportunity and instinctively bolted for the door.

'No,' he yelled, lunging full force across the floor to tackle her with his hands. He swiped at her ankles and caught hold of one. After a short tussle, she kicked herself free and turned the door handle and threw herself out of the room. She had the presence of mind to look behind. The key was in the door. She turned it half a second before he violently snatched the handle and pulled and kicked and threatened to break down the door.

Her legs turned weak. She stood in disbelief, wondering if the door would hold. He was swearing and issuing death threats behind it. *Move, Naomi, move.* In bare feet, she took hold of the banister and ran downstairs two at a time. The effort of him trying to tear the door down was banging in her ears all the way.

She was without a plan and shaking with the shock of finding herself on the free side of a locked door. Naomi landed in a small hallway with a cold quarry-tiled floor and a front door. Dim light came from a small glass window at the top of the door. She grasped the door handle and found the door was locked and needed a key. She frantically cast her gaze around. There were three oak doors, two closed, one slightly open with the light on. From the position beneath her room, the open door must be the kitchen. It was the last place he'd been. She flew towards it hoping to find keys to the car, and suddenly realised the banging had stopped upstairs.

What did that mean?

She soon found out. Behind the kitchen door was a round table dressed in a red and white gingham cloth. On it was a bowl of fake fruit and a mobile phone. Her heart leapt. With shaky hands, she picked it up. She was looking for keys and an exit now. In one corner of the kitchen was a door. She rushed to it and found a small pantry with a washing machine, a pair of old shoes and lots of shelves and empty jars. She shut the door. *Keys, keys.*

Some movement caught her eye through the kitchen window above the sink. As she glanced out she saw a denim leg in one corner of the window. *No!* He was climbing down the house and was almost on the ground. She heard him jump and land on gravel. Not wanting him to see her dash across the kitchen, she stood frozen, mind racing. She traced his noisy footsteps as he circled the cottage and put the key in the front door. With her options down to nothing, Naomi opened the pantry door and hid inside. It was black until her eyes adjusted, and smelled of onions and garlic bulbs and compost.

She held up the phone in the darkness. When she touched the screen an image flashed up of a victim, side on, surrounded by darkness, face and neck covered in blood, body zipped into a black bag. Her face was white, eyes closed, mouth open. As Naomi realised she was looking at herself, she clamped her mouth with her free hand to smother the gasp.

Had he heard it? She could hear him tearing around the downstairs of the house trying to sniff her out. He wasn't calling her, which only made her more uneasy. She stood, waiting to be discovered. She'd had nightmares less terrifying. It was eerily quiet apart from snatched rustling noises and doors creaking open. Blotting out the bloody image, Naomi brought a number pad up and tried to remember her home phone number.

Her brain was so scrambled, the number wouldn't file out. *Come on.* Her mind was as unresponsive as road kill. *Think!* After a frantic search, her brain released the area code. Once she started pressing, her fingers knew the sequence.

She put the phone to her ear, darkening the little room again. A slim strip of light sat on the floor beneath the door. Noises of him drawing closer fed through the gap. Her breathing was too heavy. Just as the phone started ringing, he burst into the kitchen. She stifled the urge to scream. The ringtone was blasting in her ear. She pressed it to her head to reduce the noise. Someone picked up the phone.

'Hello, Hamiltons.' It was Camilla. Her voice sounded almost normal, but Naomi read the pain in it. The familiarity jerked tears. Naomi stood still for a moment, eyes dripping, torn between the need to speak and the need to be silent. She daren't sniff. It dawned on her that he would notice the missing phone. She'd never escape him anyway. It was as though behind the closed door, she could see what was happening through the eye of her senses. He'd noticed the missing phone because he was striding heavily across the kitchen now.

'Hello?' Camilla's voice again, drizzled with either irritation or pain. She wouldn't stay connected for much longer.

Naomi tried to speak and found her vocal chords locked. She was equally afraid of Camilla hanging up as she was of the monster bursting in.

It had to be now. *Talk,* she yelled inside her head. Two things happened simultaneously. The door flung open with the monster, taller and more agitated than ever filling the doorway. And Naomi shouted, 'Mum?'

He pounced. She expected him to grab the phone first, so her efforts to spin away from him and guard it were wasted. Instead, he clamped her mouth before she could scream, then prised the phone from her fingers. Naomi heard Camilla's voice. 'Naomi? Is that –'

He cut her off.

'Big mistake,' he snarled. 'Big. Mistake.'

Naomi's eyes were misted with tears. Her body was weak. He stood, gripping her left arm with one hand, seething with rage, panting noisily inside his mask.

'I wanted my family to know I was alive,' she sobbed.

'Did you call anyone else?' he yelled. Naomi didn't answer. She was struggling to breathe. 'Answer me or I swear –'

'No. No,' she said.

He let go of her arm and held the phone up as if remembering he could check it for details. Naomi stood, shaking, while he satisfied himself she was telling the truth. She was desperately pleading with God in her head that she'd be locked inside her room again and left alone.

He stood silent and still a moment. The last of the daylight seeped in behind him. She dropped her head, too afraid to meet his eyes in the claustrophobic space. After what felt like a lifetime, he brutally seized one arm and marched her back upstairs. All the way, he followed her in silence. They filed into the bedroom. One of the French doors was open where he'd escaped. The curtains flapped gently. The room was cold from fresh air and smelled of open countryside.

Naomi sat on the bed and submissively held out her arms. She wanted to be chained up and left. She wanted solitude, silence, the comfort of the locked door with him on the other side of it. Her persistent thought and worst worry was him not leaving. As he wrapped the chains around her wrists again and locked them into place, she closed her eyes and held a private counsel with God about the injustice of it all.

She sat, unmoving, while he secured her wrists then went to the bathroom. He came out with her wet towel and used underwear and nightshirt. He stuffed them aggressively inside the washing bag on the wardrobe floor, then snapped the door shut. Why was he clearing up at a time like this? Too afraid to draw attention to herself, she tried to breathe silently and fought the urge to pant. Her chest felt tense. Camilla's voice was still calling her name inside her head. At least she'd given her parents some hope. They would tell Nathan and the police. It had been worth it.

'You may have just handed yourself a death sentence,' he said.

I'll face it, just get out and don't touch me.

He closed and secured the French doors then left the room, locking it noisily and deliberately behind him. He thudded down the stairs. It went chillingly quiet, leaving Naomi to wrestle with her thoughts in the growing darkness. Would anyone find her before it was too late? *You may have just handed yourself a death sentence*, was repeating mercilessly. For a pleasant September evening, the room was as chilled as the grave and Naomi sat as stiff as a corpse within it.

11

'Annabel's car could be a complete write-off,' Camilla's exasperated voice boomed into Naomi's left ear. She switched the phone to the other side and sat on the nearest thing, which happened to be the rickety wooden chair she used as a piano stool. She thought Camilla had phoned to rant about Nathan, but instead she was learning that Annie had crashed her car.

'Is anyone hurt?'

'No, no, I don't think so. A little shaken maybe,' Camilla said, typically brushing it off. 'Annabel's pride has suffered the worst bruising. If she's going to enter into a serious debate while she's driving, she needs to learn to multitask. It's the first rule of becoming a woman.'

Serious debate. Naomi didn't like the sound of those two words and didn't want to pursue the topic at all. Her mind was searching for something else to say, but Camilla spoke again.

'Maybe you can solve this debate for us.'

Too late. 'Solve what?'

'Well, it'll be a simple enough question for you. Annabel seems to think that there's no romantic involvement between you and . . . '

A pause. 'Nathan?' Naomi offered, sure that it was more a case of Camilla being unwilling to say his name than having forgotten it already. Bad sign.

'Exactly. While I was under the impression that there was something quite definite going on.'

'Definite?' she said, stalling, madly trying to organise her thoughts.

'Yes, definite.'

There was a short silence, but Naomi came back quickly. 'Why do you think that?'

Camilla sighed. 'Naomi, just answer the question please. Which one of us is right?'

'I honestly didn't hear a question.'

Naomi shut her eyes. Her jaw was tense. She couldn't fathom how Camilla could pin her into a corner like this. Why couldn't she just tell her mum to butt out like Annabel always did?

Camilla's voice turned sharp and short. 'I'll simplify: have you entered into a relationship with that man?'

Naomi had one hand pressed against her forehead now. 'He's a friend, Mum, so of course we have a relationship.'

Camilla panted hard. 'The last time I had a conversation this ridiculous I was trying to get an answer out of my local MP about plans to erect wind turbines. I'll be plainer. Has your male friend, Nathaniel Stone, exceeded the boundaries of what anyone would call friendship, and kissed you?'

Naomi could feel the heat travelling up her neck like a furnace. It reached her cheeks. She stood and walked to the window and opened it, glad she wasn't under the gaze of Camilla's all-searching eyes. 'Mum, this is embarrassing. I really don't feel comfortable answering questions like that.'

'Which can only mean he has. Oh marvellous!'

Nathan's words were tumble-drying inside her head. *Don't take any nonsense. Let her know who's in control of your life.* He didn't know Camilla.

'Mum, please. It just means I don't feel comfortable answering personal questions, that's all.'

Naomi had started to congratulate herself for calmly holding her ground when the next question, disguised as a non-question, threw her. 'I sincerely hope you haven't slept with him.'

'Of course I haven't,' she fired defensively. She felt the sting of regret as soon as the words flew out. She'd just answered both questions. Camilla would easily suss what had been left unsaid.

'Thank goodness,' Camilla said. 'In that case, you're not attached to him. The first time lives in the memory for evermore, Naomi, and with no good reason at all. The emotional entanglements can be a real nuisance. See how you got over the last one so quickly because you kept the relationship . . . simple?'

'Last one?'

'You know. Tim whatever-his-surname-was.'

'Who?' Naomi wasn't with it.

'The string player with the straw hair.'

'Tom.' Naomi remembered the months of grieving over what happened with Tom. It was anything but simple. The mention of his name sparked some anger. 'Butterworth.'

'Butterworth, yes.' Her voice softened considerably as if Naomi had soothed an itch for her. Naomi twisted her forefinger into her hair and reluctantly listened. Now Camilla had worked things out and brought Tom into it, Naomi didn't feel like talking.

'Now listen to me, this is an important time,' *here goes,* 'a pivotal time, and this is a matter of basic maths. You cannot fit him into your life. There's no room. If you don't keep up with the pacesetters, Naomi, you'll be left behind.' Naomi could picture Camilla's hand gestures to emphasise her words. 'You inhabit different worlds. It could never work. Never.' She paused for emphasis. 'Leave him to his sales pitches, yes?'

Camilla left a gap. Naomi didn't fill it, but she was listlessly searching for an excuse to get away by now. The speed of her thinking had slowed right down.

Camilla carried on. 'Have you tried the jumper on I brought for you?'

What? 'Er, no, not yet.'

'It will look very nice,' she said in a more optimistic tone, as if her second hand black jumper had saved the day and was a suitable replacement for Nathan. 'Wear it when I see you next.'

Naomi, utterly stumped for words, heard herself saying, 'I'm not wearing it for my birthday party, Mum.' Naomi released all of her breath, silently.

Camilla chipped in quickly. Small talk always bored her and the main business had been dealt with. 'Well, I've things to be getting on with. Tell him sooner rather than later.' There was no hint of a question. 'A clean break is best. Maybe I'll let Annabel know I was right on both counts.'

'Both counts?' Naomi stressed *both*, because she didn't understand.

'I was right about the relationship, and I was right that you'd see sense and end it before he starts to mean something. Annabel said you wouldn't listen. She doesn't understand you like I do. I'll ring at the usual time on Friday. Make sure you're free. I can't concentrate on a conversation if there's background noise.'

Camilla said her goodbyes and rang off, leaving Naomi staring blankly outside. She realised she was looking at static spheres of raindrops on the window.

It took time to muster the energy to even switch her phone off and redirect her focus out of the window. She leant against the windowsill and looked down at

Siobhan's window. Snugpooh, the ragged bear, was slouched on the blue pillowcase.

Before he starts to mean something. Didn't she get it? Nathan already meant everything. She wouldn't end it. No way. Stuff the consequences.

***

The day after, Naomi was back at her window in the same spot, churning the same thoughts. On the ground below, Siobhan's wide hair caught her attention. It was like a big orange flying carpet. She was running. Siobhan's usual speed was a slow to medium plod and never varied. Naomi watched Siobhan disappear around the corner.

After carrying her feelings for an evening and a morning they felt heavy. Naomi needed to offload. Lorie worked for Camilla full time, but she was sometimes available for a chat. Naomi dialled her number. Her phone was switched off.

She glanced at her watch. Nathan would be at work. She'd talked to him the night before about her conversation with Camilla and decided she needed female advice. She thought about ringing Annabel and decided she wasn't ready. With her mood so low, thinking of Annabel only brought flashbacks of her flirting with Nathan.

Naomi stood by the window for a long time, lost inside her head. She remembered she had an essay to be in for Friday, the first written assignment. She hadn't given it much thought. The work was piling up. She needed to practise several pieces, one of which she'd be playing in the main concert hall in two days' time. She was only accompanying a violinist in front of a class of about fifteen, but the thought still freaked her out. There was work to do on the difficult sections of the piece so she didn't look an idiot.

Naomi sighed. When she looked down at Siobhan's window again, Snugpooh had vanished, which could only mean that Siobhan had picked him up. Next thing, Siobhan's curtains snapped shut. Naomi checked the time. It was ten-twenty. She stepped back from the window and wondered what Siobhan was doing.

Two days later when the curtains were still closed and Siobhan hadn't been seen, Naomi started to worry.

***

Wednesday. Naomi woke up early from a nightmare. She'd walked onto the concert platform in a white blouse clutching her music, and looked down to find she was wearing only her knickers. Her feet were bare. The wooden floor was cold and sticky. The violinist hadn't shown up and Naomi had been shoved out alone to play solo. The only music she was carrying was the accompaniment to the piece they'd practised which would sound senseless without the violin. She looked out at her silent audience and noticed Nathan on the front row, smiling, giving her the thumbs-up. Lorie was beside him. Camilla sat behind them, stone-faced. Naomi looked down at her exposed legs and prayed for a way out. Her prayer was answered quickly.

She woke up in a panic. Any relief that it was only a dream was steadily replaced by the realisation that it was performance day. The only image in her mind was the small speck of a grand piano that she'd seen from the raised stands of the concert hall. In a few hours, she'd be playing it with a top-class Japanese violinist who seemed incapable of playing wrong notes. It was as though she and her violin had been programmed to avoid them.

The class began at two o'clock that afternoon. They had a final rehearsal booked for ten. That thought drove her out of bed and onto the toilet. She returned to bed, took hold of her necklace and gabbled a few words of prayer that she'd survive. Eyes closed, she pictured herself when it was over, accepting the thanks for the job like it had been no big deal. If only she could skip time and arrive magically at that moment now.

Camilla hadn't rung since Sunday. No doubt she expected that Naomi had spoken to Nathan and cut him out of her life. No doubt she thought she was being completely reasonable. Truth was, Nathan had rung every day. The texts had flown between them, making her practise disjointed and her essay a non-starter. He'd started calling her Naims. Every time Naomi thought of him, she found herself smiling.

It was a dazzling Wednesday morning. The sun was rising cheerfully without any sympathy for the fact that Naomi was sick with nerves. She still hadn't written a single word of her two-thousand word essay. A bit of research was all she'd managed. She'd be glad when the week was over.

The clock set off at a charge that day and never let up. The rehearsal at ten came and went. No worries. The morning evolved prematurely into the afternoon. At twelve-thirty, Naomi found herself in the kitchen chomping mindlessly on one quarter of a ham sandwich. It was sticking like glue to the roof of her mouth and she couldn't break it down. Bridget, the singer, came in looking like she could use a chat. Naomi didn't have the time. Not in the mood for her boyfriend problems with Max, Naomi exchanged a few words and escaped to her room.

Nathan texted at one-thirty to wish her luck. It was enough to pack her off to the toilet again. The final moments were spent in her room at her tatty upright, focussed, pumped with adrenaline, running over the difficult sections, marking the copy in pencil with anything that would remotely help; fingering, accidentals, stars and arrows at points where she needed to go back to a repeat, or shift her eyes a few bars ahead. Previous lessons learned: take no chances.

She bent the pages at the bottom where she needed to turn quickly. She was ready, except she wasn't. There was no such thing. At one-fifty, she grabbed her music and keys and headed for the dreaded concert hall.

What am I doing here?

***

Two hours later, she slumped at her laptop in her room, tired and useless, trying to write the introduction to her essay with her mind still in the concert hall. She was thinking about the two wrong notes she'd hit during twelve pages of music that had obliterated the thousands of right notes. Her mind kept replaying the two passages and she was struggling to move on. After all the panic, they'd both happened during easy sections that she hadn't bothered to worry about or over-prepare.

It had happened like this before – unforgivable slips in unexpected places. It usually took a few days to stop reliving the horror. Logic told her that no one really cared and that in the grand scheme it didn't matter. People the world over were starving to death weren't they? Her ego argued that it featured amongst the worst disasters in the history of mankind. Wrong notes were like personal earthquakes. The two today, combined, had reached about six on the Richter Scale. The only consolation was that by tomorrow it would be five, and so on. It would affect her confidence next time. Aftershocks were inevitable.

After four attempts at an introduction to her essay, she read back the latest one and decided it would have to do. At this rate, it would take a month. She had two days. One hundred words down, only one thousand nine hundred to go. She started to search for the handwritten scribbles she'd made during her research. Madeline was on her clarinet next door, not helping, repeating the same few bars. Groundhog Day!

While she was up and looking, Naomi glanced down at Siobhan's room at the closed curtains. She stared for a long moment, wrong notes and essay finally leaving centre stage. Something wasn't right. It hit her suddenly and forcefully. She needed to go and see Siobhan and ask why she'd been living behind closed curtains for two days. She grabbed her keys and phone and took the lift.

Naomi could hear muffled noises from inside Siobhan's room. She knocked and waited a while, reluctant to be pushy. She cleared her throat as she stood, listening, wondering whether to call Siobhan out loud. After a small argument with herself about shouting or not shouting and leaving or not leaving, she raised her hand to knock again and a small voice came from behind the door.

'Who is it?'

'It's me. Naomi.'

Silence a beat. 'What do you want?'

'I was just wondering . . . look, Siobhan, can you open the door please?'

Siobhan did so, slowly and grudgingly. Naomi stepped inside. The curtains were closed so Siobhan's expression was initially unclear. An ineffective lamp burned meekly from her desk. Siobhan stood in front of it now, blocking what light there was. The room, like most student rooms, was a mess.

Naomi assessed Siobhan. 'What's wrong? Your curtains have been closed since Monday. I haven't seen you in lectures.'

Siobhan shrugged. The silence hung a while. Naomi didn't know what to say, so she thought hard.

'Are you ill?'

Siobhan shook her head. It was the way she tensed her lips tightly that gave Naomi a clue.

'Has someone upset you? Is it me?'

Siobhan measured her words carefully. 'It isn't you.'

'So someone has upset you?'

'Upset isn't the right word.'

'What then?'

Siobhan dried up. They stood, looking at each other.

'D'you want to give me a clue here? I can't help if I don't know what's going on.'

'I promised I wouldn't tell.'

'Promised who?'

Siobhan froze. Naomi watched her carefully. She saw fear. 'You're afraid,' she said, 'aren't you?'

Siobhan didn't speak or move.

Naomi softened her tone. 'Sit down. Tell me what's wrong.'

Siobhan plonked herself down on the bed and grabbed Snugpooh and clutched him to her. Naomi sat beside her. 'He's going to get me,' she blurted out.

'Who is? Take a breath, come on. Tell me what happened.'

After a few moments of quiet, it spewed out, how Siobhan had seen a man loitering outside the accommodation doors looking shifty, trying to slip in.

'No one else noticed him,' she said, head down. 'Groups of people walked past him, busy laughing and talking, but I was by myself. He saw me watching him, so he did. Came over to me. He had a knife. A really big knife under his jacket.' Siobhan went quiet again. 'He told me he wanted to get in to the block. I told him I wouldn't help him. I was shaking really badly, couldn't have walked if I'd tried. He told me he'd be back, had important business to see to.'

Naomi, too shocked to speak, put an arm around Siobhan. Someone was playing a violin next door. 'That's horrifying. Why didn't you text me or something? We have to report this. We need to involve the police.'

'No,' she said, sharply. 'See, this is why I've kept my trap shut. He said if I told anyone, he'd be back and he'd find me. Promise me you'll say nothing.' There were tears in her eyes. Her hands shook as she wiped her eyes.

'OK, I promise. Look, Siobhan, I wish you'd rung me. I could have helped. A problem shared and all that.'

'You've been distracted, away with the fairies for weeks now. I didn't know why until I saw you with *him* last week.' From her tone, she'd been thinking about *him* quite a bit. 'He's coming between us.'

Siobhan saw Nathan as a threat?

'Siobhan, we're friends, OK? Nathan is my boyfriend, but that doesn't change anything with us. If you need me, I'll be there without question. That's what friends do.'

'Is that right?' Siobhan said, without a hint of sarcasm. She sounded more relieved than anything. 'I've only ever really had one friend and that's my mammy. I don't know how things work. I don't get girls.'

'Well it works like this. We're friends, so we look out for each other. OK?'

For the first time, Siobhan looked up. 'OK.'

Naomi stood up and decided to try and lighten the atmosphere. 'Are you free next Saturday?'

Siobhan shrugged. 'I suppose so, yes.'

'Would you like to come to my birthday dinner? We

can take up to five guests each and I've only invited Nathan so far. Might be nice for you to get out and have a bit of fun.'

A long hesitation, until, 'I suppose so, yes.'

Naomi turned and headed for the door. 'You know, this guy, he was probably just a drug addict or something, needing money for his next fix. I'm sure it wasn't personal. Chances are you'll never see him again. I'm sure there's no need to hide.'

'Promise you won't say nothing to nobody.'

'Course I won't.'

Naomi looked back once her fingers had twisted around the door handle. Siobhan's mouth twitched in the direction of a smile. 'Thanks, Naomi. You're a lifesaver. It's kinda nice to have a friend.'

'Yeah, it is.' Naomi hesitated, still troubled if she was honest. 'So what did this guy look like anyway?'

Siobhan didn't have to think. 'A tank.'

***

Naomi's time was squeezed over the next two days. She had to write her essay, keep up her practise, and squash in long and regular chats with Nathan. And she patiently persuaded Siobhan to leave her room and start living again. By Friday morning, Siobhan was confident enough to attend lectures and sit in the refectory for a drink, but she wouldn't venture away from the college.

Naomi still had the conclusion to write on her essay, due in by lunchtime that day. Having slept in until eleven, she had to cobble together some waffle that passed for a concluding paragraph. There was no time to wonder if it was good enough. At twenty minutes to twelve, she rushed over to the college to print it off and hand it in.

The essay was done and dropped. Feeling lighter

even though she'd only shed four sheets of A4 paper, Naomi walked out of the automatic doors and breathed more easily. It was a bright day, clear skies, almost warm. Her mood had lifted. The wrong notes from the performance weren't mocking in her head as much now. The self-torture was loosening its grip. She realised she hadn't eaten a thing that day. Starving, she found some loose change in her pocket which amounted to enough to get a bit of lunch. She decided to buy a sandwich, pronto.

Naomi crossed the road and thought about sandwich fillings. She decided on tuna mayonnaise on a crispy white roll with salad.

Loads of students were on the move. She got close to the nearest little supermarket and pulled the money from her pocket to count it again. Eyes down, someone banged into her right shoulder. She dropped the small change. The coins dispersed on the pavement. Passing people swerved to avoid them. Naomi apologised, not sure if the collision was her fault. She and the stranger, definitely a male, bent down and gathered up the coins. She was conscious of taking up his time. It took a few seconds. He deposited a few coins in her hand. It was all there, more or less, three one-pound coins, some silver.

'Watch your back, Naomi.'

'Thanks, I will.'

Naomi stopped checking the money and looked up. He'd gone. Was it someone she knew? How did he know her name? She swung round but he'd got lost in people-traffic. She'd only taken in that he was wearing a grey top with a hood. She'd logged nothing about his face or features. He was stocky. Not fat or tall, but wide. Her eyes combed over the bodies carefully, but her stranger had evaporated like a vapour trail on a summer day.

12

It was five-fifty the same day. Naomi felt agitated for two reasons: Camilla would be ringing in ten minutes and it was Nathan's weekend with Dan so she had no plans to see him until Sunday evening. She didn't begrudge Nathan being with Dan, but she hadn't seen him all week and she was getting withdrawal symptoms.

He'd begged to see her the night before, but she'd had to commit to her essay, no choice. She regretted that now. The whole weekend alone! She wished she'd been less sensible and stayed up all night writing. Even exhaustion would beat this feeling by miles. Nathan's final words about Camilla were still in her head. *If the truth is what she wants, play her at her own game and tell her straight.*

Naomi was finishing her tea in the kitchen, keenly aware of the time. Camilla's calls were always on time, to the minute. Too wound up to sit, she stood with her back against the worktop shovelling food in with a fork. She couldn't digest her baked potato fast enough. It was dry and tasteless. The beans were too hot. Her eyes ran over the messy kitchen. Her flatmates would meet her in here at ten the following morning to clear up. *Tell her straight.*

The door swung open and Bridget came in, light-brown hair scraped back in a ponytail. She wasn't wearing makeup. Her hair looked greasy and needed a wash, but it had been shoved out of the way and ignored. She was wearing tracksuit bottoms and a fitted T-shirt which said, *in case you're wondering, they're real.*

Bridget still looked in need of a heart-to-heart, which made Naomi's heart sink.

'Where have you been all week?' Bridget asked, close to an accusation. She flopped onto a leather chair beside a low table. It was centred with a salt pot and cluttered with used glasses and cups. This start was typical of Bridget – ask one or two questions then launch into her own agenda. Me, me, me! 'I've hardly seen anything of you.'

'Busy,' Naomi said, indicating her mouth was full and that she was trying her best to swallow.

'I hear you've got a new boyfriend, some hot older guy?' Bridget smiled weakly and dragged a bar of chocolate from her pocket. She always abused chocolate when she was down.

'He's only twenty-five,' Naomi said, desperate to avoid Bridget's problems, hoping to escape before she got roped in.

'Only?'

'He doesn't look it. Anyway, I haven't been busy just because of him. I've been working on my essay.'

Naomi sneaked a look at her watch. Five fifty-five.

'I think Max is seeing someone else,' Bridget ploughed on. 'He hasn't said, but you know when you can just tell?'

No, Naomi didn't know, and at the moment she didn't care and she didn't want to spend precious time talking or thinking about it. 'How do you know if he hasn't said anything?'

'See, that's the thing,' she said, leaning forward, resting her chin on one bent knee, chewing on her chocolate without offering Naomi any. 'It's more what he hasn't said. He doesn't ring me as much as he used to and he hasn't said he loves me for like fifteen days. What's that about?'

Naomi didn't know. She wanted to run over her dialogue with Camilla before she had to do it for real. How had she got sucked into this? 'How often does he normally say it?' Naomi asked, improvising, mind wandering. She put her half-empty plate next to the pile of pots at the sink.

'All the time. Doesn't yours?'

'We haven't been together long.'

Bridget screwed up the used chocolate wrapper and stuffed it in a dirty glass before proceeding to list all the amazing things about Max Lloyd and what she missed about him. 'I hate not seeing him. I hate that he's in Leeds and I'm in Manchester, it's like fifty miles away. I hate not knowing who he's with or what he's doing. It's driving me nuts.'

Naomi stole another glance at her watch while Bridget looked down. Five fifty-eight. 'Look, my mum's ringing me –'

'I don't know whether or not to get the train tomorrow and go and see him – just show up. What do you think?'

Naomi's heart was beating. Bridget was oblivious. 'I think I'd ring first. You don't want to go all that way –'

'Yeah, but I don't want him to be prepared, you know? If he doesn't know I'm coming I can surprise him. Hopefully it'll be a good surprise not a bad one. Don't you think?'

Naomi couldn't think, not with Bridget going on. 'Why don't you tell him you want to go over and see him and see how he reacts?'

'Nah. I offered last weekend and he said he was busy with assignments, but I reckon it was a load of bull –'

Naomi's phone started ringing, making Bridget jump up and shut up. Beethoven's fifth symphony blurted from the worktop. Naomi glanced down, seeing the three dreaded letters that were dancing, commanding her attention. Mum.

She looked at Bridget. Bridget stared back. 'Don't get it,' Bridget ordered.

Naomi, hassled on all sides, lifted the phone. 'Sorry, I have to.'

'Why? Who is it?' Bridget demanded. 'Is it him?' It was an accusation now.

None of your damned business. 'It's important,' Naomi said, walking, phone still blaring, reaching for the door handle. 'I'll come back.'

She left the kitchen and accepted the call as she entered her room next door. She dropped onto the bed.

Camilla talked about the house, the cats, Henry's midday naps that drove her mad, Annabel's whole life that had the same effect. She moved on to Lorie's help in the garden and the planting of hundreds of bulbs for spring. No mention of Nathan, like he'd been filed away or just forgotten. It made things harder. Naomi had prepared for a confrontation. Now she'd have to do the confronting herself.

'We're off out with Richard and Abigail for dinner tonight,' Camilla continued, talking about the neighbours – Henry's golfing buddy and Abigail, his much younger wife. 'Abigail's a bore, you know. She wastes her time watching reality TV and has the audacity to bring them up in conversation with me. Do I look like the kind of woman who's spent her life rotting in front of trashy TV, Naomi? Do I?'

'No, Mum.'

'No. What fascinates Richard about the woman I do not know. I can't think I've ever seen her in a top that adequately covers her chest.'

'Mystery solved.'

'Well,' she breathed. 'The only common ground I can find with the woman is that our husbands wear ridiculous trousers for their sport. If I catch your father's eyes wandering –'

'Mum, I really don't think Dad's interested.'

She heaved out a sigh. 'Well, I need to go and do something with my hair. I'll get Loretta to look at it.'

'Lorie still there?' Naomi asked, knowing she'd need her ear as soon as possible.

'She has to leave at six-thirty. Off out with . . . boyfriend. I hate these midlife moments where you open a memory door for a name and the room is empty.'

'Simon.'

'Simon,' she repeated. 'Have you met him?'

Naomi's eyes rolled. 'Not yet. She's bringing him to my birthday dinner.'

'That's right.'

There was a moment of silence where Naomi hesitated. It wasn't a great time to bring Nathan up. There would never be a great time. 'Mum, I need to speak to you about Nathan.' Her heart worked harder.

'Who?' Naomi imagined her in that vacant room again, name-searching. 'Oh him. Go on,' Camilla said, sharply.

Naomi closed her eyes. 'We haven't broken up.'

'You obviously weren't clear enough with him, Naomi. How exactly did you word it?'

'I haven't said anything to him.'

'What do you mean? Have you seen him this week?'

'No, I've been too busy.'

'So you haven't had chance to explain then.'

Naomi rubbed her eyes with one hand. 'Mum, there's nothing to explain to Nathan –'

'Oh yes there is. Do you want me to speak to him?'

'Mum, just listen. Please. Nathan's in love with me. I'm in love with –'

'Oh, good grief,' she shouted. Naomi lost her nerve and went quiet. She could feel her cheeks colouring and nausea stirring in the pit of her stomach. 'You've only known him five minutes. Drop him, Naomi, before you're in too deep.'

'Mum, I'm doing all my work. I've performed in the concert hall this week. I've spent time with a friend who needed help. I've done a long essay which is why I haven't seen Nathan. My work is fine. I'm sure once you get to know him, you'll see that he's an amazing person.'

'I do not want to get to know him, Naomi.' It was her warning voice.

'Why not?' It was Naomi's sheepish apologetic voice.

Camilla, refusing to explain herself said, 'Why are you doing this?'

Naomi was loathing every second of this conversation. Confrontation made her feel like digging a pit and hiding in it until the storm passed. 'Doing what?'

'Turning into Annabel. Has she put you up to this just to torment me?'

'Mum, Annabel doesn't even know about my relationship with Nathan.'

'You've always wanted to be like her. Don't think I don't know. I've seen your diaries. I hoped you'd have more sense than to want to follow her.'

Naomi couldn't speak. Camilla had read her diaries? How much? How dare she?

Camilla didn't apologise. She was finishing up the conversation now with no thought for the damage. 'I'll ask one thing. When I see you next Saturday I hope to hear you've ended this relationship. And don't tell me you're in love with someone you don't know. Ridiculous.

Get your head secured, Naomi. Think about this, would you? I'll call next Friday, usual time. Be available.'

Naomi found her tongue, but her tone was gentle like she hardly dared say what she needed to say. 'There's nothing to think about. I've invited Nathan to the party and he's accepted. So *we* will see you next Saturday. I hope you'll give him a chance.'

Camilla cut the call without another word. Naomi sat on the edge of the bed, hands shaking, thinking things through. She had no clue how much time passed before there was an almighty banging on the door. She opened it. Bridget stood, arms crossed, head cocked on one side.

'Half an hour I waited like an idiot for you in there,' she shouted, jabbing a thumb in the direction of the kitchen. 'Some friend you are.'

13

CAPTIVITY

The pink rose that stood in the thin vase opposite her bed, had wilted. It leaned, head bowed, colour fading, petals brittle and browning at the edges. It had given up. That morning the monster had noticed and removed it. He replaced it with another fresh rose, same colour, same vase, doomed to the same fate. Naomi guessed it was from the garden. How was a stupid flower meant to fill the vacant hours and make up for a husband, a family, a life? She'd have killed for a book or even a pen and paper. If she ever escaped this place, the poetry would flow.

A week had passed in solitary confinement. During that time, apart from an attempted escape which had spectacularly failed, nothing had changed and everything had changed. She was still no closer to knowing why she was in the Lake District with a psycho, or what he planned to do with her, but she did know that each new day ushered in the same feelings with new intensity. Her body hurt constantly from lack of use. Like an untended garden, ugly fast-growing weeds were threatening to overpower the delicate flowers and strangle them. Her mind felt like that garden.

Prayers for help had dried up in the jungle. Why would God want to hear from someone plotting to kill? She found herself daydreaming about ways of doing it. Her Bible reading had taught her that committing a crime in her heart was as good as doing it. She supposed God was done with her now, which made her feel painfully sad and kind of lost and abandoned, but she couldn't give up on the plan. Escape. It was all she thought about. She'd catch the monster off guard, wrap the chains around his neck from behind and lock her arm muscles, exerting all her strength until he stopped struggling. She'd take the keys from his pocket, free herself and drive away in his car. She'd visualised the whole thing from beginning to end working beautifully. It had become her fantasy and her hope. Escape. She enjoyed toying with the word in her head.

She'd prefer to do it without violence, but he'd left her no choice. In extreme circumstances, people did what they had to do. End of. Survival was the most primal human instinct. So it was only self-defence. With the prize of winning her life back, she was certain she could do it. She had to make a move before he did. Inaction amounted to apathy, which equated to danger. So while nothing changed, simultaneously nothing stayed the same. And that altered everything.

While she was daydreaming about murder, at the same time she ached for Nathan. He was always there either in pictures in her head, or on the horizon of her consciousness. Every day, she'd walked down the aisle and married him all over again. The wondering was the most debilitating thing. What had happened to him? What was he doing? Was he OK? She spent lost hours in a trace, imagining his smile, his arms around her, the way his jawline pulsed when he was tense or thinking hard; where they'd be if she hadn't been torn away from him. She imagined him searching and losing hope. The wedding seemed so long ago. Focussing on Nathan helped her through, and also intensified the pain.

In lesser degrees, she wanted a reunion with family and with Lorie. None of her college friends stayed in her mind for long. They'd parade through her head briefly then disappear, replaced by the more important people who'd defined who she was. The roots of family were deeply entrenched.

Naomi stood and walked to the French-door windows. From the look of the sky, her only clock, it was around four, four-thirty in the afternoon. The monster had done the food drop about an hour before. Naomi had intended to save some of it for supper, but had scoffed the lot. She regretted that now. The empty plastic plate lay on the red tray on the table beneath the plastic fork. She wouldn't see him again until morning.

She touched the doors just because she could, and stood examining a threatening sky with an assortment of black and grey cloud on the move. A medium strength breeze was puffing and panting, stirring the trees in the back garden and stripping them of dying leaves. They swirled around before noiselessly settling somewhere. This was the hardest part of the day, the pacing, the watching, the dreading of the oncoming darkness. It was the time her sanity felt most threatened.

It was Sunday now. Naomi had found a use for the hairgrip. Considering Jack Bauer would have escaped with it blindfolded and semiconscious, having unlocked his chains during a window of only ten seconds using one arm, she felt quite pathetic really. But this wasn't Hollywood, it was Cumbria, the wettest County in England. She'd tried the whole Jack Bauer thing and was now certain that a hairgrip in her hands was capable of almost nothing. Making any use of it was a triumph.

Using the sharp edge of one side, she'd scored the leg of the bed every day to mark the days of the week. And she'd written her name on the base of the leg close to the floor. If she ever got out of here alive, she'd never forget the single secret chore of her day in scratching that tiny line and the importance she attached to it. She'd made the lines neat and accurate and parallel, cutting through four of them when she got to five. It had been a definite highlight of the week. Apart from the shower, the fifth scoring day stood out.

She hadn't spoken to the monster since the failed escape. She often suspected he watched her for long periods through the keyhole. It made her skin tingle uncomfortably and she'd shift to one side of the bed out of view. She also sensed that he was becoming increasingly edgy. Translated into words, she picked up that he was waiting for something to happen and that things would change once it did. She could be wrong, but she couldn't deny that his anxiety transferred to her and for that reason, she hadn't provoked him by saying a word. It also meant that time to launch an attack was running out.

A routine of sorts had emerged throughout the week. After breakfast, he showered and left the house at the back and walked down the garden path in his black woolly hat, hands in the front pockets of his jeans. He climbed over the fence and took the ten to fifteen minute trek to the distant hill where he disappeared for long enough to buy a newspaper. She wondered if the house on the same hill with the billowing chimney, was a shop. He returned along the same lonely route, head down, dark hair showing beneath the hat. Despite long vigils at the window, she'd never seen another person.

He usually spent part of the morning with the TV on low. She suspected it was a cover so he could speak freely on his phone. He occasionally went out in his car. Mid afternoon, he'd bring more food, balaclava always on.

After this second daily visit, nothing ever happened except an immediate clear up downstairs. Late afternoon eventually came around, where the hours crawled painfully by until the sun sank and the room reduced to shadows. The only light she could reach was the bathroom, so she switched it on in the evenings and opened the door to brighten the room.

As she watched the dry leaves chasing around on the back lawn, she tried to remember something specific to define each day that week, and couldn't. Time had knitted together, blurring details, making her head feel sluggish and fuzzy. But she knew it was Sunday. The new academic year was due to begin in eight days, the day after she was due back from her honeymoon. It had all been carefully worked out. Her clothes had already been moved into Nathan's flat where she'd planned to begin her life with him. That thought only prompted the perpetual questions: how did she wind up here? Blah, blah, blah. At least she'd been spared the icy graveyard.

She couldn't count on it staying that way. She had to put her plan into action. Soon. Something had to change. It did, that very night, in the most unexpected way.

***

LIBERTY

Naomi tentatively knocked on Bridget's door at 11 o'clock on Saturday morning and didn't get a response. She'd failed to show at the planned clean-up session that morning. Naomi suspected her disappearance had nothing to do with cleaning avoidance and everything to do with Max Lloyd. She'd prepared a short note which she now shuffled beneath the door. It read:

Hi Bridget. I wanted to apologise for last night. I have stuff going on at home, but no excuses. It's my birthday next weekend and I'm having a dinner party at home. I'd love you to come. Hope you get things sorted with Max.

Naomi x

With no plans to do anything except work, Naomi muddled through a dull day with only books for company. Her desk was stacked with everything from orchestral scores and sheet music to books about the orchestral scores and sheet music she was studying. She did three hours of piano practise in between, focussing on what she planned to play for Nathan.

She heard nothing from Bridget that day. Nathan didn't ring either. He had specific plans all day with Dan, football then cinema. He'd warned her he might not manage to call. Naomi immersed herself in work and tried hard not to miss him. Nathan had promised to come straight to the college the minute he got back on Sunday evening. Naomi checked her watch. Twenty-eight hours to go, give or take.

That night, head aching from concentration, Naomi crawled into bed early. Oblivion meant she didn't have to be conscious of Nathan. Time flew in sleep. She had a peaceful, dreamless night, but paid the price and woke up too early. Sunday began at seven-thirty and the morning got stuck. The afternoon picked up pace. Naomi robotically did her laundry and spent an hour planning what to wear when she saw Nathan. Camilla shadowed the excitement. The only clue she got about how Camilla was feeling was via a text from Annabel, received late that afternoon. It said: 'Mum's in a real mood with me. Don't know what I've done but she's on my case more than usual. Any clues? Can't wait to jet off to Japan.'

Naomi stared at it and felt sick. So Camilla hadn't mentioned Nathan to Annabel then. Was she still living in hope that Naomi would chuck him away like an old birthday card? Rebelling was new. And nasty and uncomfortable. It was Annabel's area of expertise but Naomi didn't want advice. She'd have to work this one out for herself and tread carefully.

Naomi stood, phone in hand, rereading the message, wondering how to respond, frustrated that she didn't want to be open with Annabel about Nathan. Her thoughts strayed back in time to an unforgettable bonfire night, where she'd made a grim discovery which had burrowed deep inside her memory and refused to budge.

It was the time Naomi was boarding at school. She hadn't seen Annabel on their joint sixteenth birthday that year, so Camilla organised a bonfire party at home. Wood from a dead tree and scattered bits of dried leaves and broken branches had been piled close to Camilla's precious vegetable patch, which was at the side of the house behind a high stone wall. The fire was lit at seven on a mild November evening where a misty drizzle hung in the air and coated everything it touched.

Annabel had invited twelve school friends. All of them plus two showed up. Naomi brought only Tom Butterworth. He'd held her hand and made her feel older than sixteen. Annabel's friends couldn't believe Naomi was her twin. Naomi didn't mind that night. Bringing Tom easily made up for Annabel's fourteen girlfriends. Tom had made regular visits to the house. He'd played his viola and had earned himself a special place in Camilla's good books. He chatted easily to the girls around the fire and told a few jokes.

Low cloud steadily offloaded all that evening. The only lights in the sky were manmade. Naomi threaded through the bodies that surrounded the fire, carrying a cup of hot mushroom soup for Tom. He'd disappeared. Naomi waited, smile painted on for Annie's friends, shielding Tom's soup beneath her jacket.

After a long wait and a thorough search of the garden as well as a quick search of the house, Naomi tried to phone him. No reply. Lorie found her wandering and asked what was wrong. Naomi linked her arm and confessed that she'd lost Tom. Lorie had last seen him heading towards the back of the house with Annabel. *The back?* Naomi hadn't checked there. She turned down Lorie's offer to help track him down and set off alone.

She dumped his lukewarm soup on a window ledge and wandered round the back of the house. The biggest plot of the garden was at the front of the house. There was another huge chunk at the side, where everyone was congregating around the fire. The back had only a small amount of garden and a gloomy light on the wall by the back door. Naomi followed the path, taking care not to trip. It was a fairly new part of the house which had been extended to include a cloakroom, laundry room and wet room. The idea was to stop muddy feet being tramped through the house.

But no one ever bothered to shower in the wet room near the back door. It became a forgotten room, rarely used. Naomi picked her way carefully along the path. Obviously, no one was there. The windows were just vacant black squares.

She let herself in anyway, wiped her feet, turned on the light in the tiled hallway, closed the door. The outside noises dimmed. The house was deserted, but the warmth gave her a welcome hug. The wet room door was closed. Unusual. Naomi grasped the handle and twisted. It was locked. She wrestled with the handle, wondering if it was stiff. It didn't give way.

'Weird,' she muttered. She gently knocked. 'Tom?'

Only silence came back. She tried to open it again and couldn't. Naomi sensed her twin beyond the frozen door. Her stomach twisted into a knot. Naomi turned off the light and opened and closed the back door without leaving. She stepped into the shadows of the cloakroom opposite the wet room and leant against the wall and waited.

The wait was short. Two whispering people spilled from the room opposite. Tom was giggling.

'Has she gone?' he asked.

'Shh. Of course she's gone.' Annabel's voice. 'This isn't going to happen again, you know. Ever.'

'Feeling bad already?'

'What do you think? Naomi's my sister. Are you going to tell her?'

'Course not! I don't do guilt.' Naomi could hear the smile in his voice. She shut her eyes.

'Obviously.'

'You go out first and I'll turn up in a couple of minutes and tell Naomi I was using the bathroom.'

'You're a terrible boyfriend, you know that?'

In the silent moments that followed, Naomi detected the nauseating subtle sound of a departing kiss. She kept her eyes closed and turned to stone in the warm room.

'Stop,' Annabel said. 'Let go of me.'

'I was just testing your resolve not to kiss me again, but you can't resist, can you?'

'Oh, you reckon?' Annabel said, voice sharper. 'I want you to finish with Naomi.'

Naomi's chest clenched. 'For you? I don't see how that would work.'

'No, not for me. For her.' Annabel's voice was low, but urgent. 'Tonight was a test to see if you were good enough for my sister.'

'Yeah, right!' Tom's voice was quietly fierce. 'Are you winding me up?'

'Not at all.'

'Tonight was a test to see if you could win your sister's boyfriend. And you did. Happy?'

There was no hesitation. 'No. The fact that you followed me in here means she can do a lot better.'

'Is that your sick way of justifying yourself?'

'Finish it or I'll tell her what you're like.'

'It takes two, Annabel. Maybe I'll tell her what *you're* like.'

'Go ahead. Blood's thicker, Tom. No one can come between me and Naomi. Especially not you.'

The door opened and closed. Naomi could hear Tom shuffling around on the other side of the wall, alone.

She opened her eyes, not sure she could move. Did she let him go and pretend nothing had happened? That scenario ran into a dead end in seconds. Tom Butterworth had to leave. Now. Before he had room to deny it, or finish with her first. Naomi straightened up and stepped beyond the door. In the darkness, Tom swore. Naomi reached for the light switch and blinded him.

Tom stood, squinting against the light, shielding his eyes with one arm.

'Naomi? How long have you been – '

'Long enough.'

'What are you doing here?' he asked, dropping his arm, attempting to sound like he was pleased to see her. He stumbled forward.

Naomi glared and stepped back. Tom stopped his advance. 'Get out of here and don't come back.'

'Babe, come on,' he said, taking another step.

'Don't you touch me. I want you out of this house now, and if you don't want my dad chasing you off with his shotgun, don't speak to anyone on the way out.'

'Was this a setup by you two?'

Naomi's voice trembled. 'Leave.'

'There isn't a bus for another hour.'

'Tell someone who cares.'

Defeated, Tom nodded and backed off. He zipped up his coat. 'I only kissed her,' he said.

'Only?' Naomi yelled. 'Get. Out.'

'OK, I'm leaving,' he snapped defensively. 'You want to take a long hard look at your perfect sister and tell her to stop giving the eye to anything in trousers.'

Naomi crossed her arms. Tom turned and thundered through the door, slamming it so hard it bounced back and didn't close.

Naomi shared a school with Tom. She couldn't avoid seeing him, but it was the last time they ever spoke. The weeks after that night were agonising, like being too close to a bonfire and not being able to shift. Naomi confided only in Lorie and never confronted Annabel. She wouldn't put a wedge between them and let Tom win. It suited Naomi to let Annabel think that Tom had ended the relationship and devastated her. Annabel never suspected the truth.

Eventually the heat lost strength and the desire to hold a grudge dropped away. She was only hurting herself. Without the courage to have it out with Annie, the only thing she could do was bury it, which involved a form of forgiveness. But not for Tom. The best closure she could muster was to forget about him, or when that failed, remember his bad bits. She hated the texture of his hair. She'd always imagined herself running her fingers through a boy's hair when he kissed her. When she'd tried it with Tom, it was like a caressing a washing-up scourer. Even the colour of Tom's hair was a turn-off. She resented it when he popped up in dreams, carrying the scent of burning wood.

The memories and the feelings withdrew. Naomi's stare was still set on her phone. Annie was on the other end, waiting for a reply. She decided to tell Annabel about Nathan before Saturday, but not now. A text wasn't the right thing. Maybe during the week Camilla would tell Annie anyway. Save her the trouble.

She sent a late reply: 'If it helps, I think it's me who's bugging mum. We had words last week. Nothing serious. Explain when I see you. What do you want for your birthday?'

A reply fired back. 'Something for Japan.' Naomi screwed her face up. Great! A fruitless trudge round the shops beckoned. 'Who are you bringing to the party?'

Naomi sighed. Could she escape the subject? 'Not sure yet. Maybe my flatmates. Maybe Siobhan. Definitely Nathan.'

'Yum! Mum thought you two were an item. I told her to get real. She hasn't mentioned him since. He's not gay is he?'

Naomi stood still again, fingers hovering over her phone. What was stopping her from just saying it? She was dreading this birthday gathering. The last joint party had been the fateful bonfire one, three years before. Betrayal had left scar tissue that had faded with time, but not gone. While that night still burned on in Naomi's memory in vivid detail, she doubted Annabel remembered very much about it. Meeting Nathan had made up for all of it. Naomi thought of Nathan versus straw-haired Tom. No comparison. No contest. And she'd be with Nathan soon. Naomi smiled and her pulse ticked over pleasantly. She needed to wrap up this pointless conversation and get ready.

'Nathan gay?' she jabbed out, unable to lose the smile. 'No. Definitely not.'

***

Naomi had been ready a while when Nathan showed up

ten minutes early that evening. He stood behind the doors of the reception area in pale brown narrow-legged chinos, fingers jammed into the pockets at the top. He was wearing a cream long-sleeved top, sleeves pushed up. His hair was adorably messy on top. He grinned helplessly when he saw her and waited for her to part the glass barrier. As she released the door, he stepped forward and lifted her off the floor, squeezing her tight. Naomi forgot where she was.

'It's been a long week,' he whispered in her ear through her hair. 'I've missed you loads.'

'Me too.' They stood, locked in each other's arms, blocking the doorway. Eventually, he put her down, took hold of her hand and let her outside.

'How's Dan?'

Nathan flicked her a look. He looked so happy, it was contagious. 'Dan's fine. He's having a pretty good spell at the moment. I made sure he enjoyed his weekend even though my head was somewhere else.' He glanced at her for a lingering moment as they strolled along the pavement during the last few minutes of daylight on a chilly mid-October evening. The light was already slinking away. Naomi wasn't aware of anything but the firm clasp of Nathan's hand and the buzz of being with him. 'I couldn't stop thinking about you.'

'Really? I went to bed early last night just to stop thinking about you, but you were still with me all night.'

'I wish.' Nathan stopped walking and drew her into his arms again. There were a few people knocking around. Nathan studied her closely. 'Kissing in public is pretty juvenile, don't you think?'

'I suppose.'

He leant towards her. 'But sometimes it has to be done,' he said, finding her lips for a few glorious moments. When he pulled back, he said, 'I've been dreaming about that.' Naomi giggled. 'Well, let's say it started that way. Change the subject,' he said, glancing up at the sky. 'Have you got a piano booked?'

Naomi checked her watch. 'Yeah. In a couple of minutes.'

'Where's your music?'

Naomi pointed to the side of her head. 'In here. I memorise everything unless I'm accompanying.'

'You're amazing,' he said, kissing her forehead. 'What are you going to play?'

They started walking again. 'You'll have to guess when you hear it.'

Naomi led Nathan to one of her favourite practise rooms on the first floor. Room 180. It was the same room she had her private lessons with her teacher, Olga Kolesnikova. She was jittery as she closed the door, sat at the piano and opened the lid. Someone had left a gnawed pencil across the keys. Nathan folded his arms and stood back. She could see his reflection in the polished black lid.

'I'll have to warm up for a couple of minutes,' she said.

Nathan took another step back and watched in silence. Naomi ran up and down some scales and arpeggios until her fingers felt supple and were moving comfortably across the keys producing a quality legato sound that pleased her.

She was about to play a difficult etude in C-sharp minor. Her warm-up ended with the scale of that key. Her heart was pumping blood anxiously around her body by now. She felt warm and slightly clammy. Performing at the Royal Albert Hall wouldn't feel this bad.

She withdrew her hands from the keys, closed her eyes and drew some slow breaths, mentally rehearsing the first few bars, visualising her fingers moving effortlessly to the right notes. The thought of the ending, the newest and weakest part, broke her concentration. Now she was aware only of the piano and the gleaming white keys, waiting to burst into sound.

The piece, about three months old, had more-or-less reached the stage where she could rely on her fingers to churn out pages of notes in the right order, at speed. Her head was taking a backseat. Responses were automatic. She could just about forget notes and concentrate on quality of sound production which rested on careful listening. Nathan would have no understanding of the painstaking slog that had brought the piece to this stage in its journey, but she hoped he'd appreciate the music itself.

She opened her eyes seeing only the piano keys and threw herself without warning into the piece. It felt under control from the start. The notes were crisp and clear, the hand balance good. It progressed, relentlessly.

She began to relax; her senses were alert. She listened hard to her own playing. She could hear her teacher's voice at times, issuing the kind of instructions she gave during lessons at certain points in the piece: *less of this; more of that. Phrasing, Naomi. Tie your leg to the stool if you must, but don't blur the texture with over-pedalling.* She responded as if Olga were there, guiding her through it, drawing everything skilfully from the inside, out.

She approached the dramatic climax of the ending. *Speed of attack, Naomi.* Conscious she'd made only one tiny mistake in the whole piece, she knew this part would be the real test. Without holding back and playing safe, she unleashed all her energy into the final bars – a cascading sprint of broken chords which ended with four triumphant crashing chords.

On weak limbs, Naomi stood and turned to face

Nathan's applause. Smiling, she bowed.

Eventually, his hands stilled. 'Whoa. That was incredible. How do you remember all those notes?'

'I don't know.'

'You have to know.'

'It's like driving a car. If you tried to explain a long journey you might come unstuck, but if you get in the car you can drive where you want to go without thinking, as long as you've done the journey enough times. It's a bit like that.'

'It's unreal.'

'Did you like the piece?' Naomi asked.

'I loved it. It was brilliant,' he said, wrapping his arms around her, kissing her forehead. 'Who was it?'

'Chopin, Nathan.'

***

Nathan begged for more. Naomi refused. She led him out of the college into a murky evening, Nathan still raving about her performance. A man stood watching them across the road. Her smile disappeared and Nathan's voice faded. He was wearing a grey hooded top. It took her back a couple of days when she'd dropped her money on the pavement. He was stocky, but not very tall, unless his width only gave the illusion of him being average height. Siobhan's man? Same one? As soon as Naomi made eye contact, he lowered his eyes and began to walk away from the college, his back to them.

Nathan had gone quiet. He was watching Naomi now, following her eyes. 'OK Naims?' The guy in the hooded top didn't look back. Naomi retracted her glare and looked at Nathan blankly.

'Who was that?' Nathan asked.

A coincidence? Could it be the same person? It wasn't worth mentioning. 'No one I know.'

'You look upset,' Nathan said. 'Has he bothered you?' The man was still hurrying away, head down. Naomi shook her head.

'Sure?'

'Yeah.'

He studied her for a long moment until she forced a smile.

'OK then. D'you want to see where I live?' he asked her.

'I'd love to.'

Nathan took a lingering look down the road. Hoodie man had shrunk in the distance by now. Nathan slipped his arm around Naomi's waist and ushered her in the opposite direction, snatching a final glance over his shoulder. 'Let's go then.'

14

They weaved through the city centre and Naomi barely recognised anything until they passed Chethams, which jolted bad memories. As a pupil at Chethams she'd gone home every weekend and had never really explored the city, or wanted to. Oxford Road where the college stood, was so well equipped, she could survive off it without needing to walk for more than ten minutes in any direction. Curry Mile was in spitting distance. There was an Olympic sized swimming pool opposite the college. She'd walked to one concert at the Bridgewater Hall and thought she could find it again, probably. She'd taken occasional trips to the clothes shops and jumped on the odd tram that zipped through the streets.

Scores of people had moved into the centre over the last decade, Nathan told her as they drove along. The property developers had rubbed their hands together and got to work. New flats and apartments had sprung up everywhere and old buildings had been converted into flats. She knew Manchester had lots of water, but she hadn't seen any of it until tonight.

Nathan lived at Salford Quays in a two bedroomed second floor flat, only affordable because the rent was shared. It overlooked the canal and was a short walk from rows of bars and restaurants. He shared the place with a guy called Guy. Nathan and Guy had a double bedroom each, and otherwise shared a tiny bathroom and an open plan lounge that had a kitchen at one end. A square no-nonsense dining table divided the room.

Naomi walked around the small flat which looked

exactly like two blokes lived in it. It was minimal and trendy in a Cityish kind of way and was sort of tidy and sort of clean. Vertical blinds hung at the windows.

'This is Guy's room,' Nathan said, knocking a couple of times on a sealed white door. Silence. Nathan opened and closed the door quickly. The room exhaled a faint smell that told Naomi it needed airing – a phrase Camilla liked a lot. The only detail Naomi had gathered, was that the duvet was charcoal-coloured and the curtains striped. 'He's out a lot,' Nathan told her. 'Serious girlfriend.'

The walls were white and bare in the narrow hallway. The lounge walls told pretty much the same story except for one small black-framed picture of Manchester City's logo, which Nathan was quick to point out, was Guy's. There was a black leather sofa and matching chair, a TV, a wooden cabinet and a matching coffee table resting on a plain beige rug that lacked any detail other than colour and shape.

They wandered into Nathan's room. A pile of clothes draped over a black office chair that sat beneath a desk holding his laptop and a tower of books and DVDs. The bin was stuffed to capacity like the wicker washing basket by the desk. His double bed dominated the room and looked luxuriously comfortable. It was neatly made.

'I like it,' Naomi announced, as she perched on the bed next to Nathan and continued to scan the room. 'It's nice.'

'Nice?' Nathan laughed. 'It's a stereotypical bachelor pad. It's warm and dry. It must seem like a pit to you compared to the mansion.'

Naomi smiled. 'I don't live in a mansion, as you'll see next week.' Nathan put his arm around her and pulled her closer. 'It's just a big house.'

'Yeah right,' Nathan smiled. 'I bet your bedroom's in the west wing with an acre of garden out of the window. Am I close?'

Naomi dropped her head and laughed.

Nathan was watching her closely. 'Hey, you do want me to come to this dinner, don't you?' he asked, voice dropping, taking on a more serious tone.

Naomi looked at him, confused. 'Of course I do.'

'Why do I sense there's something you're not happy about? You've hardly mentioned it at all.'

Naomi sighed and tried to organise her thoughts. After toying with a few excuses, she decided honesty was best. 'I'm just worried,' she said, trying to picture herself in a room full of people which included Nathan and Camilla.

'Your mum?' Nathan asked. 'Has she said she doesn't want me to come?'

'She doesn't need to, but she can't stop you can she.' It wasn't a question.

Nathan reached out and touched her face. 'Do *you* want me to come?'

'You've already asked me that.'

'I'm asking again. Look at me this time.'

Naomi looked into his eyes and struggled to feel bad about anything. He didn't blink until she answered. 'Of course I want you there,' she said, 'But . . . '

Nathan had moved closer. 'But . . . you feel torn between doing what you want to do and keeping your mum happy, who doesn't want me there. And she doesn't want me in your life because I'm not good enough for you.'

'That's not true.'

'From her point of view it is,' he said gently, as a matter of fact. 'Why deny it?'

Naomi couldn't and didn't deny it. She fell quiet. 'Well, I don't care what she thinks.'

Nathan's mouth flickered, but it never became a

smile. 'Me neither,' Nathan examined her eyes. His lips were parted. 'Except that you do care, don't you? What you really meant was that you wished you didn't care.'

There wasn't time to reply. Nathan's mouth was upon hers now, silencing even her thoughts. Her attention was fixed on the warmth and movement of his mouth and the firm clasp of his arm around her middle. She felt the presence of the empty flat and their aloneness in it. The kissing intensified. Naomi pulled away. She reached for her necklace and zipped it quietly from side to side.

'Can I tell you something?'

'Course.'

'It's nothing to do with my mum.'

'Tell me,' he whispered, very close.

Naomi didn't know how to. Nathan, watching her closely, must have sensed it. 'Tom?' Naomi nodded, glad she didn't have to start a discussion by saying his name. She winced every time she said it out loud. 'He let you down – badly, you said.'

Naomi nodded again, relieved Nathan was in tune and had remembered.

'It's been on my mind,' Nathan said. He went quiet and waited.

'Well,' Naomi began. 'He two-timed me with . . . someone else. I caught him kissing her. Anyway, I broke up with him that night, but I felt horrible for ages afterwards.'

'I know the feeling,' he said, nodding, eyes focussed middle distance. He came back. 'It happened to me with the girlfriend I had before Lucy. We'd been together for about eleven months. It was with a friend of mine. Well, ex-friend.' He paused to sigh. 'The humiliation . . . Maybe that's a guy thing. I kept wondering what the other guy had that I didn't. In the end you have to let it go or it screws you up.'

Naomi managed a tight smile. 'I don't think it's a guy thing,' she said. 'I felt the same. I let it go with the girl, but not Tom.'

'Ever dream about him afterwards?' Nathan asked.

Naomi felt a surge of energy that she realised was pent-up anger. 'A lot. It drove me nuts. And now . . . ' her voice trailed off. Her head emptied.

'And now you're worried that I'll do the same, which makes you feel insecure and afraid to commit, just in case. You're not sure you could take another blow.'

'Yes,' she said, eyes filling unexpectedly. 'That's it exactly.'

Naomi blinked the tears back. Nathan took one of her hands and played with her fingers, weaving them into his own. 'Well, all I can say is that if we ever bump into Tom whatever-his-name-is, don't point him out to me if you don't want me to break his jaw. And as for you,' he said, pausing to run his fingers along one eyebrow and down her cheek, 'I promise I won't hurt you. I have the same issues. If things hadn't gone wrong with Lucy and with Judas, as I call her, I'd never have met you. So am I sorry they hurt me and let me down?' He let the question hang a moment. 'No. If it led to meeting you then it was worth it. I'd have to be insane to lose you.' Naomi couldn't speak. 'I'm not insane, but I'm in love with you which feels a bit like insanity. I'm going nowhere, OK? You'll have to trust me on that.'

A tear escaped and Nathan smudged it away with his thumb. She nodded. He kissed her again and pressed her onto her back and wrapped his arms around her until she became worried for a different reason.

'Nathan,' she said, breaking free, finding herself reaching for her necklace again. She was more conscious of it this time and it was more difficult to reach with Nathan on top of her. 'There's something else.'

'Tell me later.'

'It has to be now.'

Nathan sat up and pushed his fingers through his hair and puffed out all his breath. 'What could you possibly want to tell me right now?'

'About a promise I made. With God.'

'What?'

'I feel an idiot.' Naomi bit her lower lip. 'Remember before we got together that I promised God that if we found each other . . .' She couldn't end the sentence.

'Oh yeah?'

She paused, feeling utterly childish and ridiculous. 'I promised that if we got together, I wouldn't . . . you know . . . do anything.'

'Do anything?' He didn't get it at first. Then his mouth fell open and his eyebrows raised and it was obvious he'd just caught on. 'What?' He couldn't manage any more.

'I'm really sorry.'

Nathan panted a couple of times in disbelief. 'Why that? I mean, anything but that. Why didn't you promise to help build an orphanage or something?'

He was only half serious, but it didn't help. 'Sorry,' she said again.

'Don't apologise.' Nathan shook his head. 'Look, it's me who should be apologising. If I'd known –'

'You didn't know. Look, the promise . . . was more about me, not us. I never expected to find you. I promised God that if I got what I wanted, which was you, I'd wait until I was married before – '

'I get it,' Nathan said, fixing his eyes on hers. They were intense, as if things were churning inside his head. 'So marry me,' he said abruptly. It was Naomi's turn to be speechless. Nathan shifted quickly so that he was hanging over her again. Naomi lay back and examined his glorious face, which was unsmiling. 'Did I just ask you to marry me?' He produced a dazzling smile which took her breath.

'I think so.'

'And a minute before that I told you I wasn't insane?'

They both laughed. Nathan held her in his arms, pressing her to his chest.

'It was impulsive. You're frustrated.'

'It was impulsive,' Nathan said, 'but it feels right. Insanely right. Marry me.'

Naomi pushed Nathan back to assess his face again. 'You're not serious.'

'I think I am.'

'I can't marry you.'

'Why not?'

'Because,' she said, pausing. 'Just because.'

Nathan leant down and kissed her face all over, avoiding her lips so she could talk. 'Because?'

'We don't know each other.'

'I know everything about you. I feel like I've known you my whole life,' he said. 'Next excuse?'

'It's crazy.'

'I agree. But loads of people are crazy. It doesn't mean they're unhappy.'

'I'm a student.'

He was kissing her neck by now. 'And I have a job. I won't get in the way of your study. I have a flat here and you'll need a place to live next year. Move in with me.'

'What about Guy?'

'Compared to marriage, Guy is not a consideration. Besides, he's already talking about moving in with his girlfriend.'

'What about travelling?'

'Let's go together for our honeymoon if we can stretch to it. I have money saved, but I'm not asking my parents for any. We'll manage with what we've got.'

Naomi went quiet. Nathan took a long look at her before he kissed her again, tenderly this time, in a way that made her ache for more. Her head was scrambled, but something inside her was leaping for joy. *What's happening to me?*

Eventually Nathan withdrew and sat up. He put his head in his hands and rubbed his face. 'OK, calm down,' he said quietly to himself. 'Look, I'm sorry. I'm being selfish and stupid. Of course I'll respect your promise even though I don't get it. It's just the thought of never being able to touch you . . .' He shook his head and dropped his head in his hands and groaned. 'I'll get my head around it. In the meantime, we'll have to go out, not come here or go to your room. I can't be in a room alone with you like this, Naims. I'm a man. Once we start kissing, my instincts steer me in one direction and I've never been so attracted to anyone in my life.'

Naomi didn't know what to say.

Nathan carried on. 'I lie in here every night thinking of you, wanting you next to me. Does that scare you?'

'A bit,' she confessed, smoothing her hair. It excited her too. 'Mainly because I've never . . . you know. I don't know what I'm doing.'

'Get in,' he said, nodding his head towards the bed. 'Nothing will happen, I promise.'

After a few moments of hesitation, Naomi removed her shoes and climbed under the duvet cover and lay on her back looking at a smooth white ceiling with a dusty blue lampshade. Nathan slid in next to her and held her hand beneath the covers.

'Don't come any closer,' he said. They lay for a few still moments. The silence was kind of charged. It had an electric quality as it stretched a bit. 'Now you can't say you've never been to bed with a man before.'

'No,' she laughed.

'Plus you're fulfilling a fantasy for me,' he said, glancing sideways at her. 'It's not exactly what I expected, but then, you always surprise me, which shouldn't surprise me anymore.'

She kept her body in one place, but her neck was twisted to look at him.

'I'm really sorry.'

'Don't apologise for being different. That's what I adore about you. This is still really special for me, having you here. I wanted to prove to myself that I could lie here with you and hold your hand. Nothing else.'

'I don't want to make you uncomfortable.'

Nathan managed a small smile. 'It feels pretty good.' His smile faded. 'I'm not expecting anything from you in the way you think,' he said. 'I just want to be with you. All the time.'

'And I want to be with you, but I'm not ready for marriage.'

His grip tightened against her fingers. 'Course not.' He looked at the ceiling. Naomi continued to watch him. 'It's different for me. I've been engaged so I've already committed myself to the idea of marriage. I believe in it too. Lucy wanted children. That's why we were planning to get married. She was a year older than me and she wanted to start a family.'

'How could you afford children?' Naomi asked.

'Lucy is a solicitor. Believe it or not, we planned that I would stay at home and look after the children. We planned to have two close together before we were thirty. We even talked about names.'

'Really?' Naomi asked, feeling tinges of unexplained jealousy towards this girl, Lucy, who she didn't even know. *Don't let him see what you're thinking.* 'What names?'

'Luthan for a boy – which is a weird cross between Lucy and Nathan, Lucy's cheesy idea but, hey. And Zara for a girl. No reason. We both liked it.'

'Good enough reason.' Naomi watched Nathan across the pillow, frantically trying to derive a decent name from Naomi and Nathan. Nothing remotely worked. By the time her brain had finished juggling letters, she noticed there'd been a comfortable silence between them for a while. Nathan was eyeing her carefully.

'I don't have any regrets, Naims. I don't wish things had worked out with Lucy.'

What was the use pretending she wasn't bothered? 'Sure?'

'One hundred per cent.'

Relief flooded in. Nathan spoke again.

'I love *you*.'

It was as if Naomi heard the words in slow motion, emphasis on the last word. She watched his lips utter them, saw the words form. They hung between them now. No one had ever told her they loved her, she realised, as she lay there, dumbstruck. Those words had never been passed between any members of her family. It had taken this moment to be conscious of it.

She didn't think long about the response, it just tumbled from her lips as naturally as a running stream. 'I love you too.'

Nathan leant forward and kissed her forehead then climbed out of bed. He raked his fingers through his hair. 'Let's go to the cinema or something. I need to get out of here and focus on something other than how you make me feel and what I want to do about it. I'm proud of myself so far.'

Naomi left the warmth of the bed and stood up. She didn't say anything to Nathan as she put on her shoes, but dragging herself out of his bed had been a wrench. A part of her she hardly knew didn't want to leave.

Ever.

15

Camilla sat at her desk in the upstairs study mindlessly tapping the blunt end of her pen against a pad of paper. Trying to come up with a seating plan for the dinner party had been problematic and time-consuming. Her patience was fraying. She glanced at her watch and tutted. Four-forty.

Naomi's cat, Tess, pushed the door open and strolled in, tail up like an aerial, looking hopeful, heading for Camilla. Concentration gone, she put down her pen and removed her glasses, leaving them to swing from her neck by a thin gold chain. Camilla groaned as the cat began wiping itself all over her trouser legs.

'What gives you the idea that if you smear my trousers with fur, I'm more likely to jump up and feed you?'

Tess didn't get the hint so Camilla picked her up in one hand and dumped her on the landing and closed the door. 'Off with you.'

Tess complained outside the door. Camilla walked to the window and wondered why she felt sluggish. Two things. She was cold. Plus she didn't want to see Nathan Stone with Naomi again. Rephrase. With or without Naomi, she didn't want to face Nathan Stone again with his silky smart answers and his rugged good looks that had hooked Naomi in like fishing bait and turned Annabel's head too. Not that turning Annabel's head was such a terrific achievement.

Whatever influence Nathan Stone was having on Naomi was becoming more obvious to the point where

Naomi was asserting herself in ways that baffled Camilla. Naomi intended to inflict Nathan on the family whether he was invited or not. No discussion, no compromise. It was proof enough that Nathan Stone was no good, which in itself was a dreadful worry. Naomi was tangled in an unhealthy relationship at an important time with someone who had no understanding of music. It was a titanic problem worthy of a lot more thought and whatever action was necessary. She'd already confronted Naomi without success. What to do?

Camilla folded her arms and studied her garden. The weather had been pleasant until today. The temperature had taken a dive in the last few hours. Nature seemed to have decided to skip a season and launch into an early winter. Christmas cards and decorations had sneaked onto the supermarket shelves. The clocks were due to turn back any weekend now, shortening the days as if they weren't short enough. It was at this time of the year she missed South Africa most.

The chickens dashed across the grass, racing to be back in their pen where they could huddle together out of the stiff late-afternoon breeze. Beyond the pen, the apple trees were more-or-less bare, but the four pear trees were still clinging to plenty of fruit. Some of it lay scattered on the soil. Collecting it was a daily job at the moment. Mustn't waste. Camilla had seen too much want, to waste.

She took a small pad and pencil from her trouser pocket and jotted a note to a growing list of jobs. What she didn't take down these days could be forgotten or lost. Lists were an essential part of life and a constant reminder of age. By tomorrow, the list would become Lorie's timetable for the day.

The majestic lawn stretched out beneath her, recently mowed into squares, two-tone green. It was lush and beautiful and symmetrical. Camilla appreciated symmetry. It was satisfying, uncomplicated, consistent, reliable. Everything life wasn't.

Camilla tore her gaze from the garden, realising suddenly and urgently that there was something to do. She opened the door and almost tripped over Tess who was sitting hopefully. Camilla peered down into the hall.

Annabel drifted into view. Camilla saw the flowing blonde hair, the phone held out in front, a permanent attachment. Annabel was tapping out a message, headphones on, laughing out loud, droning some best-forgotten lyrics. Tickles, her cat, was following.

'Annabel.'

Nothing.

'Annabel.' A little louder.

Annabel stopped, turned, eventually looked up.

'What?' she said, too loudly.

Camilla signalled to remove the earphones. Annabel did. 'Could you tell Loretta I'd like a word with her in my study please?'

'Whatever.'

Camilla drifted to her room to put on an ugly brown cardigan she wore strictly indoors. Then she returned to her study and sat and waited. Lorie whisked in not long later, smiling. Camilla sent back a tight smile that was a memory a moment later.

'Have you got a few minutes?'

'Sure.' Lorie grabbed a chair and sat down opposite. Her movements were so fast always. She was a marvel, amazingly efficient. She had Naomi's colouring and trim figure. They were alike in many ways, which was one of the reasons she fitted in so perfectly. Lorie had often been mistaken for Camilla's daughter and Naomi's sister, but never Annabel. No one ever guessed Naomi and Annabel were twins.

Annabel had her grandfather's colouring: fair hair, ice-blue eyes. Camilla shook off a shiver and concentrated on Lorie settling herself.

'It's going to be a busy day tomorrow,' Camilla began.

'It'll be fine,' Lorie smiled reassuringly. 'I'm on top of everything.'

'I'm sure you are, but there are a couple of extras.'

'OK,' Lorie's face was open, ready, always optimistic that whatever problem was presented could be overcome.

'Denise, the cleaner.' Camilla clicked her fingers several times, trying to summon something more that wouldn't come. 'Her surname's gone.' She waved her hand dismissively and let it rest on her lap. 'Point is, I want you to tactfully let her go.'

For the first time, Lorie's face faltered. Some tension crept in. 'Let her go? Why?'

'I have my reasons.' Camilla paused, then decided suddenly and impulsively to share them. 'Some earrings of mine went missing last week. Little cameo studs, of all the things to take . . . They were inexpensive, but they meant something. She possibly thought that because I never wear them I wouldn't miss them. I confronted her and she reddened and couldn't look me in the eye, then denied it. This morning they magically reappeared in a place I wouldn't have dreamt of putting them.' Camilla was staring hard, not blinking. 'I won't be taken advantage of, you know that.'

Lorie sat forward. 'Camilla, Denise has got two little kids and her husband just lost his job. What if you're wrong about –'

'I'm not wrong. The timing is unfortunate, but there are certain things I won't tolerate.'

'OK,' Lorie said, voice small. 'Why do you want me

to do it?'

'For the experience,' Camilla answered. 'You know that if I had to do it, it wouldn't cause me any concern, so I've nothing whatsoever to gain. But you –'

'It'll be . . . difficult.' Lorie crossed her arms.

'Which is precisely why it's useful.' Camilla paused to assess Lorie, who was thinking hard, and frowning unconsciously. 'Plus, I'd like you to appoint another cleaner. I've already advertised the position. A few have responded. I've told them to ring tomorrow morning in between ten and eleven and I want you to deal with it. Ask whatever you think is appropriate. Use your instincts. Fill the job. Whoever you choose will be fine by me. Heaven knows my last three choices have been dreadful. What have we been paying Denise?' She tapped her forehead gently, trying to disturb her memory. Still, the name wasn't there.

'Bradbury,' Lorie offered.

'Thank you.'

'Ten pounds an hour. Too much?'

'I'm thinking not enough,' Camilla said. 'I advertised it at twelve, so it's not negotiable.'

'Twelve? For a cleaner? I know a midwife who doesn't earn that much.'

'I want a first class job doing, Loretta. I don't care about going-rates. I'm interested in a quality person doing a quality job and taking pride in the work. Like you do.'

Stuck for words, Lorie dropped her eyes and looked at her fingers, which were clasped and lying loosely on top of her legs.

Camilla went on. 'I'm also raising yours from fourteen to sixteen pounds an hour, effective immediately.' Camilla's gaze was fixed on Lorie, who looked up, stunned.

'Sixteen? I don't know what to say.'

'Nothing required. The work you do here is invaluable to me. Enough said. So you'll deal with the cleaners, one in, one out. Can I leave it with you?'

Lorie shrugged. 'Of course, yes.'

'Good.'

Lorie started to stand up. 'There's something else,' Camilla said. Lorie dropped right back in the chair and popped one slender leg over the other. 'It's . . . delicate.'

'OK.'

'What do you know about Naomi's not-so-young man?'

If there was a scramble going on to hide and amend things inside Lorie's head behind her dark eyes, Camilla didn't detect a hint of it.

'Erm.' Her voice rose. Her mouth turned down at the corners, briefly. She shrugged. 'He sounds perfect. To be fair, I'm reserving my judgement until I meet him.'

'But you speak to Naomi frequently enough that you'll have a picture I don't have. I'm not asking you to be disloyal, I just want to know what I'm dealing with. That relationship is bothering me beyond my admission even to Henry. I'm very uneasy about it.'

'Why?'

'Honestly? I don't know.'

'Look, Camilla,' Lorie said, tiptoeing carefully, stalling between words. 'I've never seen her happier, which has to be down to him. After everything she's dealt with, don't you think that counts for something?'

Camilla's forehead folded into a frown. 'Not particularly. Happiness, whatever it is, shouldn't depend upon another person, or how can it be reliable? It would comfort me far more if Naomi's happiness, for want of a better word, came from developing her talent. Her chance is now. I won't allow him to rob her.' Camilla slammed the desk gently with one hand. 'I won't.'

Lorie uncrossed her arms and tipped her palms up. 'Why would he want to rob her?'

'Why indeed.' Camilla paused. 'I've met him once. Smooth, over-confident bordering on arrogant. A person who knows how to get what he wants and will stop at nothing. I knew immediately I'd never warm to him and the feeling hasn't subsided. Now Tim –'

'Tom.'

'Yes, him. I didn't mind him. He came here the odd time. Pleasant enough boy. Good musician.'

Lorie glanced down again. This time, Camilla definitely detected a conflict. 'I don't think Tom was very –'

'I know what happened the night of the bonfire party.'

'You do?' Lorie's eyes shot up to meet Camilla's. 'How?'

'Naomi spilled it all out on paper as teenagers do. She left it on her desk one day. It was too tempting not to look through because I was concerned about her at the time. It wasn't my finest moment. I foolishly admitted it to her last week.' She shrugged. 'What's done is done.'

'Naomi will struggle with that, Camilla.'

Camilla cut in. 'It's done now. Anyway, there were pages and pages of stuff about Tom. Honestly, I blame Annabel. Obviously, I don't approve of what he did, but the point is I never got any bad feelings about him the way I do about this one. I'm sure Tom's gone on to become a perfectly adequate human being.'

Lorie's voice was quiet, but sure. 'I have to disagree. Nathan . . . Well let's say he might be a bit deeper than you think. From what I can gather he hasn't had things easy. There are things about him you don't know.'

'For instance?'

203

The pause was long enough for Lorie's discomfort to speak volumes. 'You'll have to talk to Naomi, Camilla.'

'I've tried –'

'You've tried to persuade her to dump him.' They locked eyes. Lorie held her hands up, palms flat, facing Camilla. 'Sorry, I don't want to step over the mark, but you are asking for my input and you do want me to be honest, don't you?'

Camilla slowly nodded her head, buying a little time, uncertainty creeping in.

'How do you expect her to react?' Lorie went on. 'My mum wanted me to break up with one of my ex-boyfriends and it brought us closer together. It was like we had a cause and had to take on the enemy together. The relationship lasted longer than it would have done if my mum hadn't tried to get involved. Don't make an enemy of her, Camilla. I know you wouldn't want to lose her.' There was a brittle silence. Lorie shuffled around in her chair. Camilla didn't speak. 'Is that everything?'

'I think that's more than enough.' Camilla dished out an icy warning glare. Lorie nodded, stood, crossed the floor. 'Not a word about this to Naomi.'

Lorie glanced back. 'Course not.' She opened the door, slipped beyond it and closed it very carefully behind her.

For a long time, Camilla was alone with her thoughts which were chasing in all directions. What eventually distracted her and brought the room back into focus was Henry whistling in the garden. He only ever whistled when he was pampering his precious car – the large flashy one that cost the price of a house, shone like a mirror and was impractical for shopping and general use. It was the one that turned heads and opened mouths and caused Henry to burn with pride. The same one that drew his nurturing instincts more than the children ever had.

Camilla expelled an aggravated breath and picked up the seating plan and studied it again. Her own name was at the furthest point from Nathan Stone's. She'd placed Nathan between Henry (at the head of the table) and some girl called Siobhan Dougherty. Camilla scanned the desk for a pen, found one, hovered over the page with it. She retrieved her glasses from her chest and perched them on the end of her nose and blocked out Henry's infuriating whistling.

She slashed two angry lines through Henry's name and replaced it with her own. Better. Camilla would sit at the head of the table with Nathan on one side and Naomi, opposite him, on the other. The enemy. No, she'd smile and be the perfect host and position herself directly in enemy territory. If there was one thing she'd learned from her miserable father about war, it was this: never underestimate your enemy, never turn your back on him. Always get to know your enemy in order to gain the upper hand. Draw him into unfamiliar territory and use the element of surprise. Camilla fully intended to.

***

'So, am I going to get to meet this boyfriend of yours?' Naomi asked Lorie over the phone the next day. Naomi was out shopping for a new outfit for the big birthday bash.

'Yeah, Simon's coming. I've told him all about your mum. He's a bit nervous.'

'Can't blame him.' Naomi wandered inside a shop without taking note of which one, and headed for the dresses. 'You don't seem that into him.'

Lorie laughed. 'Well, I haven't met Prince Charming like you have, but Simon's good company. We have a laugh and we share a few interests so it works for both of us. He's what I'd call . . . steady.'

'Steady?' Naomi smiled as she leafed quickly through the dresses and decided they were all ugly. 'What's that supposed to mean?' She left the shop.

'It means that the relationship isn't exactly explosive, but it's comfortable. Everyone likes Simon.'

'What's his surname again?'

'Wilde,' Lorie said.

Naomi laughed. 'A contradiction!'

'Definitely,' Lorie laughed too.

'Mm,' Naomi snorted. 'He sounds too sensible to hold your interest for long. How old is he?'

'He's twenty-seven and has a *steady job* in accountancy. Your dad will like him.'

Naomi giggled. 'Wait till you meet Nathan. He's twenty-five and has an unsteady job selling mobile phones. I can tell Mum's really looking forward to seeing him again. Not! Has she said anything?'

'No comment,' Lorie said. 'All I will say is that it's what *you* think about him that counts.'

'Do you think she'll ever accept him?'

'If the relationship lasts, I think she'll have to.'

Naomi found a vacant bench inside the shopping centre beside a bin, and sat down. There was a Subway just in front of her. She'd get a hot sandwich. For the moment, she wanted to concentrate on what Lorie was saying and couldn't multitask.

'Are we still safe to talk?' Naomi asked Lorie.

'Yeah. Your dad's out with Annie and your mum's digging in her veggie patch. I can see her through the window with her spade and her gardening face on. It's my lunch break anyway. I've had an awful morning,' Lorie groaned. 'I was supposed to be finalising the arrangements for the dinner tomorrow, but your mum had other ideas for me.'

'Like what?'

'I had to sack Denise.'

'No!' Naomi gasped. 'Why?'

'Don't ask. It was awful. She was in floods of tears. I didn't know what to do or what to say to make her feel better. As soon as she'd gone I broke down, then I had to interview for a replacement over the phone. I ended up appointing some woman called Cynthia who I've never even met. She seemed the best of the bunch. She starts on Monday.'

'What's with all the hiring and firing?'

Lorie cleared her throat. 'Don't ask me.'

'I really liked Denise.'

'Me too. Look, I've got to go. It's someone's birthday this weekend. People to see, places to go.'

Naomi smiled broadly into her phone. 'Will you be sitting next to me at dinner?' Naomi put her finger in her free ear so she could hear better.

'I honestly don't know. The whole table plan is top secret. She won't let anyone see it. My job is to sort the name labels so people know where to sit when they come in. Annie didn't want a plan, but your mum's insisting it's important. You know how everything has to be organised properly, nothing left to chance.'

'That's the one.'

'Annie's threatening to boycott the plan and plonk herself wherever she wants. It's stressing your mum no end. Your dad won't get involved.'

Naomi giggled. 'Some things never change. I bet my mum's put me at one end of the table and Nathan at the other.'

'Probably. Look, got to dash. I'll see you all tomorrow. Who are you bringing apart from Nathan?'

'My three flat mates and a girl called Siobhan.'

'OK, look forward to it.'

Naomi put her phone away. She hadn't noticed anyone drop down next to her while she was talking, she only knew now that her attention was undivided that someone was standing up and walking away from her. He was wearing a grey hooded top and had mousey brown hair. He was almost as wide as he was tall, not fat, but muscle-locked. Huge trunk of a neck. Naomi was glaring at his back in black tracksuit bottoms and white trainers. His elbows were sticking out as if he had his hands in pockets at the front of his top.

Food forgotten, Naomi stood up and started to follow him, keeping a safe distance. She weaved between bodies making sure she didn't gain or lose any ground. *What am I doing?* She wondered if she actually wanted to talk to him. Did she intend to confront him? The fact that she was pursuing meant that she intended to do something, but she didn't know what. Maybe if she could just get a glimpse of his face . . .

A couple with a pram crossed her path. Distracted for a moment, she slowed. A toy was flung from the pram. It landed close to Naomi's feet. The mother stopped to pick it up and hand it back, giving Naomi chance to clock that it was a baby boy with huge blue eyes and long lashes. When the pram moved on, hoodie-guy had gone. Naomi stumbled forward, eyes searching, clutching her carrier bag containing Annie's present, a small Japanese-English dictionary and a Manchester United sweater to remind her of home.

Someone seized her left arm suddenly. She glanced across and was confronted with the side of a grey hood.

'Look ahead,' he insisted in an unmistakable Manchester accent that sounded nasal. Naomi obeyed and looked ahead. She had no words. She anxiously tried to make eye-contact with passing strangers. No one noticed her.

'I warned you to watch your back, Naomi,' he said, confirming who he was.

Naomi turned cold. He still had hold of her and was guiding her along in a stream of disinterested bodies.

'How do you know me?' Naomi managed.

He didn't answer.

'What do you want?' Naomi tried again, terrified of him taking her from the buzz of the crowds to somewhere more secluded. She was prepared to scream and yell if necessary.

'To deliver a message.'

'What message?'

'Next message won't be words – that is the message. I'm leaving. Don't attract attention and don't try to follow me or have me followed. If you involve the police, I'll know. So don't. Understood?'

Naomi took three more faltering steps. All she could feel was relief that he was leaving. 'Yes.'

He let go and vanished through a set of steel doors that led to the car park. Naomi watched the doors snap shut and made sure he didn't return through them.

For minutes she stood, trembling, looking about her, expecting people to notice she was in pieces. They didn't. A normal Friday lunchtime carried on. People laughed, ate, talked on their phones. Music spewed from the nearest shop. It was like she was invisible and was observing from a bubble.

Struggling to breathe evenly, she eventually exited the building and began the long walk back towards the sanctuary of her little room. She pictured it as she hurried along, stealing nervous glances over both shoulders. She couldn't wait to be sitting on her unmade bed looking at the pile of clothes beneath her desk which had irritated her only that morning. Her dirty bathroom cluttered with used towels and scattered toilet roll tubes, would be a glorious sight now.

Every step, she expected him to reappear. Every person wearing a dove grey top was him. Every shoulder that brushed against her was a threat. After the most uneasy walk she could remember, she saw the familiar shimmer of the college windows in the distance and quickened her pace, feeling a rush of warm feelings for the place. The closer she got, the more the vice slackened inside her chest. She saw an orange bush not far away. She'd recognise it anywhere. She broke into a run and caught hold of Siobhan's arm from behind.

Siobhan swung round defensively, face anxious. 'Oh, it's you. You scared me half to death.'

'Sorry.'

'You're as white as a sheet. What's wrong?'

Naomi shook her head and kept hold of Siobhan's arm, which was fleshy and comforting. It reminded her of her grandma's arm and disturbed faint memories of bedtime stories from when she was little, in the days before South Africa. The memories came with some childlike feelings she tried to hang on to, but couldn't. They blurred like a chalk picture in rain, then washed away.

'Something awful just happened. Can I tell you inside?'

'OK.'

Naomi reached the halls of residence with Siobhan. She'd never felt so close to her unusual friend. Her sanctuary was in sight at last. Or was it a sanctuary? The question sneaked in and caused the euphoria to slide. Relief converted into a sickening kind of anxiety that stirred in the pit of her stomach. He knew where she lived. He'd seen where she studied. What else did the man in the grey top know about her? What if he returned with his knife?

They trooped to Naomi's room without speaking, as if what Naomi was about to say warranted a suspenseful kind of silence to set the scene.

Naomi sank into her bed and breathed easily. Siobhan perched on the piano chair and looked as though she wasn't breathing at all. She'd frozen, hands clasped together on her lap. She was a ghastly white colour apart from the freckles.

'What's going on?' Siobhan asked, tone suspicious.

'Remember the guy with the knife?'

Siobhan's cheeks flushed pink. A fire broke out on her neck. 'I wish I could forget. Built like a bus? Grey jacket? Light brown hair? Have you seen him?'

Naomi glared through Siobhan, eyes focussed beyond her. 'I don't think you've got anything to worry about anyway.'

'What do you mean? Have you seen him, Naomi?' She was pushing her long fingernails together and sliding them inside each other.

'I've seen him just now and a couple of other times. He followed me to the shops today. It's me he's after, Siobhan. Me. That day in the college, he'll have been looking for me.'

Siobhan had taken to nervously rotating her grandmother's wedding band. 'Holy crap.'

'Yeah.'

Siobhan's cheeks were glowing. It seemed like her hair was burning too. 'You know for sure?'

'He knows my name. He told me the next message won't be words.'

'Holy crap,' she said again, covering her face with both hands. 'So, what are we going to do now?'

'I really don't know,' Naomi said, feeling the sudden urge to visit the loo. 'Puts performance into perspective, ey?'

'I'll say,' Siobhan nodded slowly. 'So? Are we going to call the police?'

'No. No, not yet. I'm going to give it some thought while I'm home this weekend.'

'Puts a real downer on your birthday party.'

'No it doesn't. I won't let it,' Naomi said with more confidence and optimism than she felt.

What she was simultaneously thinking was that it was time to tell Nathan she had a problem. The man in the grey top had made his intentions so clear, denial was a luxury she couldn't afford anymore. The thought of a visit home was suddenly appealing. 'I'm going to enjoy this weekend and put him out of my mind.'

Siobhan's mouth twitched the way it did when she was attempting a smile. 'Good for you.'

After only a short pause, Siobhan screamed and pointed wildly at the floor, making Naomi jump. She removed her shoe and rushed to the offending spot and whacked the floor three times.

'Got it,' Siobhan said, panting.

Naomi sat forward and looked down and couldn't speak. Sydney, her inoffensive little roommate, had just become an ex-spider.

16

CAPTIVITY

It was the night that changed everything, Sunday, twelfth September. A storm broke out. Naomi woke up from a vivid dream, disturbed in every way by a furious scratching noise at the window. In her dream, Nathan had found her. He'd slid her rings down her finger and returned her necklace and told her he loved her and had missed her like crazy. The eerie scratching noise had snatched him away, just as he had begun kissing her passionately.

She could still feel the sensation of his lips against hers as she sat up panting, wanting him so desperately, she ached. She was tempted to collapse into tears, but held them off. She took stock, remembering where she was, realising after careful listening, that the hair-raising noise was only a tree with wind-bent branches against the window. It sounded like fingernails against a chalkboard. The wind came in violent gusts, howling savagely through the keyhole in the French doors. The sky must have been a huge dark blanket blocking out the moon and stars. She couldn't see anything at all. It was inky black, no landing light on like there usually was. There was normally a light on somewhere outside too. Not anymore. Naomi couldn't see her own hand in front of her face.

She got up and groped her way into the bathroom, finding the light-pull. She tugged sharply, but nothing happened. The power was down. For a moment, she was back in the boot of the car, the night of the wedding. She staggered back to the bed, the blackness wrapping around her mouth and throat, making her fight for air. She lifted her hands to her face, dragging the chains with her. They seemed so heavy while she felt so weak. She concentrated only on breathing, one intake of air at a time, one release. She repeated. There wasn't enough oxygen in the room. Her head was light. A feeling of sickness was spreading. She breathed harder, gulping air, scared of blacking out.

'Help me. Help me,' she heard herself saying. But her voice was distant. She sounded like someone else. A torrent of rain whipped the glass. The wind hurled it against the window until she couldn't hear her own voice. She was gripping the bed covers between her fingers, nails digging into her palms.

She hadn't heard the key turn in the door, or seen the door open, but suddenly she sensed someone was with her in the room. She held her breath, wondering if it was her imagination. The bed lowered as someone sat down carefully, confirming her suspicions.

Naomi started to breathe more steadily. After a while, the sickness eased. Her breathing steadied to normal, which confused her. Something was telling her she should be panicking, but the presence of another person was having the opposite effect.

The rain continued to pelt the glass. A crack of thunder almost shook the house. She wasn't afraid anymore, but suspected she should be. She reached out and found a warm body. His chest was hard beneath a thin top. Her hand moved up to a muscular shoulder and down a defined bicep until she met with the flesh of his lower arm. It was so familiar.

'Nathan?'

Either he didn't answer, or she couldn't hear him

against the driving rain. Needing to get closer, Naomi shuffled toward the heat of his body. Her fingers reached out and touched his face, meeting with rough stubble around his mouth. In contrast, his hair was soft. She pulled it gently through her fingers. A blinding flash of light revealed him for a micro-moment. She'd moved so close, she only really got a glimpse of his eyes. They were Nathan's at their most blue, but his hair had grown down his forehead. The darkness covered him again. She returned to his face, fingering the contours of his eyes, nose, cheekbones, mouth.

'Nathan,' Naomi said, having to raise her voice to be heard.

He put his mouth to her ear and breathed. 'Calm down.'

'I've missed you so much,' she said.

His arms surrounded her, squeezing her to him, tracing her spine with one finger. She couldn't hold him the way she wanted to. The chains held her wrists, making it impossible.

Water started dripping from the ceiling onto the bed and into her hair in huge cold droplets. He took hold of her wrists and fumbled around in the darkness until her hands were free. She enjoyed the freedom of rotating her wrists, but they ached and felt cold. Naomi found herself being lifted off the bed into his arms. She hoped she wasn't dreaming. She wrapped her arms around his neck and tucked her head beneath his chin.

'I knew you'd find me.'

She expected him to head for the stairs and to take her away from this house, but as he walked through the door and out onto a creaky landing, another spark of light revealed a white wooden banister, a green carpet, a black window with sliding rain in straight lines, and two other doors. The vision was gone in a heartbeat. During her brief escape, she hadn't taken in any details about the landing.

He walked past the stairs and carefully guided her through a doorway inside another room and laid her on a bed. The thunder was drawing closer and becoming ferocious. The bed was still warm. Whose bed? When he placed her down, he didn't join her. She didn't know where he was.

'Nathan?' she hissed.

A long pause. 'I'm here,' she heard, faintly. It was definitely Nathan's familiar voice, but he wasn't close.

'Lie next to me.'

'I can't.'

Naomi didn't understand. 'You're not leaving?'

She had a long wait for the answer. 'I have to.'

'No.' She leapt up and found him after two paces. Her arms circled his neck, but he stood stiffly. 'I'm so cold. Hold me, please,' she begged. 'Don't go.'

She rested her head against his chest and listened to the rhythm. After a short delay, his arms folded around her again, pressing her tightly with his large hands that spread easily across her back, warming her body. Her arms tightened around his neck. They breathed against each other. His pulse was quickening. After more than a week alone, she was melting. It wasn't enough. She guided his face towards hers. She could feel his breath on her now, but he was resisting a connection.

'Kiss me.'

She was waiting, eyes sealed, when another intense flash of lightening came and went. It left her seeing spots of white light. She felt the first contact as their lips touched. Sensing his reluctance, she held him there. Her fingers ran through his hair and twisted. She pressed the back of his head until the contact was firmer. Finally he responded and parted his lips, pressing tentatively at first, then more readily than she was used to. She was eager to match him. This was a different Nathan. His kisses, normally reserved and controlled, had never stirred her like this. It held the excitement and intensity of the first time, but better. She was sure that they'd never really lost themselves in each other until now. She couldn't feel the cold anymore. The trauma of the past week lost impact. Resistance gone, she pushed her fingers more roughly into his hair, knowing she couldn't hold back as she had in the past. Knowing she didn't need to.

As they stumbled towards the bed, she found herself tugging at his top. Clothes were a barrier. He took hold of her wrists and unpeeled them from him and stepped back. 'No,' he said, breathing hard. 'No. Stop.'

His voice was throaty. She was barely tuned in to it when she wanted him so badly. Naomi reached out and found him. 'We're married now.'

He pulled free and moved back. 'Listen to what you're saying.'

The tone of his voice shocked her, but Naomi still stumbled after him in the dark. The rain was easing into a more steady patter. The thunder was moving on. As she found him, he took hold of her arms and held them firmly.

'You're confusing me, Nathan.'

'That wasn't the intention.'

'Don't you want me?' she asked.

As the rain reduced further, there was an uneasy stretch of quiet. 'Not while you think I'm someone else.'

Naomi stood, feeling the strength of his arms holding her. She couldn't clear her head. She felt no fear, just a deep sense of pain that weighed her down until she couldn't stand. He supported her as she fell onto him and broke down.

'You told me you were Nathan.'

'You knew I wasn't him.'

'No,' she yelled, sobbing. 'No. I saw you.' Naomi started pounding his chest with her fists. He allowed it and stood firm, not moving or defending himself. Naomi felt her knees buckle and she collapsed onto the floor.

He reached down and gathered her up and set her down on the bed. She curled into a tight ball. She assumed he was still standing there, waiting behind his veil of silence. Light flooded the room from the landing. Power returned in a burst that left Naomi squinting. She was lying on a double bed facing a window with closed blue curtains. An alarm started up somewhere.

It was like returning to the real world from a land of dreams. She heard him fly from the room and down the stairs to quieten it. Naomi sat up, frantically wiping her eyes, forcing herself to think. There was no time to regret things or think about the consequences. She was free.

She leapt from the bed and ran out onto the landing. He was already striding up the stairs, two at a time. She froze as she looked at the top of his head, her senses sharp and alert, heart pounding. He raised his head and looked at her. He stopped too. She could only stare. He was young with clear skin, defined cheek bones and a strong jaw line. He had Nathan's eyes, though his mouth and nose were set differently. His hair was darker, longer and had more movement, but he was as tall and as well-built. She couldn't stop looking at him.

'Dan?'

He gripped hold of the stair rail. His eyes closed for a long moment, then opened. They were bluer than Nathan's and striking against his darker hair and eyebrows. His voice finally made sense. She'd heard it occasionally in the background when she'd been on the phone to Nathan, that deep voice of Dan's. Why hadn't she realised the obvious? Even his movements mirrored

Nathan's now she thought about it, and the shape and size of his hands, which she'd watched every day.

'Why?' Naomi whispered. 'After everything Nathan's done for you.'

'He betrayed me,' Dan said, jaw clenching.

'Do you know who I am?'

'Of course I do,' Dan said.

'Did Nathan tell you we were getting married?'

Dan puffed out an aggravated breath. 'Evidently.'

Naomi struggled to find words. 'How could you do this?' she said slowly. 'He loves you and this is what –'

'Don't talk to me about love. No one loves Nathan like I do. That includes you.' Dan fixed his eyes on her now and set a serious expression that jabbed her with anxiety. Naomi didn't dare disagree. 'Some things are unforgiveable. This time, he's gone too far.'

'*He's* gone too far?' Naomi felt herself filling with fear now. 'Have you been taking your medication, Dan?'

Dan was breathing hard through his nose. A storm crossed his face, but his tone of voice defied it. 'Of course I've been taking my medication,' he said, quietly.

'Dan, this is wrong. We shouldn't be here like this. Look, this is not your fault –'

'Damn right it's not,' he said, starting to move towards her in measured steps.

Naomi crossed her arms and stiffened. 'Listen to me,' she began, keeping her voice as reasonable as possible, 'you have to take me back to Nathan, OK? Tonight. You have to let me go.'

Dan continued towards her, eyes tormented. He stopped right in front of her. In bare feet, she felt so short. Her instinct was to run, but there was nowhere to go. He searched her eyes. Dan's eyes looked wild and dangerous the way Nathan had described them. He shook his head. His eyes glazed with tears. A pool formed at the bottom.

'It's too late.' He paused. 'Too late.'

Naomi's heart was rattling inside her ribcage. The rain was still lightly falling. The wind still whistled through the trees. 'Dan, what have you done?'

The pool overflowed and tears rolled down his cheeks. 'The only thing I could do,' he yelled in an eruption of temper. 'He left me no choice.'

Naomi, shocked, stepped backwards. Dan pulled at his hair and his face creased in agony. He wiped his eyes and looked at her again. Their eyes locked.

Gathering her courage, Naomi moved to him and took his hands. 'Dan, calmly, we're going to sit down and talk about this, OK?'

'Stop treating me like a freaking retard,' he shouted, jerking his hands away. 'I'm not going to hurt you, OK?'

'I know you're not,' she said with no certainty, trying not to turn away from his terrifying eyes.

'What happened in the bedroom just now wasn't an accident,' he said, waving one arm around wildly. 'We both wanted it to happen. Don't you see this is impossible for me too? I have feelings for you. Get it? I. Have. Feelings.' He was clutching both fists to his chest and pounding in time to his words. 'You think I'm on some sick pleasure trip while you're up in that room, but I'm trying to work things out, OK? And I don't know what to do.'

He wasn't making sense, which made perfect sense when she reminded herself this was Dan. Naomi thought of Lucy, Nathan's ex-fiancée. Naomi had been sure over the past week that the monster had a very clear plan and that she featured in it strongly. To discover that there was no plan at all except to detain her and feed her and spy on her and watch her shower, stunned her. Dan had taken on more than he could manage. He was panicking. He turned his back on her and stamped towards a small window on the landing where droplets of rain were trickling. A silk flower arrangement stood on the sill in a green vase. Eventually, Dan turned and walked towards her. He stopped a safe distance away and didn't speak.

'Dan, I need to know what's happened to Nathan.'

Dan brushed past her into the bedroom like he couldn't look her in the eye anymore. She'd fantasised about a moment like this where he was vulnerable, where she could spring a surprise attack. That time had now come and had also gone. Unbelievably, Dan was family. Naomi tried to pluck that thought from her mind and throw it away.

'You really do not want to know what's happened to Nathan, trust me on that,' he said in his rich deep voice that reminded her he wasn't Nathan. He was calmer now at least.

Naomi didn't trust him. At all. Dan frantically wiped his eyes and Naomi tried to inject some gentleness into her tone. 'I've got to know, Dan. And you need to own up to the truth. I admit I'm terrified of what you might tell me.'

Dan turned sharply and directed his eyes at her again. He slowly shook his head while the tears kept pouring. For a week, Naomi had thought he was incapable of emotion. So far, she'd been wrong about everything. Dan was inconsolable. His lips were quivering as he fought to hold himself together.

'You should be,' he managed.

LIBERTY

It was late afternoon. The house was a hive of frantic activity. Annabel was packing for Japan. Everyone except Henry was feeling the heat. Guests were due to arrive at seven. Six courses had been carefully selected by Camilla with Lorie's help. The Italian chef who was providing his services for the evening, had turned up with a teenage assistant, his son. They dragged in three ugly foldable tables that Lorie had the job of dressing and disguising.

One of the many things stressing Camilla was that, with sixteen sitting down for dinner, they were being forced to use the only two sets of dining chairs they had. They didn't match. They weren't even the same wood. Lorie had a generous budget to mask the problem any way she could. She'd assured Camilla that by the time she'd finished, there wouldn't be a problem with the tables or the chairs. Camilla was unconvinced, which meant she was flustered.

Camilla had left Lorie to sort out the table and chair problem alone and busied herself with a list of other jobs. When she returned to the dining room at five-fifteen, Lorie wasn't there but the room was transformed. Camilla stood in the doorway, transfixed. A few helium-filled balloons had been tastefully placed. The eight-seater dining table that normally occupied the room had been removed to make way for the three tables that now lay in a row in the centre of the room and looked incredible.

Camilla inched forward for a closer inspection. The tables were covered in deep red tablecloths to match the main colour in the curtains. At the centre of each of the outer tables was a tall thin vase, holding two carnations, one dark red, one cream. At the centre of the middle table was an exotic flower arrangement. Cream petals were scattered around the three vases. The table was fully set with their best dinnerware. There was a tiny box beside each of the plates. Camilla was curious enough to lift a lid. She found two sugared almonds, one white, one pink.

Camilla touched the serviettes, artistically arranged inside the wine glasses, the same thick linen as the tablecloths, the same deep red. The back of the chairs had been covered in pieces of cream satin and were gathered into a kind of rosette at the back and secured with red ribbon which hung down. Lorie had even bought padded seat cushions which were tied to the backs of the chairs and masked the difference in the wood. Small candles dotted the room. One thing was still missing: the name labels. Camilla had collected them from Lorie. This job she'd do herself. Not trusting Annabel not to rearrange them, Camilla kept them inside her pocket and decided to leave it until the last minute.

Camilla could hear Annabel thudding around upstairs and wondered when Naomi would be arriving with . . . *him*. She glanced at her watch and her expression tightened. It was almost five-thirty. Time to get changed and drag Henry away from the football league tables to do the same. Marriage often felt like having an extra child, especially since Henry had retired. He'd regressed into a lost little boy who enjoyed dawdling time away and playing before his afternoon nap. Pathetic really, for a man so capable. The outfit Camilla had selected for him was waiting patiently on the bed.

Camilla took one last look behind her, glancing at the end chair where she'd be sitting beside the man who'd strode into Naomi's life and assumed pole position. *There are things about him you don't know.* Well, whatever secrets Nathan Stone was hiding, Camilla thought as she left the room, she was going to dig them up.

***

There was a crisis from the outset, a very unexpected one. At twenty to seven with everything on track –

though not a single guest had arrived, including Naomi – Camilla dragged herself from her seating plan and the placing of the table tags, to investigate a commotion in the hall. Unusually, Lorie was agitated with somebody, which drew Camilla from the dining room. The musicians had arrived. One of the four was Tom Butterworth.

After observing for a moment and taking in the details, Camilla said, softly, 'I'll deal with this, Loretta.' Camilla, dressed and ready for the evening, felt it only appropriate that her speaking voice should reflect her appearance.

Lorie turned. 'Camilla, I'm so sorry. I had no idea Tom was part of the group. I can show him the door.'

'Which may be a dreadful mistake,' Camilla said, as she weighed up two boys, two girls, who were standing looking sheepish and embarrassed, clutching their instruments and their music stands to their bodies as if they weren't sure there was a point putting them down.

'But Tom – '

'I know all about Tom,' Camilla said, eyeing him, letting him know that whatever tricks he'd performed in her home in the past, had not been forgotten. When Tom shifted his stare, Camilla turned her attention to Lorie. 'You have to understand that viola players are an essential part of a string quartet and don't grow on trees. It isn't going to be possible to replace him at this stage.'

Lorie's cheeks were slightly flushed. Her hair, normally up during the day, was long and full and she was beautifully dressed in a fitted knee-length low-cut dress that was tangerine-red, like her lip colour.

'I'll check on the chef,' Lorie said, heading for the kitchen. Camilla returned her eyes to Tom Butterworth. He couldn't stand it and flicked concentrated glances to the floor. The other three stood still, utterly confused.

'Look, Mrs Hamilton,' Tom began, trying to align a steady gaze. 'I only knew we had a booking for tonight. Until I got in the car, I didn't even know where it was. I'm sorry – '

'Please,' Camilla cut in, one hand raised. 'Naomi will be here at any moment and I don't want a scene. My girls turn nineteen today and tomorrow and you're here to create an atmosphere conducive to a pleasant evening. Don't try to speak to either of them. If that's agreed, I see no reason why we can't proceed as planned. Can you do your job without distraction?'

He nodded uncertainly. 'Yes.'

Camilla indicated that they should follow her. 'Very well, then. I'll show you to the dining room so you can set up. Music to begin promptly at six fifty-five please. I hope you haven't brought that dreadful Cannon in D by Pachelbel.'

Nobody responded. Camilla pictured the exchanges of glances behind her. 'I suspected as much,' she said, looking behind to check they were still following. They were. Plus, they were looking very worried. 'It isn't a favourite of Naomi's, or mine,' she said, stopping at the door, allowing them to pass into the dining room. 'If you'll set up in that corner,' she said, indicating the area furthest from where Naomi would be sitting opposite Nathan. 'I'll leave you to tune up. Back to the tables if you would, Tim.'

***

It was the first time Naomi had been home in weeks. Nervous for obvious reasons, she directed Nathan through the open gates and down the drive at quarter to seven. Bridget, Megan and Madeline would be travelling together in a taxi, and had grudgingly agreed that Siobhan could share the ride. Naomi didn't know who was at the house, but having already done her hair and makeup, she planned to sneak in through the back door and change into one of three evening dresses. Having cut her shopping trip short, she hadn't bought anything new.

It amazed her that Nathan, looking divine in a black suit and plain grey tie, showed no evidence of nerves. Nathan reached for her hand and squeezed gently. 'It'll be fine,' he said with a reassuring smile and sideways glance. 'Don't worry.'

'I'll be glad when it's over,' Naomi blurted out.

Nathan said nothing until he'd pulled up in front of the house and killed the engine.

'The mansion,' he muttered.

'Is it what you imagined?'

'Exactly.' Nathan turned his body and his attention to Naomi, and his back to the house. 'Listen to me. This is your birthday. You won't see Annie for a while after tonight. The whole thing will be costing a small fortune. I'm sure your mum will put her own feelings to one side tonight to make it special for you two. There's nothing to worry about, OK?'

Naomi looked at him and some calm returned. She still hadn't told Annie about Nathan. There was something else bothering her more.

'You OK?' Nathan asked. Naomi realised she'd been quiet for a while.

'I need to tell you something.'

Nathan took her hand again and held it. 'Sure, what is it? You look upset.'

'Well it's really freaking me out. Nothing's happened. Not yet.' Naomi paused. Nathan waited. 'Someone's following me.'

'What?' Nathan swallowed. 'Who? When?'

'You remember the guy who was eyeing us when we

came out of the college that time?'

Nathan's eyes searched the roof of the car. 'Oh yeah?'

'Him. Yesterday, I saw him while I was out shopping. He followed me until I noticed him, then he took off and I followed him. I lost him, then next thing he had hold of my arm. He said he had a message for me, but didn't give me one, he just left. It scared me half to death. It was a relief to get away from Manchester today.'

Nathan's face had hardened. 'Is he a student? Anyone you know?'

'No. I have no idea what he wants. He turned up at college with a knife not long ago. Huge guy.'

'A knife? I'm going to sort him out,' Nathan said, aggressively.

'Did I mention he was huge? Please –'

'Just leave it with me. If he shows up again, I'll put him in the picture. Maybe he just needs to know you're not available.'

'I didn't get the impression he wanted to go out with me, Nathan.'

'He's a guy. What else would he want?

Naomi thought about it. 'I honestly don't know.'

'Don't worry about it. I promise I'll sort it out.' He paused until his face readjusted and had softened. 'Now you promise me you'll enjoy tonight.' He was studying her carefully.

Naomi dropped her head. 'I'll try.'

'Not good enough.' Nathan paused. 'Have you told Annie about us yet?' Naomi shook her head. 'I don't get it.'

'I don't either.'

Nathan released her hand and lifted her chin. 'Let me speak to her,' he said. 'I'll have a quiet word and that will be that.' His face relaxed into a half smile. 'It's time she knew we're together.'

Mum thought you two were an item. I told her to get real. It was humiliating to admit to him that Annie couldn't imagine Nathan seeing Naomi as girlfriend material. She wondered how Annie would react to the news and felt the onset of panic. Naomi nodded her head, relieved that she didn't need to face the look of disbelief in Annie's eyes when she found out.

'Fine. Tell her,' Naomi said.

'She won't be surprised,' Nathan said, reaching into the darkness of the space behind his seat. 'Now, onto more important matters.' He produced a box about the size of a shoe box, wrapped in ribbon and a bow. 'I know it isn't your birthday till tomorrow, but . . .'

Naomi took it and undid the ribbon. It felt quite light. Inside was another smaller box similarly wrapped, then another and another. By now, Naomi was laughing. 'You haven't actually got me anything have you!'

'Keep going.'

Four boxes later, Naomi was swimming in boxes and was down to a small navy-blue jewellery box. She hesitated and looked up, feeling the softness of the velvet lid. 'I hope you haven't spent too much on me,' she said.

'Open it,' he said, reaching for the car light above his head, switching it on.

Naomi lifted the lid to a stunning square-shaped diamond ring. The stone was too big to be a real diamond. She tugged it free of the box and examined it, holding it up to the light. 'Wow. It's beautiful. It looks so real.'

'It is real,' Nathan said.

'No way.' Her jaw dropped.

'Three carat solitaire diamond set in platinum,' Nathan went on. 'Do you like it?'

'Like it? It's the most incredible ring I've ever seen.

How did you afford it?'

'I won't lie. It cost me everything I have in savings. My trip will have to be postponed for a while.'

'Nathan –'

Nathan touched her lips. 'I wanted to, Naims. It's only metal and a stone. It doesn't justify how I feel about you, but I've asked you to marry me and I meant it. You're holding the proof. For now,' he said taking the ring from her and sliding it down the fourth finger of her right hand, 'it just means that I love you, that I'm committed to you and that I'll respect your promise with Him Upstairs. If you ever decide to switch it to the other hand, I'll be very happy. If you never do, I'll still love you.'

Naomi looked down. The ring fit perfectly. Her head was in a spin. 'I don't know what to say.'

'Just as well,' Nathan said, checking his watch. 'It's time you got changed.'

'Nathan,' she said, pausing to look at him. He lent her his eyes. 'Thank you doesn't seem enough.'

Nathan leant over and kissed her cheek. 'It's more than enough for me. Are you ready?'

Naomi took a deep breath then exhaled, 'No.'

17

They slipped through the back door, Naomi painfully conscious of her ring, sure it was flashing like a lighthouse beacon. Lorie was alone in the kitchen, Naomi hugged her, introduced her to Nathan and dashed off to get changed. Time was short. She picked a beige-coloured silk dress she'd bought in the summer and used for her last recital with the Junior Royal Northern. No one at this party had ever seen it. The recital had gone well so the dress held no nightmarish memories. Her accessories were black and sparkly: earrings, bracelet. She wouldn't part with her necklace.

Music had started playing downstairs. A surprise. Nice touch, she smiled. Annie wouldn't be impressed, but then a rock band over dinner would hardly be right. She took a last check in the mirror and found she was humming along to what was being played downstairs: Handel's Water Music.

The upstairs was empty as Naomi clutched the bannister and made her way down the main staircase into the hall. Her new diamond sparkled as it caught the light. The platinum was chunky, the stone huge. Naomi couldn't even guess at a cost. Camilla would think it was fake and had cost a fiver. Time to go downstairs and join what sounded like a buzzing crowd.

Nathan was waiting in the hall with Lorie and another guy.

'You look amazing,' Nathan whispered as she reached the hallway. He turned to finish his sentence about football to the shy-looking guy beside him, who was about the same age. Lorie was linking the guy's arm.

'This is Simon,' Lorie said, at the same moment Naomi worked it out.

Simon was wearing a navy suit and a sensible haircut parted on the side. He lunged forward nervously and shook Naomi's hand. 'Nice to meet you.'

Lorie noticed the ring and gasped. 'That new?'

'A present from Nathan,' Naomi said, finding herself colouring. Lorie held Naomi's hand up and stared, open-mouthed.

'Mum's coming,' Naomi said, snatching her hand away at the formidable sight of Camilla emerging from the dining room, the picture of elegance in a mauve chiffon dress and a double row of pearls.

'There you are,' Camilla said, gliding towards them in a cloud of perfume, smile painted on. Naomi found she was hiding her hand. 'I thought you'd got lost.' Her eyes flicked up and down. 'Not your colour that, Naomi. Drains your complexion.'

'I think she looks beautiful,' Nathan said.

Camilla's attention shifted to Nathan. 'She always looks beautiful, Nathaniel, but certain shades enhance her natural colouring more than others. It is Nathaniel isn't it, your proper name?'

'I was christened Nathaniel, yes.'

'Well, it's good of you to come.' The brief smile was tight. 'We're about ready to sit down for dinner. Everyone has arrived, so my list informs me.' She faced Lorie. 'Loretta, you've done a first-class job as always, but I insist you relax now and consider yourself a guest. I've told myself do the same. The chef assures me he has everything in hand.'

Camilla filed off to the dining room. Everyone followed like sheep. The dining room was littered with bodies, most of them around Annabel who was talking animatedly and entertaining her little audience. She stood out in a short pale-pink dress, thin straps across the shoulders, glossy pink lips, hair free-flowing, wavy, full. Only Siobhan stood alone, wearing the same outfit as she had to the Freshers' dinner. She was on the peripheries of the little group that made up Naomi's flatmates, but they weren't including her.

As soon as Annabel spotted Naomi, she stopped talking midsentence and rushed over to hug her. Nathan got a tight squeeze too, a very long one for a virtual stranger. It was interrupted by Henry clinking his glass with a spoon. Naomi looked round in time to see Camilla snatch it off him. She jabbed a few words into his ear. Henry responded by raising his voice and saying, 'Good evening everybody.'

A hush settled over the room. The musicians stopped playing. All heads turned to Henry, who was wearing a black bowtie, black suit, crisp white shirt. Camilla had fixed a neutral expression.

'It's wonderful to have you here tonight on the occasion of Annabel and Naomi's nineteenth birthday.' Henry paused to consult a small piece of paper in his hand. 'We've borrowed the best chef in the area. He's brought two able assistants.' Henry indicated to the doorway where an Italian-looking man stood in a white apron, pin-striped. He nodded slightly.

Henry glanced at his paper. 'We're going to be entertained over dinner by our string quartet. They've been playing together for two years now, they inform me.' All eyes fell on the corner of the room where three of the four players stood, instruments in hand to acknowledge the comments. Another polite wave of applause.

'Now,' Henry said, 'we limited the girls to five guests each. Annabel could have brought a hundred, but the shortlist for the night includes Lydia, Barney, Dominic, Holly and Erica. Naomi has brought five new friends from college.' Henry needed his list this time. 'There's Megan and Madeline, Bridget and Siobhan and, where is he?' Henry searched the room unnecessarily. Camilla squirmed as the silence stretched into a few seconds, forcing Nathan to raise his hand. 'There he is. Nathan.' Camilla loaded his ear with some information. 'Who is not from college,' he added. 'Our other two guests just there,' he pointed Lorie out, 'are Lorie Taylor and her partner, Simon Wilde. Lorie has looked after, first, our girls, and now the running of house for almost seven years. She knows the place as well as we do and is responsible for much of the planning tonight. She's like a third daughter to us.' Camilla nodded approvingly. 'As most of you will know, Annabel jets off to Japan for a new adventure in her gap year,' he glanced at his watch, 'in about thirteen hours. We'll miss her very much, but wish her all the best. Just come home in one piece please, darling, and don't bring an army of new friends. You have quite enough.' Henry finished, looking at Annabel. People clapped and laughed. 'So if you'd like to find your places at the table. Let battle commence.'

Naomi found her name. Nathan found his. Siobhan plonked down beside Nathan looking completely miserable about the whole evening, which didn't necessarily mean she wasn't enjoying herself. To Naomi's left was one of Annie's male friends, Barney. He was opposite Siobhan, who didn't know where to look. Lorie was exactly in the middle opposite Simon, and Annie was at the other end of the table beside Henry, who had the end seat not far from the string quartet. Megan and Madeline were close to Annie. Bridget – who'd recently split from Max and was still in the life's-not-worth-living-without-him stage – was opposite

Dominic. There were seven seated on each length and Henry was at the far end.

The music started up again – Bach's Air on a G string. Naomi noticed there was only one vacant seat now to her right and to Nathan's left. She looked round the room and found the only person still standing.

***

Camilla had offered wine three times to Nathan. Three times, he'd declined and filled up with water instead. Camilla eyed him while he chatted politely with Siobhan about her favourite repertoire for the flute and life at the Royal Northern and Manchester in general, and before that, in Dublin. Two courses had gone by. Camilla had considered telling Naomi about Tom Butterworth. Tom's back was to the table. His straw hair was much shorter than it used to be, and darker too, if she wasn't mistaken. He hadn't looked round once. He was an excellent string player doing a sterling job, minding his own business. There seemed little point drawing Naomi's attention to him. Even Annabel, who was only about six feet away from Tom, was so disconnected to the music that Tom might as well have been a robot. She was lost in conversation, always. No, things were running smoothly to Camilla's left. Naomi was chatting happily to Barney. Camilla was waiting to make her move to her right now.

When Nathan was distracted with food and had stopped talking to Siobhan, she said, 'So you studied philosophy Nathaniel?'

Nathan swallowed his food and made brief eye contact. 'I did, yeah.'

'Was it useful?'

'Extremely.'

'What attracted you to such an abstract subject?'

Annabel collapsed into loud giggles at the other end of the table, but Camilla kept her eyes firmly fixed on Nathan.

Nathan drew breath. 'Well, basically, I had no interest in pursuing well-trodden paths. I've always had questions. I wanted answers and I wanted to study the art of critical thinking and reasoning. Thinking is so underrated, don't you think?'

'Can't say I've given it much thought,' Camilla obliged, with a smile.

Nathan reciprocated. 'Exactly. We live in crazy times. We're bombarded with advertising and endless marketing and people are being brainwashed. I didn't want to be a puppet without really stopping to analyse what I'm doing and why. Politics winds me up. It's all about image and sound-bites and who looks the best in public. It's a huge pile of utter nonsense. There's no real democracy in this country. My opinion only.'

'I see,' Camilla said, taking a shallow sip of wine. 'I agree that there does appear to be an awful lot of hot air and little substance. Who's best at question-dodging and who's most skilful at being dishonest while prattling on about integrity, is an enormous problem for sure.' She stopped talking and looked at him very directly. 'So did you find answers to your questions?'

'There are always answers,' Nathan said. 'Just not enough intellectual brainpower to grasp things.'

'And what are these burning questions you have?'

Nathan stopped eating and held her eyes. 'How to apply logic to life. How to avoid deception. How to filter what's real from what's not. How to recognise truth, if truth can be defined. If truth exists at all. Then there's existence itself . . .'

'Rather deep.' Camilla took another swallow of wine, dabbed her lips.

'Ever heard of Carnegie?'

'I've heard of Carnegie Hall in New York.'

'Named after Andrew Carnegie who paid for it to be built. He started life as a nobody, but became one of the wealthiest men in history.' Nathan paused. 'I once came across one of his quotes. He said, "The man who acquires the ability to take possession of his own mind may take possession of anything else".'

A short pause. 'Thought provoking,' Camilla said.

'Absolutely.'

Camilla was unsettled beneath Nathan's gaze. A change of subject, perhaps. 'And why don't you drink, Nathaniel?'

'The short answer is I don't want to,' he replied, setting about his food again.

'And the long answer?'

He nodded thoughtfully. 'My brother has an alcohol problem. I resent what it's done to him and my family. My way of exacting my revenge is by refusing to drink. It's probably not very logical.'

'Understandable though,' Camilla said, managing a smile that she hoped would relax him. 'Tell me about your family.'

Camilla knew she had his full attention, but he kept her waiting by pouring more water and placing the jug carefully down before he spoke again. 'I've got a younger brother, the one I was just talking about, Dan, who's twenty-three.' He shrugged, as if that was that! 'Just the two of us.'

'Is he still at home?'

'Er, no. He has a flat. He lives by himself.'

'Naomi has never mentioned him or your parents to me.'

Nathan looked her in the eye while his fork twisted pasta lengths. 'She's never met my family. I don't have a good relationship with my parents.'

'Oh?' Her eyebrows rose, inviting him to go on.

'It's complicated. Dan's got schizophrenia and my parents virtually abandoned him when he needed them most. He might not have turned to drink with their support. I spend every other weekend with him now. I can't be a hypocrite and have a relationship with them after the way they've treated Dan. That's why Naomi won't be meeting them anytime soon.'

Naomi was still holding a conversation with Barney. She didn't seem to be listening. Camilla kept her voice low. Nathan guided his fork inside his mouth.

'Do they even know about Naomi?'

Nathan, mouth full, shook his head. 'Not yet.'

Camilla had about stopped eating. 'Without wishing to sound insensitive, is your brother any sort of a danger?'

Nathan emptied his mouth before he replied. 'Not to me. But he doesn't cope well with new people and his behaviour can be unpredictable sometimes. That's why I daren't introduce him to Naims. It wouldn't be good for either of them.'

'Naims?' Camilla said, irritated, feigning confusion.

'Naomi.'

'I don't like to shorten names.'

'Whereas I do,' Nathan said, unapologetically. He even smiled.

Camilla drew a long breath and blotted her lips with a napkin. The pasta – long multi-coloured ribbons with mushrooms and ham – was deliciously tasty, but was loaded with cheese and cream and left a film of grease.

'Grandparents?' Camilla pressed.

'The only one alive is my mum's mum, who moved to the States with her second husband before I was born. I've only met her a few times.'

'So you're not a close family.'

'I'd say we *were* close before Dan was ill. Things changed after that. Unexpected problems can blow families apart, can't they? What about you?'

Camilla was thrown. 'I beg your pardon?'

Nathan settled a steady gaze on her. 'What was your relationship like with your parents?'

Camilla hesitated, struggling to find the part in the script where he questioned her. It wasn't there. 'When I was young, my father was in the army away from home a lot,' she babbled, saying more than she meant to. Her neck felt hot. 'My mother was rather detached, let's say.'

'So you weren't close either. You'll understand that families can be complex.'

'This is becoming rather personal,' Camilla said, patting her lips again.

'I'm sorry,' Nathan looked up. 'I thought we were having a personal discussion. It's as exposing for me to share details about my life and family as it is for you.'

Camilla cleared her throat. 'Well my parents aren't my entire family, Nathaniel. I have a family of my own now. And I'm very proud of my girls.'

Nathan took another sip of iced water. 'I'm sure you are. Naomi is so talented. She played for me last week.'

'Did she?' Camilla asked, not sounding pleased suddenly. She leant closer to ensure privacy. 'Has she told you how important music is to her? How she must give all her concentration to these few college years before her chance to develop and improve slips away? Do you understand my daughter's potential and what is important to her?'

Nathan looked at Camilla for a long time, as if he was struggling to select the right words. 'I hope so,' he eventually said. 'But I'm not a musician so maybe I don't fully understand. Why don't you tell me what's on your mind?'

Encouraged, Camilla pushed the remaining food to one side as if she'd lost the patience and the appetite to finish it. Naomi was leaning across the table engaging Siobhan in conversation. She seemed oblivious. Camilla placed her cutlery in the middle of her plate and shifted her chair a little closer to the right. She'd longed for an opportunity like this. She may not get another.

'If you think anything of my daughter, you'll understand that her world is not yours,' she explained, like he was three years old. 'Music is a discipline. Her devotion has come at the cost of being popular and having friendships and the kind of social life Annabel has always had. Naomi is not like other girls. She's never followed the crowds or time-wasted as teenagers do. All her work . . . it has to mean something in the future.' She paused for emphasis. 'It has to count.'

'Or else?'

Camilla frowned. 'Or else it'll have been for nothing. Don't you see?'

Camilla paused to search Nathan's eyes, hoping for a flicker of comprehension.

Nathan didn't oblige, though he said, 'I agree.'

Camilla let go of some tension. 'Good, then you'll understand why –'

Nathan cut in. 'That is, I agree with the part that she isn't like other girls. That's why I fell in love with her. And I agree that her music training has come at the cost of relationships, but I don't think that's been a choice for her. She was miserable alone. She consoled herself with her necklace and three prayers a day. I don't think she'd have labelled it as misery at the time, but now she has friendships and a relationship with me, she can compare the difference and she wouldn't turn the clock back.'

Camilla was struggling to keep her voice down now.

'You barely know her.'

'*I* barely know her?' Nathan gave up on eating. Shock pinned Camilla to her chair. What was he insinuating? She wasn't sure she could move, she was only sure she was desperate to. Nathan took advantage of the silence. 'I know how I feel about her and how she feels about me. I know that she loves music and she's an incredible pianist, but that performing terrifies her. Do you know how anxious she becomes before a performance? Can't eat, can't sleep. She struggles constantly with self-doubt. She has low self-esteem. She beats herself up for days for making tiny mistakes.'

Low self-esteem? My Naomi? The heat around Camilla's neck was increasing. 'I think you're grossly exaggerating,' she managed, with effort.

'I don't think so,' he said, so quietly it unhinged her. 'If anything, I'm understating it. Her problem is she's never been able to tell you because she's terrified of disappointing you. It's as if a weakness of any kind is unacceptable.'

Anger flared inside Camilla, which she fought to suppress. Her breathing quickened. Her fists clenched. *How dare he?*

Because Camilla said nothing, Nathan carried on. 'I know she feels guilty whenever she cries. I know she's so loyal and responsible she worries about letting people down. I know that music isn't her only passion and that she loves literature. She writes the most amazing poetry. Have you ever read her poetry, Camilla? Is it alright if I call you that?'

Camilla's eyes were set, unblinking. 'Absolutely not, no.'

'What would you prefer me to call you?'

Naomi glanced over, grasping Camilla's attention. Too late, Camilla realised the need to soften her face.

'What are you two whispering about?' Naomi asked, forehead creasing.

Camilla recovered quickly. She must, for Naomi's sake. 'Nothing important,' she said, voice unnaturally light. She stood up and lifted her glass of wine. 'I was just thinking how it was high time your father got to know Nathaniel a little better. Maybe I'll stop hogging him and offer to swap places so they can have a talk.'

Naomi smiled cautiously. 'That's a nice idea, Mum. Is everything OK?'

'Of course. Everything's perfect.'

18

Five excellent courses had gone by. Coffee and handmade chocolates still to go. Henry dabbed his mouth and drummed the bulk of his belly with both hands. Camilla threw a disapproving glare the full length of the table. Henry stopped. His shirt buttons were straining and his trousers felt tight all round. Time for new trousers, perhaps.

It had been an exceptional meal. The chef had not disappointed. His two helpers had coped very well. They'd been polite and efficient, no mishaps. Henry was toying with the idea of dragging the three of them in, to heap upon them some well-deserved praise. He'd already decided to add a giant tip to the final bill. He poured himself another glass of wine, the fourth of the night, roughly.

He'd enjoyed a lengthy chat with Nathan about football, cars, cricket, cars, politics and cars. Smashing lad! Camilla had caught his eye from time to time as if she was observing carefully. Henry, having not a clue why there was concern in her eyes, reassured her by smiling warmly each time. He didn't see how she could possibly be dissatisfied with the evening when it had run so smoothly.

It was eight forty-five. The musicians had been booked for two hours and would be leaving shortly. The timing had been perfect. Camilla excused herself and stood and left the room. Henry had only one thing in mind. He turned to Nathan.

'While we're waiting for coffee, d'you fancy taking a

quick peek at my girls?'

Nathan stood up and placed a hand on Henry's shoulder. 'What are we waiting for?'

Henry clapped Nathan on the back, which drew Naomi's attention.

'Where are you two off to?'

Henry grinned. 'One guess. And if your mother asks where we are, tell her we'll be back any minute.'

Naomi rolled her eyes. 'Hurry.'

Henry took Nathan into the hall and looked about him without speaking. It smelled of strong coffee. He took an enormous bunch of keys from a nearby drawer and sneaked Nathan out of the front door like a thief. The moon was behind ghostly shifting cloud, no stars. They passed Nathan's car, Lorie's Mini, then Camilla's Honda Civic beside Annabel's recently-repaired VW Golf, and continued to the back of the house to Henry's purpose-built garage. Henry buzzed open the remote-control door, flicked on the main light and disabled the alarm that was beeping. Three gleaming cars were lined up like school children, facing the front.

Nathan stuck his hands in his trouser pockets, and wandered in. 'Whoa. Three?'

'I've been very fortunate, Nathan. I've earned a substantial income all my life and we've inherited a great deal of money from both sides. Camilla thinks my little collection is obscene.'

Nathan laughed. 'I'm feeling impolite. Aren't you going to introduce us?'

'With pleasure,' Henry said, hunting through his keys.

He led Nathan to the middle of the three cars, by far the smallest. 'Here's the old girl, my classic 1957 Ford Thunderbird.' Henry opened the door of an immaculate shiny white sports car with a bright red interior, only two seats. The hood was down so everything was visible. He climbed inside, sat at the wheel and looked up at Nathan, who was examining the dashboard. 'I picked her up in an auction twenty-five years ago for twelve hundred pounds. My father babysat her while we were in South Africa. I couldn't part with her. She needed some work, but see what a bit of TLC can do. Worth nearer thirty K now.'

'Impressive. Just for show or do you ever take her out?'

Henry grinned. 'I take her out on warm sunny days, just locally. She's only my bit on the side.'

'I take it this is the main girl then?' Nathan smiled, heading for a black Rolls-Royce.

Henry stepped out of the car and hurried to catch up. 'That's right,' he beamed. 'Stunning isn't she? Absolutely beautiful.'

He disabled the alarm and signalled for Nathan to get in, driver's side.

'Sports car?' Nathan asked, though the hood was up.

They started to climb into a cream leather interior. There were two individual seats in the back.

'Yes, convertible. Rolls-Royce Phantom, 6.7 engine. Twelve months old. Every man's dream. Purrs like a kitten. Every time I turn her on, I fall in love all over again. I'd take you for a spin if I hadn't had a few.'

Henry reached across and switched the engine on. 'Hear that?'

'Just.'

'That's what I'm talking about,' Henry said, nodding. 'Magic. Once you've driven one of these, nothing else comes close.'

'Just as well she's grounded then,' Nathan said. 'I have to drive my Vauxhall Astra home later.'

'Quite,' Henry chuckled, then pointed to the third car on the far side of the Ford. It was a navy blue, highly polished, five door saloon. 'That's my everyday drive. Beautiful car in her own right. Jaguar XJ. I used to think Jags were top dogs, until I test drove this one.' He patted the seat. 'Stole my heart. Had to have her.' They sat in silent awe for a few seconds until Henry added, quietly, 'You know, Camilla doesn't understand this passion I have. I'd like to be able to polish my cars without the daggers flying out of the kitchen window via my wife's eyes.'

'Do you understand her passion for growing turnips?' Nathan asked.

Henry laughed suddenly and helplessly. 'Not a bit.' The laughter died down until the silence of a still evening returned. Henry turned to Nathan, who was holding the steering wheel and staring ahead. 'Having said all that, family comes first. Hobbies and interests are one thing, but the most important thing to me is my family, Nathan. My girls, my *real* girls . . . ' Henry shook his head, unexpectedly finding his eyes had filled and his voice was trembling. He got a grip. 'They're everything to me.' He paused. Nathan was thoughtful, looking straight at him now. 'I know it's only been a few weeks with Naomi, but –'

'I love her,' Nathan cut in. 'You're her father, so I should tell you I've asked her to marry me. Done properly, I really should have consulted you first.'

Henry felt lightheaded. How many glasses of wine had he had? 'Marriage?' he spluttered.

'She didn't accept,' Nathan said. 'She isn't ready and I understand that. But I'm ready for her. I'm older. I know what I want and she's the one. You know when you just know?'

Henry thought about it, struggling to straighten his thoughts. Camilla's face filled his mind and Henry found himself nodding and saying, 'I do,' like he was at the altar. 'But why marriage? And why now?'

'I know it's a big deal. Look, this is private, but you know Naomi has certain . . . principles.'

'Principles?' Henry's head was woolly.

Nathan cleared his throat. 'Naomi isn't like any other girls I've been out with. She's made a commitment to save herself until . . . '

His words trailed off, but comprehension finally dawned on Henry. 'Oh, I see. I had no idea.'

'So of course, I'll respect her,' Nathan said, looking directly at Henry. 'But I hope it explains why I proposed. She'll need a place to live next year and I have one. The students in her year are already looking at housing. I'd like her to be with me, but she won't move in unless we're married. So I found myself asking her to marry me. It wasn't planned, but it feels so right. This week, I spent everything I had on a ring in case she changes her mind.'

Henry was trying to unscramble his head. It felt clear while they were chatting about cars and sport, but now . . . 'You haven't mentioned this to Camilla, have you?'

'Hell, no,' Nathan said. 'I did mention that I'd fallen in love with Naomi and that was too much for her.'

'It would be,' Henry said. 'Best not to say anything about, you know . . . '

'I agree. In any case, Naomi isn't ready so it isn't relevant. I just wanted you both to know what Naomi means to me. I think I upset Camilla and I'm sorry about that.'

'Ah,' Henry said. Finally things added up.

'She objected to me calling her Camilla too. That was two major blunders in the space of a few sentences. The third came when I asked her if she'd been close to her parents. She swapped seats with you after that.'

'Ouch,' Henry said, drawing a noisy breath.

'She asked me about my family first. I got a bit

defensive. Things aren't great between me and my parents. I didn't intend to upset her,' Nathan said.

'Touchy subject for her too. Even I don't venture down that avenue,' Henry said, realising he was almost whispering. 'You weren't to know. Look, I appreciate your honesty. And please call me Henry.'

'I didn't mean to cause trouble.'

'No, no, of course not. She's very protective of Naomi after what happened in South Africa. Did she tell you?'

'Naomi did. I can't even imagine.'

'It was awful,' Henry nodded and drew a few more raspy breaths. 'And then her experience with school here. Well, it's a relief to me that Naomi's looking so relaxed and happy. Camilla's never seen her like this before and it's causing her anxiety. She thinks musicians have to be uptight all day long or they aren't serious enough. That's how Naomi used to be when she was home. She spent hours alone practising in the music room, or reading upstairs. Between you and me, I never thought it was healthy, because she never seemed happy.'

'She wasn't, Henry.'

Henry nodded thoughtfully then jutted his hand out in Nathan's direction. Nathan shook it. 'I want to thank you for respecting my daughter and bringing her sparkle back. She's very precious to me. Not every guy would stick around under her conditions.'

'Like I said, I love her.'

'I can see that,' Henry said. Suddenly, he could also see something else. Camilla was standing in the garage doorway, stone-faced, still. 'Oh, help us.'

'Dare I give you some advice?' Nathan muttered between his teeth.

'Please do.'

'Don't defend yourself, just apologise. And blame

me if it helps. I can't sink any lower tonight.'

***

The musicians had ended with 'Happy birthday to you'. Everyone joined in and sang. Camilla had been furious that Henry had missed it. Naomi noticed the red blotches on her neck and knew Henry was in for it.

People were leaving the table now. There were gangs of empty bottles. Lorie was helping to clear up with Simon. Annie was getting louder. She demanded at top pitch that some decent music be played now. Naomi smiled and shook her head, automatically flicking a glance at the string quartet to see if they'd heard.

The musicians were packing their instruments away quietly in the corner. One of them looked familiar as she saw him in profile for a millisecond. Then he was crouching down again, busying himself on the floor, back to her. Naomi moved a little closer. He reminded her of . . .

The fingers of two cool hands that carried the faint scent of leather, covered her eyes from behind. A sexy voice shot some warm breath into her ear and said, 'When can we be alone?'

Naomi grinned. Nathan let go. She turned round and had to stop herself from wrapping her arms around his neck and kissing him. 'I thought we'd talked about that.'

'My memory's faulty when you look this good.' Her arms were by her side, but Nathan discreetly took hold of both hands. His fingers ran over her new ring and he smiled and looked down. 'Nice ring,' he said. 'Where did you get it?'

Her smile widened. 'It was a gift from this hot guy I'm seeing at the moment. Can you keep a secret?'

He narrowed his eyes. 'Depends what it is.'

She moved closer. 'All night I've been thinking how it might look better on the other hand.'

Nathan's eyes widened. 'Are you serious?'

'Well, I'm seriously in love with this guy and I'm wondering what's holding me back.'

Nathan pulled her to him and spoke into her ear again. 'I happen to know he's seriously in love with you too,' he whispered. 'Naomi Stone. Has a nice ring to it, if you'll pardon the pun. And no, I wouldn't be able to keep a secret like that.'

Naomi laughed. Nathan pulled back.

'Like I said, I'm only thinking about it,' Naomi said.

'Good enough.'

'So, has my dad been boring you?'

'Not at all. We got along great, which is just as well when I stuffed up so sensationally with your mum.'

'She can be impossible. I'm sure you did your best.'

Nathan shrugged. He was distracted suddenly, looking over Naomi's shoulder. When Naomi followed his gaze, Annie was walking out of the room, alone. 'Right,' he said. 'Time I had a little chat to your sister and put her in the picture so you can stop avoiding her.'

'I haven't been avoiding her.'

Nathan looked into her eyes. 'Oh, you reckon?'

Naomi detained him. 'What are you going to say?'

'Come on, Naims, she's not blind. I shouldn't need to say much.'

Naomi was nervous, but she let him go. Nathan left the room. Naomi could only stare after him blankly. He'd done an amazing job with Siobhan over dinner, chatting to her, drawing conversation from her so naturally. He was amazing with people. Naomi adored him for it. Suddenly remembering the need to look out for Siobhan now dinner was done, Naomi cast her gaze across the room in search of her. She could see Megan and

Madeline standing together, and Bridget who was getting very friendly with Annie's friend, Dominic. But she couldn't see Siobhan.

Naomi was about to go and ask the girls if they knew where she was, when Henry appeared, carrying a wad of cash. Henry chatted to Naomi long enough to gauge her approval about every aspect of the evening. Assured she'd had a wonderful time, he excused himself to pay the string quartet before they left.

The viola player straightened up and turned round. Naomi froze. He did too. His horribly familiar face winded her. Tom Butterworth, the cheating rat who'd poisoned a hundred dreams, was staring at her across the room.

The noise faded. The bodies felt far removed. Every body, that is, except Tom Butterworth's. Despite not moving, he seemed so close and so colourful and tall. It was as if there was only the two of them in the crowded room. Naomi stiffened and continued to stare him out. In her head she was screaming, hoping he could read her eyes. *How dare you come here? Turn around and get out.* Tom Butterworth didn't back down. Her instinct was to run, but no way was she going to move. Her house, *he* could run.

Tom began striding towards her. The compulsion to vanish overwhelmed her. She stayed still. Her heart was thudding by the time he stood, close up, right in front. He'd grown. Having been forced into a confrontation, she was determined to speak first. She hoped an opening sentence would occur to her. She snatched the first one that came along.

'When I told you to get out of my house, I meant for ever.' Her tone was calm, but cold.

Tom, in white shirt, held up his hands in surrender. There were wet patches under his arms. 'I don't want to cause trouble.'

Naomi was repulsed. 'The fact that you're here causes trouble. How've you got the nerve to come back?'

He tried to reach out and touch her arm. Naomi pulled back. 'Naomi, it was three years ago. If you'll give me the chance, I only want to apologise –'

'No chance,' she said firmly. 'I don't want to hear it.'

Tom snorted a couple of heavy breaths. 'What do you want from me?'

'Get out and leave me alone.'

'Fine,' he said, throwing his arms up. 'I've done my job. I'm going. For a so-called Christian, you're not very tolerant or forgiving.'

Naomi felt her mouth drop open. She also felt two warm hands press down on each of her shoulders from behind.

Nathan's voice, barely holding on to calm, said, 'You watch where you're throwing your accusations, mate.'

Tom clenched his teeth and looked at Nathan. 'We're trying to have a private conversation here. I'm sorry, who are you?'

Naomi found her tongue and answered for him. 'Nathan Stone. He's my fiancé,' she said softly, discreetly swapping the ring onto the other hand, then shifting to Nathan's side. She took his hand without taking her eyes off Tom. Nathan squeezed it firmly, no need for words. 'Nathan, this is Tom Butterworth.'

'Oh yeah!'

'Your fiancé?' Tom said, not quietly. 'Since when?'

Nathan edged closer to Tom. He was a couple of inches taller and far more athletically built. 'None of your business.'

'Fiancé?' came a voice behind Naomi. It was so filled with horror, Naomi didn't recognise it.

She turned. Annabel stood hands on hips. 'I thought I was coming to have a word with you about your boyfriend, but fiancé? What the hell?'

Naomi could feel her cheeks colouring. This was exactly the reaction she'd been dreading from Annabel.

'Annie, I was going to tell you about us, but –'

'But what, Naomi?' Annabel shouted. Her stare was intense, face set tight. 'You thought maybe you'd get him to come on to me first, so he could humiliate me and knock me back and tell me he was my twin's boyfriend?'

'I did not come on to you,' Nathan intervened. 'I asked you for a quiet word. That isn't an invitation, Annabel. You led me into Naomi's piano room. I just wanted the chance to properly explain that Naomi and I are together.'

'You took my arm,' Annabel said, forcefully.

'I propped you up so you didn't collapse,' Nathan said, quietly but firmly.

'This is priceless coming from her,' Tom piped up, eyeing Annabel. The room hushed except for the drama going on in the centre of it. All the strength drained from Naomi. All eyes were on them. There wasn't a hole in the floor to crawl into, but she looked for one anyway. Camilla had just returned with Lorie and Simon. 'She did exactly the same thing with me, then blamed me for it. She's unbelievable.'

Annabel turned her attention to Tom, the shock of seeing him registering for the first time. 'And what the hell is he doing here?' she yelled, pointing at him, fixing a glare. 'How dare you tell Naomi about that?'

'She knows. She's always known,' Tom yelled back. 'She was there that night, Annabel. She heard everything.'

'You, with Tom?' Nathan asked Annabel. 'How could you do that?' He turned to Naomi. His voice softened. 'Why didn't you tell me it was Annabel?'

Naomi said nothing. Camilla charged forward, red-necked. She reached the scene. 'We're going to sort this out calmly, and privately.' She threw Henry a vicious look then lowered her voice to a whisper. 'Not another word in here, you four. Hear me? Follow.'

Camilla marched for the door. Tom, looking bewildered, filed behind. Naomi, still attached to Nathan, followed. It was a long ten paces. At the door, Camilla turned and paused, waiting for Annabel, who hadn't moved. Her arms were crossed. After a wordless glare, Annabel followed too.

'Music, Henry.'

Without speaking, Camilla led them, heels clicking, to Naomi's large piano room, which had an assortment of chairs and a display cabinet holding music trophies and certificates. Dance music started up in the dining room. Camilla closed the door and indicated for everyone to find a seat while she remained standing. Everyone sat. She eyed them all individually.

'I'm utterly speechless,' she eventually said, pausing to purse her lips.

'I doubt that,' Annabel muttered.

'Not another word from you,' Camilla snapped. She glared at Annabel until she looked away. Then Camilla found Tom. 'I suspect you started this.'

'I didn't,' Tom protested mildly.

Camilla cut in. 'I should have allowed Loretta to throw you out, instead of which I told you specifically not to speak to either of my daughters tonight. Which part of that didn't you understand?'

'Knowing he was my ex-boyfriend, why did you let him stay?' Naomi came in, voice shaky. 'What was he even doing here in the first place?'

'By some cruel coincidence I managed to book a

string quartet which included him.'

'Or were you hoping I'd get back with him and finish with Nathan?' Naomi asked.

'Of course not,' Camilla said, outraged. 'After what happened with Tom, I knew there was no chance of that.'

'How do you know what happened?' Annabel said, despite the warning.

Camilla's neck glowed. She paused. 'Naomi's diary.'

'Mum!' Annabel and Naomi yelled in unison. They were incapable of any more.

The word hung a while until Tom spoke. 'Look, Mrs Hamilton, can I just say, Naomi saw me tonight, or I'd have left without speaking to her. I didn't mean to cause trouble. I only wanted to apologise.'

'You accused her of being intolerant and unforgiving,' Nathan said. 'How's that an apology?'

'That was after she told me where to stick my apology and told me to get out. For ages, I've wanted to say sorry, and – '

'Yeah right,' Naomi said. 'How about, "I don't do guilt." Those words sound familiar to you, Tom?'

'You forget that she was there too,' Tom said, hurling an outstretched arm and finger at Annabel.

Annabel, head down, said nothing.

'You're wrong,' Naomi shouted, surprising herself. 'I've spent every minute trying to forget that fact, and I can't.'

Naomi's voice cracked on the final two words. Nathan stood and pulled Naomi to her feet. He put his arms around her and Naomi leant into his chest and collapsed into tears. Her sobbing was the only sound.

'Naomi, you're embarrassing yourself. Pull yourself together,' Camilla hissed.

'She has a right to be upset,' Nathan said, impatiently. 'She was worried about tonight when she should have been looking forward to it. I promised her everything would be OK. Then he shows up, her sister gets too friendly with me and she isn't even allowed to be upset about it.'

'I've never been so disrespected,' Camilla said.

'I didn't get too friendly with you,' Annabel screamed.

'You tried to kiss me, remember?' Nathan told Annabel under his breath.

'You wanted me to.'

'No, I didn't.' Nathan looked away from Annabel and switched his attention to Camilla. 'If you want to be respected, it has to be two-way,' he said more calmly. 'I'm sorry, but there has to be consistency. You've been against us from the start and you've shown me no respect at all, which has upset Naomi more than anything that's happened tonight.'

'How dare you,' Camilla said.

'I hate this family,' Annabel yelled, standing up. 'You're such a hypocrite, Mother. This is crap – all of it. I'm sick of taking the blame for everything around here. Shall we all stop pretending, just for once?'

'Don't you speak to me –'

'I'll speak to you any way I want because I'm a person too. Disown me if you want to. I'm leaving anyway,' Annabel screamed, the veins on her neck bulging. 'How much was Naomi's piano?'

'I beg your pardon?'

'We came in here, me and him,' Annabel yelled, jabbing a thumb in Nathan's direction. 'We both knew why. He went to the piano and played a couple of notes and said that he'd never realised a piano could cost forty-five grand. I told him it was only fifteen, like my car. He told me Naomi had said it was forty-five thousand. So, let's have the truth.'

Nathan pulled away from Naomi and looked at her. 'I'm sorry, I assumed she knew.'

'You assume too much,' Camilla said.

'So do you,' Annabel bellowed at Camilla. 'Everything's secretive in this house because nobody is honest. No one's allowed to be, and everyone's miserable because of it,' Annabel assaulted Camilla with her eyes.

'Naomi needed an excellent instrument –'

'Fine,' Annabel screamed, 'I get it. Why didn't you just say so instead of trying to pretend you were treating us equally when you never have? Naomi's the golden girl. It's Naomi this, Naomi that. No one is good enough for Naomi. You're treating him like he's stolen the crown jewels or something,' she said, throwing her arm in Nathan's direction again. 'Naomi's the most talented person in the whole world. If only I was more like Naomi, I might have a chance of being successful in my life. You even prefer Lorie to me,' she said, tears streaming down her cheeks. 'I've had it my whole life. The only way I can deal with it is to pretend I don't care. Well, I'm done with pretending.'

Annabel broke down and couldn't carry on. She buried her head in her hands. It was Naomi who went to try and comfort her. 'Annie, I'm sorry.'

Annabel pushed her away and looked at her, ice-blue eyes streaming. 'About what, Naomi? About being Mum's favourite? About everyone being so disappointed in me because I can't ever measure up to you?' She paused. 'I'm sorry I kissed him three years ago,' she said, gesturing at Tom. 'I was young and stupid and thought I could prove to myself, just once, that I could have what you had. I felt horrible about it straight after. But I swear, I wouldn't have gone anywhere near him tonight if I'd known you were together.' She threw a dark glance at Nathan. 'Why didn't you just tell me? Why didn't any of you just tell me?'

Naomi covered her eyes with one hand. 'I thought you'd think I wasn't good enough for him. I've always felt inferior to you.'

Despite the tears, Annabel laughed, then cried harder. 'See what you've done to us, Mother, by trying to control our lives and mould us into the perfect daughters, you've only succeeded in screwing us up.'

'No,' Camilla said, some uncertainty creeping into her tone. 'I've sacrificed everything for you girls.'

'You've manipulated us,' Annabel said, throwing her arms up wildly, letting them crash down. 'Me and Naomi are finally managing some honesty, and you're still deluded.'

'Annie, that's unfair,' Naomi said, gently. 'Mum only wants the best for us, you have to see that.'

'Does she?' Annabel said. 'Then why don't you share your wonderful news? I'm sure she'll be ecstatic.'

'Annie, please,' Naomi said.

'If she wants the best for us, then why are you so afraid of her?' Annabel said. 'Go on and tell her what I found out before she walked in. I've still got a few things to pack before I can get out of here.' She looked at Camilla. 'Sell my car and keep the money. I don't want anything from you.'

Annabel staggered to the door, opened it, slammed it shut behind her. Camilla, who'd lost the ability to speak, didn't move. No one spoke. Tom, the only one still sitting, stood and muttered something about needing to leave. He apologised again on his way through the door. Camilla set her stare on Nathan and Naomi until Nathan spoke up.

'We're engaged.'

All Camilla's features seemed to open in alarm. There was another long silence.

'Since when?'

'Tonight,' Nathan said.

'Are you pregnant, Naomi?' Camilla asked in a small voice as if all the air had been sucked from her.

Naomi shook her head. 'I've told you we've never slept together.'

'Then why?'

Naomi looked at Camilla in her chiffon gown, standing, head low, almost bowed. Her fight had gone. Naomi was seized by a sickening mixture of heaviness and sadness and couldn't answer.

Nathan took Naomi in his arms again and rested his chin on her head. 'Because we're adults and we love each other and we won't be told we can't be together. I'd prefer to have your approval, but with or without it, I'm determined to make her very happy.'

19

CAPTIVITY

After hours of fits of rain, Naomi became conscious, suddenly, that it had stopped. The incessant pattering at the window had abated, leaving a kind of damp and heavy silence. Dan was slumped beside her on the sofa where they'd spent the night in senseless exchanges, Dan never able to reach the point or answer the questions Naomi had asked about Nathan. He wouldn't explain why he'd collaborated with another man to take her at knifepoint to a cemetery before bringing her to a beautiful cottage in the back of beyond. She hadn't concluded if he'd meant to kill her and changed his mind, or if a well-laid plan had gone wrong. Dan's mood was unpredictable. He was agitated and upset. She didn't feel to push him.

For hours, he'd communicated by muttering fragments of information, which she was now trying to piece together. She was certain about only a few things: that Nathan was in terrible trouble and that Dan was terrified about it and had not known what to do but run and hide, taking Naomi with him. Nothing added up. He'd stare at her at times with his wild eyes and ask, 'Don't you see?' She didn't, and was forced to admit it, which only aggravated him more. Dan would revert to holding his head and crying. It had been a bizarre few hours and Naomi was filled with a horrible sense of foreboding. *What am I not understanding here*? That Dan was not in his right mind was the clearest thing, which was, in itself, a huge and immediate problem.

As the first morning light penetrated the closed curtains of the dim little sitting room, making the lamplight less effective, Naomi was feeling a growing urgency to get away from Dan. She came to her senses, having been utterly lost in rambling thickets of thought, and realised he'd gone quiet. She slowly sat up and studied him, head dropped back against the sofa. Dan had drifted into sleep. His face didn't look peaceful or rested. It looked as though his expression, retaining the subject of their last conversation, had frozen and his eyelids had closed. He reminded her so much of Nathan.

Naomi stood carefully. Dan didn't move. His mouth was shut, but he was inhaling deep breaths through his nose. His chest was heaving steadily, fingers locked loosely across his body. Naomi moved noiselessly to the door, which was slightly open. She took hold of it and opened it just far enough to slip through. She paused in the hall to listen, chest drumming a heavy beat, which she was sure would rouse Dan. The only other sound was the slower pulse of a ticking clock, which she found on the wall beside the front door, brass pendulum swinging rhythmically beneath. It was almost quarter to seven.

The front door had an unclosed heavy curtain beside it on a black rail. Naomi, desperate to leave, weighed up the door. It was bolted at the top. Unwilling to risk the noise of moving the bolt, she tiptoed into the kitchen to look for keys and a way out of the back. There was nothing on the table but the bowl of fake fruit. She scanned the kitchen surfaces for keys, a phone, anything useful. Again, nothing.

She headed for the back door. There was a single key in the lock. The sight of it brought a surge of energy. Naomi took hold of the key and slowly turned it anticlockwise. After a click, she held still and looked over her shoulder. Nothing had changed. Dan wasn't following. Only now did it occur to her that her feet were bare. She hesitated, mind divided. She knew where she'd seen shoes – in the small pantry on the other side of the kitchen. Was it worth diverting for them? She stiffened for a couple of seconds, cursing her inaction, simultaneously picturing the sodden fields after a night of endless rain. She needed shoes. She flew to the pantry door, opened it, found the shoes stacked up in the corner. They were too big. They were also the only option.

Naomi picked them up and returned to the back door, shaking with the need to leave. She took hold of the door handle and took pains over slowly opening it. A breath of fresh morning air invited her out. She inhaled deeply. The birds were chattering in the trees. Every second she took over carefully closing the door, she expected Dan to appear and seize her again and lock her in the bedroom. She couldn't go back to the chains. She wouldn't.

Beyond the back door, four rows of big square flagstones were laid across the full width of the house. An ornate cast iron table and two chairs sat on them to the right of the door. Beyond that, a step led to a crazy-paved path edged with bedding plants, which ran the length of the garden. Part of this path had been in her view from the window and was painted in vivid colours in her memory.

Naomi could see the familiar wooden gate at the end of the garden. Holding the shoes in one hand, and not wanting to wear them until she was clear of the path, she raced for the garden gate and went through it.

Another look back assured her that Dan wasn't following. Hands trembling, she shoved on the shoes. She was wearing the jeans and the zip up fleece top. It was a damp, chilly morning. The evidence of a deluge of rainfall was everywhere. Beyond the garden, Naomi plunged into the wet field and began to hurry away from the house as quickly as she could. Her shoes were being sucked into mud. There was a swollen stream to her right.

She pictured a pretty village behind the distant hill, with low stone walls, a couple of shops, a pub and a few houses. She'd make it to the newsagent. With luck, it would be open already. She'd tumble inside a cosy little shop with a friendly shopkeeper who knew all the locals. She'd make herself known and borrow a phone and call home. The only number Nathan had was his mobile. She'd never memorised it.

Lines of possible conversations were ringing in her head as she avoided the swamps and tried to keep moving quickly. Slicing into her plans and her peace was a faraway yell that stopped her heart.

'Naomi.' Then more forcefully. 'Naomi.'

She glanced behind. In the distance, Dan was charging down the garden and simultaneously climbing into his shoes. Naomi sped up. The shoes were loose. Now she was being less careful, cold mud was sloshing inside her shoes.

Stay upright. Don't slip. She hurried on, the air lifting her hair. It carried the promise of distant farms and drew more pictures in her head. She'd settle for any destination that was away from Dan and the cottage and the bed with seven scored lines in the leg.

The sky sat low and overcast; the hidden sun seemed impossibly distant. The field was loosely wrapped in a carpet of mist, so vision ahead was limited. As long as the house was directly behind her, she knew she was heading in the right direction.

She threw another glance over her shoulder to check the position of the house. Dan was gaining ground. Her concentration faltered. Naomi twisted her ankle and fell.

Panic was a powerful anaesthetic. The pain was delayed, but came after she rose quickly and charged on, yelping every few steps.

'Naomi. Stop. No,' Dan yelled.

The cottage was invisible behind her now. Suddenly, the mist rolled back enough for her to see the outline of a building. The thought of the end of the chase made her realise she was breathless and aching. Dan's voice was becoming clearer.

'Naomi, stop,' Dan was screaming.

Naomi wouldn't. She wanted the world to know that despite a dead week, she was alive. The building was taking shape, details of the brickwork emerging. Her legs were feeling the strain of running up a steady slope. Adrenaline pushed her to the top. Dan was only a few metres behind. The stone building was right in front. Beyond that, there was a sleepy road and a row of cottages on the other side of it just as she'd imagined. A few parked cars lined the little street. There was a red phone box on Naomi's side and a post box opposite. Her chest expanded with the joy of seeing simple things she'd never cared about.

Naomi sprinted down the slope and to the front of the stone building. It wasn't a shop, but a double-fronted house. Dan was right behind her, unwilling to yell. She found the shop across the road, on the end of the row. She darted across the road, praying the shop was open.

Dan was ten metres behind.

'Naomi,' he hissed. 'No. Please. Stop.'

Naomi ignored him and lunged for the shop door and threw herself inside. She was panting heavily into a warm empty room.

She stood, trembling, expecting Dan to burst through the door breathing his threats. He didn't. A voice called from a back room. 'With you in a minute.'

A tall fridge to Naomi's left held dairy products and cans and bottles of drink. To her right, the whole wall was littered with newspapers and magazines. She stared at the colourful prints and the bold black words on the front covers and the blood drained from her head. She managed two faltering steps forward and seized up. Nathan was looking at her from the front cover of a national newspaper beneath a headline she could not accept. She heard the bell signal the opening of the door behind her. Dan was entering the shop cautiously. His features were fading. She had no strength to run. The room was losing colour and definition, closing in. Dan lunged to catch her just as the shop, like a candle, blew out.

***

It was the day after the party. Nathan woke up to the sound of his phone in his luxuriously comfortable double bed. He looked around the bland bedroom of his flat and looked forward to a day when life would be less of a struggle. He had ambitions far beyond this pokey flat. He picked up his phone. The date said: Sunday, twenty-third of October. It was nearly nine O'clock. It was Naomi's birthday. A text message from Naomi was staring at him. He opened it. It said: 'So sorry about last night. Sorry for not telling you about Tom and Annabel. Sorry about Annabel and my mum. I'm dying with embarrassment. Annie left early without saying goodbye. It's times like these when I'm glad I won't be a Hamilton for much longer. Can you forgive me?'

Nathan smiled and replied: 'It's your birthday, remember? Happy birthday! Don't apologise. None of it was your fault. I'm glad you won't be a Hamilton for much longer either. I'll be round to collect you soon.

Where are you now?'

Within a few seconds, a reply had come back. 'I'm still in my room. Haven't dared venture downstairs yet.'

Tired of texting, Nathan dialled. She answered. Nathan said, 'Hey babe. Can you talk?'

'I'm locked in my en suite bathroom, about to take a shower. It's weird being back in this house. It's been ages since I slept here.'

'You looked hot in that dress last night.'

'I wore it for you.'

Nathan smiled into his phone and settled back in bed, one arm behind his head. 'I know you did because you knew I'd be struggling to take my eyes off you and concentrate on anyone else.'

'So it worked?' Nathan could hear the smile in her voice too.

'How could it not?' he said.

'I love the ring. I really really love it.'

'Good,' Nathan said, thinking it was time he got up and showered too. 'I can't wait to go on honeymoon. Where would you like to go?'

'I don't care as long as we're together. I'm thinking hot and exotic. I'm thinking villa, close to the sea, with private beach. White sands. I'm thinking no phones or interruptions for at least a week. Are you picturing this?'

'Very clearly,' Nathan said. 'How soon can we go?'

'Patience, Nathan. It needs careful planning. It's going to take time. It'll be a church wedding. Churches are booked for months ahead. Then there's the reception. Loads to organise.'

Nathan crossed his legs. 'You're boring me with details. I want a small wedding. As few people as possible. All I really want is to be on that beach with you.'

'Me too. What about Dan though? Will he be a

problem?'

'No. I'll talk to Dan, maybe include him in our plans somehow. He always listens to me. Look, got to go. I'm due at the house soon to pick Naomi up. Will you still be there?'

'Of course.' Lorie grinned to the empty room and turned on the shower and slipped out of her robe. 'If you touch her before the wedding, I swear I'll kill you.'

Nathan laughed. 'You're so sexy when you're jealous. Same rules for Simple Simon.'

'Simon bores me rigid but he's insurance to keep you on your toes. I'll dump him before the wedding if I can stomach him that long.'

Nathan stood up and opened the curtains. 'You'd better.'

'I have to say,' Lorie said, 'mentioning the cost of the piano was genius.'

'Not as genius as booking Tom Butterworth. How did you manage it?'

'Camilla booked him,' Lorie said. 'All I did was provide the phone numbers. I rang round until I'd got his quartet, then I gave Camilla four numbers, only one was still open for booking.'

'You're incredible. You know that?'

'Yes, but I still think the piano bombshell topped Tom. It'll blow them apart for ages. Annie's stubborn. She won't back down easily.'

'Good, then the coast is clear to plan the wedding with her out of the picture.'

'Correct. Henry loves you, by the way. Camilla's furious about it.'

Nathan laughed. 'Result. With the family at war, Naomi can't wait to get out of it. This is going to be simple.'

'Don't relax,' Lorie said. 'I've got rid of the cleaner,

Denise. She was getting too familiar with Camilla. The new one is nice, but dim. Don't underestimate Camilla, she's sharp. I think it's time you infuriated her by apologising. Do it publicly and sincerely then she can't tell you where to stick it. It'll weaken her case with Henry that you're the devil incarnate.'

'Fine. I'm going to take a quick shower then I'll be round. Maybe I'll pick up some flowers on the way.'

'Bring her roses. White. Open, but not fully. No less than a dozen. Have some foliage added.'

'I'll have them professionally arranged and finished with ribbon.'

'Perfect.'

A short pause. 'By the way, Naomi's been threatened. I'll have to produce some money.'

'Wish I could help, but I'm as broke as you are.'

'Not for much longer. Have you asked Henry about the loan?'

Lorie's voice came back at its lowest pitch. With the shower pelting behind her, she could only just hear Nathan. 'I'm going to speak to him when I'm showered and dressed.'

'Do it before I arrive. I need that money, yesterday.'

'I daren't ask for more than ten.'

'That's only half.'

'Best I can do. Wish me luck.'

Nathan stood up and walked to the window, looking out on a dull morning that didn't dampen his mood. 'You don't need it.'

He switched off the phone and headed for the cramped bathroom in the flat. As he passed the second bedroom, he rapped sharply on the door. 'Hey, Dan, you awake? Congratulate me, why don't you. I'm officially engaged.'

***

Naomi couldn't remember much of the walk back to the cottage, but she did remember, as Dan steered her through the back door, that being back there brought relief. It fulfilled an immediate need to sit down and settle the sickness in her stomach.

There were two brown leather sofas in the small sitting room. Naomi was slouched on one in a trance; Dan sat on the other. She was staring at the open fireplace, eyes blurred into logs and surrounding cream tiles and wood frame. She felt like she'd shrunk inside a little corner of herself and that the outside had hardened into an unresponsive shell. Her eyes weren't taking in information except in blurred pictures. Her head was firing the image that had capsized her world. She was still seeing Nathan's tear-stained face with a turquoise ocean behind him that had apparently just claimed his young wife's life. The headline said, *Bride Lost in Paradise*. There had been a tiny picture in a black square in the far right corner, of Naomi in her wedding dress with Nathan.

Naomi hadn't realised that Dan had left the room until he returned and dropped down next to her and heaved a loud sigh. He was holding a black mug that smelled of tea. She looked down at it robotically. That it looked very milky was her only thought.

'Drink this,' Dan said. 'It will help with the shock.'

Naomi took the mug and clasped it between two hands, barely feeling the weight or substance of it. With Dan watching her closely, she obediently sipped. It was too sweet. Dan said nothing until she'd finished drinking and he'd taken the cup off her and put it on the floor.

'We were lucky you weren't seen at the shop,' he said. Naomi didn't answer. Dan held on to a few seconds of silence before he said, 'Naomi, I'm really sorry.'

Naomi resumed her intense study of the fireplace. Her right hand held on to her left, but she was strangely numb. 'Are you schizophrenic, Dan?'

'Is that what he told you?' She heard Dan shift a little in his seat. 'My medication is for asthma. Nathan's the only sick one of the two of us.'

'So you never scared Lucy away?' Her voice was unreasonably calm.

'Who the hell is Lucy?'

Naomi dried up for a few seconds until a gut-wrenching pain bowled into her from nowhere. 'Why?' Naomi suddenly exploded, shifting her gaze out of the window. 'Why?'

Dan didn't speak. The peaceful countryside, disconnected from the atrocity, held no answers either.

'Did he have any feelings for me . . . at all?'

'He isn't capable,' Dan said. 'I'm sorry.'

'None of it was real?'

'It's not your fault. You never stood a chance.'

Naomi glared at Dan now. 'What's that supposed to mean?'

Dan's eyes were moist. He wiped them. 'You were set up from the start. You were as good as married before you ever stepped foot in that hotel the night you met him.'

Vivid scenes and feelings from that evening flooded back. Siobhan's freckled arms, a walk to the toilet with the magical sound of Gershwin, her chance meeting with Nathan in his crisp shirt with the black cuff links, the hope that he'd talk to her and leave some droplet of information about himself. *As good as married.* The words got stuck. Naomi found herself focussing on Dan's eyes again. They were unblinking. Vivid blue with pale hazel flecks.

'I'd never seen Nathan before that night.'

Dan shook his head. 'He knew you'd be there. He knew you'd use the toilet eventually. And if you hadn't, he'd have found you anyway. He knew everything about you before you said a word. He knew about your parents, your sister, your cat, your course, your past, and your future. He even researched classical music. You were set up to meet your dream guy and like I said, you didn't stand a chance.'

Naomi's head jolted back a few centimetres. 'Who told him?'

Dan's head dropped. 'Think about it. Who knows your family so well she's virtually part of it? Who else could it be?'

'Lorie?' she barely managed any sound. 'No. Why would she do that?'

Dan covered his eyes with one hand. 'They've been together since before you met Nathan.'

Naomi seemed to crystalize, then shatter into tiny shards. When she'd gathered a few pieces of herself, she stood up just to see if she could. She tested the movement of her legs and stumbled to the window and put her hands on the narrow sill for support. Dan must have followed because she felt a warm hand on her shoulder. 'Get your hands off me.' She lashed out and connected with his face behind her.

Naomi stared out of the window at a green world with a grey topping. Beyond that she saw no details. 'Naomi, I'm sorry, OK?' Dan raised his voice. 'I've protected you for a week, but now you have to know the truth. It's time.'

Naomi spun round wildly and yelled in his face. 'Protected me? You chained me up for seven days. You're a sick pervert.'

'I had to chain you up.' Dan was rubbing his face on one side. 'You had to believe I was dangerous and could hurt you. I was protecting you. I didn't want you seeing my face, because I knew you'd be reminded of *him*.'

'Nothing you say makes any sense.'

'When the guy came round, why didn't you scream for help?'

Through a film of tears, Naomi shouted, 'Because I thought you'd hurt him if I did. I was scared, Dan.'

'Exactly,' Dan matched her tone. 'And because of that, you're still alive and no one's seen you.' He paused. 'I was scared too.'

'You? You tortured me by leaving me alone with nothing to do.'

'Entertaining you wasn't on the agenda,' Dan yelled. 'I was distracted with the more pressing job of saving your life. Believe it or not, watching you suffer was too much for me. I couldn't hack it. All my instincts were screaming at me to help you. To hold you.'

'I thought I was going to die, Dan. I lay for hours every day wondering how I might kill you before you killed me. You made a monster out of me. You were a monster. Why didn't you just tell me what the hell I was doing here?'

'I couldn't. Until last night, there was nothing to tell. Imagine in that car park when I took you, if I'd said, "Hi, I'm Nathan's brother. Please come quietly with me and do what I say and I'll save your life because a week from now your husband's going to fake your death thousands of miles away with your best friend, and the only chance you have of surviving is if we fake your death first. OK"?' Dan paused, breathing hard. 'You weren't supposed to live. You should be buried in that cemetery where no one would ever look for you. All week, I've been waiting, wondering if they'd do it, when they'll do it, and how. Then yesterday, after a week on honeymoon, they actually did it.'

'They?' Naomi said, brain sluggish.

'Yes, they. It's been meticulously planned. She'd go in your place. They have your rings, your necklace, your clothes, your phone, your passport. They went out there to fake your death. She's been posing as you for the past week, sending your parents and your sister texts from your phone. Your family haven't been mourning, Naomi, they thought you were having the time of your life. As far as Nathan knows, you're dead in a cemetery in England. I had to send him a photograph to prove it. The guy at the cemetery was there to witness the job. As far as the rest of the world knows, as of today you're lost at sea and everyone feels sorry for poor Nathan Stone who lost his pretty young bride in a tragic accident. No one will ever look for you because you're dead, Naomi. Not presumed dead. Dead. Gone.'

'You could have stopped them.' Naomi felt her legs give way. Dan reached out and seized her arms. He held her a moment and she was helpless in his arms. Dan manoeuvred her back to the sofa and set her down.

'I couldn't do a thing. If Nathan finds out you're alive, we're both as good as dead,' Dan said, voice a little calmer. 'Lorie will be back in England soon on her own passport. She went out using yours. They think they've got away with murder. She'll be at your parents' house later today, comforting them, manipulating them the way she always has.'

Naomi wove her fingers inside her hair and pulled. 'I've lost everything. Everyone,' she said. 'I don't even feel like a person anymore. I have no identity . . .'

'Of course you do.' Dan ventured an arm around her shoulder. Naomi didn't object. Her strength had gone. Dan's hand grazed her shoulder in small movements. Her eyes filled with tears. 'I risked everything,' Dan said. 'The choice was your life, or Nathan's. If you rise from the dead, his life is finished, but he deserves to go to prison.'

Naomi closed her eyes, shutting everything out. Dan continued to stroke the top of her arm. 'I want to speak to my parents and –'

'Too dangerous.'

'Dan, we need to call the police.'

'You don't understand. We're only safe so long as you're dead. I'm sorry, I know it's crap.'

'What are you afraid of?'

Dan looked at her very closely now. Tiny muscles moved inside his jaw. Nathan had the same habit. 'Look, prison is the best case scenario for Nathan. Worst is that the men who've had a hold over him will think he's double-crossed them and punish him. Then they'll turn their attention to us. We're not safe. I don't know what to do, but you must not be seen.'

Naomi's chest felt tight and heavy. 'What men?'

'Nathan's a liability. He gambles. Poker player. He's been involved with a dodgy crew in Manchester he hooked up with, innocently enough at first. They're involved with organised crime, shady business dealings, protection rackets, you name it. There's a whole world out there, Naomi, that you know nothing about.'

'Nathan?'

'You don't know him. Look, I've done all I can to help him. I'm a junior doctor in my last year of training. I work at the hospital. I've lent him money. I've begged him to break free of them and he's tried, but it's not that easy. They don't want to let him go, but they offered him a deal. One game of poker. If he won, he got his freedom, with conditions. If he lost, he'd owe them twenty grand with no way of paying it back. Like a lunatic, he took the odds.'

'And lost,' Naomi said.

'Course. How could he not? They don't do mercy, or

give second chances, they just collect.'

Naomi thought back to the man in the grey hoodie all those months ago, who'd followed her, but who'd disappeared once Nathan had talked to him.

'There was this guy who used to follow me –'

'The collection man,' Dan said. 'If Nathan hadn't coughed up when he did, you'd have been hurt or killed as a warning to Nathan. He's only part paid what he owes Solomon thanks to your dad, with money lent to Lorie to help with her sick mother.'

Naomi dropped her eyes to the floor. 'I can't take this in.'

'I know,' Dan said quietly. 'Such an almighty mess. Nathan's up to his eyeballs in debt. His lifestyle's way beyond his means. He owes me money, my parents, thousands on credit cards, student loan, overdrawn at the bank. Everyone's after him for money with interest, including Solomon.'

'Who?'

'Vincent Solomon, leader of the gang. Nasty piece of work. And Nathan had no way out until he met Lorie, who told him about your family. You became his ticket to freedom.'

Naomi looked at Dan without seeing him. 'My granddad's money?'

Dan nodded.

'But the ring?' she spluttered.

'Is my mum's,' Dan said. 'I'm furious about that. It was a gift from my dad for their thirtieth wedding anniversary. Nathe stole it and had it made smaller for you.' Dan shook his head. 'I nearly decked him for that one. My poor mum is still cursing herself for losing it.'

'Why do you protect him from her?'

'I don't,' Dan said, frustrated. 'I protect her from him by keeping quiet. I'm in the middle while Nathan looks after number one. He has no conscience.'

Naomi didn't speak again until her tears cleared up. 'So what are we going to do?'

'I haven't worked that part out yet. I've got the house for another week if we need it that long.'

A mobile phone went off. Dan snatched it from his pocket and stared at the screen.

'Oh great, it's him,' he said.

'Nathan?'

'I need to get it. If I don't pick up, he'll wonder why.' Dan held up a warning finger. 'Don't even breathe loudly.' He sucked in some air, stood up and pressed the receive button. 'Hey, Nathe.'

Naomi could hear Nathan's familiar voice on the other end, triumphant, ecstatic. 'Hey, Dan, how's it going? Did you see the headlines this morning? Loads of journalists, bro. Like bees round honey.' He laughed. Naomi's stomach knotted up. Her mouth ran dry as the truth finally bit hard.

'I can't believe you did it,' Dan said, tone expressionless.

'Now, Danny-boy, I'm going to take that as a compliment,' Nathan said. 'I think I've just had the best week of my life. You know, Lorie's incredible. It really felt like we'd just got married, you know?'

'Did you want something?' Dan cut in, wandering away from Naomi. It wasn't far enough. Nathan's voice was still echoing round the room.

Nathan laughed again. 'Don't be like that. I'm going to be stuck out here for a few days answering questions, playing the desolate husband and ordering the seas to be searched for my missing wife. The police are showing a vague interest, but things are pretty slack around here, to be honest. They've said they'll do what they can, no promises. Anyway, I was ringing to say that Lorie's on her way back to England now. Once she's consoled the Hamiltons etcetera, she's going to pay you a visit. She's bringing your money.'

'I've told you I don't want it. I don't want to see her either.'

'Dan, come on. We couldn't have done it without you. Time to celebrate. Take your cut. Enjoy it.'

Dan didn't respond. He stared at the floor, one hand against his forehead.

'That's the spirit,' Nathan said. 'She'll be in touch. Where are you anyway?'

'On holiday.'

'Respect,' Nathan said, voice full of enthusiasm. 'UK?'

'Yes.'

'Whereabouts?'

Dan hesitated. 'Lake District.'

'Living the dream,' Nathan laughed. 'Things are going to change from now on, Danny. When she's over her jetlag, Lorie will drive out to see you, wherever you are.'

With his back to Naomi, Dan switched off the phone and tensed. When he eventually swivelled round, there were tears in his eyes and an angry red patch on his right cheekbone. And Naomi was too thunderstruck to muster even a grain of guilt.

20

Lorie spotted Henry sitting alone in the lounge watching the sports news and an analysis of the previous day's football results and league tables. Having taken Annabel to the airport at some unearthly hour, he was yawning and sipping on a mug of tea. Camilla was in the garden gathering fallen leaves in her green Wellington boots. She would mask the disaster of the previous evening by staying detached from the family and avoiding a discussion of the previous night. Even from a distance, Lorie could read Camilla's body language and knew she would be wearing her stiffest expression, keen to demonstrate that life goes on, and that in the face of difficulty, the tough get on with it.

Naomi was still upstairs. Lorie smiled for no one's benefit but her own. She could not have orchestrated it any better. She opened the door and strode into the room. Henry tensed and looked round then settled back on the sofa, relieved that it was only Lorie.

'Did Annabel get off OK?'

'Fine thanks, petal.' He glanced at his posh watch and smothered another yawn. 'She'll be in the air by now.'

'That's good,' Lorie said, sitting down. 'Look, Henry, I need to talk to you about something, but if now's not a good time I can –'

'Now's fine,' Henry cut in obligingly. He smiled, briefly, then let it drop.

Lorie clasped her fingers together. 'Well, it's a bit delicate. I really should be speaking to both of you, but after last night, I'm not sure Camilla –'

'Quite right. You know my wife. Things are best left for now. What's troubling you?'

'Two things actually,' Lorie said, dragging her hair behind her ears. 'One is about me, and one about my mum.'

'Oh?' Henry said, forehead rising, eyes opening. 'Well, age before beauty, how's your mother?'

'She's been diagnosed with cancer,' Lorie said, lowering her gaze to her lap. She twisted her fingers.

'Cancer? That's terrible.' A pause. 'I'm sorry. Will she be alright? I mean it's marvellous what they can do these days.'

'I know,' Lorie said in a small voice. 'Please don't say anything to anyone. My mum's still in denial. She thinks the doctors have got it wrong.'

'Won't breathe a word,' Henry assured her in his most sincere voice.

'So, I've been thinking that I want to spend more time with my mum, and also that I should go to university to do nursing. I know I'm twenty-six, but it's never too late is it? Applications need to be in very soon, but I won't be able to start until next September, so I'm giving you plenty of notice.'

'Oh,' Henry said, momentarily stumped for words. 'I see. No, of course it's never too late. Camilla will be devastated to lose you. You're quite irreplaceable you know.' He stopped to digest what he'd been told. Lorie waited. The TV plugged the silence. 'But you have to think of your own life and your future and I have to say you'll make a first class nurse.'

'Thank you,' Lorie said, smoothing her hair, crossing her legs. 'So here's the really delicate part, I want to take my mum on holiday, just me and her. There are a few places she's always wanted to see. After her treatment, I want to make sure she sees them. I have a policy that matures next year and I wondered if it would be possible to borrow the money in advance. I completely understand if –'

'No need to explain,' Henry said, holding up a podgy hand. 'It's the least we can do. We'd like to think after the years of service to our family that we can help you out with yours.'

Henry stood and walked to a drawer and withdrew a chequebook. 'Name your figure,' he told Lorie.

Lorie drew a silent breath. 'I'm so grateful. I can have a legal document drawn up, promising to pay the money back by September.'

'No, no,' Henry chuckled. 'Good grief how long have we known each other?' His pen was poised by now.

'Is ten thousand too much?'

Henry responded by scribbling away. He finished by penning his loopy signature at the bottom, then he prised the paper carefully from the book and walked across to where Lorie was still sitting, hands in lap. He thrust the cheque firmly in her direction stopping just short of her face. 'There you are, flower. Let's hope your mum has a lot of years left with us yet.'

'Thanks, Henry, you're so kind,' Lorie said, taking it from him.

'Not at all. Now you just let us know whenever you need time off to take her places. Family first.' Lorie offered a sweet smile. Henry returned to his position on the sofa beside his newspaper. 'Is Naomi down yet?'

'No, she's still in her room,' Lorie said.

'Bit of a shock, the engagement last night. Did it come as a shock to you?'

'Absolutely.'

Henry grunted in response.

Lorie added, 'He seems a great guy though. Naomi's sensible. I'm sure she knows what she's doing.'

Henry rubbed the back of his neck. 'Oh, I agree. It's just the suddenness that's thrown me. Still, I can't argue with his reasons. There aren't many men like him around. She could do a lot worse.' He sighed. 'I'm more concerned about Annabel at the moment, to be honest.' Henry shook his head. 'Thank goodness you'll be around for the next few months to help organise the wedding and to support Camilla.'

'I'll do everything I can to make things easier.'

Henry stood and ambled to the window to check that Camilla was still busy. 'Between you and I, we have money aside for when the girls either get married or reach twenty-five. We decided it would be whichever came first. It's hard enough becoming an adult these days with all the debt and the financial pressures. Alfie, Camilla's father, left her in excess of two million pounds when he died. His father was a jeweller, you know. Alfie took over the business when he came out of the army.' Henry turned round to look at Lorie, who reacted as though she knew nothing about this windfall of money that had had her plotting with Nathan over the past few months. 'Camilla won't touch the money for her own reasons, so we'll halve it between our girls.'

Lorie ensured she looked lost for words. 'Wow, that's incredible. A one million pound wedding present?'

'One point one to be precise. It should ensure their security, set them up with a nice home and give them a little to put on one side.'

'Do you think Nathan will accept it?'

Henry started to walk towards her, hands in pockets. 'I've been thinking about that a lot since last night. He seems very independent, a man of principle. Maybe the best thing to do is just to put a cheque in the wedding card and say nothing in advance, no fuss. I don't want him thinking we're trying to run his new life with Naomi.'

'Or give it to them before the wedding so they can make plans, maybe buy a house. Between me and you, Naomi tells me that Nathan worries about money. He's very careful with it. If you explain that it's an inheritance from her grandfather, it's impossible to refuse, don't you think?'

'Yes, you're right,' Henry said, taking his seat again. He looked relieved to be able to talk about it with someone. 'Yes, Camilla permitting, I'll give it to them before the wedding. Don't mention any of this, will you?'

'No, of course not.'

Henry nodded, satisfied. 'Camilla will probably tell you herself at some point, but especially not a word to Naomi. I'm hoping it will be a nice surprise.'

Lorie stood up. 'Who wouldn't be delighted? Look, I'd better get on, but don't worry, secret's safe. I'd hate to spoil the surprise.'

A car was coming down the drive. The noise of the engine caught Henry's attention. He looked out of the window. Nathan stopped the car and got out, carrying two large arrangements of flowers. One was white, the other red, Naomi's favourite colour. *Well done.* Camilla was eyeing him in the distance, but she didn't stop working.

'Is that Nathan?' Lorie asked, feeling her heart gathering speed. She tucked the cheque inside her trouser pocket. 'I'll let him in and call Naomi down.'

'Yes, thank you, Lorie.'

To hide her smile, Lorie turned quickly and hurried for the door. Job done. No problem.

***

Naomi woke up in her small room in the halls of residence with her scattered belongings, too many holding reminders of the weekend. She'd left her room as an eighteen-year-old student and returned as a nineteen-year-old woman with a fiancé and a nasty family rift on her shoulders. Not forgetting that for reasons unknown, a weird guy in a hoodie was lurking in the shadows.

Her head throbbed through lack of sleep. Her eyes swivelled painfully in their sockets while she scanned the room in a daze. Everything was as she'd left it. The same people played the same instruments next door. The same clothes littered the floor. The same music still sat open on her piano ready to practise. But it was like waking up in a foreign place – as though she'd been caught in a desert storm which had shifted the sands and the contours of the landscape so completely, she'd lost direction.

The uncertainty of the future was responsible for the tightness in her chest. Would Camilla and then inevitably Henry, refuse to support her in her decision to get married, and leave her stranded and alone? Would they force her to choose between Nathan and them? Would Annie disappear into a vast continent to find a new life with new friends and a new and less complicated family? Would Camilla begin a new routine of something far worse than demanding a set speaking time each week, and not call at all?

These questions and more charged through her mind like rush hour as she recalled the parting scene of the day before, her birthday. Camilla had stood – reminding Naomi of a closed shop during a still evening: lights off, shutters down – speechless and emotionless at the door as she and Nathan left. She'd muttered her quiet goodbyes as if they might never see each other again, and stood beside Henry without movement or expression as Nathan had driven away. Naomi had endured the nauseating feeling of knowing she had devastated her mother and divided her parents. She'd left without the assurance of a continued relationship, without the promise of so much as a phone call, the same way Annie had left the previous night.

It was a bright day. Naomi reached behind her and slid a curtain to one side, which immediately cast shadows over one half of the room. She held up her left hand and studied her ring. She twitched her hand and watched a display of light and colours as the sunlight caught the surface. The ring still felt heavy and invasive on her finger as it shimmered like a little star. It was stunning, beautiful. It didn't muster a smile, not even an inner one.

Since the previous day, she'd been through cycles of feeling angry that Camilla had ruined the occasion, to feeling that it was less to do with Camilla and more to do with the circumstances. It was as if the elements had colluded to bring a concoction of cruel things together, creating the perfect conditions for a storm, a storm which could have been avoided if only Tom Butterworth had not been at the party; if only he hadn't spoken to her; if only Annie had not drunk so much; if only Nathan hadn't mentioned the cost of the piano. The thoughts continued on a circuit leaving a trail of regrets.

The question that was troubling her was this: did she really want to marry Nathan, or had she got engaged to spite Tom Butterworth or to prove to Camilla that she could make her own decisions? Was there a tiny part of her that was relieved that Annie had been humiliated enough to finally face up to the past? *For a Christian, you're not very tolerant or forgiving* – Tom's words. In her head. Loud and angry. Naomi reached for her necklace and zipped the cross from side to side, toying for the first time with the idea of taking it off. The burden of being a hypocrite felt too heavy.

Her phone rang, dragging her back to her room. Naomi extended her arm slowly towards her phone and lifted it up. It was Lorie. Lorie was about the only person she could bear to speak to right now.

She pressed the button to receive the call. 'Hi.'

'Why the long voice?'

Naomi sighed. 'The weekend was a disaster, with a capital D.'

'What?' Lorie laughed. 'I was calling to congratulate you properly and say that I think you've done the right thing.'

'Really? I was half expecting a lecture about insanity and what I've done to my family, and I probably would have listened.'

'Come on, Naomi. Nathan's amazing. I mean, don't take this the wrong way, but he's sizzling hot, he's charming, and he's obviously madly in love with you. What more could you want?'

A ghost of a smile appeared on Naomi's lips before it got away. 'He is pretty special isn't he?'

'It's what you have together that's special. Your dad is fine about everything. He really likes Nathan. By the end of this week, your mum will be used to the idea too. Don't worry.'

Naomi twisted her finger into her hair and rotated. 'Did you see her face when I left? It's haunted me.'

'She was back in the garden straight after. Honestly, she's fine. She just needs a bit of space to get over the shock. Annie will be fine too once she's calmed down. She left a message this morning to say she'd arrived safely, which cheered Camilla up. Trust me, everything's going to work out fine. I'll smooth things over for you at this end.'

Naomi breathed more easily.

'Look,' Lorie continued, 'you can't keep living your life to please other people.'

'Meaning my mum.'

'Exactly. Look, I love your mum, you know I do, but I'm going to give you some advice now. I'm speaking from experience with my mum and because I know yours so well.'

'I'm listening.'

'Mums don't know how or when to stop mothering. You've got to take the lead, OK? As long as you keep acting like your mum's daughter, she'll keep treating you like a child, like she has the right to make decisions for you.'

'So what shall I do?'

'What *you* want to do. No one can make that call but you, Naomi. You're entitled to make decisions and have them respected. My humble opinion is that you should be celebrating about Nathan, not apologising for him. If I were you, I'd be showing my ring off. This has to be about you and Nathan, not you, Nathan and Camilla. Let me manage things here. I'll make sure everything works out perfectly.'

***

It had taken a few days for the bank to clear the cheque and arrange for Lorie to collect ten thousand pounds in cash, after which she handed it over to Nathan.

Nathan parked the car alone, found his way out of the dim car park and deposited his used chewing gum in a metal bin that was dirtier than it was ugly. He walked briskly, head down, along a quiet Oxford Road. He passed Manchester University on his right. The music college was across the road a little further up. His fists were screwed up in two tights balls inside the pockets of his lightweight jacket. Naomi didn't know he was going to be around. He didn't want her to see him. She was not part of his agenda today.

The weather had turned bitterly cold. Gusts of a vicious wind pushed icy fingers into Nathan's back penetrating his thin jacket and, beneath it, his thinner shirt. He barely noticed, didn't care. The object of his whole concentration lay straight ahead about twenty metres in the distance: a tank of a guy, Damien Carter, in his trademark grey jacket, propping up a lamppost, facing the opposite way. The height advantage Nathan had over him was levelled by Carter's width.

Nathan filled with loathing at the sight of him and clenched his fists more firmly, feeling the tension run the full length of his arms and into his shoulders. His teeth were crunched together. With parted lips, he breathed through his teeth, billowing out visible warm air that got lost to the cold; his eyes were focussed and narrowed. As he got closer, he released his right hand from his pocket. Exactly alongside, Nathan took hold of Carter's trunk of an arm and swung him round and carried on walking. Carter, taken by surprise at first, jerked free, then cooperated and kept up pace.

'Touch me again, I'll knock you out,' he snarled.

Nathan, not wanting to push his luck, didn't speak. They carried on walking in hostile silence.

'You'd better be leading me to a bundle of cash,' he added. 'My instructions, if not, are to break your arms.'

Nathan's step faltered, but he covered it. He glanced to his side and straight into the guy's dark eyes. They were small and glassy and dead. He looked like a shark and moved like he was king of his territory – top of the food chain. Nathan broke eye contact and said nothing.

They reached a multi-storey car park. Nathan pulled ahead and led him out of daylight and into the still gloom of level zero. They waited for the lift without speaking. When the doors opened, Nathan stepped inside. The shark followed. They took the short ride to the fifth level. The only sound was the low hum of moving machinery. When the lift jerked to a stop and the doors opened, the shark floated out, swivelling his predatory eyes, covering every angle.

When he was satisfied they were alone, he settled his eyes on Nathan. Nathan led him to his car parked close to the lift door, opened the boot and cast his eyes from left to right. Still alone. Nathan held out a small canvas rucksack.

'Ten thousand in cash.'

After a hesitation, shark guy said, 'You owe twenty.'

Nathan dumped the bag into the guy's wide front. 'I know exactly what I owe and I'll pay with interest if he'll give me more time. When I get married, I'll give him another fifteen K. That's a twenty-five per cent profit.'

'Get real.'

'I don't have the rest,' Nathan hissed, right in his face, a few spots of saliva showering him. 'I'm out of options for now.'

The shark wiped his face and glared, then squared up to Nathan. 'Maybe I'll just break one arm then. Left or right?'

'Look –'

'If I go back to Solomon with half his money, he's going to come after you big time. And it won't be my problem.'

Nathan felt faint. He suppressed the panic and made sure it didn't reach his eyes. 'I'll treble what I owe him. I'll give him another thirty K if he'll wait. No bank will give me a loan right now. Just stay away from Naomi Hamilton before my investment gets cold feet.'

'You had to know we were serious.'

'As if I didn't know that. I'm getting the money together, but my fiancée is strictly off limits. If she walks, none of us will get paid.'

'Not my problem.' Carter took hold of Nathan's right arm near the top and squeezed.

Nathan's palms were slippery. 'Tell Solomon I'll get his money as soon as I can get Naomi up the aisle, maybe before. Thirty grand.' Carter looked as unimpressed as he was unconvinced. Nathan panicked. 'Plus a car,' he said off the top of his head.

The dead eyes narrowed with mild interest, the thick eyebrows pulled low, the grip loosened a little. 'What car?'

'Rolls-Royce. Convertible. Top of the range. I'll find a way. Just tell Solomon it will be worth his while to wait. Then we part company for good. No more ties.'

'If I find out this Rolls doesn't exist –'

'I sat in it last week beside two other expensive cars. It exists.'

He nodded his head economically. 'I'll pass the message on. No guarantees.'

With that he released Nathan, turned, scanned the car park until Nathan relaxed, then turned back and bludgeoned his right fist into Nathan's middle. Nathan doubled up in agony and fought for air. Carter, without a backward glance, disappeared through a door that had a diagram of a staircase above it.

Nathan stumbled and collapsed against the car bonnet and waited until his breathing had steadied. He fell inside his car, shaking all over. When he'd recovered as much as he was going to, he dialled Naomi's number. The answering service came on. Nathan forced a light unconcerned tone and left a message.

'Hey, babe, it's me. Just to let you know, I've seen your hoodie guy and we've had a few words. Turns out he thought you were someone else. You won't be seeing him again so don't worry, OK? Catch you later. Love you lots.'

Nathan threw his phone onto the passenger seat and reached for his sunglasses to cover his eyes. Behind the shades, it was as dark as night. The engine roared to life at a flick of his wrist. Nathan clutched the steering wheel with both hands and watched the door where the predator had just disappeared. One hand caressed his stomach. 'That's right, just keep walking and don't come back,' he muttered. Nathan revved hard, reversed, then screeched away, relieved that for now, it was over.

21

Despite Lorie's fighting words plus a steady stream of comforting comments from Nathan which got Naomi through a few uneasy days, by the end of that week when Camilla had still not called, Naomi was wondering if she'd stick to the usual arrangement of calling at six on Friday evening. Or maybe it was an attempt to convince herself that normal rules still applied and that past routines would continue. It was Friday today.

For once, she was anxious for six to come. She was anticipating the call with a strange intensity that was new to her. It felt more like suspense – the desperate kind of suspense that grows like a tumour throughout a period of waiting and half-hoping, half-dreading. It wasn't anger she felt, more abandonment and an increasing lack of identity. She needed a few words of assurance or acceptance from the only person who could give it, to the point where every text message or phone call that wasn't from Camilla brought a surge of disappointment that burned a depleted supply of energy. It was Nathan's weekend with Dan. Naomi had no plans beyond being available to take Camilla's call – a call that had to, for sanity's sake, come.

For now, a dull morning was dragging its feet. Naomi was sitting in a History of Music lecture, a dot in a large cluster of first-year students taking notes. The lecturer was prowling the floor and talking animatedly about the harmony and disharmony of twentieth century music, with particular reference to Stravinsky's Rite of Spring and the stir it had caused at the debut performance in

1913. Naomi, claustrophobic in the dingy lecture studio, longed for daylight, fresh air and an end to the morning and a lecture she wished she'd never attended.

Finding it impossible to listen to the lecturer above the din of her own thoughts, she saw him lunging for the piano to demonstrate sections of music, but barely heard it. It was as if the sound was drifting in from a faraway room through a door which was opening and closing.

Suddenly, she had to get out. Just plotting her escape improved her mood. She glanced at the aisle. Three people separated her from the steps that would lead her down and then out through the door to the lecturer's right and into freedom.

She shoved her stuff roughly inside her bag, attracting a few turned heads and half-interested glances. Embarrassed, but more determined to escape now she'd made a move, she stood and fed her way slowly and apologetically through legs and books and bags. Bobbing noiselessly down the steps brought a glorious sense of release. The long walk to the door led her finally to the exit and rewarded her with a view of a window and easy deep breathing. It was in the narrow corridor a few metres beyond the door that her muscles unlocked just as her name was called from behind.

Naomi knew the voice well, but it only got as far as pulling her from a distant place as she swung round. Siobhan was walking towards her in no rush. Siobhan only had one walking speed, which never varied. It was a medium steady plod, in musical terms, *andante*. Naomi found herself waiting for Siobhan instead of Siobhan quickening her step to catch her. She'd hardly seen Siobhan since the party and Siobhan had only sent polite congratulations, via text, about the engagement. Maybe she was jealous, Naomi thought as Siobhan reached her, unsmiling, her stuff bunched up in one hand as if she'd gathered it in a rush. Naomi turned and carried on at Siobhan's pace, which didn't suit her mood.

'Can we talk?' Siobhan asked without making eye contact.

Naomi made an effort to accommodate the fact that Siobhan was incapable of reading her. A more sensitive person would have taken one look and backed off. 'Now?'

'It's a good a time as any.' *For you, maybe.* 'Shall we grab a coffee?'

'Fine.'

They switched course and went to the refectory, ordered two drinks. Naomi found the most solitary seats available and slumped down opposite Siobhan.

Naomi glanced at her watch discreetly as Siobhan settled. The time was gradually creeping towards lunchtime. It was almost eleven.

'So?' Naomi said, keen to hurry things along.

'You don't look happy,' Siobhan blurted out.

'Of course I'm happy,' Naomi countered automatically.

Siobhan sighed and held her cup to her lips and blew without sipping. 'I've something to say. It's not going to be easy.'

'OK,' Naomi said, her interest slightly stirred, not necessarily in a good way. Her guard was still up.

'I think you're making a mistake.'

Naomi felt her mouth open slightly. 'I'm sorry?' But she'd heard perfectly well.

The question only invited Siobhan to repeat herself. 'I think you're making a mistake.' It was said in the same monotone, only slightly slower.

'With Nathan?' Naomi automatically asked, sounding more calm and reasonable than she felt. Why had she asked another question when she felt like yelling at Siobhan that she'd already said too much? She could feel the bubbling onset of anger now.

'Hear me out,' she began, before pausing to weigh Naomi. 'Look, I wasn't going to say anything, but I've been thinking about it all this week, and I've decided I have to. It would be much easier for me to keep quiet and say nothing.'

Naomi paused then decided to speak her mind. 'Before you say anything else, can I ask you something?'

'OK.'

'Are you jealous of my relationship with Nathan?'

Siobhan drew breath to reply quickly, then changed her mind. She crossed her arms, leant back in her seat and pouted sulkily at Naomi. 'I suppose the answer is yes and no.'

'Yes, because?'

'Because you're one of the only friends I've ever had and because I didn't want him spoiling things or changing you or taking you away from me. And because I care about you.'

Naomi found herself locked in a glare with Siobhan. 'You don't even know Nathan. I thought friends stuck together. It's like you're in league with my mum or something.'

'That's ridiculous, so it is. It's because I'm your friend that I'm being honest with you.' She paused, lowered her tone. 'I've got a confession to make. Let me say my piece, then you can do what you want with it. Up to you.'

Naomi was hating this conversation. Hating, hating it. She resisted the impulse to stand and run. All week she'd been bracing herself for an epic battle with Camilla, and seeing as it had seemed unavoidable, she'd dreaded and wanted it in equal measures. But she was unprepared for a full-on dress rehearsal with Siobhan.

'What confession?' was the best she could manage between clenched teeth. She'd reached a point of resignation. She picked up her drink to give her something to do. Her hands trembled with fury.

Siobhan lifted her cup again and sipped. 'I was in your piano room when Nathan came in with Annabel.'

Naomi frowned over the top of her cup. This was unexpected. 'What? Why?'

'They didn't know I was there. I'd gone to the loo after dinner and seen your piano through an open door. It was curiosity that took me inside. I just wanted to look at your music room, your sacred place where it all happens, so to speak. I don't know why. No reason.'

Naomi placed her drink down and tucked her hands beneath her legs to warm them and stop them from shaking. Her back was aching through tension. So was her head. 'And?'

'And I recognised Nathan's voice outside the room. I didn't want him to catch me being nosy, so I panicked and ducked behind the closed curtains behind me.' She stopped to recall details and insert her nails inside each other. While Naomi waited, her engagement ring dug into her leg. 'The first thing I heard him say when the door closed, was, "It's good to get away from the crowds." I was sure he must be with you. I was about to step out and own up to the fact that I was there until Annabel giggled and said, "It's always quiet in here except when Naomi's home. No one ever comes in. What can I do for you?" I was standing there, frozen, so I was, trying not to breathe too loudly. I was sure one of them would hear me. I could hear Annabel's heels as she walked. They came to the piano, right near me. Someone played a few notes.'

Naomi was starting to feel queasy, but she fought it, telling herself that her uneasiness was only the memories from the fateful bonfire night, being disturbed. Siobhan's tale was sickeningly familiar. But there was a crucial difference. Nathan hadn't encouraged Annabel. Nothing had happened. Knowing the end of the story made it bearable as Naomi sat there, unmoving, with the ring pushing into her skin.

Naomi realised Siobhan had gone silent. 'I already know about all this,' she said.

'From who?'

'Bits from Annabel, the rest from Nathan,' Naomi said, resenting the disturbance of painful private memories.

'Well as a witness, I'm telling you my version of events. OK?'

It wasn't OK, but Naomi found herself nodding and locking her fingers together beneath her backside.

Siobhan put her drink down. 'OK, so Nathan said, "who'd have thought a piano could cost forty-five grand." Annabel laughed and asked him where he'd got that crap from – that the piano was only fifteen grand. He told her he'd got it from you. That he was sure he was right. There was a bit of a silence. I thought they'd heard me, but then I heard the piano lid going down and Annabel standing up and walking away. I moved sideways so I could see through a tiny gap in the curtains. Annabel looked at him over her shoulder with her come-on eyes and said something like, "I'm sure you didn't ask me in here to talk about pianos".'

Siobhan paused to check on Naomi and ask if she was OK.

'I know that nothing happened, Siobhan, so you might as well finish your story.'

'OK, well Nathan appeared in front of her, very close, bodies almost touching. He told her she was drunk. She laughed and put her arms around his neck and said she knew very well what she was doing. Nathan touched her waist at the sides and slid his hands all the way up to her arms. He waited until her head had dropped to one side and she was moving in to kiss him, I swear she was. Then he unpeeled her arms from around him and told her he was with you.'

Naomi was aware of the drumming inside her chest. The need to get away was overpowering. 'Is that it?' she asked quietly as if she was in full control and nothing Siobhan was saying was having an impact.

'Pretty much, except Annabel swore at him. She glared at him in disbelief. He didn't apologise. I swear he was struggling not to smile. He calmly turned his back on her and walked out and closed the door. Annabel burst into tears, then dried her eyes and rushed after him in a rage.'

Naomi consciously wiped her face of all expression. Sad as it was, it turned out that Siobhan was a trouble-causer who would use an opportunity like this to twist the truth and make Nathan look bad. Naomi gave herself permission to resent Annie occasionally, but she felt like killing anyone else who found fault. Naomi took in Siobhan's wide hair resting on her shoulders and decided that she wasn't a good friend after all.

'Say something,' Siobhan said, appealing to Naomi through her piggy little eyes that barely held any colour.

Naomi couldn't look into them for a second longer. 'I'm going to my room. Please don't follow me.'

'OK.' Siobhan dropped her gaze and said nothing more. Naomi collected her bag and stood up. Her legs felt heavy. Forcing herself to move, she made it out of the college, along the pavement, into the reception area and up the lift to the sixth floor and into her room without clocking a single detail of the journey.

***

After a long stretch of glaring at a bare wall from her bed and feeling time crawling by, Naomi twisted her head in search of her phone. She picked it up. Two-forty.

'Stuff it, they're my parents,' she muttered out loud. 'I have a right to ring them if I want to.'

Tough words, but did she, really? was the thought that nagged her while she flicked through her mobile phonebook searching for Camilla's number. The easier option was to ring Henry. Except it wasn't Henry's voice she needed to hear. She wondered how she'd begin the conversation and felt the gulf that divided her from her parents. Her dependency on them gave them a kind of power that left her exposed and vulnerable. When she'd most needed their support, they'd crushed her simply by doing nothing at all. How could an absence of words be so cruel? She clutched her phone to her chest and lay back on her pillow again. A few frustrated tears slid down the side of her head and settled inside her ears. She mopped them up with her sleeves and started to think hard.

The issue ran much deeper than dependency. Earning positive words from Camilla had become a quest. She couldn't separate her hours of music practise and school revision from the hope that Camilla would notice. Her pathetic life had been about surviving off rations of hard-to-come-by praise. It had landed her in a music college. *Do I even want to be here?*

The worst thing was realising that most parents of her friends were more like attentive servants. There was a constant flow of money and phone calls that asked the tireless question: are you alright? For Naomi, the parent-child differences had been marked like a netball court her whole life. She must not step over this or that line. She must not enter a forbidden part of the court that her position didn't allow. She must not break rules. Or what? Annie had always answered that question: be labelled a huge disappointment.

Naomi scrolled to the top of her address book to Annabel's number. Seeing her name pricked more tears. It had taken this moment to understand that Annie wasn't rebellious, she just had the courage to be herself. Naomi could see it suddenly and clearly. She needed to speak to Annabel. Now. Maybe they could be a team too. When the phone started ringing, she sensed Annie a breath away and felt elated.

Annabel answered frostily and told her it was quarter to eleven at night, then asked her what she wanted. Naomi delivered her little speech without a break and told Annabel she loved her and missed her. Annabel began to sob. Naomi allowed the kind of pause that seemed to bind them together and make everything better. When Annabel was able to speak, she told Naomi she loved her too.

'Look, I'm sorry about the piano.' Naomi was crying now too.

'I don't give a toss about the piano. But because I care about you, I'm telling you that you've got to get that ring off your finger and dump that loser who's conned you into getting engaged. I'm telling you he's no good.'

Naomi closed her eyes, determined to stay calm. 'Annie, you're bound to feel angry with Nathan –'

'I'm angry because he's managed to get engaged to my sister when he doesn't deserve her.'

'You don't know him. If you knew –'

'Naomi, wake up. I'm begging you.' Annie's voice had turned suddenly urgent. 'I know guys. I know enough about him to know that he's no good. He'll hurt you really badly if you don't end this now.'

Naomi wiped her tears and took the phone away from

her ear and stared at it. Annabel's voice flowed from it, faintly.

'Naomi, are you still there? Can you hear me?'

Naomi extended her forefinger slowly and disconnected her twin and threw her phone across the bed.

22

Lorie could feel her phone vibrating against her leg from deep inside the pocket of her jeans. It was an impossible time to take a call or even find out who it was. She turned to Nathan and told him her phone was ringing. He shrugged and smiled and twisted his neck to kiss her. She met his lips. It was a strain when they were both jammed inside a carriage of the most famous roller coaster in the country. Lorie traced the red track to the highest peak where the other train was tipping over the sixty-two metre drop and would plummet at seventy plus miles an hour. Screaming drowned the roar of the train.

'You can see why they called it The Big One,' Lorie said, stomach fluttering.

'Wait till you see the view from the top.'

'I'm going to shut my eyes.'

Nathan laughed. 'Don't you dare.'

The train lunged forward. The track was more than a mile long. Nathan took her nearest hand. She glanced at him, giggling like a kid and tossed her windswept hair behind her with her free hand.

In the last moments before the big drop, Lorie watched the sea and the dying sun on the horizon which spread an apricot light over a small patch of dark water. The moon was out too, in its thinnest form, looking like a glowing smile that had been painted into the night sky by a child. Darkness was gathering, bringing the magic of Blackpool at dusk during autumn, the season of the illuminations.

The second before the train plummeted, leaving her stomach behind, Lorie wished she could freeze the moment and properly take in what she'd had to absorb in a flash. The Golden Mile stretching from the South Pier to the North, blazing with a million colourful dancing bulbs; dressed-up trams ferrying countless bodies up and down the ancient tracks; the Tower in all its glitzed-up splendour in the distance; red lasers slicing the skies.

After a mad couple of minutes, the train screeched to a stop and they tumbled out of the carriage and staggered away arm in arm.

'Awesome,' Lorie said, sticking her hand in Nathan's back pocket.

Nathan squeezed her shoulder and laughed. 'Want another go?'

Lorie nodded. They weaved their way through moving bodies and found the end of the snaking queue.

Getting away from home for the weekend meant complete freedom. Lorie could dissolve into crowds and not have to worry about knowing anybody. Almost. There was always a chance that probability would throw up a freak meeting with someone she knew. Actually, the risk almost added to the buzz of being in conspiracy with a guy she couldn't stop watching. She never got tired of looking at his face and studying every wondrous part of it. Being so helplessly in love with him made her lightheaded sometimes.

After a weekend with Nathan, she felt like Cinderella after the ball. She'd float into work in a daze, knowing she couldn't afford a slip. She must be as steady and reliable as the time on Henry's Rolex watch. It must be as if Nathan Stone hadn't strolled into her life and flipped her world.

So anonymity was a relief. On alternate weekends, they escaped to some getaway under the pretext of Nathan caring for his sick brother, a clever plan which meant that Naomi, having sacrificed Nathan to a nobler cause, knew not to call. It was precious time together that moved too quickly and came around too slowly. It was time spent in a frenzied haze of complete happiness; a time when they were aware only of each other, where they lived out fantasies and plotted moves and sketched out their future together.

It was Nathan who reminded Lorie she'd missed a call as he stood behind her in the queue, both arms wound tightly around her neck, chin resting on the top of her head as he breathed warm air on her. Lorie took her phone from her pocket and found the call was from Naomi. She dialled to receive her voicemail without telling Nathan, who was lifting her hair from one side of her neck and making gentle contact with his lips.

By the end of Naomi's message, which Lorie struggled to hear word-for-word, she'd gathered enough to know there was a problem. She tensed. Nathan noticed. He released his grip on her, allowing her room to move. She did an about-turn in his arms until she was facing him. He fenced the sides of her face with his strong hands.

'Hey babe, what's wrong?'

'Not good. Your fiancée wants me to spend the weekend with her because, well something about Annie. Because you're away with Dan, she needs me to call her back asap. All I know is she's upset.'

'No,' Nathan yelled, not in answer, but as if he was letting go of an anguished cry he couldn't hold in. He released Lorie's face and thumped his head with the palm of one hand and left it there. 'Why does she have to be so needy?'

Lorie held her voice down and suggested he did the same. 'Because we've engineered it that way so that she'll want to cling to you for security.'

Nathan spun away from Lorie, agitated. 'Ignore her.

What can she do about it?'

'We can't ignore her. It isn't me who should be comforting her, it's you. You're the one she really wants.'

'You want me to call her?' he asked, appalled.

Lorie sighed. A bubble had burst. The euphoria was leaking away and Naomi was to blame. 'It's not what I want that matters. It's what has to be done. Let's go somewhere quieter.'

Nathan snatched her hand and tugged her along as he found a route through the crowds. They made their way to a quiet hotel on a back street where they were staying on the second floor in room fifteen. The hotel reception was dead, apart from a short bloke who stood by the desk waiting for attention. He kept eyeing his watch every few seconds as if rehearsing the point he intended to make when someone showed up. From here, there was no sense of the thousands of bodies that milled around in the carnival atmosphere not far away. They dropped onto the bed and looked at each other and listened to the silence of the small room.

'So, now what?' Nathan said, eyeing her seriously.

Lorie shrugged. 'We need to rethink. Something has happened with Annie. Naomi's upset. As far as I know, Camilla hasn't spoken to her since the engagement last weekend. She's an immature kid with a desperate need to feel accepted by her parents. We had to expect a few waves. She's feeling the heat.'

'My heart bleeds.'

Lorie took one of his hands and played with his fingers. 'One of us is going to have to go back.'

'What? No,' Nathan said firmly. 'This is our time.'

'Not yet it isn't,' Lorie said, knowing someone had to be patient and reasonable. She felt like being neither. 'We knew things might get sticky. If she's not convinced that you're besotted with her, why should she risk losing her family to marry you? This is a job, Nathan. There are going to be sacrifices.'

'Hell,' he hissed, withdrawing his hand from hers and throwing himself backwards until he was sprawled out, arms above his head, eyes pointing upward. 'Why can't she talk to her friends? Isn't that what girls do?'

Lorie didn't respond except to smooth her hair. She stood up and checked herself in the mirror and watched herself talk. 'This is what we're going to do. I'll ring her now and tell her I'm away with Simon for the weekend. We'll go out. Eat. Jump on a tram. Have some fun. Later, you can call her and say Dan's doing well and ask her how she is. She'll tell you she's feeling awful. You'll sympathise and tell her she's very important to you – more so than Dan – and you'll come to the rescue by promising to be back in the morning so you can deal with the problems together. She'll try to be brave. You'll insist on being there.' Lorie turned her back on herself to look at Nathan, who was still staring blankly at the ceiling as if he was struggling to accept some terrible news. 'Got it?'

He didn't look at her. 'What if I don't want to?'

'What's that got to do with it?'

Nathan emptied his lungs and half sat up, resting his weight on his elbows, lips pouted irresistibly. Lorie couldn't stay away. She dropped down beside him, half amused.

'We've still got tonight,' she said. 'Why waste it on tomorrow's problems?'

Nathan focussed his eyes on hers and his face softened.

'It isn't enough.'

'It'll have to be. You've got some serious work to do. Annie's pretty much out of the picture, but it's time you turned the charm on with Camilla before she decides you're not having her father's money.'

'She wouldn't!'

Lorie raised her eyebrows in response.

Nathan almost smiled. 'She takes the bait so easily. Winding her up is amazing fun.'

'I can think of better. You'll be thanking me once we have more than a million in the bank, plus a windfall of insurance money and no more worries. Persuade her you're worth her inheritance or all this will be for nothing.'

Nathan fully sat up now. 'That sounded like an order.'

'It was. From now on, you don't put a foot wrong around her, you hear me? When she tells me I've got a wedding to plan, I'll know she's accepted it. She hasn't mentioned it once all week.'

Nathan took her face in one hand. 'I'm going to take that as a challenge.'

'Good.'

'I'm going to break the ice-queen's shell.'

'Good.'

'Why are we talking about Camilla?'

'Good question,' Lorie whispered, closing her eyes in anticipation of Nathan's lips. He was drawing closer. 'I hate the thought of you kissing her. Do you enjoy it, Nathan?'

She could feel his breath now. Because he didn't answer immediately, Lorie opened her eyes. He hovered, very close, the hint of a smile on his lips.

'You've asked me that a hundred times.'

'And you've never answered it once.'

***

Camilla was in the garden because she felt best when she was using energy and because she enjoyed being there, or so she kept telling herself despite a firm awareness that she was acutely miserable, and cross, and had been dodging outside every day to be out of Henry's way.

His acceptance of Naomi's engagement and his insistence that Camilla should do the same, meant that every time she looked at him she found it impossible not to feel maddened by his patronising little smiles and his infuriating attempts to make her feel better, all of which were successfully having the opposite effect. She was tired of him patting the space next to himself on the sofa as if she'd be grateful to drop into it and offload her heart's weight into his ear. And if he offered to make her one more cup of tea!

She didn't want to offload, at least not to a man who was still whistling and caring for his cars and talking about golf at a time of crisis. A man who couldn't see that Naomi getting engaged to a man she'd known for weeks required a husband/wife emergency conference followed by strategy to bring the girl to her senses and kick the imposter out of the family before he took root. If that wasn't enough, there was Annabel. Camilla sighed loudly, knowing no one would hear her.

Whenever she thought of Annabel, she was filled with a gnawing emptiness that stole her appetite and made her feel nauseous. It only lifted when she distracted herself with other things and closed the door on Annabel, which she managed only in small chunks every day. She'd tried to call her, three times. Three times she'd got a pre-recorded message in Annabel's friendliest voice, inviting her to leave a message, promising to return the call. So she'd left three messages, asking Annabel to reply. Each one had been ignored.

Her life couldn't have crumbled more sensationally or in a shorter space of time. Naomi was bound to defend her position by standing by Nathan, so why bother calling her? Annabel's refusal even to talk to her had been enough to put her off ringing Naomi. Naomi's situation could never be win-win. There was no solution or compromise.

All Camilla could feel whenever she thought of . . . *him*, was raw anger that fired her to the point where she was constantly on the verge of ripping into Henry for doing nothing more than grinning at her. *He* was affecting her marriage, not least because he'd wormed his way into Henry's good books. The only way Camilla could hold back her rage was by putting on a jumbled assortment of hideous clothes and escaping to the garden where the trees seemed to have more sense and compassion than Henry, and where she could violently channel her energy into stabbing and raking and digging.

Having done all of the above for a couple of hours, and finding herself too warm despite a chilly day, Camilla was feeling calmer and was feeding the chickens and checking for fresh eggs. A car eased down the driveway and had her craning her neck to see who was daring to visit.

As far as she knew, they weren't expecting anyone. Camilla's face was set hard against a medium-strength breeze that carried the kind of drizzle that coated everything in a damp film. Her hair must be awful. She became aware of her ugly cardigan, her grubby nails and her green wellies caked in filth. A silver car slipped past the big oak with the tree-house, and past her row of neatly trimmed laurel bushes. All her suppressed feelings resurfaced when she realised it was *him* with Naomi.

From a distance, she watched as they got out of the car, spotted her, waved – or at least *he* did – and sauntered arm in arm to the front door. Henry had already opened the door. He hugged Naomi, shook Nathan's hand and beckoned for Camilla to join them as if the prodigal son had returned and the fatted calf needed slaughtering. They disappeared inside the house and closed the door, leaving Camilla to imagine what was going on inside.

For the first time in a long time, Camilla had an urge to turn her back on her life and run. Without even an outline of a plan, she had an impulse to throw down her gardening gloves, turn her back on the house and the people in it and wander irresponsibly through the front gate.

Even as the idea was taking shape and Camilla was imagining herself standing at the bus stop a couple of hundred metres away and using the few coins that had been jangling around in her pocket all afternoon, she was heading for the wet room at the back of the house. She'd take a rare shower in there and delay having to face Nathan Stone.

The hot shower did nothing to clear her head or arrange the thoughts inside it. Camilla towelled herself almost dry, put on a bath robe, slipped quietly to her room via the back staircase, and dressed. She combed her hair, stepped into some low-heeled shoes and walked carefully down the stairs, trying to soften her expression.

Two minutes later, Camilla found herself alone in Naomi's piano room with Nathan Stone. Had she agreed to speak to him privately? It was more a case of being so stunned by his request, she couldn't find an objection. From there he'd taken her silence as agreement and ushered her out of the room. And here she was with him now, cross with Henry for allowing it.

When he turned and looked at her and said nothing, Camilla said, 'I'm certain I have nothing to say to you.'

'I understand,' Nathan said, at a distance.

'Do you?' Camilla said, without conviction.

Nathan wandered over to the window and looked over the garden. Eventually he turned to face her from the other side of the room. 'I only want to apologise,' he said.

'Again?' Camilla stood tall and refused to drop her gaze.

'I'd just like a chance to make my position clear. OK?'

Camilla said nothing, so Nathan went on.

'I know it seems like we're rushing into a very serious part of life without –'

'We? Did you propose to each other simultaneously, or did one propose to the other?'

Nathan offered a tight smile. 'I proposed to Naomi. Look, I can see things from your point of view. If Naomi was my daughter, I'd be worried too.'

Camilla glared at him. 'Do you have any children?'

'Of course not.'

'Then don't tell me you understand my point of view.'

'Fair enough.' Nathan paused. 'Can I explain *my* viewpoint then? I'd really like things to be better between us.' He took a few steps forward.

Camilla didn't budge. She was aware of her breathing and was consciously taking in controlled amounts of air. 'I've heard all about your reasons. Henry's told me this week several times. It makes less sense to me each time.'

For the first time, Nathan looked puzzled. 'Why's that? Can't you see that I'm just trying to respect Naomi and wait until after we're married –'

'What I'm having trouble with, Nathaniel,' Camilla jumped in, voice sharp, 'is that you seem not to understand the meaning of respect. You would have respected her far more by not asking her to marry you at all. Put a different way, you could have accepted her decision to wait until marriage, without proposing. Her decision to wait doesn't mean you have to marry her. It doesn't mean you're right for her either.'

'It doesn't mean I'm not. I love Naomi.'

'So you keep saying.'

'I've been brought up to believe that love is the most important thing.'

'Really? And somehow you gleaned this wonderful lesson from a mother you don't speak to and who ignores your brother and who knows nothing about your relationship with my daughter?'

Nathan drew a few deep breaths. 'That's very personal,' he said, fighting to keep calm.

'But accurate,' she said.

'Actually,' Nathan replied, 'I have talked to my mum about Naomi and about our engagement. I've kept it from Naomi because I don't want to upset her. My mum's response wasn't good.'

'Well that's a relief.'

He paused to sigh. 'Like I said, the relationship between me and my parents is strained and it causes me a lot of distress. I'm sorry if that spills out defensively sometimes like it did at the party. Basically, they don't want to be involved in the wedding.'

Camilla dropped her head. 'Well, if there is going to be a wedding, that isn't an option, I'm afraid.'

Silence. Camilla glanced up. Nathan's eyebrows had sunk. 'What do you mean?'

'They *are* involved whether they like it or not. I need to contact your mother and speak to her.'

'She won't want to speak to you.'

'Let me worry about that.' Camilla marched over to a small lamp table with a single drawer at the top and withdrew an A5 sized sheet of paper and a new pencil. 'Can you write down her phone number please?'

'That's not a good idea.' Nathan paced forward a couple of steps but made no attempt to take the paper and pencil. 'Look, I want to make things right with them and I want them to meet Naomi, but they need some time. How about e-mailing her?'

'For something this important?' Camilla asked. 'No. An e-mail is not appropriate.'

'Well how about I give you the address and you can write to her? My mum needs time to digest things.'

'So do I, but no one considers that.' Camilla sunk into thought while Nathan stood motionless. 'Fine. I'll write to your mother. In the meantime, I won't let your relationship with Naomi come between mine with her.'

Nathan took the pencil and paper, finally. 'That's good. She hates being distanced from you. It'd be great for you two to understand each other better.'

'Don't patronise me.'

'Honestly, I wasn't trying to.' Nathan began scribbling while Camilla waited in silence. She glared at the crown of his head and had an unhelpful urge to whack him with the nearest lamp. He handed her an address with a smile. Camilla studied it so she didn't have to look at him. 'Thanks for listening to me,' he continued in a polite tone. 'I was hoping we could make a fresh start.'

Camilla looked up and glared. 'Whereas I've been hoping for a clean break.'

Nathan's smile faded, but he held his tongue. 'What can I do to prove to you that I only want the best for Naomi?'

Camilla didn't hesitate. 'Walk away.'

'I'm afraid I can't do that.'

She eyed him icily, willing him to read all the things she'd thought, but hadn't said. 'That's what I'm afraid of too.'

23

CAPTIVITY

For a few days Naomi had been in a daze and Dan had continued to keep her alive by patiently feeding her, bringing her drinks, insisting she go to bed even if sleep was hard to find, keeping her separate from a world that believed she'd left it.

The truth and reality of her new life was impossible to ignore or accept. For three days, the news told some part of the fairytale turned tragedy. She learned how, after a week alone with Nathan in the beautiful deserted beach villa they'd chosen and booked together, they'd got on a cruise ship.

Nathan, interviewed shortly after the 'accident' had spoken between sobs about how, on the late evening of the first night, Naomi had felt lightheaded and unwell and had left the bar area and gone to the deck for air. The couple they'd been speaking to in the bar had been interviewed and had told the same tale, how Naomi had sat beside Nathan, head low, shades to cover her eyes, pale and subdued. The man had suggested she might have sunstroke or food poisoning. Naomi had stood and said air was all she needed. Nathan had offered to follow. She'd refused and told him she wouldn't be long.

One of the eyewitnesses, a woman with a French accent, told how she'd seen a young woman leaning against the back end of the ship, alone, long dark hair lifted by a stern breeze. She was wearing a distinctive yellow dress, she remembered, that tied in a knot behind her neck with two silky ribbons that hung down her bare back. The girl had stepped out of her high-heeled sandals which were abandoned on the deck.

A different woman in a polka dot top told how she'd been in her cabin and had heard a scream around eleven-thirty at night. She went out onto the deck and discovered a pair of strappy black sandals. She'd been unable to find out who they belonged to, until Nathan, frantically looking for Naomi, had found the woman holding Naomi's shoes. He'd scanned every inch of the ship and couldn't find her. By the time the captain was informed, there was no way of knowing what time she'd disappeared. It was only clear she was no longer there.

After three days of following the story and the desperate attempts to search for her, and watching Nathan's Oscar-winning performances as he climbed aboard boats and helicopters to accompany the rescue party, the journalist covering the story announced, sadly, that Naomi was presumed dead and that there was little hope of ever finding the body. Naomi, a poor swimmer, was afraid of deep water, she'd reported. Naomi could only imagine how her family was feeling having to listen to it all.

The last report showed a different reporter standing outside the Royal Northern near the start of the new term. Naomi Stone, she'd said, should have been starting here as a second year student. The words 'live from Manchester' were at the top left of the screen. The camera had shifted to the left. Siobhan was standing with the reporter in her favourite blue jumper, her big hair draped over her head and shoulders like a small animal taking a nap. She wept helplessly throughout the interview and could only repeat over and over that Naomi was the best friend she'd ever had. That was the final report before the story rested. Since then, Naomi had become withdrawn. She was sitting on the sofa studying the knots in the wood of the floor when Dan came in from the kitchen carrying a glass of juice.

'We have to talk,' he said in a gentle tone, setting the juice down in front of her.

Naomi's eyes moved to the blank TV screen which reflected the room. 'What about?'

'The thing we've been avoiding. Lorie is coming tomorrow and we need a watertight plan. Where you'll go, what you'll do, how you'll know when to come back. Maybe I should get you a mobile phone. You'll have to leave the house while she's here. And you can't be seen. Agreed?' When Naomi didn't reply, Dan added, 'I'm sorry to have to talk about this when you're feeling so bad.'

Naomi sat up straight. 'I haven't been avoiding it.'

'What?'

'Nathan and Lorie. I've thought of nothing else since I found out.'

Dan looked puzzled. 'And?'

'It's time they faced up.'

'Naomi, I agree, but think about this. Nathan will say you faked the death together for insurance money. No one can prove Lorie was involved, at least not quickly. There's no proof of the gang's involvement because no one's been hurt. All the police will know is that you're alive when you're supposed to be dead. And if certain people get hold of that information, all hell could break loose. I've thought about this endlessly and there's no solution that doesn't carry horrible risks.'

Naomi looked at Dan. He looked at her. 'So let's take a risk. When she comes here, we fasten her up and call the police.'

Dan's face tightened. 'And say what? Even if she's arrested, she'll be allowed to make at least one call. One call is all she needs to set a ball rolling that won't stop until you're back in that grave and me with you.'

Naomi dropped her head. 'The two people I most trusted . . . '

'Are in fact psychopaths,' Dan finished. He squeezed her hand then withdrew.

'Don't let her come here then. We need more thinking time.'

Dan's voice was patient, soft. 'It's not as simple as that. If I put her off it looks like I've got something to hide. And she'll come anyway.'

'I don't want to see her, Dan.'

'I'll make sure you don't.'

Naomi shook her head. 'I've been meaning to ask, who was the guy at the cemetery?'

Dan put his thumb nail between his teeth. 'I didn't even know his name. He was a professional hit man. Someone Vincent Solomon knew. Nathan paid him to find a fool-proof way to dispose of you and make sure you were dead. Apparently a freshly dug grave in a cemetery was the ideal place. He's done it before. An old guy was buried the day before the wedding. The grave was full, would never need to be opened again. Don't ask me how they find out all this stuff.'

Naomi shivered. 'If he was a professional, why did it fail?'

Dan sighed. 'Because Nathan made a big mistake – telling the guy that I'd pull the trigger. I distracted him, told him to check we were alone then fired two shots into the soil. The gun kicked back so hard, it hit your head. It took me by surprise. I've never handled one before. Anyway, I covered you in blood and pretended to wretch. He was too busy ogling your body to bother checking your head.'

'How sick is that?'

'Tell me about it.'

Naomi swallowed. 'Whose blood?'

Dan sighed. 'Mine. I had it in a blood bag ready to spill. The drug I gave you slowed your pulse so it would be hard to detect if he checked. He didn't. Some pro.'

'I can't believe you did all that for me.'

'I was so scared of him not leaving. He wanted to . . . touch you, even after he thought you were dead. He was an animal. I had to threaten him with the gun. I kept telling him to take the rings, that I'd finish the job. I'd buried you up to the neck before he left. Then I had to pull you out, leave a neat job and carry you to the car. Getting you through the railings took ages. He got the rings back to Nathan quickly, for Lorie.'

Naomi dropped her head. 'Why didn't they just get married and leave me out of it?'

'You know why. Money. Greed. Nathan was in a financial mess and involved with a dangerous bunch who owned him, big time. Lorie provided the answer. They constructed a plan that made them look good to the gang, gave them some credibility. To each other, it was an elaborate game. Their secret. They fed off each other. I love Nathe, but he's sick. He's incapable of feeling guilt or remorse.' Dan shook his head. 'My poor mum has no idea what he's capable of or who he's been involved with. She thinks he's wonderful, that we share a nice little flat together and watch TV in the evenings. Her and my dad pay the rent.'

'I thought he shared with Guy.'

'He's a compulsive liar.'

'Couldn't you have talked some sense into him?'

'Don't you think I tried?' Dan asked, remaining patient. 'For months, all I knew was that he'd marry you then divorce you after a short time and make money. I never knew the plan was to kill you until . . .'

Naomi's heart started to pound. 'Until?'

'A week before the wedding.' Naomi couldn't reply. 'After I'd objected as strongly as I could and battled with my conscience about not calling the police – they'd have denied it, of course, and there was no evidence. I didn't even know who was supposed to be killing you. I decided that the only thing I could do was get involved and stop it happening. Nathan had to deliver what he'd promised them.'

'Me, dead?'

'No.' Dan closed his eyes, opened them, blinked a few times. 'The rest of the money he owed and your dad's car. Nathan wanted freedom. He wanted to cut ties with them for ever. Paying his gambling debt was nowhere near enough. He had to buy his way out. That cost your dad's Rolls Royce, sold online before the wedding for three hundred grand to a guy in the south-east, no questions asked. Lorie was the last in the wedding car, wasn't she?'

'What? No, my mum was last out of the house.'

Dan waited.

'Oh, no, Lorie had forgotten her flowers,' she went on, 'so she ran back in the house to get them.'

'And at the same time,' Dan continued, 'she unlocked the back door, leaving it clear for a guy called Noel Beresford to go into the house while you were all out for the day, and help himself to the spare keys your dad has to the garage and his car. Lorie gave them the alarm code number and copies of the car documents. Your dad will have concluded he couldn't have switched the alarm on that night. All they had to do was wait until your dad brought the car home, then they could help themselves. The cleaner got the blame for leaving the house open and the light off. She got the sack the next day. The insurance company won't pay out because there was no break in.'

Naomi was boiling with anger.

Dan finished. 'The car was taken at about midnight. By the early hours, it would have been down south and your dad would have woken up to his car gone without a trace.'

'Unbelievable.'

'It was spotted by a traffic policeman, travelling at nearly a hundred and thirty miles an hours down the M1. He caught the registration number, but not the car. The police turned up at your parents' house the following morning. That was the first your mum and dad knew about the car. The police will never trace the people who took it, or pin it on Nathan and Lorie. Your dad struggled to get the police to even take it seriously enough. They've got better things to do than chase stolen cars, even expensive ones. And now you're dead to them, the car doesn't matter at all. All part of the plan.'

Naomi was struggling to take it in. 'How do you know all this?'

'Lorie's been in touch with your parents. Nathan's kept me informed. He thought the whole thing was hilarious. He was on a high because the sale of that car meant freedom for him from those lunatics. Everything had gone smoothly. The last thing was to fake your death, which he thinks has been successful too.'

'How could anyone conceive of all that?'

Dan shrugged his shoulders. 'I've told you, he's not right up here.' Dan tapped the side of his head. 'Nathan's incredibly intelligent and he likes a challenge. He likes to mess with people's heads. The more intricate the game, the better. I've protected my parents from him, but he has a talent for finding trouble. I've tried so hard to protect Nathan from screwing up. And I couldn't do it, not since he got involved with that lot, and gambling.' Dan's voice was failing. There were tears in his eyes.

Naomi softened her voice for Dan's sake. 'He told me it was you who got involved with a bad crowd.'

Dan, in tears, shook his head.

'Nathan deserves what's coming to him. And so does she,' Naomi continued, finding she couldn't utter Lorie's name.

'Too right.' Dan wiped his eyes angrily. It occurred to Naomi to put her arms around Dan just as they both tuned in to a car crunching across the gravel outside. 'Stay here.' Dan jumped to his feet. 'Whoever it is, I'll get rid of them.'

He vanished from the room and was back in seconds.

'You need to hide, now,' he hissed urgently.

Naomi's legs were weak as she got to her feet. Her vision vanished then came back. 'Hide where? Who is it?'

Dan's hands were shaking. 'The pantry? No, the upstairs needs checking for traces of you.' Dan was tugging on her arm with no real sense of where he wanted her to go. Naomi jerked free. 'Go in the bedroom and lock the door.'

'Dan, who is it?' Naomi asked as loudly as she dared.

Dan froze for a moment. His face was without colour. 'It's Lorie.'

Naomi's eyes narrowed. 'We have the advantage here, Dan.'

'But we don't know how to use it.'

A car door slammed outside. Naomi didn't move. 'I'm not hiding from her.'

Dan's eyes opened wide. 'Naomi, I'm begging you.'

***

The flight had been a blur. Annabel had talked to no one, looked no one in the eye. She'd refused the food and drink she'd been offered and couldn't account for the passing of a lot of tortured hours. She knew she hadn't slept. She knew her back and neck ached from tension.

Since Henry had rung to tell her of Naomi's death and tearfully call her home, the passing of time had mysteriously changed. She'd entered an existence parallel to the one she'd always known – a place where she felt suddenly detached and invisible, where thought and movement happened only in slow motion and sleep never came; where she could watch everyone else scurrying around like insects and feel certain that whatever they were doing didn't matter half as much as they thought.

After sobbing and screaming and hurling questions at her lonely room until she'd emptied, Annabel had gone still and wondered if she'd ever move or speak or eat again. The thought of Naomi being claimed and buried in some unknowable part of a vast ocean, plagued her. She'd never escape the horror of it. Annabel lay stiff and disabled, thoughts adrift, mind lost at sea, limbs incapable of response. When her brain had agreed to function enough to rouse her muscles, she'd switched on her laptop, booked the first flight to Manchester and slung some stuff wearily into her two suitcases. Stunned by shock, the only thing she'd consciously armed herself with, was her passport.

She'd written a note for the couple who'd rented her a room for the past year and who were away on business, then packed up her old life and robotically taken a taxi to Tokyo airport without saying goodbye to anyone.

The descent registered when her ears began to hurt and she was forced to yawn for relief. The greyness of north-west England was smothering the plane like a thick woollen blanket. Rain was slopping heavily against the windows. Having noticed that much, she slipped back into a trance and imagined what it might be like when she saw Camilla. The plane, struggling through dense cloud, was juddering violently and shook the unhappy thought away. More depressed by the thought of living than dying, Annabel was calm, or numb. She visualised the plane being pelted by lightning, then nose-diving and plummeting to the ground through stormy clouds and erupting into unquenchable flames. If only.

She didn't look out of the window or wonder how she felt about being back in England. She knew it didn't matter anymore. Whichever continent was beneath her feet wouldn't relieve the heaviness that slurred her footsteps or reduce the pressure in her chest that was worse to bear than any physical pain. She just wanted to be home now, back to familiarity and all the things she'd grown to think were dull and unsophisticated. Back to the only two people who'd understand.

Henry met her at the airport alone, and gathered her into his arms. Did this mean Camilla resented that of the two girls, Annabel was the one left? Did this mean she couldn't look at her? Tears she'd held on to for sixteen hours, broke out. Henry joined in. They stood at the busy meeting point, sandwiched between Annabel's upright cases, sobbing into each other's shoulders, unable to move. It was only when someone interrupted, apologised and asked if Annabel was Naomi's twin and if he might ask a couple of questions that Henry snatched hold of the cases and hurried Annabel to the car.

Camilla was peering out of the front window from the downstairs study when the car came to a stop at the front of the house. It was dark by now and moonless and starless. Annabel found she couldn't move. Camilla stumbled outside and made her way in front of the car to Annabel's side and opened the door. Annabel, managing to stand, fell into Camilla's open arms. Exhaustion overcame her during the silent moments where Camilla caressed her back and allowed her to cry without expecting her to be strong.

Camilla eventually led her to the warmth and light of the house. As they passed through the front door together, Annabel muttered some apology for past behaviour. Camilla did the same, adding that it didn't matter, that nothing mattered anymore except that she was safely home.

Camilla offered to put the kettle on and Annabel got stuck beside the small hall table that held a potted orchid and a burning lamp. She stared at the painting above it. She didn't notice herself. She examined Naomi to her left, hair parted in the middle without a fringe and falling loosely, unblemished forehead, dark eyes shining innocently and a sweet smile, reminding Annabel how she'd been willing to please the guy who'd taken the picture with the intention of painting it, but that she'd been too shy to speak to him. Her long fingers – trained and shaped even then to tease incredible sound out of her piano – were just out of the shot, but Annabel remembered, suddenly, that they'd been clasped together on her knee. One shoulder was slightly raised, betraying her self-consciousness behind the smile.

Annabel gripped the table with both hands, dropped her head and was swamped by a wave of pain. The house pressed in on her with its memories and its hidden treasures and its reminders in every corner, of Naomi. The comfort she'd expected from home, didn't come. There was only crushing guilt. She wondered as she thought and pictured it just a couple of rooms away, how she'd ever face the accusing tone of Naomi's piano.

***

With only a few seconds, Naomi flew to the bedroom and looked over it with a critical eye. Everything looked undisturbed. Footsteps pressed on gravel outside. She rushed into the bathroom and cleared a couple of long dark hairs from the bath. Since learning the truth, she'd used the same bedroom with the bathroom without the chains. The bed had been unbolted from the wall and moved to its original position, the holes filled in. Every day, she made the bed and straightened the bedroom in case they needed to leave quickly. Every time they'd eaten, Dan had carefully and immediately washed the pots and put them away. She had virtually no clothes to worry about. The few clothes she had were in the wardrobe.

It was there she hurried to next. She took hold of both wardrobe doors at the same time and opened them. As she looked at the couple of items in the wardrobe and the bag that still held her dirty underwear, there were three equally spaced knocks at the front door.

'Think,' she hissed to herself. She couldn't. *You could lock yourself in the bedroom.* She rushed to the bedroom door and turned the key. There was nothing she could do but climb inside the almost empty wardrobe and try to close the doors. Sitting inside the locked room, in view of anyone curious enough to look through the keyhole, didn't seem like cover enough.

'Coming,' she heard Dan call from downstairs, which she took as her final warning. Pulling the doors towards her simultaneously, then letting go just before they trapped her fingers, worked. They snapped shut, leaving about half a centimetre of a gap that would allow some light once her eyes adjusted.

As Dan opened the front door, Naomi slid down the side of the wardrobe and quietly settled into a sitting position, knees to her chin. Her body was trembling. Anxiety or anger? Both. She wrapped her arms around her legs to comfort herself then wondered how cool Dan was feeling downstairs.

'Lorie?' she heard Dan's voice feigning surprise, but not pleasure. 'You're lucky I was in. What are you doing here today?'

Naomi only caught snatches of her response. 'Needed someone to talk to,' and then, 'bored without Nathan,' stuck in her mind so that she missed everything else.

Dan led Lorie into the kitchen right beneath her, making Naomi conscious of the need to be still. She realised that Dan was letting her in on the conversation, which she followed closely and heard almost word-for-word.

'This is nice. You'll have to show me around,' Lorie said.

Dan said, 'Later,' then, 'you've got a suntan since I last saw you.' Diversion tactics.

'Well I've been away with my mother of course,' she said, using the official story. 'Obviously I couldn't go before the wedding, so we booked to leave the day after. She was desperate for a bit of sun after all her treatment, so we went to Spain for a week.'

'Let's hope Camilla never wants to see the holiday photos,' Dan said, sarcastically.

'At a time like this?' she laughed.

'Doesn't Camilla know your mum?'

'They've never met. Put the kettle on then, it's freezing out there.'

Dan scraped a kitchen chair. Naomi imagined him getting up and having to think about making drinks. 'How are Henry and Camilla?'

'As you'd expect,' she said, tone light, 'in bits.'

The words winded Naomi. Tears wet her knees

quickly. She stifled the snivels. There was a long silence before Dan said, 'Do you really think you're going to get away with this?'

Lorie laughed, suddenly. 'You're involved, Danny. Do I think we're going to get away with it? We have. It's over. We mixed with no one out there. Spoke to no one. Nathan shopped alone and brought food back to our little place close to the sea. It was so romantic. A few people saw us together, at a distance, lying on the beach or taking a walk, but we were so careful. I wore shades the whole time, even on the ship. You've seen people on the news being interviewed, telling in their broken English how in love we were.'

'How the hell did you manage to fake her death and have eye witnesses.'

Lorie laughed again. 'Genius, hey? It was easy. One week together alone, then board a ship and fall overboard the first night before anyone has a chance to recognise me.'

'I know a very good psychiatrist,' Dan broke in.

'So book yourself in, Danny,' Lorie laughed again, 'you could do with a new perspective. So, anyway, I dyed my hair blonde, became someone else, got off the ship when it docked, worked my way back to the airport, came back using my own passport. Simple.'

Dan must have been speechless because he said nothing. Eventually, Lorie spoke again.

'What are you doing out here in this isolated house, Danny?'

There was a long pause. 'Thinking.'

'What about?'

'What a mess this all is.'

'Mess? I don't think so. Nathan's free. You've got nothing to do with this, officially. You can get back to your job at the hospital. Henry and Camilla think I'm starting a degree course. Nathan and me, we'll let things settle for a few months. Nathan needs to be visible. Then we'll start a new life abroad. Maybe buy a few houses, rent them out. If we invest carefully, we'll never have to work again. For Nathan, no more gambling or involvement with Solomon's crew. A new start for everyone.'

'Except the Hamiltons.' Another drawn out pause. 'Don't you ever stop to think about what this has done to them?'

'You did it.' Lorie's voice was unconcerned, amused if anything. 'They have money, another daughter, they'll survive. They'll probably sell up and go back to South Africa. I've brought you some money. Nathan's paying you fifteen grand for the job, plus the five he owes you. Here's twenty grand. Enjoy it.'

'I don't want twenty thousand landing in my account, thank you.'

'Whatever you say,' Lorie said. 'But you're a murderer looking after ill people, think of that. And think of the headlines if you go soft on us and start thinking about a confession.'

'I won't be confessing anything. Don't worry about that.'

'Good.' Some shuffling around. 'Well at least take this then.'

'My mother's ring. How thoughtful! I'll smuggle it into the house so she can puzzle over why it's shrunk.'

The next sound took a while to register. It had gone quiet downstairs. Another car was approaching the house. Naomi heard Dan scrape the chair forcefully and get to his feet.

'There's someone here.'

Lorie was following him out of the kitchen. 'You're jumpy, Danny. Cool down and stop acting like a convict.'

'I came here for peace and quiet,' Dan said, not quietly. Naomi realised quickly that the rest of his sentence was for her. His voice was raised. 'It's the guy who owns the house. I forgot he was coming to mend a tap upstairs.'

'So let him mend it,' Lorie said in the same tone.

It took Naomi a couple of seconds to grasp that she had to unlock the door. She quietly opened the wardrobe door and crawled onto the wooden floor and silently stood. By now, Dan was greeting someone at the door. Naomi fumbled inside her pocket for the key and tiptoed to the lock. She noiselessly pushed the key into the hole and turned. That done, she crept back to the wardrobe.

Out of the small gap, Naomi could see a bit of the room. The owner, obviously not wanting to intrude for longer than necessary, came straight up to the bedroom and stopped and turned to look behind him, right in front of the wardrobe within Naomi's narrow view. Naomi took shallow noiseless breaths and kept very still. She heard more footsteps. Dan walked in. She was sure Lorie was following.

'Any problems when that torrential rain fell?'

'No,' Dan lied.

'You've put the bed back I see,' the guy commented.

'Yes,' Dan said after a small hesitation. Naomi clenched her jaw. He carried on speaking before the guy could say anything more. 'I'll leave you to it. We'll be downstairs if you need us.'

'You were in the bath last time I came to do this job,' the guy commented with a small chuckle. Naomi closed her eyes and bit her lip. She pictured him looking straight at Lorie. 'Nice to meet you this time.'

The man proceeded to the bathroom and closed the door. Naomi wasn't aware of anything but the noises he was making. After a few minutes, he came out, descended the stairs, said a few things in the hall, and left.

Dan returned to the kitchen with Lorie and offered, loudly, to make her some food.

'Don't change the subject, Danny,' Lorie said in a voice that was half playful, half determined to draw the truth. 'Who's been sharing your peace and quiet?'

'No one.'

'Yeah right,' she said, forcefully. 'She coming back?'

'I mean, no one I'm prepared to discuss.'

'Who is she?'

Naomi could hear cupboards clattering.

'Just a girl I met in a pub round here. A local, OK, Mum?'

'And she came here because she needed a bath?'

'No, Lorie. She stayed the night with me and had a bath the following morning, OK? Any more questions that are none of your business?'

'Are you seeing her again?'

'Tonight. I thought you were coming tomorrow, so I invited her for dinner. She'll be here at six-thirty, by which time you'll have gone.'

'I was planning to stay over in the spare room.'

'Well, tough. If you're going to show up unannounced you'll have to accommodate my plans. In any case, I don't think Nathan would approve.'

'Nathan sent me here to keep an eye on you, to check you're OK after everything that's happened. He's concerned about you. He knows you can be a bit . . . sensitive. He told me to stay as long as necessary.'

'Job done.' A cupboard door slammed shut. 'I don't need you to babysit me OK? I'm enjoying being on my own and having a bit of company if I choose, when I choose. And I'll do that with whoever the hell I want. I don't need my brother's permission, and I certainly don't need yours.'

Another chair scraped the floor. 'Fine,' she said, nonchalantly, 'In that case, my job here is done.'

'Like I said.'

'I'll leave you to prepare for your guest in peace. I can explore the area on my own while it's still light, then make my way home. I have an important job tomorrow. Solomon needs paying. I'll show up nice and early to keep him sweet. That's the reason I couldn't come tomorrow.'

'Why didn't you just say?'

'I preferred to surprise you and to see what you're up to.'

'What are you, my mother? Time to leave, Lorie.'

They were in the hall where it was more difficult to listen. As far as Naomi could tell, there were no goodbyes at the door. The door opened, then closed. An engine started up. A car, which Naomi pictured to be Lorie's royal blue Mini with the union jack roof, pulled away until there was nothing but silence. Dan ran up the stairs. Naomi waited for him to give her the all clear. She heard him close the curtains before he opened the wardrobe doors and pulled her out, telling her he'd sensed her in there. Naomi found herself wrapped in Dan's arms, feeling his heartbeat and his hands moving up and down her back.

'Did we do the right thing letting her go?' Naomi said.

'We had no choice. She has to pay Solomon or it will hit the fan big time. Once Solomon has his money, I'll rest a bit easier.' They broke apart and looked at each other. 'Do you think she suspected anything?'

Naomi looked at him carefully, arrested by the colour of his eyes. 'I thought you were amazing.'

***

Lorie stopped the car half on the narrow road, half in long grass behind a low stone wall that didn't seem to have any cement between the stones. She wasn't far from the solitary cottage where Dan would be entertaining his guest in a couple of hours. She was out of view of the windows. She killed the engine and looked at the house bathed in the low light of late afternoon. Two birds were squabbling on the roof.

Lorie drew her phone from her coat pocket and struggled to get a signal. She called Nathan, keeping an eye on the house.

'Hey babe, how goes it?' he said after three rings.

'Not sure,' was Lorie's careful reply.

'Have you seen Dan?'

'Yep.'

'Did he accept the money?'

Lorie switched the phone to her other ear. 'Not a penny. He took the ring though. I'm sitting outside a cottage in the middle of nowhere, where Dan's apparently found himself a girlfriend. He thinks I've left.'

'Girlfriend?' Nathan sounded confused.

'A local, apparently. Been for a sleepover.'

'No way. Dan's slow with girls. He's never brought anyone back to the flat. It takes him for ever to ask a girl out, let alone make a move on her.'

'That's what I thought.'

'Did you challenge him?'

'Kind of. He told me to butt out. He's seeing her again tonight. He was keen for me to leave.'

Nathan was quiet a moment. 'Dan's just committed a major crime. His previous crime before that was having a biscuit after he brushed his teeth. I can't imagine his mind is on girls right now.'

'That's what I thought,' Lorie said a second time.

'You don't think he's desperate to confess to someone? How did he seem?'

'A bit jittery. Mostly OK. He's bound to have regrets. That's Dan.'

'Something's up,' Nathan said, pausing to clear his throat. 'Stick around and find out what it is and who this chick is. Follow her when she leaves. Find out where she lives and what the deal is. If anything seems suspicious, call me. And don't let Dan know you're still around.'

24

LIBERTY

It was a lukewarm day at the end of June, the day of Naomi's end-of-year piano recital, the final ordeal before she could complete her first year. She had to perform for twenty minutes without music. She'd already accompanied two other first-year students that week, Siobhan one of them. Naomi was exhausted from worry and work. She'd slept three hours the night before and woken up at four in the morning to a Mozart symphony blasting inside her head that she couldn't turn off or turn down. She'd tried to erase it by mentally rehearsing her recital pieces. It hadn't worked.

She sat in the recital room now beside Nathan. Siobhan had come to listen and lend support. She was sitting alone a few rows behind. Naomi could feel Siobhan's eyes on her. Unable to resist the pull, she glanced behind and found Siobhan looking directly at her. Siobhan nodded once, stone-faced. Naomi smiled in response, conscious of Nathan, who was likely the cause of Siobhan's frostiness. It was the first time they'd seen each other since the party.

Camilla had wanted to come to the recital, but only students were allowed in. Naomi had shown up with Nathan, hoping he'd be taken for a student. No one questioned him. Naomi was the first after lunch. They sat waiting for the two adjudicators now, Naomi warming her hands in Nathan's, trying not to overthink her pieces. Cold hands were useless for playing. She could barely even mentally play the first few bars of her Bach prelude, the opening piece. She took her engagement ring off and asked Nathan to look after it. In an effort not to panic about a crucial part of her memory that seemed to have gone missing, she thought of the last few months instead, and wondered where the time had gone.

Engagement had started painfully. Everyone except Lorie had been in a conspiracy against them. Things had gradually got better and relationships had gone through a healing process thanks to time. Well, mostly. Naomi couldn't think of a specific day or event where Camilla was suddenly fine that she was marrying Nathan, but there had been a gradual shift which meant that they could now talk about plans and dresses and menus without Camilla's hair bristling. Naomi had Lorie to thank for the defrost.

It turned out that the lingering problems were with Annabel. Time had changed nothing there. Annabel had been home once, at Christmas. She'd stayed for two weeks, giving Naomi time to persuade her to be a bridesmaid. It hadn't worked. Annie had said, "He's not good enough for you. I'm not playing happy families when he's divided us. I've told you what I think of him. How many more times?"

Naomi had tried to convince Annabel she was wrong; tried to offer all the reasons why she'd misread intentions. Annabel hadn't budged. Camilla couldn't forgive her for it. It was nine weeks to the wedding now and Annie had stuck to her resolve: she would not be a bridesmaid or condone the wedding by attending it. She'd even decided that life and work in Tokyo suited her so well she'd be staying out there a second year.

Camilla's response to Annabel's response had broken their relationship. Seeing each other over Christmas had only given them the perfect chance to tear into each other face-to-face and dredge up past problems and pain. Camilla had insisted that Annabel, like herself, had no choice but to accept the wedding and make room for it in her plans. Annabel disagreed. She claimed the right to have a choice and told Camilla, more brutally each time, that she wouldn't be anyone's puppet, and where she, Camilla, could stick her threats. Annabel dug a trench. Camilla dug one too. Naomi was stuck in no-man's-land trying to call the two of them together. There was no truce, not even on Christmas Day.

Naomi had to accept Annabel's choice without taking sides. She begged Camilla to restore some harmony. Camilla couldn't. It was Annabel who'd created the discord after all. When Annabel returned to Japan, Camilla gave up on her. She stopped e-mailing, stopped trying to mend things over the phone, wouldn't entertain the idea of Skype, whatever that was. If Annabel was determined to be so pig-headed and selfish, she was on her own. Naomi knew that Henry rang her regularly and privately. He left messages for her on her Facebook account and followed her latest pictures. Camilla had stopped talking to Naomi about her twin. It was as if Lorie had taken her place as a second daughter.

Naomi didn't know she'd sighed until Nathan squeezed her hand.

'Don't worry, babe. You're going to be great.'

Naomi snapped into the present and tried to smile. 'It's not that.' She leant into Nathan's ear. 'Hey, can we go to your place after this. I need to talk to you.'

Nathan looked at her. They'd been to Nathan's flat a few times in the nine months they'd been together, and never returned to his bedroom.

'Everything OK?'

She lowered her voice almost to nothing and nodded. 'We're never fully alone and I need it right now.'

Nathan rubbed the hand he was holding, with his other hand. 'The place is a mess.'

Naomi rested her head on his shoulder and suddenly and desperately wanted to be there with him, whatever it looked like. 'I don't care. When this is over, I want to get away from here.'

He kissed her cheek and his hand brushed the side of her leg at the top, generating feelings which lingered longer than the contact. She ached for the ordeal to be over and at the same time, dreaded it coming.

'OK, babe.'

The two adjudicators entered the room and Naomi stiffened with an intense sense of dread.

***

Nathan slotted the key in the door and apologised again for the mess. Floating in a liberated state of relief, Naomi assured him she could not have cared less. She walked into the narrow hallway of the flat ahead of Nathan and the quietness of the place stood between them for a moment and felt more than pleasant.

'You played really well,' Nathan said for the third time, interrupting the silence. 'You were awesome.'

Naomi turned and smiled over her shoulder. 'I was distracted. It helped me for some reason.'

'Drink? Food?'

'Neither,' Naomi said, walking into the small lounge. There were a few papers, shoes and magazines scattered around, plus the occasional cup, but it wasn't half as bad as Nathan had prepared her for.

'Guy not in? I haven't met him yet.'

'He's a workaholic,' Nathan said, gathering up envelopes and anything else preventing her from sitting.

Naomi sat down. Nathan settled next to her, then

twisted his body to face her. 'What's wrong, babe?'

She let go of all her breath. 'Nathan, you know I love you very much . . .'

A hesitation. 'Why can I feel a *but* coming?'

'Not a *but*, just a nagging feeling I need to talk about. I was sitting there before the performance thinking of my first year, of Annie out in Japan, how she won't come home. Thinking of something Siobhan said that I've never mentioned.'

'What's that?'

Naomi took his hand. 'You remember my birthday last year?'

'How could I forget?'

'Well, Siobhan was in my piano room when you went in there with Annie. She told me what happened.'

Nathan paused to think. 'She was there?'

'Behind the curtain.'

'Why?' Nathan sat up straighter. 'And why have you never mentioned it?'

Naomi shrugged. 'I suppose being in the same room as you two today brought it back.'

'Look,' Nathan said, locking fingers with her, 'I've told you what happened with Annie, in detail.'

'I know,' Naomi said, pausing to wonder if she regretted the conversation already. 'It's just that Annie's story matches Siobhan's and Annie is so determined that I shouldn't marry you . . . I really thought she'd come around.'

'Naims, listen,' Nathan said, drawing much closer, placing one hand at the top of her leg and leaving it there. 'Annie wasn't in possession of her mind that night. Whatever she got in her head is only her warped version of the truth, not the actual truth. I'm sorry she's got the wrong end of the stick and won't let go, but I swear nothing was ever going to happen. I wasn't even tempted.'

'I believe you.'

'OK.' His face relaxed. 'So what's the problem?'

Naomi dropped her gaze. 'What's bothering me is that Siobhan was convinced you upset Annie deliberately and led her on. Annie said you treated it like a game, as if she was a plaything. That's why she can't move on.'

'Utter garbage,' Nathan fumed. 'Why would I do that?'

'I had to ask.'

'It comes down to my word against hers and she was drunk and I don't drink. 'Listen, Naims, look at me.' With effort, Naomi did. 'Do you trust me? Because if you don't there's nowhere to go in this relationship.'

Naomi felt the onset of panic. 'Of course I trust you.'

'What more is there to say then? And as for your so-called friend, it's obvious she's as jealous as hell even though she thinks she's Mother Theresa or something. Fact is, you're slim, she's not. You're engaged and happy, she's not and never will be. You're hot, she's definitely not. You have money, a nice house. Need I go on?'

'Please don't. She is my friend.'

Nathan's voice rose. 'Oh you reckon? I'm telling you now, I'm not having that . . . girl at the wedding.'

'Nathan please –'

'No,' he shouted. 'She's tried to come between us and stir trouble. What right has she, that miserable ugly bitch?'

Naomi was stunned. Nathan's eyes looked darker. 'I've never seen you like this before.'

Nathan dropped his head and lowered his voice. 'I'm sorry. I just hate to see you unhappy. I know I'm over-reacting.' He found her eyes again. They looked more natural. 'The problem is I love you too much.'

'I didn't know you had a temper.'

'Neither did I,' Nathan said. 'I suppose when you care about someone so much, it can arouse feelings you didn't know you had. Can you forgive me? Please?'

'Course.' Naomi melted and put her arms around him. 'Hey, it's OK.'

She pulled back to look at him. His eyes were still troubled. He touched her face and pushed her hair back. 'We can't have secrets. I might be furious, but I'm glad you've told me what's on your mind.'

'Actually, I haven't yet.'

Nathan waited, inches from her lips, expression serious.

'Nathan, my family is divided and yours don't even know we're getting married. I'd feel so much better if I could at least meet your family. I'm not expecting much, honestly.'

'I'm going to talk to Dan soon, I promise. You're right, we can't get married without telling him. But I still don't want you to meet him. When we're married, things will have to change. I can't leave you every other weekend to spend time with Dan. He'll have to understand that we'll be visiting him together, just for a few hours.'

'It will be a big change for him.'

'I know,' Nathan sighed. 'That's why I keep putting off talking to him.'

'What about your parents?

Nathan paused. 'Babe, they already know.'

'They do?'

Nathan nodded. 'I didn't want to tell you because I didn't want to hurt you. I'm sorry, but they don't want to be involved. They've said they won't come.'

'They don't even want to meet me?'

'Apparently not. Your mum has been trying to

contact them. She's written to my mum twice and only had a short response, which was negative.'

'I don't believe it.'

'They're being stubborn, like Annie. I've always taken Dan's side not theirs, and now they're punishing me. It's a pride thing. There's nothing I can do. Sorry.'

Unexpectedly, a pool formed in Naomi's eyes at the bottom. Her voice shook. 'Can I tell you what's really bothering me Nathan?' She went on without waiting for an answer. 'With all this going on, do you think we should go ahead? Do you think we're doing the right thing?'

He drew closer, slowly. His eyes dropped. Naomi couldn't focus on him and closed her eyes too. A tear escaped her right eye as her head fell to one side. His hands were holding her neck. His voice was tender. 'I know we are.'

Naomi savoured a rare and special moment, of being alone like this with Nathan. He never normally allowed it. The problems drifted as he reached her lips and whispered her name without kissing her. His hand slid down her back and drew her closer. Naomi's pulse was driving hard. She didn't have to lean very far forward to meet his lips. He edged back, delaying. 'What do you think?' he whispered.

Naomi found she couldn't think so she nodded instead. Nathan took command and kissed her fiercely, crushing her to him. The alarm system that normally operated inside her head was switched off. She was aware only of a torrent of pleasant sensations, the pressure of Nathan's warm hands, the blissful movement of his mouth. Naomi bound herself more tightly to him. He pushed forward and laid her flat. His hands were travelling now.

'Nathan?'

As if pulled out of a trance, Nathan sat up and pushed his fingers through his hair. 'I'm sorry. I know I shouldn't –'

Naomi sat up, covered his lips with her fingers, covered his lips with her lips, pulled back just enough to speak. 'Nathan, it's OK. Don't stop.'

He kissed her again, but she could tell his brain was functioning now. He withdrew and stood up, panting hard. 'No. No. We shouldn't. We can't do this.'

Naomi was confused. 'Why not?'

'Because we decided. Because waiting is important to you, so it's important to me.'

'Nathan, we're engaged. I do want to wait, or I did. But right now, I want you more. I need you. I struggle to feel that you're mine sometimes. I want to feel close to you.'

Nathan sat down again and took her in his arms. 'Oh babe, I'm always here. I don't let myself get too close to you because I can't control myself when I do.'

'I'm going to repeat your words to me when we first met – stop trying.'

He squeezed her tight. 'No. We're not going to do this because you're worth the wait. Nine weeks, Naims and we'll be on honeymoon. I've dreamt about taking walks on the beach in the evening with you, then making love to you all night. I never pictured us on this sofa on a lousy summer day in England with a dirty mug digging into my leg.'

Nathan produced a stained cup and held it up. Naomi had to laugh.

The heat died down. 'OK, you win.'

Nathan touched her face with his fingers and produced a winning smile. 'Hey, you're not getting cold feet are you? I never pictured myself on that beach or in that bed without you.'

'No,' Naomi said. 'My feet are toasty warm.' She looked at her watch. 'In fact I'd better not stay too long. I have a dress fitting with Lorie.'

'What's it like?'

'Not telling.'

'What colour is it?'

'White.'

'For purity,' Nathan said.

'The only thing keeping me pure right now is your amazing restraint. I wish Annie knew you like I do.'

Nathan reached inside his pocket and held up her ring. 'Don't forget this, soon-to-be Mrs Stone,' he said, pushing the ring back onto her finger.

'How could I?' Naomi smiled. Her mood had transformed. The doubts had been miraculously swept aside. She slid her ring back on.

'Hey, don't tell anyone that we got a bit carried away just now,' he said.

'Who would I tell?'

'I don't know. Lorie? Friends tell each other everything, don't they? I'd just like things to be private between us.'

'My lips are sealed.' She leant forward to kiss him, briefly. 'You know, I can't wait for the wedding.'

Nathan stood up and drew her into a final hug. 'I'm looking forward to the honeymoon much more.'

***

It had been a forty minute drive to reach a town called Bury on the north side of Manchester, a side Camilla had never had reason to visit. Frequently and frantically, she kept consulting a piece of paper with scribbled instructions lying flat on her lap. Her glasses, only needed for reading, were on and off and hung round her neck.

Henry had begged her to make life easier by taking his Jag with built-in sat-nav. Camilla had refused. She wanted to use her own car, not that flashy thing, she'd told him, and she didn't want to listen to that nameless woman bleating out instructions in her patronising voice either. With the help of a simple map, she could rely on her own intelligence, thank you.

With a pleasant mixture of relief and satisfaction, Camilla signalled to make her final turn. She intended to report to Henry that she hadn't made a single wrong turn all journey. She'd been so distracted by instructions, it wasn't until now that she focussed properly on the area. Confusion crept up on her. She drove slowly down the narrow avenue, too slowly for the red car making its point up her bumper, concentration divided between searching for number forty-four and noticing how appalling the houses were.

The odd numbers were on the left. She pulled over to allow the red car to pass, then continued, eyes on the houses to the right, passing the twenties, then thirties, stopping outside a tired-looking quasi semi that needed everything doing. She was trying not to stare in case anyone had seen her stop, but in one lingering glance she'd clocked that the paint was peeling, the windows were dirty, the curtains were barely open and hung unevenly, and the front door, a faded green, had no number and was identifiable only from the house numbers either side. The tiny front garden was chaotic and without colour, except for dandelions that poked through every crevice of the broken paving stones.

Only Henry knew about her visit. Camilla hadn't discussed with Naomi or Lorie the need she felt to try and reason with Nathan's parents in advance of the wedding. Convinced she could say something to alter their minds, she'd planned the visit without invitation, determined to come away with a commitment from them not only to attend the wedding, but also to help pay.

She didn't want to cause bother. She'd planned how polite and reasonable she'd be; how she'd accept a cup of tea offered in an already-imagined delicate floral cup sitting on a saucer. But as she looked about her and smoothed her pinstriped trousers that matched her navy jacket, her well-rehearsed scene died. She felt overdressed. In no rush to knock on the green door, she slowly undid her seatbelt, put her glasses in her bag and wondered if she'd made a mistake.

Nathaniel Stone, who talked about philosophy and music and literature as if he was master of all three, could surely not have been raised in a house like this. Now she was taking in the whole street, she realised that most of the houses looked shabby and neglected, like a mish-mash of odd socks, old worn ones that had lost their other half. There were more wheelie bins stranded on the pavement than there were flowers in the gardens.

From her bag, Camilla withdrew the short letter she'd eventually drawn from Nathan's mother. She'd put it in her bag as she would a hospital appointment letter. She looked at it now to delay getting out of the car. It was almost three months old, dated 3rd April. It was articulate, written in careful handwriting on expensive paper. It was not the kind of letter that Camilla imagined could be produced from behind dirty windows and an ugly front door. Holding it down below window level, she checked the address and ran her eyes over the two paragraphs again. It read:

Dear Mrs Hamilton,
I appreciate your reasons for writing to me and I apologise for the delay in response. I'm sure Nathan has

explained the family problems, which I hesitate to share with anyone outside the family. Seeing as it now looks as though the wedding will go ahead and our families will come together through marriage, I want to be clear that Nathan and his brother Daniel have chosen to remove themselves from our lives. We see them occasionally on their terms. As a mother, you'll understand how hurtful and debilitating this feels. Without going into detail about the reasons for this rift from our point of view, which are lengthy and complex, I need only say that my husband and I have grown to accept the situation and move on with our own lives, given it was the only option.

I hope you'll accept our decision to be absent from the wedding in September. There are no bad wishes. We will be sending a gift, but we feel that our being there would dredge up the recent pain of ill-feeling, which is unfair to Naomi on her special day. Daniel is too unwell to attend in any case, so we will be on duty during the wedding weekend and honeymoon period. We'll look after him if necessary. I hope this clarifies our position.

Regards,
Valerie Stone.

'Clarifies?' Camilla said out loud, putting the letter away, 'it's as clear as mud.'

Since the letter had dropped through the door, Valerie Stone's words had done nothing but plague Camilla and confuse her on the position of Nathan's parents. She couldn't understand how they had no bad feelings, but were willing to miss their son's wedding. How they wanted the best for Naomi – a girl they hadn't taken the time to meet – on her special day, but they were willing to hurt her by shunning her. How they were willing to care for Daniel in Nathan's absence, but were unwilling to visit him regularly when he had a serious illness. And how they were planning to send a gift, but had not offered to contribute a penny to the wedding. Something wasn't right.

Having only ever heard Nathan's side of the story, a side she had no faith in, she'd grown determined to hear about the other half of the Stone tale. It was more than an interest by now, it was a compulsion. There was something else. Having failed with Annabel in every possible way, Camilla had sympathy for Valerie Stone. It was all too easy to understand how quickly things got out of hand and pride strangled the life out of relationships. Valerie's perspective would be different. And Camilla felt hopeful of unearthing the real Nathan Stone, if she could get to his roots. His attempts over several months to be more-than-reasonable and ever-so charming had made her more suspicious of him if anything. He wasn't real.

Camilla opened the door and stepped onto the drab street. She put her bag carefully over her shoulder and made her way to number forty-four that had no number. There was no bell either. She took hold of the door knocker, tapped three times.

She heard heavy footsteps. She straightened and took a breath. A young man in a red football shirt and a bloated face, only twenties, answered the door and looked at her blankly.

'Daniel?' Camilla ventured, though he looked nothing like Nathan.

He frowned. 'No.'

'I'm sorry, I'm mistaken. I'm here to see Valerie if I may.'

He paused to gawp at her and shuffle his feet. 'You've got the wrong house, I reckon.'

Camilla felt some relief. This man in front of her with his bulbous hairy belly showing beneath his shirt belonged here. Valerie Stone didn't.

Camilla, not one to waste time, turned. 'Sorry to have troubled you.'

***

Lorie was passing Camilla's bedroom later that day. She caught enough of one sentence to make her stop and listen hard.

'Not a penny from them either. I'm telling you, Henry, something's not right.'

'You must have got the wrong house. I told you to take my car.'

Camilla raised her voice. 'And I've told you I had the address in the woman's own handwriting right in front of me. There was no mistake.'

Lorie's heart almost stopped.

'If Nathan's brother is ill, maybe he just wasn't responsive enough to understand what you wanted.'

'Oh for goodness' sake, Henry, ill or not, the lad must know his own name. I asked him if he was Daniel. He said not. He looked as much like Nathaniel as you do.'

A pause. 'There'll be some perfectly logical explanation.'

'Well, I'd like to know what it is,' Camilla shot back. 'What's been logical about any of this so far?'

Lorie had heard enough. She raced downstairs out of the way to dream up a way to make Henry's words and not Camilla's, make sense. Lorie's first instinct was to contact Nathan. A problem shared, etcetera. But it wasn't the right place to do it. She needed to call him with a solution, not a problem. And fast.

As the beginnings of a plan started to germinate, Lorie realised with a sinking feeling that she'd have to get directly involved. She didn't see any another way. It would be risky. She thought of September when all of this would be a memory, when she'd leave work and Naomi would be gone and Nathan would be hers for a heavenly week away – a time they could really begin to plan a future. She felt calmer. It was a necessary risk.

25

Later that night, Lorie was alone in her flat staring at a dinner she'd pecked at and couldn't eat. Nathan would be home by now. She abandoned her food and reached for her phone.

Two rings, Nathan's voice, 'Hey, gorgeous.'

'We've got a problem.'

'Go on.'

'Camilla took a trip to see your mum today and met your mate, Dave.'

'What?' Much shriller than before. 'Why?'

'Because, reading between the lines and I didn't hang around for many, she's not convinced.'

'The interfering old cow! What does she want?'

'Money, for one thing.'

'Hasn't she got enough?'

'Not the point. She obviously doesn't buy the explanation we sent her about not going to the wedding. We're going to have to up our game.'

'Game's over by the sound of it.'

'No, it's not. We just need to stay ahead. Find out exactly what Dave said to her. Hopefully nothing, I'll take it from there.'

Nathan was silent a moment. 'Are you saying I'll have to tell my mum I'm getting married?'

'No, you can't do that. If your mum gets with Camilla, the game will be up in seconds. If your parents come, they'll expect Dan to be there, which will blow the cover altogether. I never saw it getting this complex.'

Nathan panted. 'So what's the plan?'

'I'm going to call Camilla from an old phone of mine. I'll have to pose as your mum. Your job is to get some money.'

'What? How?'

'Any way you can. Borrow some off Dan, he has some savings.'

'I already owe him five grand.'

'He knows you can pay him back. Just get some money. I'll have to offer them some. This phone call's going to be make or break.'

'When are you going to do it?'

'Call Dave. Get back to me so I know what the damage is. I've got to do it now before I lose my nerve.'

***

Lorie had heard Valerie Stone speaking to Nathan over the phone. She'd spent her first ten years in North Wales and retained a hint of a Welsh accent that had struck Lorie when she'd shared the earpiece of the phone with Nathan and listened to her. Lorie stood and practised Valerie's accent out loud, in a tone that was higher pitched than her own. In case Valerie Stone and Camilla were ever to talk to each other in the future, it was best to be as authentic as possible. It had been a policy between Nathan and herself, to keep the lies simmering as close to the truth as possible. No false names. No obvious blunders. As she practised Valerie's accent, she remembered that Nathan had mentioned his gran was ill – the one who lived in Florida with her second husband. His parents were thinking they might have to go over there. Perfect. She could use that.

She ranked this moment as she held the phone in her hand preparing to press the numbers, as the most important and the most nerve jangling of her life. She held her breath, trying to suspend time itself. When she let the air out slowly, time proceeded again.

'Just do it,' she told herself. 'You know her better than her own husband.'

Ten seconds later, Camilla was on the other end of her phone and Lorie was due on stage and felt enough stage fright for the opening night at the West End. 'Mrs Hamilton?'

'Speaking?'

'It's Valerie Stone here. I hope you don't mind me calling.'

A surprised moment of silence. 'Not at all. It's such a coincidence. I called round today at what I thought was your home and a young –'

'You went to that dreadful house on Wentlock Street?' Lorie said.

'Yes, that's right.'

'I'm sorry you wasted your time. We rented it temporarily. We've had extensive work done to the house starting with the roof, and had to move out for a few months. They told us the work would take six weeks then blamed the weather for the fact that it took them more like sixteen. Typical, I'm told.'

'Nathan never explained that,' Camilla said.

'He's not exactly in touch with things around here.'

'Of course not.'

'Look, I'm calling with an apology and an offer. We've agonised over our decision, Mrs Hamilton, but we're sure we won't be coming to the wedding. I realise how that must seem. Things might be different in the future, who's to say, but for now, it's settled.'

'And what if –'

'Sorry to interrupt, but nothing you can say will make a difference. I've discussed it with my husband so many times. You'll understand this is difficult even to speak about?'

'I do understand.' Camilla hesitated. 'Won't you at least meet Naomi? It's very important to her.'

Lorie stood up and started to pace the floor in search of the right words. 'Yes, we intend to, but something's come up, something urgent. My mother lives in the States and has been taken into hospital. They're still doing tests, but my stepfather says it's serious. We have a flight booked, one way. They need help with medical bills. We'll stay out there as long as we can afford. I really can't think beyond that at the moment.'

'I understand,' Camilla said again.

Lorie was stumped for a moment. She'd been expecting some polite disagreement, a mild battle at least, but Camilla was being her most reasonable self. 'Thank you,' Lorie said, to buy some time. 'But we would like to help with the wedding financially. Please don't tell Nathan, he might not approve. He has a thing about not accepting money from us. I have no amount in mind because I haven't been involved in the arrangements, but I'm open to suggestions.'

'It's all taken care of,' Camilla said, shocking Lorie again.

'I'm sorry?'

'Really, Mrs Stone, I appreciate the offer, but I think you have enough on with repairs to the house, flights to America and medical bills. We're happy to cover the cost if you're in agreement.'

Lorie was shaking one fist in the air in triumph by now. 'That's just too generous –'

'No it isn't,' Camilla said firmly. 'I insist. You go and see to your mother and I hope things can improve at this end when you get back. Really, Naomi is a lovely girl. I'm sure she'll want to bring the family together and not divide it further.'

'Mrs Hamilton –'

'Camilla. Please.'

'Camilla, I'm very grateful.'

'The pleasure is ours.'

After a few more pleasantries, Lorie finished the call and shouted out in relief. Her hands were shaking with the elation. She phoned Nathan back, sure she'd burst with the news if she didn't share it.

Nathan, 'Hey, how did it go?'

'Just call me brilliant.'

'Really?'

'I had her eating out of my hand, it was awesome. She doesn't even want any money. It would be their pleasure, Camilla told me, to pay for the lot.'

Nathan laughed. 'Unreal. How do you do it?'

Lorie smiled to herself. Impressing Nathan never got old. 'Never mind that, I have a question for you and it's time you answered it.'

'Not that one again,' Nathan said, sickeningly sounding like he was up for some fun now the crisis had passed.

'Yes that one. It's nine weeks to the wedding and you've been seeing her for nine long months, longer than we intended. I've chucked Simon out of sheer boredom and because I'm more attracted to a Big Mac than to him.' Nathan laughed again. 'Now don't dodge the question – do you enjoy kissing her or not?'

Nathan turned silent until it became uncomfortable for Lorie.

'I'll take that as a yes then,' she said, frostily.

'No, I'm just thinking.'

'You shouldn't need to think.'

'Look, babe, it's a job. It's not the worst I've ever had and no one could call her ugly. Great body.'

'Nathan,' Lorie sighed, deflated suddenly, nausea

clutching at her insides. She wanted reassurance. She wasn't getting it. The only way she could save face was to take charge. 'I'm only going to ask you one more time –'

'Is that a promise?' Nathan joked.

Lorie carried on in the same tone, refusing to be drawn in. 'Do you enjoy kissing her, yes or no?'

She could never tell what Nathan was doing on the other end of the phone. Was he squirming, smiling, sweating? She'd have betted on him smiling from the vibes she was getting. His games went too far sometimes.

'Babe, come on, I'm a man –'

'Yeah, I've noticed,' Lorie snapped, before cutting Nathan off. She collapsed onto the sofa and broke down. Having made her point, she held on to the phone, ready to take the call when Nathan rang to apologise and tell her, finally and emphatically that kissing Naomi meant nothing. She decided she'd let it ring a while before she answered. Lorie waited, she sobbed, she ached, she waited some more. The crash after the high was a hard landing. As time stretched on, she wondered if she hated him as much as she loved him. He didn't call.

***

It was much earlier than Camilla's normal bedtime. She slid between the freshly laundered bedding beside Henry, who was smiling from behind his latest crime book that had a dagger on the cover drenched in blood.

'Didn't I say there'd be a perfectly logical explanation?' he said, glancing up.

Camilla was too tired to think of a good comeback, so she said nothing. It was a good kind of tired. Since her conversation with Valerie Stone, she'd felt a loosening in her muscles. Her mind was more at peace. Having found some answers to months of solution-seeking, her body was telling her it was time to take a well-deserved rest. The mental energy spent on Nathan and Naomi, and Annabel, had been exhausting.

'She seemed like a very nice woman,' Camilla conceded.

'Why wouldn't she be? Nathan's a very nice lad,' Henry said, patting her arm with hot fingers. 'Families aren't perfect as well we know. Stop fighting now, love, and let things be. Buy yourself an outfit and a hat. Start to look forward to it.'

Camilla settled into her two feather pillows, back to Henry. 'It won't be complete without Annabel there.'

Henry placed a very warm hand on her and left it there. 'Tell her that. Speak to her. She might be stubborn at first, but she'll see sense. The longer this silence goes on between the two of you, the harder it will be to put right. Mm?' He rubbed her arm vigorously beneath the duvet and finally let go.

'How often do you contact her?' Camilla asked, grudgingly.

'Every week,' Henry said. 'She's doing well, working hard, lots of friends, you know Annabel.' He paused. Camilla had nothing to say back, especially because she found that she had a painful lump in her throat. 'Come on, love, time to bury the hatchet and make a fresh start. Mm? If she knows you've accepted Nathan, maybe she'll do the same. Maybe she'll come home.'

Camilla swallowed a few times to steady her voice. 'When did I ever say I'd accepted him?'

Henry's hand was back again, even toastier. 'What do you want from him?'

It was a fair question. During the silence that followed, Camilla repeated it to herself. She'd been quiet so long, she didn't know if Henry was still listening or was back with his book. She thought she was answering in her head, but realised she was speaking out loud when she heard her own voice.

'I don't trust him.'

A short pause. 'What's this really about, Camilla?'

Camilla could feel her defences prickling. She hadn't meant to head towards a conversation like this. She squirmed free of his hand. 'What do you mean?'

'Your issues with trust. The way you distance yourself from anyone who crosses the line. The way you must be in control. The way you struggle with intimacy.'

Camilla turned to glare at him. 'That's not true.'

'You know it is.'

Camilla, too furious to express herself, turned her back on Henry again and shuffled to the cool edge of the bed.

Henry's voice was gentle. 'I'm trying to help.'

'Is that right?'

'Yes. Think of this wedding as a fresh start. Our girls have left us, Camilla, suddenly. It's a wrench. It's hard to adjust, but we have to look to the future and embrace the changes whatever they might be.' Henry snapped his book shut and cleared his throat. 'We have to trust Naomi to Nathan and we have to believe Annabel is making the decisions that are right for her. We have to let Lorie go very soon too. Stop battling what we can't change. Acceptance is the way forward.'

Even in her silent mutiny that prevented her from responding, she accepted he was right. What else could be done? The wedding date was rushing towards them. The plans and events that were keeping her busy daily now, meant that long summer days only flashed by. Naomi had finished her first year. She was due to pack up and come home that weekend. The next time she returned to college, she'd be married.

Camilla sighed and found herself thinking out loud again. 'I suppose it's time I bought an outfit.'

Henry moved right over to Camilla's side of the bed and wrapped one arm around her. 'That's the spirit, love. And isn't it time we gave them the money too?'

'Not while I'm still living in hope of them changing their plans.'

'Camilla,' Henry said, 'have you ever seen a couple more in love?'

Camilla avoided the question. 'I suppose a lump sum would get them a home. I can't think of Naomi starting married life in that dreadful flat of his.'

'We can't dictate how they spend the money. Once it's gone, it's no longer ours. This Saturday, when Naomi comes home, let's prepare a nice dinner for her and invite Nathan round and have a cheque ready. I can sort it out. What do you say?'

Camilla was trapped and felt claustrophobic. Loving gestures had a habit of leaving her feeling this way. 'On the condition that you remove yourself to your own side of the bed and don't invade mine again, I say let's do dinner and hold the cheque off for now.'

After a delayed moment where Camilla held her breath, Henry obliged and Camilla resumed breathing.

'Whatever you say. But call Annabel, would you? That can't wait.'

Henry took Camilla's silence as a positive. He leant over and flicked the switch on his lamp, plunging them into darkness. He could smile freely into the blackness without the risk of being questioned. Things were coming together, finally.

***

Lorie had hung around waiting for Dan's dinner guest for

long enough. Without the engine running, she was cold. Without having brought anything but a bag of mixed boiled sweets, she was hungry too. She wanted to stretch her legs, but she daren't wander around. She'd been planning to take a look at the girl, then find somewhere to eat and return later. The girl was an hour late. Maybe she wasn't coming. In her indecision and her need for company, Lorie found herself calling Nathan again.

Nathan answered sleepily. 'This had better be good. I've got a flight tomorrow. I need to sleep.'

'My heart bleeds,' Lorie said, mimicking a phrase Nathan often used. 'I haven't moved since we last spoke. Dan's girl never showed and I'm getting pretty sick of hanging around.'

Nathan yawned. 'Is it dark there?'

'It's England. Of course it's dark. And damp. And cold.'

'You might have missed her.' He sounded bored. 'Walk up to the house, take a look through the windows. If you have no joy, ring Dan on a pretext, see what he says.'

'Have the reporters stopped hounding you?'

'Yeah, it's all died down. It's over. Only call me back if you have to tonight. Definitely call me after you've done the drop at Solomon's tomorrow.'

Nathan hung up. Lorie panted sharply, got out of the car and resisted the urge to slam the door. She wrapped her jacket around her and climbed with care over the nearby wall. The house was at the bottom of a little grassy bank. Lorie advanced steadily towards it, passing through a row of conifers. By the time she reached the bottom, the long wet grass had penetrated her shoes. She wasn't dressed for this. She hadn't planned on a spying mission in Cumbria while Nathan lazed in paradise. Lorie found the path in front of the house and ran down it on tiptoes. An outside light lit the way and fortunately wasn't movement-sensitive.

There were two windows either side of the front door. One glowed, curtains closed, the other was unlit, curtains also closed. Lorie crept round the back of the house into darkness, keeping her complaints in her head. The kitchen window had a roller blind, she remembered, which was all the way down. Beside the window was the back door. She tried the handle. Locked. Frustrated and with no options, Lorie bent down to look through the keyhole. Light from the hall fed into the kitchen. She had a limited view of a thin slice of the kitchen table with a gingham table cloth and the kitchen door behind it, which was half open. Her eyes returned to the table. At an angle, she could see keys and a phone.

Suddenly, she could hear a voice, Dan's drawing closer. So Dan was not alone. Her instinct was to back off and run, but she fought it, assuring herself he wasn't likely to exit the back door. Dan passed the kitchen door and she could hear him running up the stairs. The bathroom light went on above her head. A plan occurred to her in a rush.

Hoping to draw the girl into the kitchen, Lorie rang Dan's mobile. She watched it light up as the ringtone sang out from the table. Lorie was crouched and still. Dan called from upstairs.

'Leave that.'

'Come out of your hiding place,' Lorie whispered to herself as she continued to wedge her eyeball against the tiny opening. The phone's answering message came on – Dan's voice.

'Crap,' Lorie whispered, out of ideas now. She disconnected and redialled and continued to watch.

'Come on, come on.'

No one came. By the time Dan thudded down the

stairs again, the answering message was telling her she was through to Dan's phone, blah, blah, blah. She cut him off. Dan came into the kitchen, flicked on the light, picked up his phone, looked at the screen.

'Two missed calls from Lorie,' he said too loudly to be talking to himself.

Silence in response. Lorie was confused. Why would some girl in the other room care who 'Lorie' was? Had Dan talked? Instead of leaving, Lorie was suspicious enough to hang around. It was risky being this close to Dan, about two, three metres at the most. An adrenaline surge fired through her. This was ridiculous. What was the worst that could happen? A shadow appeared on the floor behind Dan. The girl would be visible if only Dan would shift.

That was Lorie's last thought before the world stopped revolving. It seemed to happen in slow motion – Dan, eyes on his phone, moving out of view, clearing the way for Lorie to stare at the dark-haired girl in the doorway wearing jeans and a zip-up tracksuit top. Lorie's pulse banged in her ears. For a frozen moment, she couldn't understand. Her eyes were deceiving her. Or, she was dreaming. She'd wake up soon with the sound of the sea drifting through the open windows, Nathan already out for his morning swim. She'd tell him of this nightmare back in chilly England.

The next horrifying sound brought her to her senses, dragging reality back. Her mobile phone on 'silent', buzzed and vibrated in her hand. Lorie dropped it with the shock. It crashed to the ground. No. Lorie looked down in panic at Dan's name. She snatched up the phone and rejected the call. The back of the phone was missing. No time to search. No time to think. She had to leave.

'What was that?' Dan's voice from just inside the back door. Lorie bolted to the side of the house just as she heard the back door opening.

'Shh.' Dan's voice again. She could picture him standing in the doorway listening with the attention of a predator on the hunt, scanning the length of the murky garden. She wasn't safe where she was. If Dan took a few paces and turned the corner, she'd be in full view. At the same time, she was too afraid to move or breathe loudly.

'Probably an animal.' Naomi's voice, low. *Dead Naomi?*

'Stay here,' she heard Dan say in a hushed tone.

She knew she had to move, no choice. As noiselessly as possible, she made her way to the front of the house and ran for the cover of a horse chestnut tree, which was on the house side of the stone wall. Every panicked step to the tree, she expected Dan to pierce the night air with a yell. She made it a couple of seconds before Dan, brandishing a torch from his mobile phone, came into view. Lorie ducked behind the tree and crouched amongst a mass of spikey conkers, short of breath. Her palms were clammy.

Suddenly aware that Dan might call again, she scrambled to switch off her phone. Lorie couldn't move. She daren't even peep. The rough bark of the tree scratched her back. She closed her eyes. All Dan had to do was discover her here and it would be over. All he had to do was climb the grass verge to see her parked car. Months of planning would be obliterated.

Maybe it was too late already. The unthinkable had happened. Dan had betrayed Nathan and spared Naomi, making Dan the enemy. Lorie had to reach safety. She had to reach Nathan. Had Dan spilled to the police? Would they be waiting outside her flat when she drove home? Logic told her that the fact that Dan was in hiding with Naomi meant that the secret was still intact. Dan wouldn't risk going public.

Lorie covered her head with both hands and ordered herself to stop thinking. One thing at a time – she had to get away without Dan knowing what she'd discovered. She had to wait until the small circle of light that was being flashed around the grass to her left, had disappeared.

She sat there long after the light had stopped searching the grass. Eventually on liquid limbs, she stood. The wall was a few paces away up a small incline. She ran for it and threw herself over as quickly as she could. There was a small grass mound on the other side, which met with the road. Head low, Lorie ran in the direction of her car. The comfort of reaching it was all she wanted now. Though the lane was badly lit, she could see the dark outline of the rear of the car not far away.

Lorie pulled her keys from her pocket as she stumbled along. She fired up her phone, waited for a signal and redialled Nathan's number. It rang once, twice, three times, four.

'Come on, come on, pick up,' she hissed as she neared the safety of her Mini.

26

THE BIG DAY

It was the first Saturday in September and was pleasantly warm, more so than it had been all August. The beautiful blush in the morning sky that announced the rising sun dimmed Dan's mood. The atrocities that would be committed today didn't deserve a glorious prelude of colour or a fanfare of birdsong. Dan hadn't slept all night and hadn't wanted to. Afraid to shut his eyes and find in the next instant that hours had evaporated into nothing but nightmares, he'd lay in the dark stillness through the creeping minutes, feeling the pulse of passing time so consciously, he'd slowed it down.

Dan tried to reckon the number of hours he'd slept that week and could find less than fifteen. It had been seven days since he'd discovered that Lorie and Nathan had been hatching a plan. They weren't just plotting to devastate the life of Naomi Hamilton, they were planning to end it and rob her parents of a small fortune. Dan had overheard a phone call from his room. Nathan had the gruff-voiced guy on the other end of the receiver, on loudspeaker. The guy was telling Nathan, as casually as if he was explaining how he'd fix the washing machine, how he planned to take Naomi out and how no one would ever either find her or look for her.

Nathan and Lorie's job was to fake her death somewhere far away, a week later. Providing Lorie could make it out of the country posing as Naomi, no one foresaw a problem. Handing over Henry Hamilton's car and playing a part in the murder of his daughter, plus coughing up the thirty thousand pounds he still owed in gambling debts, would ensure Nathan's freedom from a group of criminals who'd held him hostage for too long. Neither side wanted to see or hear from the other again. If Nathan delivered everything he'd promised, after the wedding, all was square.

Dan had sat paralysed in his room, listening. Faking an accident? Murder? Nathan was many things, but not a killer. He waited until the call ended then came out from his hiding place. Lorie was on the sofa, Nathan pacing the room. Dan erupted in his quietest voice, even though he knew that the couple who lived next door were away on holiday.

'Murder?' he hissed at Nathan. 'Are you out of your mind?'

'Mate,' Nathan said, striding towards him, clasping Dan's shoulder close to his neck, 'it's going to work.'

'Take her money if you must, but don't take her life,' Dan tried to reason.

'Hey, I'm no murderer, you know that. No one will ever pin it on us. That's why we're hiring someone else.'

Dan was speechless for a few moments. 'Are you missing the point here?' Dan's voice was rising. 'Planning to divorce her was bad enough.'

Nathan smiled apologetically. 'Yeah, two problems. Lorie didn't want me sleeping with her first, plus I thought it'd be better if Solomon had some insurance that I can be airtight once we part company. I'm making a fresh start, Danny. I thought you'd be pleased. No more gambling, no more debt. It's a new life, with a sacrifice, granted, but –'

'A human sacrifice, Nathan. Just because you're not killing her yourself doesn't mean you're not responsible.

You intend to fake her death and go public? You're perverting the course of justice. You're stealing a ton of money. You're committing murder by proxy. You're insane, both of you.'

'I'm telling you, we can pull it off,' Lorie chipped in, casually. 'No problem.'

Nathan nodded in agreement.

Dan turned from Lorie in disgust. He refused to even look at her. 'I don't care if you can or can't, this is wrong,' Dan said.

'Right and wrong isn't black and white.' Nathan's tone had a threatening edge. 'Solomon's taken over my life with a game of poker. Is that right?'

'You knew the risk. You took it. You lost.'

'And now I'm taking my life back.' He paused. 'And there's a job vacancy for you.'

Dan stared at him incredulously. 'What the hell are you talking about now?'

'We need a digger to assist Carter.'

'Digger? Who's Carter?'

'Damien Carter. Solomon's right-hand man. He'll arrive at the cemetery with Naomi the night of the wedding and the grave will have to be open and ready. For practical reasons, she'll need to walk to the grave herself and be killed there. Someone will need to seal it once she's in, and ensure they're not seen.'

'What grave?'

'Irrelevant. There are always funerals on Fridays. We need a full grave, one that won't need to be reopened. Carter will have his ear to the ground, if you'll pardon the pun. A cemetery is the perfect place for a dead body, so I'm told.'

Lorie laughed. 'Genius.'

Dan glared at her, then Nathan. 'You really think I'm going to get involved?'

'You know what's going down so you're already involved.'

'And you expect me to turn a blind eye?'

'I know you won't, which is why I'm bringing you in. Nothing major. You'll just be a small player on the peripheries.'

Dan shook his head in disbelief. He was feeling queasy. 'Leave me out of this.'

'You're overreacting,' Nathan said, 'which makes you a liability. If you don't agree to come on board, Dan, I might have to force the issue.'

Dan's mouth had dried and was gluing together. 'Meaning?'

'If I tell Solomon you're in the know, he'll want to cover his tracks, which isn't a happy position.'

'Don't tell him.'

'Don't make me tell him.'

Dan couldn't speak at first. Nathan allowed the silence. 'Are you saying what I think you're saying?'

'I'm saying come in from the cold and join the circle. It's warmer. You don't want to get on the wrong side of Vincent Solomon.'

'I don't want to get on any side of him, Nathan.'

Nathan ignored him and carried on. 'And don't imagine you can tip the police or the Hamiltons off either. I'm telling you now, the safest thing you can do is play a small part. Then we're all happy. We divide the money. Life moves on.'

Dan's tongue had lost its purpose. His mouth was open. All he could do was pant at intervals. Eventually, he said, 'You set me up. You wanted me to hear that call. You're trying to dirty my hands in a mess that's all yours. I've got a career. I save lives. I've only ever tried to help you, Nathan, and this is what you do?'

Lorie was looking at her nails. Nathan was looking

into Dan's eyes without flinching. 'Sign up.'

'Screw you,' Dan said, hurling a final look at his brother. He stormed into his room and heavily slammed the door.

'That went better than expected,' Dan heard Nathan say to Lorie.

Seconds later, Nathan opened the door, propped up the doorframe and spoke softly and infuriatingly reasonably. 'I'm going to give you twenty-four hours to get your head together, bro. Don't think about doing anything stupid. You're way out of your depth. Any wrong move puts lives in danger. Remember what you're about.'

Nathan closed the door. Dan stared at it blankly. *And sitting idle is handing a death sentence to Naomi Hamilton.*

***

Dan spent the first twelve hours lying on top of his bed in a misty rage. Sleep never approached. His hands shook with fury. Betrayal – a black and filthy word. His head couldn't absorb the fact that Nathan was prepared to drag him through the mire by blackmail. Like oil on water, it clogged and swamped his mind making rational thought impossible.

By the end of twenty-four hours, loyalty for Nathan having died, he'd reviewed every legal and moral avenue and had come up with only one solution: he could not allow Naomi Hamilton to be murdered. Beyond that, he had a sketchy plan which didn't involve the police or properly consider the future. He knew from what Nathan had told him over months, that one wrong move could have devastating results. Crossing members of this group caused 'accidents'. They were men of action without conscience. Nathan deserved to go to prison for his stupidity, but he didn't deserve to die. Dan had reached a point of resignation. He would put himself on the line to try and stop them from mindlessly killing.

Six days before the wedding, Nathan came back to him for a decision, as if there was a choice. Dan had done a shift at the hospital and was exhausted with the lack of sleep. He lay flat on his bed, one arm draped across his forehead, not wanting Nathan anywhere near him.

'I'm sorry it's turned out this way, bro,' Nathan said, almost sounding sincere, perching on the end of Dan's bed with a can of lager in his hand. They were alone in the flat. Dan felt something close to hatred, but suppressed it. 'I didn't want to drag you in, but it had to be done. I promise after the wedding, it will be over.'

Dan shot him a look. 'What do you want me to do? Thank you? Tell you everything's going to work out fine?'

'No,' Nathan said slowly, 'but I have to deliver. Don't let me down.' Dan kept quiet. 'It will be worth your while financially. Plus I'll pay you the five grand I owe.'

'I'm not in it for money.'

Nathan shifted on the bed. 'So you're in?'

Dan was looking down, drawing lines on his bed cover. 'On my terms, not yours. I'm not doing any digging or stealing or sealing of graves. I'll collect Naomi and deliver her to the cemetery. Then I'm leaving. I'm not hanging around to witness a killing.'

Nathan stood up, too excited to sit. 'Someone will need to bring the rings back to the hotel for Lorie. Then that's it, I swear.'

'Fine. But that's all I'm doing. Take it or leave it.'

'I knew you'd see sense.'

Unbelievable! 'If anything goes wrong, you won't

see me for dust, Nathe. It's going to be your problem if it hits the fan.'

Nathan grinned. 'Nothing will go wrong. Naomi will want her necklace. I'm going to make sure it stays in the car. You'll be standing by in a balaclava waiting for her to come back for it. I'll text you when she's on her way down. The car won't be in view of any security cameras. You'll tell me if the car park isn't clear and I'll delay her somehow. You'll take her to the cemetery. Agreed? Lorie will be with you until Naomi has gone, then she'll come back inside the hotel with me. No one will know she's not my wife. Simple.'

'Simple,' Dan echoed, sarcastically. 'Now get out and leave me alone. I've been working all day. I need to sleep.'

'Do me a favour, Dan,' Nathan said, enjoying himself now. Dan glared at him as if to say *what now*? 'Before you leave her at the cemetery, show her your face. Introduce yourself and tell me about her reaction.'

'What? What the hell for?'

'Humour me. I think about stuff like that.'

Dan glared at Nathan a moment while his stomach churned relentlessly. 'You can go now.'

'Think about it.' Nathan happily left the room and Dan lay back and – with sleep not remotely on the horizon – reviewed his skeletal plan for the hundredth time. Naomi would never reach the cemetery. He'd snatch her from the hotel and take her somewhere secluded until he could work out what to do next. Once Nathan realised she hadn't been delivered, he'd abandon his plan to travel with Lorie and call Dan. Nathan would be livid, but Dan would negotiate her return her on conditions of a divorce and not a death. The Rolls-Royce would be stolen as planned. The crew would get their prize. They'd be satisfied. Dan would have to turn a blind eye to that. Nathan would already have the Hamiltons' money in the bank. Naomi would think that Nathan was the hero and that she'd been kidnapped and returned for a ransom. She'd never know Nathan was responsible. Loosely, that was Dan's counter plan. He went online and started looking at lonely cottages and ways of detaining her so she couldn't possibly escape.

***

Two days before the wedding, Dan had booked emergency time off work built on a sob story, and had helped himself to a few packaged needles and enough anaesthetic to knock Naomi out for days. He'd found a cottage in the Lake District that ticked the boxes. From the pictures, it even looked like it had old-fashioned internal doors with keyholes. He'd booked it for two weeks. He'd had to buy some wrist restraints from a revolting joint with obscure windows, and be served by a woman who had more body piercings than teeth. He modified his purchase with extra long chains so Naomi could reach the bathroom. He bought a few essentials for her, hardly daring to believe she'd ever reach the stage of actually needing and using them. He'd bought a bolt for the bedroom door, just in case. He'd hidden everything inside the spare wheel of his car having filled up with petrol and checked the tyres; he withdrew as much money as he had.

Dan was beginning to hope that things were going to work when one comment from Nathan sent his plan into orbit. It was Thursday evening. Dan was making a show of reading a medical magazine while Nathan watched Top Gear and ate Ben and Jerry's ice cream with a small spoon straight from the tub, and swigged a bottle of beer. He was in a fantastic mood. The Hamiltons had finally handed over the long-awaited cheque.

'Carter is going to follow you to the cemetery just to watch your back,' he said without averting his gaze from the TV. 'Another guy will be at the grave.'

Dan was crumbling inside and trying hard to muster the ability to speak. He looked up casually from behind his magazine. Nathan didn't meet his eyes. 'I don't need an escort, thank you,' he managed.

'Whether you need one or not, Carter insists on shadowing you.'

Every part of Dan's airtight plan was deflating. 'He can get stuffed.'

'Even stuffed, he'd find a way to make sure you deliver. They're professionals, Dan. Standard procedure. Deal with it, don't fight it.'

Dan found he couldn't reply, not now his tongue felt thick and useless. Deal with it? He was a junior doctor. His only experience with 'professionals' were with medical people who extended and enhanced lives. He stared through his magazine, focus beyond it, words a meaningless black blur. Nathan, taking his silence as agreement, stood up and changed the subject.

'Good news. I've got a best man, my mate Dave from Bury. Let's hope Camilla doesn't recognise him. And I've finally told Mum and Dad I'm getting married,' Nathan said. 'I didn't want it to be a shock to them when it all kicks off. It's bound to make the headlines unless the Queen hands the throne to Charlie.'

'What did they say?' Dan managed. He could feel the blood draining from his head and wondered if he'd pass out. The room was losing colour and clarity. There was a shortage of oxygen too.

'What can they do from the States? It's worked out perfectly. They think the wedding has been thrown together in a rush. I told them we'd have a reception when they get back so they can meet Naomi. Mum's too distracted with Gran to fight a battle.'

'Whatever,' Dan said, attempting to sound vague, struggling to remain conscious. 'When this is over, return her ring.'

'What do you take me for?' Nathan said, with mock sincerity. He did Dan the favour of standing, hurling his spoon into the sink from several metres away, and announcing he was packing some clothes. He turned on his way to the bedroom. 'Oh, and by the way, slight change of plan. I've told the pro we've hired that you'll pull the trigger.'

'What?' Dan couldn't say anymore. He could barely see.

'I've got a balaclava in my room, and a gun. It isn't loaded. It's just for show to shut her up if you need to. The pro will have the loaded gun, with a silencer. Aim and fire. Simple. And don't forget to introduce yourself to her first. Her face should be a picture. In fact, have a camera ready.'

Dan stared at Nathan, but could only see his outline. 'What the hell have you told her about me?'

Nathan laughed and calmly strode off to his room, while Dan doubled up, lowering his head, gasping for air, fighting the urge to vomit with the smell of cookie dough ice cream too close.

***

So here Dan was on the morning of the wedding in the wake of a bright dawn, exhausted, fearful, the heaviness in his chest a constant reminder that so much was at stake. He didn't want to get up and acknowledge that the dreadful day was beginning. Staying in bed, eyes fixed on the opposite wall behind which Nathan was sleeping, held it at bay. His revised plan was so full of risk and danger, his heart trembled whenever he went over it. It could backfire. He daren't think about it. He daren't not. Must it happen at all, this crazy wedding?

Daylight fuelled Dan's limbs until he twitched with restlessness. All week he'd planned how to save Naomi without properly questioning the insensibility of it all. Pumped with emotion and resenting the fact that he hadn't heard Nathan stir all night, he found himself bouncing out of bed and heading for Nathan's room. His only plan was to make Nathan see the insanity. His legs moved purposefully forward and only faltered outside Nathan's room. He closed his eyes and landed two clear taps on the door.

The bed creaked. Nathan was conscious. Dan opened the door and caught sight of a dark suit hanging from the curtain pole where weak light was finding a way in.

Nathan looked round, facing Dan framed by the doorway. Nathan squinted at him without sitting up. His voice was croaky. 'S'up, Dan?'

'Don't . . . ' he stopped. His throat constricted; his voice shook with the effort of speaking. He swallowed. 'Don't do it. Back out. Break her heart.' Nathan stared, blinked some more, looked as if he was struggling to know what day it was. 'Take the car. Rob the house if you must while it's empty, but don't go ahead. It's madness –'

'Hell, Dan. House won't be empty if there's no wedding.' Nathan turned his back on him angrily. 'What time is it?'

'Ten to seven.'

'Wedding's not till three.'

'Time to undo it.'

Dan waited for a reply and wondered if Nathan had drifted.

'You're worrying me, Danny,' Nathan eventually said, almost in a whisper. 'If I can't trust you –'

'Trust *me*? You betrayed and blackmailed me and hung me out to dry. This isn't about me or you, it's about crime and murder, Nathan. Use your head.'

'I have – and constructed the perfect plan.'

'It isn't perfect, it's evil. Back out.'

Nathan unearthed himself suddenly and flung the covers back. 'You don't understand these people. They're the evil ones, Dan. If not her neck, it would be mine.'

'Run then. Take the money this morning and disappear. Make sure they never find you.'

There was no hint of indecision. 'The cheque hasn't cleared yet so there is no money. Anyway, I've built myself up to this, Dan. Earned it. It's been brewing for a year. By next week, I'll be famous. And rich. And free. I'm looking forward to it.'

Dan dropped his head. Trying to reason with Nathan was hopeless. Futile.

Nathan carried on. 'Accidents, you know, they happen. Tragic. At least she'll have had a blissful week of marriage first. The press will love it. It'll sell. People will talk about it for a few days then forget. I'll slip into the background, broken. Lorie and I will find comfort in each other. I'll gradually restart my life. I'll ring Camilla now and again for old times' sake.'

'What if they want their money back?'

'You reckon they'll be thinking about money with their daughter gone? Henry was clear when he handed it over that it isn't theirs anymore. I'm telling you, Camilla looked relieved to see the back of it. Weird, or what?'

'You're a lunatic. I'm ashamed to call you my brother.'

'Whereas I'm proud of you for keeping a cool head so far.' For the first time, Nathan came close to smiling.

His voice was infuriatingly composed, which disarmed Dan completely. 'I'm just a person in trouble with a brilliant plan, is all, Daniel. And it's almost over. So if you intend to back out, say now.'

Dan's hands were trembling. His legs were unsteady. 'There is no backing out. You've made sure of it. So I'll be in the car park, Nathan, and I'll make sure she isn't violently hurt on the way to her grave. I'll make sure her death is quick and painless.'

'Whatever turns you on.' Nathan was watching him carefully, as if he was weighing up his suitability for the job. Nausea stirred in the pit of Dan's empty stomach and the feeling rose, but he didn't deflect his eyes.

'If we're done, I could do with tweaking my speech,' Nathan added, yawning, 'the one that thanks my in-laws for all their support and generosity and thanks my wife for being born and agreeing to spend the rest of her life with me, which is about the point I turn my attention to the chief bridesmaid and how stunning she looks.' This reference to Lorie made him smile openly and wipe the sleep from his eyes. He'd stopped looking at Dan with suspicion at least.

Dan stared helplessly. 'Aren't you the tiniest bit anxious this could go badly wrong?'

Nathan's eyebrows sunk for a second, then bounced back. 'No.' He paused to noisily scratch his crotch under the covers. 'See, there's a backup plan for every stage except Lorie passing for Naomi at passport control. What are the chances of them looking at her properly? Have you ever noticed those guys, eyes numbed by hours of looking at little books and a thousand faces that look alike? I could probably pass for her myself.'

Nathan settled down again. Dan closed the door and found his legs taking him to the sofa where he crashed down. He swallowed the sickness away and forced himself to confront the fact that he needed to prepare. A grave had been selected in a sheltered spot on the edge of a large batch of graves beside a row of trees. A rough diagram of how to reach it had been passed to him, along with the details on the gravestone. He had the day to plan the route and visit the cemetery in north Manchester. After dark when the gates were locked, entrance, he was told, could be made over a short wall through a broken railing. The diagram showed the route in red arrows from the road through the railings, to the grave.

Nathan volunteering Dan to do the shooting had been an advantage. Dan would take the gun. It would be dark. He'd position himself so he could put the bullet elsewhere. He'd need blood and distraction tactics so the guy wouldn't closely scrutinise the wound. He'd read enough to know that bullets make neat entries and messy exits. The drug he'd give Naomi would pull her pulse right down. Thinking about it brought on palpitations. He'd take beta blockers to dull the shakes and deceive his nervous system that he was preparing for neither flight nor fight when he could face both. Composure was essential when failure wasn't an option.

***

Naomi awoke to a bright morning, an endorsement if she needed one that even nature was smiling down. Why wouldn't it? She'd kept her side of the bargain with God, thanks to Nathan. He'd produced heroic self-control.

Lorie was in the room next door with her bridesmaid's dress. They'd chosen it together, a romantic white A-line gown in chiffon, only knee length, with a deep red sash that tied at the back and tumbled down the full length of the dress in two crimson satin streams. The neckline, like Naomi's, was low and V-shaped with two thin straps covering each shoulder.

Naomi flew out of bed and opened the curtains. Sunshine filtered in and danced in shadows on the wooden floor through a tree outside her window. Henry was getting out of his Rolls-Royce in his old dressing gown. He'd brought the car to the front of the house to attach some white ribbon. Henry was driving the four of them to the church. A hire car wasn't necessary.

Henry stroked the full length of his car with a yellow cloth and vanished out of view. Naomi went to her wardrobe to look at her dress and imagine Nathan's reaction when she reached him at the altar. It was fitted down her body to her hips, where it became full and fell an inch from the floor. At the back, a train fanned out with the same detail of pearl and lace that surrounded the waist in a wide band.

The morning passed with Lorie in a haze of pre-wedding pampering. They shaved, moisturised, plucked, painted and filed. Henry and Camilla were doing their own thing in another part of the house. Paths occasionally crossed.

The flowers arrived, bringing everyone together to scrutinize button holes for the men and two stunning bouquets of crimson-coloured calla lilies and white roses interspersed with Bear grass. The calla lilies were the same shade as Lorie's sash; rich-coloured, a type called Red Embers native to South Africa. Naomi had carefully researched the flowers, which were pale pink at first blossom, then turned dark red over time. They symbolised deepening love and passion. Scrolled petals formed almost a heart shape that arched and peaked at the bottom like dripping blood. She imagined casting them over her shoulder.

At midday, Lorie suggested makeup and hair in that order. Naomi's mobile rang from her bed. Lorie, who seemed more nervous than Naomi, jumped up to get it. She passed it over cautiously.

'It's Annie.'

During the few moments that it took for Naomi to reach out for her phone, a scene paraded through her head of Annie waiting to be collected at the airport. Naomi wondered if she'd changed her mind, unable to stay away, and come home.

'Hi Annie,' she said, desperately hoping.

'Please don't tell Mum I called.'

Naomi let all the air out of her and slumped on the bed. One sentence told her everything and flattened her. 'I won't.'

'Look, I know this seems lame – me not being there when you're about to get married. It isn't because I'm too busy or too far away. I wanted to be there, Naomi.' A pause, then some snivelling. 'I really wanted to be, believe me.'

Naomi steadied her own voice. 'Why didn't you come then?'

'I've thought about it loads.' She sighed and blew her nose. 'But I can't witness you tying the knot with Nathan. I'm sorry. I'll probably regret it and if I do it'll be my own fault, but at the moment, the further away I am, the better. I wouldn't be able to keep my mouth shut if I saw him again. Plus things are awful with Mum. Everyone's better off without me. It's your day.'

'Annie –'

'Let me finish. But, you're my sister and I really want you to be happy, so I'm ringing to say have a fantastic day and don't spoil it by thinking of me, OK?'

With Naomi too choked to respond, Annabel carried on.

'You've always been brainier and more sensible than me, so let's assume I'm wrong about Nathan and that you're going to have a great life together, OK?'

'I trust him,' Naomi sniffed.

'That's good,' Annabel sighed. 'So, tell me, are you still a virgin?'

Despite the tears, Naomi collapsed into laughter and blotted her eyes with a screwed-up tissue she found on the bed. 'Thanks to Nathan, yes.'

Annie laughed too. 'So weird. Let's hope after tonight you're not both having second thoughts.'

Lorie was watching intently, but was unsmiling. Naomi knew she could hear everything and found herself colouring. 'I'm sure it will be fine.'

'Fine? I'm expecting fireworks. You've waited long enough for some action.'

Naomi turned her face from Lorie and busied herself by collecting her makeup bag from her dressing table. She couldn't lose the smile. 'Well, I'll let you know,' she said.

'You'd better. And enjoy your day. Make it one to remember. Looking forward to seeing the photos. Don't tell Mum I called.'

After blowing Naomi two kisses down the phone, Annabel had gone and Naomi could once again sense the miles between them that had vanished while they were talking. Naomi turned to face Lorie with an emptiness inside her that only Annie had the power to cause, and fill. She dried her eyes. Crying had always been forbidden, or, when that failed, ignored.

Naomi's attention was won by Lorie taking a large butterfly clip from her hair and allowing it to tumble. It had grown six inches in two days.

'Your haircut is just like mine and it's the same colour. What did you do?'

Lorie smiled. 'I've had extensions and coloured it. I thought it would look nice for the photos. What do you reckon?'

'It looks great.' Naomi dragged Lorie to the mirror and they stood, side by side, Lorie standing just a couple of centimetres shorter than Naomi, hair and eyes the same shape and shade. 'We could be twins.' Naomi said.

'Except you look younger and your eyes aren't as close together as mine and you have higher cheekbones and better boobs.'

'What do you weigh?' Naomi asked.

'Eight stone, two.'

'Same, give or take,' Naomi said. She turned to Lorie. 'You've always been more like a sister than a friend. Don't ever lose touch just because I'm married and you're at uni. Do you promise?'

'Naomi, we're family, right? You've always been the sister I never had.'

They moved together and hugged. Naomi didn't know why she got the strangest feeling that today marked the end of something. Feeling tearful all over again and childlike too, she clutched Lorie.

Lorie gave her a very wide smile when they came apart. 'I'm so excited,' she said, taking Naomi's hands, squeezing them gently. 'Is all your packing done?'

'Yep, everything's ready to go. White underwear in the overnight bag with my nightgown. I've got the perfume we chose.'

'You'll be covered in confetti when you get to the hotel. Trust me, you'll want a shower to freshen up. Your soap bag has everything you need to look and smell fabulous. Are you nervous?'

Naomi thought of her end-of-year recital. 'I'm a musician, Lorie. I've done worse things. Plus I haven't rushed to the toilet yct, which is a very good sign.'

'Just enjoy every moment.'

'I intend to.'

Lorie turned to the mirror. Naomi caught her eye in it.

'So do I.'

Lorie slipped behind Naomi, lifted her hair and told her to take a deep breath. 'Brace yourself,' she said, taking hold of the clasp of Naomi's necklace from behind.

Naomi grasped the cross that had hung around her neck for eight years without ever coming off. It was her way of delaying the moment and preparing herself.

'Let go,' Lorie said, into Naomi's hair. 'Put it in the soap bag with the perfume and put it on before the big moment tonight after your shower.'

Naomi still clung on. 'I'll feel naked without it. I've always been protected –'

'It's called superstition.'

'To me, it's called faith.'

'It'll only be for a few hours and I'll be with you the whole time. After that, you can wear it for the rest of your life. You won't want to go to bed without it tonight.'

'No, no way.' Naomi watched her fingers reluctantly release her cross. Lorie soundlessly unfastened it, removed it and tucked it inside Naomi's hand. She replaced it with another necklace of pearls and diamonds – loaned by Camilla, inherited from her grandmother. A family heirloom. Something borrowed.

'There. Painless so far?' Lorie asked. Unsure, Naomi could only stare at herself until Lorie took her arm. 'Come on, time's pressing on. Let's not keep Nathan waiting.'

***

Camilla was last out of the house. She was reluctant to leave. She paused and looked behind her for no reason that she could fathom. End of an era, she told herself, and all that sentimental rubbish. She also told herself with insistence, to be practical and leave the house without further delay.

She busied herself by drawing a small sheet of paper from the drawer in the hall table. Leaning against the table, she penned a note to Cynthia the cleaner, who had not been invited to the wedding, but had been asked instead to come that day and clear up any wedding-preparation debris and strip the beds that Naomi and Lorie had slept in the previous night. Neither would be likely to stay there again and Camilla couldn't stand the thought of stumbling upon Naomi's room as she'd left it, with all the clues of her last moments there. She preferred to find it cleared and tidied. She hadn't once been in Annabel's room since Christmas. It was easier that way. Camilla let go of a sigh. Her short note said:

Cynthia,
Please clear and tidy the two upstairs bedrooms as discussed. When leaving, ensure all doors are locked and the hall light is on. Thank you. See you Monday as usual.
Camilla.

Camilla glanced up at the picture of Naomi and Annabel. A lump tough and painful as cement thickened in her throat. She picked up her white gloves and put them on. She straightened her hat. Her new beige handbag that perfectly matched her shoes, was beside her on the floor. She collected it. Her clacking heels echoed across the wooden floor as she headed bravely for the door, trying to summon a smile from a faraway place, leaving the silent house to its own private memories.

27

Naomi was holding the thin back of a phone she'd found sticking up from a crack in the paving stones by the back door. As Dan searched the back garden, Naomi concluded quickly that the remnant in her hand, was Lorie's. She was familiar with the make displayed in very faint lettering and two parallel scratches in the top right corner.

So Lorie knew. Maybe she'd warned Nathan already. News could spread at the rate of a forest fire. She'd always known too much and been too close. She'd always used it for her own advantage. Not this time.

Naomi hurried down the garden and found Dan beyond the gate frantically splashing light onto every dark corner. She took hold of his arm and he swung round, ready to attack.

'It was a phone,' Naomi whispered. Dan breathed out and relaxed. 'Lorie's phone.'

His eyebrows crunched together. 'Sure?'

'Certain.'

'What do we do?' Dan's voice was quiet, but not calm.

'We find her. Now. We can't let her leave.'

Beyond a row of spaced-out fir trees – which looked like great black giants in the darkness – on the border of the garden, a grassy embankment led to the low stone wall. Naomi lunged for the firs and squeezed between them, catching her arms. Dan followed. The slope was steep just at this point. Naomi scrambled up and hopped over the wall. There was a small dark shape tucked into the side of the road not far away. Even in poor light, the Mini was unmistakable. So Lorie was still around somewhere.

'Got her,' Naomi whispered to Dan who was right alongside.

'Now what?'

'When she comes out of her hiding place, we'll be waiting.'

'She has to be that way,' Dan whispered, indicating beyond the car to the rear.

They moved quietly to the front of the car, which was half lodged in long grass. They crouched. The wait was short. Someone was trotting up the deserted lane, panting hard. Naomi peeped out and confirmed to Dan that it was Lorie. She was holding her phone out in front of her as she ran, pressing buttons.

'Now, before it's too late,' Naomi mouthed.

The footsteps drew closer. Dan held his palm out to Naomi, universal sign for *hold still*. He pulled a penknife from his pocket and opened it out. When Lorie was right up to the car, they heard her say, 'Nathan, it's me.' Dan leapt out and seized her from behind. Lorie screamed and dropped her phone. Out of pure luck, it skidded Naomi's way. While Dan wrestled to restrain Lorie, Naomi scooped it up off the road. Lorie, in a desperate attempt to warn Nathan, started screaming that Naomi was alive.

Naomi straightened up. Dan had Lorie pressed against the car, one arm twisted up her back. She yelped. He released a little pressure.

Dan turned to Naomi. 'Did you cut Nathan off or does he know?' Naomi shook her head. There was a tense silence. 'Naomi?' Dan's voice was frantic.

'He knows,' Naomi whispered.

'No,' Dan yelled suddenly. He pulled Lorie slightly away from the car and rammed her hard against it. 'You could have walked, Lorie. But you had to come back here didn't you? And now we're all screwed.'

Lorie half turned, spat at Dan, missed. Dan pushed her arm up her back again until she cried out.

'You've betrayed your own brother,' she said. 'How could you do that?'

Dan inhaled a few noisy breaths. 'Your best friend is here in case you hadn't noticed,' he said, pulling Lorie free of the car, shuffling her round until Naomi was face to face with her a couple of metres away. 'You remember her don't you?'

Naomi paced forward, closing the gap. She glared at Lorie. Lorie glared back.

'How dare you lecture Dan on betrayal?' Naomi was standing in front of her now. Dan held Lorie's arms. 'You're finished, Lorie. You failed. You had everything once, and now I'm going to leave you with absolutely nothing.'

'I'd love to see how. Nathan knows exactly where I am, and it won't be long before he sends someone out for me,' Lorie said, out of breath. 'You're out of your league, Naomi. You've no idea what you're fighting here.'

'All I have to do is walk into a police station.'

'So why haven't you then?' Lorie hissed. She didn't wait for an answer. 'Because Dan's warned you that the consequences of being seen are too risky and that Nathan has powerful connections that you two don't stand a hope against. And because you're naive and stupid.'

'Oh, you think?' Naomi lashed out and back-handed Lorie across the face. Lorie struggled to fight back, but Dan held her tight. 'That one was from me.' Naomi slapped her hard across the other cheek. 'And that was from my parents who've loved you like you were their own daughter.'

'Bitch,' Lorrie screamed.

Naomi moved closer. 'Well, it's amazing what it does to a person being tricked into marriage, then being snatched and buried alive, then being taken and tied to a bed and being left for days with nothing to do but think. And then finding out that the people you loved most were responsible, and the person you loathed most was your only real friend. You kind of find yourself in a situation like that. I recommend it. In fact, I'm betting Dan could arrange the same treatment for you too.'

'Let's do it,' Dan said, pressing the blade of the knife into Lorie's neck until she didn't dare move. She drew shallow breaths.

'I know you won't hurt me, Dan. You haven't got the guts.'

'I've sliced into dead people plenty of times, and you're dead to me already.'

'Take her to the house. I'll bring the car,' Naomi said.

'We can't stay here,' Dan said, panic in his tone. 'Not now. Don't you see?'

'We can't go anywhere tonight, Dan,' Naomi argued. 'Besides, we have a hostage which gives us some leverage. We'll use her if we have to – if she's worth anything to anyone.' She stretched out one hand in Lorie's direction for the keys.

Lorie glared at her and held on to them. 'You unbelievable bitch.'

Naomi took a step closer and leaned her head forward until they were almost nose-to-nose. 'I haven't even started yet, but I think I'm learning the ropes. I'm not that innocent girl you followed up the aisle in my sister's place before you took off with my husband, Lorie.'

'Husband,' Lorie mocked. 'He was never yours. He was never even attracted to you.'

'Sure about that?' Dan cut in. 'What if Nathan enjoyed having two girlfriends?' he shot into Lorie's ear. 'Nothing turns him on more than playing games with peoples' heads. You know that better than anyone. When your jealousy didn't drive him crazy, Lorie, it amused him quite a lot.'

'You know nothing about our relationship,' Lorie yelled.

'Then how would I know this, "Do you enjoy kissing her, Nathan?" And he never answered your question because it entertained him too much to see you beg and then throw your little tantrums.'

Lorie tried to lash out, but Dan restrained her. The knife cut into her neck and started to ooze blood. 'So I'll answer your question, Lorie, seeing as Nathan never will. He loved being with Naomi and especially kissing her. She never tried too hard to impress him the way you had to, and the fact that he could never have her meant she drove him wild. So he was never yours either.'

Lorie, who'd been flicking her attention away from Naomi's eyes, glared into them now without blinking. Naomi said, 'I was with him for an hour in that hotel room, Lorie. He didn't expect me to live, so how do you imagine we passed the time?'

Lorie shook her head and breathed hard. 'You did nothing.'

Naomi managed to smile. 'Nothing? All that pent up frustration over months. What, you think he turned me down when I stepped out of the shower and didn't bother to get dressed?'

Tears of rage pricked Lorie's eyes.

Naomi carried on. 'You think I didn't know how to seduce him? The fact that I had no experience was what made him want me most.'

'The only way he wanted you was dead.'

'You know, looking back, it didn't feel that way to me. Nathan was very keen to make the most of what time we had left.'

Dan leant into her ear again. 'Nathan uses people, haven't you noticed? You served his purposes once, and now you're no longer useful to him. Knowing Nathan, I'd say the relationship has run into a dead end.'

'You're lying, both of you,' she yelled, eyes still on Naomi. 'We'll soon find out where Nathan's loyalties lie. I know he loves me.'

'He doesn't know the meaning of the word,' Dan replied. 'Now move it. Time for bed.'

'I have to get the money to Solomon.'

'You should have thought of that before you came here.'

'I have to settle it by tomorrow. Let me go.'

Dan hesitated, so Naomi stepped forward. She took hold of Lorie's arm and prised the keys from her hand. 'You're going nowhere.' Dan started to march her away, but he looked anxious as he glanced over his shoulder.

'Lovely view from the window,' Naomi called.

Naomi got into Lorie's car, blocking the verbal abuse Lorie was hurling back at her. Satisfied she'd convinced Lorie that Nathan would send a search-party, Naomi found a smile had settled on her lips as she considered the real truth: that Nathan knew nothing. The battery had dislodged as soon as Lorie dropped the phone. Naomi assembled it and switched it on. There was a message from Nathan, which said, 'Why aren't you picking up? What the hell was the screaming about? Any news about Dan's girl?'

On the screen in bubbles were the previous few messages they'd exchanged. Naomi got the picture pretty quickly. She pressed the screen to reply. 'Tripped in the dark. Hurt my ankle. Dropped my phone. Dan was bluffing about the girl. Nothing happening. Staying in B&B. Off to bed now to put my leg up. I'll set off early tomorrow to deliver the money to Solomon.'

Boiling inside, it took a few seconds for Naomi to muster the composure it took to finish with two of Lorie's signature kisses. Having managed them through gritted teeth, Naomi sent the message, switched off the phone and fired the car engine.

***

After an hour of yelling and stamping her feet, Dan went up to the room where Lorie was secured, and sedated her. Dan re-bolted the bed to the wall and moved it so she could use the bathroom. He returned to Naomi in the small sitting room. They looked at each other for a few moments without speaking, then he sat beside her on the sofa, arms spread over the back either side. He looked exhausted.

'She's right,' Dan began. 'We're out of our league with no way out. And we're not safe here anymore.' Naomi half smiled back at him. 'What do you know that I don't?' he asked.

'Nathan knows nothing. No one's coming to save her skin.'

Dan sighed in relief. His head dropped forward and he pushed both hands through his hair. Naomi produced Lorie's phone and showed him the recent messages, stopping before the one she didn't want him to see.

'However much she winds you up,' Naomi continued, 'do not tell her that Nathan isn't coming.'

'I won't.' He relaxed and tipped his head back against the Chesterfield sofa. 'Why did you lie when I asked you about it?'

'Instinct. I thought we could use it.'

Dan reached out and found her hand. He covered it with his and squeezed. Dan's hand was strong and warm. Naomi looked down as Dan tentatively weaved his fingers through Naomi's and held them there. Naomi allowed it. Seconds stretched on until, eventually, Dan let go.

'Sorry,' he said.

She was watching him. 'I'm not.'

He looked at her now with his piercing blue eyes, expression serious. 'Naomi, you know I have . . . feelings for you. I know the circumstances are awful, but I can't help it. I'm not expecting –'

'Dan,' Naomi absorbed his gaze. 'Things are . . . complicated, you know? I'm not even sure who I am right now.'

Dan nodded reflectively. 'Well, I think you're amazing.'

Naomi half smiled. 'Nathan said that to me once.'

'Difference is, he didn't mean it.' Naomi went silent a beat. 'Can I ask you something?'

'Sure.'

'On the wedding night, did you and Nathan actually – '

'No.' She dropped her head. Dan stroked her hand.

'Sorry to ask. I just needed to know. I wouldn't put anything past Nathan.' He paused. 'I'm so relieved.'

'Me too.' Naomi swallowed, gathering the courage to voice what was troubling her. 'Dan, tell me the truth, did Nathan really enjoy being with me?'

Dan closed his eyes, opened them. 'Honestly, I don't know. I'm sorry. I heard her asking him a couple of times. I heard him dodging it in his typical way. I know Nathan and how he thinks. I wasn't going to let her humiliate you, so I unleashed some ammunition I knew would hurt.'

'You and me both.' She couldn't add anymore. She should have despised Nathan, but it was easier to blame Lorie and see Nathan as a victim, which was also stupid and illogical. Time to start thinking with her head.

'I'm sure of something though,' Dan said, pulling her from her thoughts. 'For what it's worth, kissing you was the best moment of my entire life.' He paused. Their eyes locked. Naomi found herself mesmerised by the colour and intensity of them. 'Even though you thought I was my brother.'

Naomi shook her head. 'At some subconscious level, Dan, I knew you weren't Nathan.'

'Really?'

Naomi smiled weakly. 'Nathan has never kissed me like that. I don't think he's ever wanted me that badly.' Her smile fell away and she eyed Dan seriously. 'And I've never wanted him as much as I wanted you that night.'

There was a charged silence where the only sound was the measured persistence of the hall clock. Eventually Dan cleared his throat and looked away and changed the subject. 'So, what are we going to do about her?' He flicked a finger towards the ceiling even though Lorie's room was not directly above.

'We're going to finish her. Finish this. Clear up the mess somehow.'

'And how're we going to do that without ending up with a bullet in our necks or the police believing you were as much involved as Nathan?'

'I have an idea, but I want to think it through. Do you have a computer?'

'Course.' Dan rushed to his room and appeared within seconds with an iPad. 'What now?'

'A few days before the wedding, my parents gave us a lot of money. We set up a joint bank account and deposited the cheque.'

'Why didn't he just transfer Solomon's money to him?'

Naomi shrugged, but her mind got working. 'I'm guessing a guy like that strictly wants cash, which I'm guessing takes time. I'm also guessing Nathan wanted me out of the way before he took a chunk like that out of our account.'

Dan squeezed her shoulder.

'Let's hope he hasn't changed the password,' Naomi added.

'He thinks you're dead. Why would there be a need?'

Naomi logged into the bank's website and tapped in a user name and password. The screen went blank. Naomi held her breath.

'Thank goodness,' she said as the account details flashed up on the screen. A transfer had been made six days before, of fifty thousand pounds payable to Miss Loretta Taylor. There was still more than a million in the account.

'Bingo,' Dan whispered, looking over her shoulder. 'This is proof of Lorie's involvement. It's taken her a few days to convert it into cash. Twenty for me, the other thirty for Solomon. She must have it with her.'

'Give me your bank card, Dan.'

'What for?'

'I'm about to transfer a large sum of money.'

Dan reached inside his pocket for his wallet and produced a bank card. 'Do you know what you're doing?'

'Yes. I'm stopping Nathan from getting his hands on my mum's inheritance, so it's going into your account for safekeeping.' She looked steadily at Dan and tried to take the card off him, but he held on. 'I know I can trust you.'

'Of course you can trust me,' Dan said. 'But when Nathan notices it's gone –'

'It will be too late,' Naomi said.

'Too late for who?'

Naomi eyed Dan, but dodged the question until he finally let go of the card.

'I'm only sorry I won't see his reaction.'

'You're making me nervous, Naomi.'

Naomi made no comment as she read Dan's details and emptied all the money into his account except the twenty pounds Nathan had put into the account to activate it. She handed the iPad to Dan. 'Done. I'm tired now. I need to sleep. Can we talk tactics tomorrow?'

'First thing,' Dan said, standing up. 'I'll go and change my bed for you. I'll sleep down here.'

Naomi stood up too. 'No need. I'll be fine down here.' She looked at him and could see the objections in his eyes. 'I don't want to be anywhere near her upstairs. I don't trust myself.'

Dan considered it a moment and his face softened. 'OK.'

***

It was impossible to know when the right moment to leave would arrive. Naomi was lying on the sofa the way she had been for hours: on her back, wide awake, fully dressed, afraid of making a noise. She was clutching Lorie's car keys and her phone – her only source of telling the time – which she was checking every few minutes. For what seemed like an age, Naomi had stayed still and waited, listening, distracting herself by going over fine details in her head. It was almost three in the morning when everything upstairs finally settled into quiet. Dan, directly above her, had stopped turning over in bed.

At eight minutes past three, she got up to quietly locate something to write with, and on. She padded into the kitchen armed only with Lorie's phone for light. She found a print-off of the cottage details that Dan had brought for the address and which was blank on the back. Beside it was a pencil and Dan's bunch of keys. Naomi scribbled Dan a note, which she read back in her head.

It said:

Dan –

Whenever you find this, don't leave the house or try to follow me. I'm not bailing on you, but let Lorie believe I am and play the role well. If I'd talked the plan over, you wouldn't have agreed to take any risks. We can't hide any more.

I have Lorie's phone. Wait for me to call you. If Nathan rings, stay calm, get out of earshot of Lorie. Tell Nathan she never showed. Deny she's been here at all.

I can never repay you for saving my life, but I can try to sort out the mess from here without dragging you further in. Trust me OK? I'll be in touch.

N.

Should she add a kiss? She wanted to, but decided not. Naomi quietly removed a key from Dan's set. It was the one that was most familiar, the one that filled her head with memories and her eyes with tears. She blinked them away and returned to the small lounge where she sat, back straight, waiting on the sofa for a few more solitary minutes. Nothing happened. The house was as silent as a sepulchre. Almost. The clock spewed its robotic rhythm from the hall. Naomi could see the pendulum swinging in her mind's eye. In her head, she counted down from five, stood up, then advanced stealthily towards the kitchen again. She'd probably never see this house again. It was seared onto her memory.

The key was in the lock in the back door. She slid Lorie's phone inside her pocket and clutched the keys to prevent a noise. She crossed the kitchen and paused to listen. With concentration, she could still hear the clock. One click and the key turned in the lock. One gentle slide and the bolt across the top was free.

Naomi let herself into the back garden and took pains to close the door. She picked her way through darkness to the front of the house. She unlocked the car and cringed as the four lights flashed suddenly. Naomi hurried to the car on tiptoes and got inside. She switched on the engine, slid the car into first, and quietly pulled away without looking back. The expected call from Dan never came. Two and a half hours later, Naomi had pulled into Salford Quays and was getting out of the car and looking round at the black windows of Nathan and Dan's flat.

The dark water was shimmering with pools of yellow light from a line of lampposts. She went to the boot of the car and found what she expected to find: piles of money zipped up in two plain black bags. *Her* money. She picked the bags up. They weren't particularly heavy. On her way up to the flat, she checked the message on Lorie's phone which she'd hidden from Dan – the one that contained Solomon's address and warned Lorie that the deadline for payment was up at midday the day after. Even a second late was too late. The 'or else' part of the message wasn't needed. The address was in Gatley, South Manchester. What made her shudder was that it was only about seven miles from home.

There was another message from Nathan with a flight number and time to pick him up discreetly from the airport. It had been five days since the farcical tragedy. It was old news now, and old news had a short life in the public's memory. Would Nathan fly home to a gathering of interested journalists a week after the event? She doubted it.

Naomi scanned the starless September sky where the west was still black and the east was flushing pink. It wouldn't be long before the city sprung to life and the mechanics of a hectic day began to hum. She found the door and remembered the code to the building and entered at five forty-six. Relieved to have made it safely, she carried the money to the second floor and let herself into the flat, seeing no one en route. She closed the door and paused to inhale the familiar scent and feeling of the place. Her legs buckled.

She stumbled into the unlit bedroom and crawled into Nathan's bed in the dark, fully clothed. Aware of the nearby wardrobe containing all her clothes and shoes, she broke down. Her head filled with recent scenes of hauling all her things into the flat with Nathan, until she sunk into sleep.

Her dreams were jumbled and senseless. It was the phone, still in her hand, that alerted her and brought her back to Nathan's bed and the room that was littered with her stuff and now drenched in daylight. The light was too bright for early morning. She'd missed a message from Dan and there was a message from Nathan. She read Nathan's message first. 'Waiting to hear from you. By now you'll be on your way to Solomon's. Don't go inside. Leave the money with whoever answers the door and get away from there. Report back to me the minute it's done so I can relax. See you tomorrow. X'

Naomi sat up sharply in bed and tried to shake off the drowsiness. Her eyes burned. Dan's message was three hours old. 'My prisoner is yelling the house down about owed money. She's scared, Naomi. I've told her you've taken the money and run. I hope you know what you're doing.'

Naomi, still half-dead with fatigue, replied to Dan, 'I hope so too. Gag her.'

She rose from the bed and hurried to the wardrobe to find the right thing to wear. There was no such thing. Still, having to settle on something, and quickly, she pulled out a bold red blouse, a tight black pencil skirt and long heeled boots, and the whole time she prayed that God would forgive her for what she was about to do.

28

Camilla stood outside Naomi's bedroom, hand on the door handle, trying to work up the courage to open the door. It wouldn't come. Head bowed, eyes closed, she felt a gentle hand on her shoulder. She looked round to find Annabel, red-eyed, hair in untamed curls around her face.

'Haven't you been in there yet, Mum?'

Camilla shook her head. 'Not since the wedding day.'

'I haven't been in either.' Annabel moved to Camilla's side and watched her mum's bony hand resting on the door handle, knuckles white. Annabel covered Camilla's hand with her own. 'Together?'

Camilla's eyes flooded with tears. She couldn't help it. Annabel pressed her hand until the catch was released and the door swung open. They stood hand-in-hand in the doorway, not daring to go in. Camilla scanned the room cautiously, noting how Cynthia – the woman she'd sacked for negligence – had left the room exactly as instructed. The bed was carefully made. The curtains that framed the two parallel windows had been prettily arranged. Naomi's dressing table had been tidied. Cynthia had gone to the trouble of leaving an arrangement of flowers in a crystal vase. The flowers had wilted.

Annabel tugged gently on Camilla's arm. They walked inside the room together and looked round without speaking. The bathroom door was ajar. Naomi's fluffy white bath robe hung on the bathroom side of the door. At the sight of this, Camilla broke down. For days, she'd kept herself intact in front of the family. Now Annabel stood watching her, open-mouthed.

'Mum, are you crying?' she asked, needing confirmation.

Camilla nodded. Annabel took Camilla in her arms and held her. They stood for minutes until Camilla led Annabel to the bed and they dropped down.

Camilla mopped her eyes and looked at Annabel. 'Can you ever forgive me?'

'For crying?'

'No, for falling short as a mother and failing to accept your individuality, because I was too short-sighted to appreciate it.'

Annabel didn't respond. Her eyes filled with confusion and fresh tears.

Camilla carried on. 'I want you to know,' she began haltingly, 'that I've never favoured Naomi above you.' She stopped. Annabel listened in silence. 'I've always loved you both equally, but . . .' she swallowed and allowed the tears to fall without checking them, 'you remind me of my father, Annabel. You have his eyes, same colour.'

'I don't understand –'

Camilla held up a palm. 'Of course you don't. How could you?' she said gently. 'I never intended to tell anyone, but now he's gone it's time I offloaded.' Henry was standing in the doorway. Camilla didn't know how long he'd been there. She signalled for him to join them. He might as well know too.

Henry sat beside Camilla. 'I've always known about your father,' he said.

'You have?'

Henry nodded and placed an arm around Camilla's shoulder. 'He admitted it to me before we went to South Africa. I think he knew he might never see you again. He said that when the time was right I should tell you he was very sorry.'

'What about?' Annabel asked.

Camilla looked steadily into Annabel's eyes and took her hand. 'He was cruel. I had no label for it back then, and no vocabulary to explain myself to anyone even if I'd had the courage.'

'Granddad?'

'Yes. You know, the house where I grew up was Victorian. It had a cellar. If my mother was out, he'd shut me in there in the dark for doing the slightest thing wrong. The first thing I saw when he opened that heavy door, was the colour of his eyes. He was older than my mother. Served in the Second World War and brought all the damage home with him. He was distant, impossible to please, vicious temper. Occasionally it got out of control and he'd lash out, especially if I cried.'

'I got the impression he was quiet and withdrawn.'

'In later years, he was. He'd never let me practise the piano because of the noise. I desperately wanted to play, but he'd stop me and I'd end up retreating to the garden and studying the plants. I grew to love them.'

'I hardly remember him,' Annabel said.

'I took you and Naomi to South Africa when you were small because I didn't want you to remember him. We came back once he'd died. Part of me feels guilty about that.'

'I thought we came back because of what happened to Naomi.'

At the mention of her name, Camilla's chest felt too heavy. Her eyes refilled and a feeling of utter devastation pressed down. 'That was only part of it. I didn't really want to come back, but once he'd gone, I thought I should look after my mother, what was left of her. And now I can't stop thinking that if we'd only stayed over there in a safer part, Naomi would still be . . . '

'Mum, this is not your fault. We all feel guilty. I should have come back for her wedding.'

'That was my fault too,' Camilla said, gripping Annabel's fingers.

'No Mum, honestly, that decision was all mine. I couldn't face Nathan and I feel terrible about that now. Did you see him being interviewed last week? He's heartbroken. Imagine how bad he feels that he wasn't with Naomi when she . . . you know. Apparently, he offered to go on deck with her, but she refused. He'll always relive that night. He'll never forgive himself.'

Camilla shrugged. Henry gave her a silent squeeze. 'A mother wouldn't have taken no for an answer. I have no room for Nathan's feelings, Annabel, when I can't come to terms with my own.'

'You can't blame him, Mum. He did everything he could to find her. He has to fly home tomorrow without her.'

'I don't blame him, I just regret the day she ever met him. In any case, you're my priority, not him.'

Annabel wiped her eyes. 'Don't worry about me.'

'I will always worry about you. I'm sorry I've hurt you, Annabel. I am. I like to appear competent and measured and controlled, but the truth is it's a veneer to cover the fear and pain that never leaves me.'

Annabel swallowed hard. 'I get it, Mum.'

'I never told Naomi that I loved her.'

'You didn't need to, Mum.'

Camilla allowed her head to drop. 'She rang me, Annabel. The last time I heard her voice, she said just one word. My name. She sounded anxious. She got cut off. It was the night she went missing.'

'Mum, come on, we've been over this. She was probably excited, not afraid. The signal from the phone was bad. She was cut off, that's all.'

Henry chipped in quietly, 'Annabel's right, love.'

Camilla shook her head firmly. 'I'll never forget her tone of voice. It bothered me enough to check the time. It was quarter to eight in the evening. Caribbean time that would be quarter to three in the afternoon. She wasn't even using her own phone. Why is that?'

'What are you getting at Camilla?' Henry asked.

Camilla had never shared the thought until now. 'What if she was pushed?'

'Murdered?' Annabel went quiet for a long time. 'Who'd do that?'

Henry sighed.

Camilla, having voiced the dreaded thought, couldn't add any more.

'No,' Annabel said, eventually, 'It makes no sense.'

'Nothing has made sense to me for a long time now. I feel like I'm losing my mind.'

Annabel twisted her body and faced Camilla. 'Mum, listen, I've been thinking. Instead of sitting in the house all day like useless people, maybe me, you and Dad, and Lorie and Nathan, should organise a service for her at the church where she got married. Don't you think? We can play her favourite music, read one of her poems, invite her friends. She deserves a proper funeral.'

Henry said again, 'Annabel's right.'

'Funeral?' Camilla shot up. 'No, no, I can't,' she said, heading for the door. 'That's as good as giving up. There's a reason why she rang me distressed. Until I find out what it is, there'll be no talk of funerals. No, I need to fly out there and look at things for myself.'

'There's nothing to look at but a vast ocean, Camilla. Please.'

Annabel sighed. 'We've got to accept she isn't coming home,' she said to Camilla's back.

Camilla paused by the door and glanced round, eyes flooded again. 'I'm sorry, I just can't.'

***

Naomi pulled up on a well-to-do residential street with wide pavements that were edged with a strip of grass and a row of trees that hung over and arched across the road. She looked at the address on Lorie's phone. This was the house, number fifty-seven. She looked at it while she unfastened her seatbelt. It was detached. Dark brick, large bay windows with pretty stained glass in the front door that centred an open brick porch. There was a silver Mercedes on the drive. It was eleven fifty-seven. Three minutes to the deadline.

Naomi reached for her packed handbag and got out of Lorie's Mini. Her eyes were hidden behind huge sunglasses. She hurried up a herringbone-paved driveway without breaking into a trot. Before she reached the door, it opened. There was nobody in the doorway. A black mat sat behind the door that led to a marble tiled hallway with white walls filled with modern art.

Stunned, she hesitated before stepping inside. A pumped up body appeared from behind the door and indicated she step forward. Her pulse quickened. It didn't take her long to comb her memory and come up with a threatening guy in a grey hooded jacket. He had glassy dead eyes, non-descript colour. He was wearing a plain T-shirt that might well have been painted to his body. Biceps bulged beneath the sleeves. His shifty movements were chillingly familiar.

'A minute more and he'd have sent me out looking.'

Naomi swallowed. 'Nathan is still out of the country,' she said, for something to say.

'It's our job to know where Nathan is while he owes

402

us money,' he said.

She kept hidden behind her sunglasses and decided she was safer in silence.

'Brought the money?'

'Yes.'

'In cash?'

'Yes.'

'He's waiting for you in the card room.'

Naomi wouldn't have known where the card room was, but Lorie obviously did. She'd been here before and met these people. Naomi hesitated long enough for the big ugly guy to flicker his funny-coloured eyes in the direction of a door to her left. She noticed all the doors off the hall had keyholes. She imagined whoever lived here securing the doors at night before going to bed.

She stepped ahead of him into a huge bright room. It had big windows front and back and covered the length of the house. She took in a dark wooden floor, plush black leather sofas, black cast iron fireplace, more artwork on more white walls and a glass table close to the rear window. There was a door on the far wall that she would have assumed led outside. When she thought back, there was a garage on that side of the house. Beside the door was a heavy bookcase. She wondered if it doubled to cover the door. Seeing as it was the only other door in the room except for the one she'd just come through, she crossed the floor towards it.

Alone, she took hold of a polished silver door handle and pushed open the door. She was met by a hidden room with a view of the back garden. She guessed it was built behind the garage. The walls were lined with books on fitted book cases. From one glance, there was a mixture of fact and fiction with a section on history and Nazi Germany. Breaking up the books on the wall opposite the door, was a desk with box files and a flat computer screen and keypad, and a safe tucked into the corner. The back of a big black leather chair obstructed her view. In front of the window was another low glass table holding a pack of cards, face down, surrounded by six easy chairs.

A calm voice from inside the chair said, 'I don't like to be kept waiting.'

Naomi drew breath. 'Neither do I, so let's get this over with.'

The chair swivelled round. He was no older than about thirty. Slim, short fair hair, pale skin, sky-blue eyes that were intently watching her. His fingers pressed together like a steeple in front of his face. He was dressed in crisp dark trousers, white shirt open at the neck, polished black shoes. She was better able to hide the shock from behind her sunglasses. She didn't know what the face of an evil person was meant to look like, but she'd never pictured this guy, living on a regular street in an immaculate home that looked out on a beautiful landscaped garden that even Camilla would have been proud of.

She stood free of the doorframe, resisting the urge to slump. Silence. Either he was as shocked as she was, or she was expected to speak next. She had time to collect her thoughts and become more anxious.

He spoke first. 'Courtesy is very important to me, Lorie,' he said, standing, walking towards her, stopping just in front. He was shorter than Nathan by about four inches. 'An apology might be appropriate.'

'I'll have to disappoint you. Honesty is more important to me than courtesy.' He was close enough to reach out and touch. Naomi pushed her glasses on top of her head and looked him in the eye. 'It's Naomi Hamilton. I don't think we've ever met, but I feel as though I know you. One of your minions followed me, spied on me and threatened me not long ago, which wasn't very polite.'

He didn't respond immediately. His expression was unreadable. 'You're dead.'

'Is that a wish, or a threat?'

'I was led to believe it was a fact. Have you come alone?' he asked, eyes narrowing and shifting.

'Yes.'

'If you're lying to me –'

'Why would I do that? I didn't have to come here. No one in the world but you and Dan Stone knows that I'm alive.'

Again, he stared at her without speaking. She held his eyes.

'You're beautiful,' he said, as if he was thinking out loud. 'I could blissfully get lost in those eyes for a very long time.'

She didn't react, but her nerve faltered. She'd dressed for confidence, not appeal.

He switched subject. 'OK, you've got my attention. What are you doing here, Mrs Stone?'

'I'd prefer it if you didn't call me that.'

For the first time, a ghost of a smile played on his lips. 'Fine by me.'

Naomi broke eye contact and took her bag from her shoulder and emptied the contents onto the glass table to her right. Forty-five thin bundles of fifty-pound notes fell out. Each bundle held a thousand pounds, easily countable. She'd reserved five thousand for Dan. He glanced at the table, but didn't budge.

'Forty-five thousand,' she said. 'I'm here to pay Nathan's debt and cut ties for good.'

His eyebrows twitched. 'You realise he arranged to have you murdered? His idea.'

'Yes.'

A pause. 'You say he doesn't know you're alive?'

'That's right.'

He frowned. 'You're not about to give me a sickly sermon on the virtues of love and forgiveness I hope.'

'I wouldn't waste my breath.'

'In that case, I'm intrigued. You've succeeded in surprising me, which happens pitifully rarely,' he said. 'Tell me what you're doing here.'

'It has to stop now. You've taken my dad's car, and every penny you've had from Nathan has come indirectly from my family, including that.' She flicked a glance at the table. 'So, I intend to forget we've ever met and go home to my family. Nathan and Lorie will be punished by law for faking my death. Because I'm alive, no one's going to look your way, are they? I don't ever want to have to look over my shoulder again. And I want the same for Dan Stone. The only crime he's committed is saving my life.'

He smiled, fully now. 'You're very demanding.'

'It's been a stressful couple of weeks.'

'I can see that.' The smile vanished. 'I like women who know what they want.' He lowered his voice and shuffled closer. 'Do you realise what a vulnerable situation you're in here, Naomi?' He eyed her carefully up and down. 'You've come alone – entered the lion's den, you might say. No one knows you're alive.' He paused. 'You're an exceptionally attractive girl with no one to watch your back.' His voice had dropped to a whisper. His mouth was inches away. Naomi didn't recoil.

He continued. 'Some girls get a kick out of danger. They're not attracted to the nice guys who get them flowers and write poetic verses. They go for the bad boys to inject a little excitement into their lives. Are you one of those girls, Naomi?'

'No.'

He smiled. 'So, you're a good girl then?'

'I try.'

'That's good.' He eyed her again, in no rush. 'See, guys like me, when bad things go down, we like to come home to girls like you.' He leant forward, tilting his head, stopping an inch from her lips. Naomi swallowed hard. 'With your permission, I'd very much like to kiss you.'

She didn't move. 'I'm married. I'd very much like it if you didn't.'

'We both know your marriage is meaningless.'

'When I stood in church with God as my witness, it wasn't meaningless to me. So until –'

'You're a shrewd negotiator, Naomi, don't hide behind God. How about one kiss and you can have your money back and leave. What do you say?'

They were breathing the same air. Naomi, aware of the scent of her own perfume, wished she hadn't worn any. 'I agree I'm in a vulnerable position. One kiss can easily lead to other things.'

'What things?' Naomi said nothing. 'Describe them to me.' Naomi held her breath. 'Naughty things you've never done?' he dragged out in a throaty voice. He paused. 'Unless . . . Nathan . . . showed you a thing or two before he sent you to your death.' Naomi didn't move. 'You're exciting me, Naomi.'

Naomi drew a little air. 'I don't want you to kiss me, so ignoring that would be very rude indeed.'

He coolly backed off, unruffled. He was smiling, in fact. Was it all a game? A test? Her heart was inconsolable. Her legs could barely support her weight. She battled to hold her nerve.

'OK. Let's do it your way and be honest then. Your husband owes me thirty thousand, not forty-five.'

Naomi paused to calm her breathing and control her voice. 'I know that.'

'So . . . I'm struggling to work out why I've earned a bonus.'

'You haven't yet.' Naomi leant against the doorframe for support now. 'I was hoping for a favour.'

He sat carefully in the chair again, easing her discomfort a little.

'A favour? Does it involve Nathan?'

'Yes.'

'You know, I'm very disappointed in him. He'd have made a great business partner, but he wanted out. It took an awful lot of persuasion to let him go.'

'I know. We paid.' Naomi collected her bag from the table, a signal she was ready to leave. 'Maybe what I have in mind will be satisfying for both of us.'

'There's an irony here, Naomi, don't you see it?' She shook her head. 'Nathan was good. You're better. Plus you have more guts and nicer legs.'

Her only thought was to get out as fast as possible. 'Do we have an agreement or not?'

'I'm in,' he smiled widely, opening his arms. 'What man except an idiot could refuse you?'

'I'll be in touch.'

'The sooner the better.'

***

Naomi stopped the car around the corner and took out Lorie's phone and called Dan. She kept checking that no one was following her. She was trembling all over when Dan answered, sounding out of breath.

'Naomi, I've been panicking. What the hell are you up to?'

'It's all sorted. No one's going to pay the ultimate price, but debts have almost been paid.'

'Almost?'

'Nathan and Lorie are going down, Dan. Are you prepared for that?'

'Yes. I agree we have to turn them in.'

'We won't need to turn them in.'

'Meaning?'

'You'll see. Look, I've got to get out of here. I'm going back to the flat to pack my things, then I'm going to Lorie's flat to retrieve anything from my life she's taken.'

Dan breathed loudly down the phone in relief. 'Be careful, OK?'

'Of course. What's happening there?'

'She's like a wild animal. I mean she's not just furious, she's ferocious. And she's afraid.'

'Progress. Prison doesn't reform people, Dan. By the time I've finished with both of them, they'll have a small inkling of what they've put me through, followed by plenty of time to think about it.'

'I've got to be out of the cottage by tomorrow.'

'Perfect. Nathan will be back in the UK by then. He'll very much want to see Lorie. Pack your things. Tie her up. Throw her in the boot. Bring her back. I'll tell you when and where once a plan's in place. And don't panic or back down on anything.'

'I promise.' Dan cleared his throat. 'Naomi?' His voice had a tender edge.

'Yeah?'

There was a heavy pause. 'Doesn't matter.'

'Yeah it does.'

Dan didn't reply.

Naomi read the silence. 'I miss you too, Dan. See you tomorrow.'

***

Nathan was standing in the queue ready to board the plane home, aware of the eyes on him. Having done all he could to locate his lost bride, he was going home to try and rebuild his life without her. These were his thoughts as he arranged what he hoped was a suitable expression. There was an unusual hush in the line of people who were allowing him to the front as if they were collectively responsible for his loss. It was VIP treatment. Very nice! He was absorbing the apologetic glances, the mothers who silenced the whispers of the kids and told them off for staring.

Something was troubling Nathan though, making his pained expression easier to fix. He hadn't heard from Lorie. UK time, it was six pm. She should have delivered the money to Solomon hours before and let him know the job was done. Time and again he'd tried to contact her and got nowhere. Had she run into trouble? Been late? It was unthinkable. The most logical thing was a communication problem, but still he felt unsettled. The flight to Manchester with a pit stop in New York was eighteen hours, during which time, he wouldn't get a signal. His phone was infuriatingly silent. And to think that the last time he'd spoken to Lorie he'd been anxious to be rid of her . . .

'Sir?' An attractive English stewardess with very red lips and glossy tied-back hair dragged Nathan from deep thought and invited him to follow her. When they were free of the line of people and heading directly for the plane, she said, 'The Captain has instructed me to offer our condolences and upgrade your flight to first class. If there's anything we can do to make the flight easier or more comfortable, please don't hesitate to ask.'

She was walking slightly ahead. From behind his dark shades, he admired her figure in a tight navy skirt and slightly transparent blouse. The way she moved her hips when she walked mesmerised him. Her legs were toned and shapely and perfectly tanned. The delightful view was marred only by his desperation to hear from Lorie while there was still time. When she took a glance over her shoulder, Nathan offered a strained smile as if nothing could ever compensate for the pain.

'That's very kind. Thank you.'

His phone vibrated in his pocket just before they reached the open door of the plane.

Finally. He resisted looking while he was shown inside and up a short flight of stairs to his luxury seat.

She indicated that he should sit down and make himself comfortable. Now his spirits had lifted a bit, he took time to notice that her name badge said 'Jess.'

He sat down. She leant a little closer as if lowering her voice marked respect. She smelled as good as she looked. 'Can I get you a drink?'

'That would be lovely, Jess, thank you,' he said sincerely. 'Whisky and dry.'

She nodded and hurried away. Nathan withdrew his phone from his pocket. It was a message from Lorie just as he'd hoped.

'About time,' he muttered, opening the message.

His mouth went dry. Even sitting down, he felt dizzy. He could only stare.

The stewardess returned with the drink that clinked with ice. 'Sir? You don't look so good. Are you alright?'

He mindlessly took the drink and downed it in two big gulps. His hands were shaking. 'Another, please.'

After a short delay, she left again. Nathan looked down again at the message in his hand. It said: 'Couldn't have done it without you. Thanks for all your help. It's been fun. Xx'

Nathan logged on to the internet and hurried as quickly as he could into the website of his bank account.

He jabbed out user names and passwords. Details arranged themselves on screen. He stared. His balance was twenty pounds. He thought he might be sick. He logged into Lorie's account, having to fight to remember her password. Her account details lined the screen. The account was empty. Nathan wanted to scream out loud. She'd withdrawn the fifty thousand they'd transferred to her account. There was no sign of the rest of the money. Lorie had a secret account somewhere. Of course, she must have.

The stewardess returned, looking concerned. She handed him another drink, which he took without thanking her and gulped quickly. He needed cold water on his face.

'Is there a toilet I could use?'

'This way.'

Nathan disappeared inside a pocket of a bathroom and locked the door. He splashed his face with water and sunk onto the toilet seat. He fought for a signal, found Dan's number and dialled it. Dan answered after a few rings.

'Dan, I'm in trouble.'

After a short pause, Dan said, 'How?'

'Lorie has done the dirty on me. Sly cow has taken off with all the money,' he whispered fiercely. He sighed and shut his eyes. Hearing it out loud seemed to double his anxiety.

'How do you know?' Dan asked.

'How do you think – the account's empty. So is Lorie's because she's got fifty grand in cash. I've got to catch up with that bitch before Solomon catches up with me. Where did she go after she'd been to see you?'

'Nathe, she hasn't been here.'

'What?'

'She didn't show.'

'I know she came. She described the cottage, said you were seeing some girl.'

'Girl? Girls are the last thing on my mind. What you know is what she told you.'

'She was supposed to give you Mum's ring.'

'Like I said, she didn't show.'

'I'm going to kill her,' he hissed, the full impact hitting him about now. 'I trusted her.'

'Trust is a risky business, so you've always told me.'

Nathan wasn't listening. 'You've got to help me, Dan. We're brothers.'

No assurances came back. Nathan's agitation grew with the silence that followed. 'Nathan, I told you that if you ran into trouble, you'd be on your own this time.'

'We're in this together. If I go down, you're going with me, Daniel. You *and* her. You've committed a murder don't forget that.'

There was another short pause. 'I only ever tried to help you, Nathan. I trusted you and you crapped on me from a great height.' Dan sounded close to tears.

Nathan was unmoved. 'Don't go soft on me now,' he whispered fiercely.

'Bye, Nathan.'

Dan cut the call. Nathan was pumped with enough rage to punch something, preferably Lorie's face. He didn't even have the luxury of yelling. He thought of Lorie, thousands of miles away with a head start and all his cash. Plus a ring worth thousands. He captured his wild eyes in the mirror. He stared and asked himself a pressing question: *Do I hunt the bitch down or try and get off the plane.*

29

It was a smooth landing at Manchester when the British Airways flight from San Juan to Manchester via New York, touched down an hour late at eight-thirty in the morning through clear skies. Nathan had played the part well of a bereaved person who'd lost everything and was about to face a painful and uncertain future, because there'd been no acting required.

He'd never know that Jess the stewardess, would go home and report to her parents that Nathan Stone had been distraught and had not slept all flight, but had sat upright in a trance staring blankly into the abyss of black space beyond the window, unaware of everything. He hadn't been so bad, she reported over lunch that same day, when she'd seen him before the flight, but had deteriorated the further away he went from his bride's final resting place. Nathan would never know that Jess and her mum had spent a few silent moments pitying him, before Jess turned in to bed for the day and her mum went to the gym. He'd never know that the story the day after that, had become distorted enough to include him sobbing all journey.

Apart from staff, Nathan was last off the plane, and last to the terminal to reclaim his luggage. He was in no hurry. Leaving the safety of passenger-only areas to a public meeting point where Solomon or one of his crew might be waiting to collect money Nathan no longer had, was hardly inviting.

Nathan watched his suitcase pass him four times on the carousel before dragging his stare from the snaking black belt and retrieving it. He wheeled it to the gents where he hung around to kill time. After a spell in the toilets, he wandered into the baggage hall again and dropped onto a hard bench for another cowardly wait.

The sensation of his phone vibrating, dragged his concentration from a trampled sweet wrapper on the floor. A text message three words long chilled his blood. From Solomon, 'You can run . . .' But you can't hide, he finished off in his head.

Nathan looked about him as a random sample of the general public trailed luggage around. No one was paying him any attention as he sat, head bowed. The hall was constantly filling and emptying – the people themselves on a kind of conveyor belt. His forehead felt moist, like his hands. *Pull yourself together,* he told himself sternly, trying to rally himself into some action. *If they're waiting for you out there, sitting here isn't going to save your skin.*

He pulled his wallet from his hand luggage and counted his English cash. Was there enough for a taxi to his flat, if he got that far? He had nineteen pounds thirty-eight pence. It would get him somewhere. He hadn't thought he needed to reserve any cash when Lorie should have collected him. The free drinks on the plane had preserved what bit he had, mercifully. The thought of Lorie and the need to track her down, gave him the energy to stand.

He dragged his suitcase towards the exit and held back until he could tag on to a group of people. He emerged head down. It was stupid to think that like a child playing hide-and-seek, if he hid his face no one would see him. At six feet three, he was as conspicuous with his head bowed as not. Nathan chanced a glance at the scattering of faces who were gathered together in small clumps, waiting. He scanned desperately while working to appear casual. He looked down for a split second before stalling mid stride and re-searching the faces with a sense of alarm. He'd seen someone, a girl who was slow to file out of his memory and into his mind because she'd been deeply stowed. Buried, in fact.

His eyes flicked over a dozen faces, twice over. Three times. She wasn't there. Was she ever? He looked beyond the bodies and could see no one scurrying away. He was tired. Maybe mad. Maybe stressed too. *Naomi? Use your head, idiot.*

Glancing occasionally over his shoulder, Nathan proceeded on shaky legs to a vacant taxi outside the front door. As he got into the back of the car, lugging his case behind him, he noticed a blue Mini ahead in the road with a Union Jack roof. Nathan stared anxiously after the car as it drew further away, but he made out the registration plate. It was definitely Lorie's car. Nathan was tempted to yell the clichéd 'follow that car' line, but he was worried he might be recognised. Staying in character was essential.

He had no thinking time, so he said as calmly as possible, 'A friend should have collected me but I was late out. I can see her car straight ahead. Can you try to catch her up so I can hitch a lift back?' The driver did an impressive wheel skid and set off in pursuit.

'Why don't you call her?' he suggested as they gained ground.

Nathan hadn't decided if he wanted to let Lorie know he'd seen her or not. What he was definite about was the need to know where she was going. Had she seen him? He thought not. He suspected she'd come to the airport to check out whether or not he'd returned, and given up once he'd failed to come through the terminal. No, on balance, he decided it was more advantageous to track her from a distance, so he slunk back in his seat and made a mock call on his phone.

'She isn't picking up,' he told the driver.

'Sensible.'

'Just follow her please.'

'Shall I honk my horn?'

'Best not. I don't want to startle her,' Nathan said, honestly.

Nathan was close enough to see Lorie's long dark hair with her new extensions. In the mirror all he could see was a large pair of black sunglasses. If he'd been driving the taxi, he'd have been tempted to ram into the back of her hard. Being this close to her made his insides simmer with hatred and – he couldn't deny it – hope. Pursuing Lorie was as good as following his money and now she was in sight, so was the cash. He was going to corner her and make her sweat. And for her greed, she'd get nothing. He'd have to pay Solomon an outrageous sum to appease him. Any amount was a small price for freedom. Plus, he'd taken life insurance cover with Naomi. There was another pay-out to look forward to later on.

As expected, Lorie picked up the M56 and progressed towards Manchester Centre. He wanted to ask the driver to create some distance, but daren't. Conscious that the driver might work out who he was before long, he stayed cool and detached, answering questions in minimal sentences to keep up pretences.

A few minutes later, it occurred to Nathan that the taxi was being followed by the same model of a black Volvo he'd seen at Solomon's place. He shifted behind the driver's seat until he could watch it in the wing mirror without turning round. He hoped for a coincidence until the car got so close, he could make out enough of the driver to recognise him. One of the crew. A huge guy like Carter, this one a red-haired guy called Leon Chambers.

Nathan slid a little further into his seat and nursed a growing sense of dread. Lorie signalled to come off at junction six. Where the hell was she going? He'd hoped she was going home, but she was heading for the A538 which led through Wilmslow to Alderley Edge and the Hamiltons' house. He couldn't follow her there. What was she up to, the conniving little cow? It was time to call off the chase. It wasn't all bad news. He knew where she was heading.

Nathan suddenly remembered he was exhausted. He smothered a series of yawns. He had to collect his car and hunt Lorie down before taking a much-needed rest. He'd have instructed the driver to take him home, but he needed to shake off Chambers. Wearily, he told the driver to stop following the Mini and head for the city centre instead. Once he'd shed the shadow, he'd jump on a Metrolink tram back to the Quays.

To save time, he paid the driver over his shoulder just before the car stopped at traffic lights. He jumped out without looking back, and headed for the nearest department store to get lost. It was two minutes before he realised he'd left his case. He cursed under his breath and his mind ran over what he'd lost. His flat key was in his wallet in his pocket, beside his phone and passport. With a million quid, he could replace shorts, T-shirts and beach towels. The priority was to get to Lorie.

Nathan wasn't being pursued. He grabbed a navy baseball cap from a bargain bin and parted with a couple of quid for it, saving enough for the tram. The giant shop had four floors and three doors on the ground floor. He took the exit on the opposite wall to where he'd burst in fifteen minutes before and found himself on a quiet side street. He put the cap on and worked his way cautiously to the main road to check if the door was being guarded. It wasn't. Not long later, Nathan jumped off the tram at

Salford Quays and searched for the parked Volvo, which he couldn't see.

Result. With some relief, Nathan entered his apartment building at ten-forty and made his way to the second floor. His hand was unsteady as he unlocked the door and hurried into the hallway. Back against the closed door, he stood for a moment absorbing the blissful peace of home. During a few deeply drawn breaths, he detected a whiff of floral perfume. It was so subtle he lost it straight away and couldn't recapture it. Nathan wandered towards his bedroom and stood in the doorway. Naomi's things had vanished. Lorie had taken every last stitch of it.

He checked the cupboards. Not a trace. Fury rose in him again. He'd been planning to visit the Hamiltons with a few items of Naomi's clothing, a nice gesture as Lorie herself had told him. Keep them sweet. Tiredness fled from him. He was going to find Lorie. Immediately. Nathan snatched his car keys from the side of his bed.

'Going somewhere?'

His heart flipped.

Vincent Solomon was leaning against the doorframe, hands in smart trouser pockets. He always looked ready for a business meeting. The fact that he'd come without sending someone wasn't good.

'How did you get in here?'

'Does it matter?'

'Look, it's not my fault. Lorie was meant to pay you and she took off with the money, but I know where she is and I'm going to track her down right now. Then I'll come straight over to your house, I promise.'

He eyed Nathan carefully. 'I'm tired of excuses, Nathan.'

'I'm going to get you the money.' He held up his keys. 'Now. First opportunity.'

Solomon's smile chilled Nathan. 'Because I'm a reasonable man, I'm going to keep this simple. You have until midnight tonight to get my money, and you can add twenty thousand for my trouble.' Nathan was surprised it wasn't more. 'Fifty thousand, Nathan. For one hundred thousand, you can have your brother back.'

'You have Dan?'

Solomon didn't reply.

'So that's how you got in here.'

Solomon straightened up.

'Locate Lorie. Get my money. Bring her to the cemetery around midnight. I'll meet you there with Dan.'

'Cemetery?'

'Yes. I don't want you at my house, not now you're a celebrity. Besides, your wife will appreciate a visit I'm sure. Don't fail. Final chance, I promise you that.'

Nathan nodded, relieved. Solomon left.

***

Dan locked up the cottage for the last time and posted the keys through the letter box as the landlord had instructed. He threw his bags on the back seat, glad to be leaving. Lorie was secured in the boot as Naomi had instructed. There was one more thing still to do.

Dan opened the boot to find Lorie squinting into daylight on her back. Her hands were tied in front. She was lying on the pillow Dan had provided out of charity. He stared at her. She tried to yell something, frustrated as hell with the inability to form words.

Dan calmly delivered his carefully planned line. 'Nathan's dead, Lorie.'

Saying the words out loud had an impact on Dan, even though he knew they weren't true. His eyes swam. Lorie's spurted tears. She made as much noise as the cloth around her mouth would allow.

Dan shut the boot and wiped his eyes as he climbed into the driver's seat. He turned on the radio to drown out his thinking. Two weeks had felt like two months. He swigged a can of Red Bull to keep him sharp. It would be evening by the time they got back. Dan shoved his car into first and pulled away from the cottage without a desire to look back.

***

Nathan had been desperate enough to ring the Hamiltons. He'd spoken to Henry and under intense pressure, had had to act the grieving husband all over again. He'd rung for one purpose only: to find out if Lorie was at the house. After an excruciating twenty minute conversation where Henry had wept like a baby and Nathan had felt obliged to join in, he'd manoeuvred the conversation onto discovering that Lorie hadn't visited for several days.

What? Where the hell was she?

Nathan had been to Lorie's flat. No joy. He'd rung her a dozen times and not got a response. He'd sat outside the flat until late afternoon before giving up and driving by every other place he could think of. She was in none of them. He'd even, heaven only knew why, driven past Simple Simon's in the fading late-afternoon light. No Mini. He went back to recheck the flat – hers, then his. No sign. He tried her phone another dozen times.

Hungry and exhausted, he'd driven aimlessly round the city centre until every street and every person looked the same. Necessity halted the search. Nathan crawled into a station and filled his car with enough petrol to leave his bank account running on fumes. With a cheque for one point one million going in, he hadn't arranged an overdraft facility. He begged the use of the toilet and bought an energy drink and a bar of chocolate and used t hem quickly.

He returned to his car, noticing that the sky was moonless and that the onset of darkness had brought a stern easterly wind that cut through his coat. Crispy leaves were blowing into the forecourt. Nathan hunched into his jacket and zipped it to the top. He glanced at his watch. Almost nine-fifteen. He screeched out of the station to begin another desperate search, not daring to count how many hours he'd been awake.

At ten-thirty, Nathan stopped by the side of the road. Which road? He didn't even know where he was. Confused and disorientated, he smashed his hands into the steering wheel with both hands and shook it violently, screaming every foul word his vocabulary could muster. Tears of rage blinded him.

It helped release some tension, but he felt an idiot, even alone. He hadn't cried in a decade, maybe more. 'Man up,' he yelled to himself, clearing his eyes. 'Quit acting like a fairy.'

The mist cleared from his mind. No time for self-pity. He scrambled a plan. He hadn't been to Alderley Edge, the last place Lorie had been headed. He had no real hope of finding her there. She could be in Timbuktu by now and probably was. The clock was speeding up. For the hundredth time, he cursed himself for not following her while he had the chance, and set off in search of a road sign. Last throw of the dice. Plan B was to get as far away as possible. It would be a death wish to show up at the cemetery without Lorie. He had no wish to die. Dan had made his position clear, so Dan was on his own.

Nathan had the sneaky suspicion he was being followed from a distance, but couldn't prove it. It was more of a hair-raising feeling. He found and trawled the streets of Alderley Edge and roamed round the deserted centre. Why had Lorie come here? Maybe it was a decoy to throw him off course. Maybe everything he'd done today had been a big fat waste of time and petrol. It was gone eleven by now. The roads were as empty as Nathan's head; the sky as dark as his mood. He sat at a crossroads. *Quit the search or run?* Two minds weren't better than one. His phone signalled a text. He was alone on the road. He jerked the handbrake up and opened the message. It was from Solomon. It read: 'Time's almost up. You're being shadowed. Don't try and run. And don't be late.'

Nathan stared at the words and panted hard. He had nothing to say in return. Suddenly conscious that he was at a T-junction and wondering who was trailing him, he snatched a look in his rear-view mirror to check for cars. Nathan caught sight of a small car turning down a side street. It looked like a Mini. It was a long shot. Nathan, fired and desperate, did a U-turn and screeched down the street in pursuit. He made a right turn and ahead of him in the road was a blue Mini. He sped along until the registration plate was in view. It was Lorie's car. No doubt at all. He could see her in the front seat with her new hair extensions.

Unable to believe his fortune or keep composed, Nathan laughed out loud. Time to let Lorie know the game was up. Nathan found her number, dialled. He watched her reach across to the passenger seat and look at her phone.

'Pick up,' he whispered. 'There's a good girl.'

Nathan flashed his headlights at her three times and positioned himself just inches from her back bumper. Eventually, Lorie put the phone to her ear and answered without speaking. Nathan smiled. 'See the car up your backside, Lorie? Guess who?'

It was too dark to see her face. She said nothing.

'Make one wrong move and I'll hit you so hard, that flimsy little box will fold like cardboard. So we're taking a little detour to Naomi's cemetery where Solomon is waiting to collect his cash. Do you have it with you?'

After a short pause, there was a murmur. 'Mm.'

'That's good. Lead the way. No more smart moves, Lorie, or you won't see another daybreak. I'm pretty certain I'm being shadowed too. You don't have a hope.'

Nathan cut her off. He wanted her to sweat. He hoped her hands were shaking. He hoped she was going to suffer badly. He steadily kept about a metre or so behind. The cemetery was a half hour drive. He'd make it before midnight, just. He was alert, always expecting her to make a break for it, but she kept moving steadily, glued to his front. He saw her looking regularly into her mirror and regretted he wasn't close enough to see the fear in her eyes.

***

Naomi led Nathan down a route she'd travelled two weeks before, a route she'd never seen. Her heart was pounding erratically as she drove down the eerie country roads that led, as her sat-nav promised, to the tree-lined stony lane. Solomon's car sat at the end of it close to the imposing pair of locked gates.

Damien Carter emerged from the Mercedes as she pulled up with Nathan close behind. Carter strode over and pulled her from the car and put something over her head that felt like a rough sack. Some small holes had been picked so she could see. Otherwise, she could have been going to the gallows.

Naomi had no script from here, no plan. A reunion at the cemetery had been discussed, no details. The police were supposed to take over from there, but how events would transpire was worrying her now. Nathan arrived by her side. Carter ordered him to get the money. Nathan opened the boot. She heard him unzip the bag then zip it up.

'Solomon's waiting in the graveyard.'

Naomi could see to walk, just. She took the familiar route to the broken railing and was ordered to climb through. The stinging nettle that caught the back of her hand was the least of her problems. Nathan followed with Carter. They weaved through bushes and picked up a concrete path where they walked in silence. The memories made a powerful return as they turned onto a narrower path then filed through gravestones across the grass. The earth was soft underfoot. The scent of fresh flowers belonging to the dead, hung in the air.

'So this is where my wife's been hiding,' Nathan said, trying to break the ice with Carter, who didn't want conversation. Naomi could feel the tension between them.

Carter let go of Naomi's arm and told Nathan to guide her the rest of the way. Carter moved ahead. She couldn't see Nathan, but she felt him brutally take hold of her left arm. It was the same arm he'd lightly touched the night they'd met.

'You crossed the wrong person, Lorie. I can't even begin to understand why,' Nathan hissed in her ear. He was squeezing her arm painfully now and she was gasping and trying to pull away. 'I don't know what Vincent's got planned for you, but I'm going to enjoy watching.' He leaned closer until she could feel the warmth of his breath through the rough canvas. 'And just so you know, she beat you in every way: hotter, sexier, younger and richer. And I loved kissing her. And it didn't stop there. The hotel room on the wedding night. She was gagging for it. Pity she never got chance to tell you every sordid little detail.'

They stopped walking. Nathan stopped talking and released her by shoving her forward. Naomi's mind was on Solomon. She'd put her trust in a psychopath who couldn't be trusted. The insanity of it occurred to her about now. Where was Dan? Naomi swivelled her head until she found Vincent Solomon standing by a grave. The moon had shown up too, plus one bright star. There was a spade thrust into the loose earth at the top. Her pulse responded.

'Nathan. Good to see you again,' Solomon said, voice light and unconcerned, taking charge. 'Good day?'

'It's turning out better than it started.'

'For me too.'

'So this is where my wife is?'

'Exactly. She's listening to every word.'

Nathan sniggered. 'Carter has your money,' he said with confidence. 'If we can finish the job, I can get to bed.'

'I think we should finally put this business to bed. It's gone on long enough.'

The bag changed hands.

'How much?'

Nathan cleared his throat, stalling. 'Unless she's taken any, there should be fifty grand. If there isn't, I'll make it up, you have my word.'

A slight pause. A raised eyebrow. 'And what about your brother?'

'What about him?' Nathan shot back, rhetorically. 'Where is he?'

'Close,' Solomon said. 'Very close.'

'As close as my wife?'

'Almost.'

Naomi's heart was hammering beneath the sack, which was scratching her face. Her head felt hot and itchy. Maybe it was time to unveil herself and get the hell out of there. Maybe Nathan and Lorie had been punished enough. She found she couldn't move.

Nathan laughed and carried on. 'You haven't buried him already?'

'No, I'll bring him out. Plus, I have a little surprise for you.'

'Oh?' Nathan said, half curious, half cautious.

Naomi wondered if it was her cue to lose the mask. She hesitated because Solomon was looking in the opposite direction. From beyond a distant tree, Carter emerged with Dan and Lorie, whose head was covered with a sack. Naomi found Nathan through the eye slits. In profile, she could see the look of confusion. His eyes were narrowed and fixed on the growing figures in the moonlight. Nathan swallowed hard and said nothing.

When they were all standing together, Nathan was still staring at Lorie trying to see beyond the cover at the face that lay beneath. He barely even noticed Dan.

Solomon took the lead again. 'So, I don't think we need any introductions.'

Nathan couldn't speak.

'It's rude to stare, Nathan. Courtesy, remember. Eyes off the lady.'

'Who the hell is that?' Nathan asked, in a voice that implied he barely wanted to know.

Lorie was whimpering beneath the bag. Dan pulled it free of her head. Nathan's mouth fell open. Lorie was gagged. Eyes and nose streaming. Dan released the cloth from round her mouth.

'They told me you were dead,' Lorie sobbed, wiping her face, gasping, eyes blinking, stumbling towards Nathan. Nathan didn't move. Nobody stopped Lorie's advance as she tried to hurry into the safety of Nathan's arms. But he was a statue, stiff and unyielding. She looked into his eyes. 'Dan told me you were dead,' she repeated, desperately trying to reach him, failing. 'She stole my car and the money.'

Lorie raised her arm in Naomi's direction.

'Not quite the reception you'd expected,' Solomon said. 'Manners, Nathan, she's relieved to see you.'

Nathan was winded. He turned to Solomon in slow motion, then to Naomi. Unable to find his voice, he nodded at her vaguely.

Her moment had come. Naomi pulled the bag from the back of her neck and threw it down and shook her hair.

Nathan stared, eyes wide. Naomi stared right back. 'Hey Nathan. Been chasing ghosts all day?'

There was a silence where nobody moved. 'You?'

'Me. From the moment you stepped off that plane, you were always going to land up in this cemetery tonight, right in the spot where you sent me. I brought you here, not the other way around.'

Nathan turned to Dan. 'You . . . and her.'

'You didn't seriously think I could hurt her,' Dan said.

'I didn't think you'd get a choice,' Nathan stammered.

'There's always a choice, Nathan,' Dan threw back.

Solomon broke into applause and a small chuckle. He looked at Naomi. 'You were absolutely right. This has been very satisfying – so much so, I'd have done it for free. You've let an incredible girl go, Nathan. What were you thinking? She's beautiful. She's smart. And very soon, she'll be rich and single. You took out life insurance, isn't that right? What you don't know is that it's difficult to make a claim without a death certificate, so you'd have been struggling to claim. But, if you don't make it tonight, she's sure to get one.'

Naomi had her eye on Dan who looked anxious to step forward and say something. Naomi warned him not to, through her eyes. The only relaxed one was Solomon.

'So, what now?' Solomon said, rubbing his hands together, looking about him.

Naomi stepped forward. 'Now we call the police. I'm leaving with Dan and these two will get what they deserve.'

'Stick around for the show,' Solomon said, not a request, a new edge in his voice. 'It's early, Naomi. I'm just loosening up.'

Solomon unzipped the bag and littered the contents on the ground. Only a small amount of money fell out along with bundles of cut up newspapers bound with rubber bands.

'Tut, tut,' Solomon said, collecting five small bundles off the floor. 'Only five thousand. And this is Dan's money, isn't it? None for me.'

He strolled towards Dan and deposited the money in his hands. 'You should always pay your debts, Nathan. Rule number two.'

A pearl of sweat was betraying Nathan, slipping down one side of his forehead. Lorie tried to hold him, but he brushed her off. Solomon strode slowly towards Nathan, eyeing him carefully. Carter shifted closer to Dan who threw the money down and skipped free of Carter to Naomi's side. He firmly took hold of her hand. Solomon hadn't noticed. His whole focus was on Nathan.

'You know what this means, don't you Nathan?'

Nathan had lost the ability to speak. He twitched his head from side to side.

'Means the debt's outstanding. And the interest keeps mounting. And if you have no way of honouring it, someone's got to pay, right?'

Solomon from nowhere, produced a handgun. Nathan

stepped back, palms rising. The terror in his eyes moved Dan into action.

'No, come on,' Dan said. 'There are other ways.'

Solomon swung round and wouldn't let Dan speak. 'Don't come another step closer.'

Naomi shrugged Dan off and moved between Nathan and Solomon. She turned to Solomon, the gun close to her chest.

'Look, I thought we agreed no more violence. I paid the price for Nathan's freedom so he could be tried by law. Not this. Please, don't hurt him.'

'You got that right. *You* paid, not him.' Solomon had a chilling look in his eye, especially when he smiled as he did now. 'It was never about money. We understood that. You wanted him to suffer. I was happy to help.'

He sidestepped Naomi and put the gun to Nathan's head. Lorie screamed. Carter clamped her mouth and held her firm. Nathan drew a huge amount of air as if it might be his last. Naomi dropped to her knees. Dan fell beside her.

'Please don't hurt him. I instigated this. I'm responsible. I'll give you all the money I have,' Naomi pleaded.

'It's not about money. It's about justice.'

'This isn't just,' Naomi yelled from the ground. 'Kill me if you have to hurt someone. No one even knows I'm alive.' Naomi glared at him defiantly.

Dan threw his arms around Naomi's head to protect her. 'Naomi, no. You don't know what you're saying. I'm not going to let you –'

'You can't stop her.' Solomon said, withdrawing the gun from Nathan's head. He stepped back from the group and laughed. 'This is amazing, Nathan, isn't it? Have you ever seen a more charitable pair? It's a novelty for me, I have to admit.' He eyed Nathan carefully now. 'I always thought we'd make a great partnership,' he said to Nathan.

Nathan nodded, confused, a glint of hope in his eyes along with the fear. His expression said that he was suspicious of another chance. What was the catch?

'Maybe it's not too late. Let's solve our first problem. Interesting one, isn't it?' Solomon asked Nathan, who didn't answer. 'Two people falling over themselves to offer their own lives as a ransom. Two people whose lives mean nothing to you. I can't choose.' He held the gun out to Nathan. 'Take it. There's one bullet. You choose where to put it.'

After a delay, Nathan accepted the weapon and looked down at it like he'd never seen a gun and didn't know how to use it. He had a crazy look of euphoria though.

'One shot, Nathan. There's your wife who's in possession of all your money. She shows up alive, you're screwed. There's your brother who saved her life and betrayed you. There's even Lorie who landed you in this mess by going to see them when she should have paid me first. Big mistake.' He eased his way face-to-face with Nathan, almost nose-to-nose. 'But then there's me. And I own you now. And I want to see how you work under pressure. So make your choice. Be decisive. Grave's ready. Ten seconds.'

Nathan tried to step back and create some distance, but Solomon moved when he did, with him. Nathan's eyes flicked wildly round the group as if he was weighing up his options, one by one.

Solomon began his slow count. 'Ten, nine, eight . . . '

'Don't be stupid, Nathan,' Dan yelled. 'Put the gun down. It's over.'

Nathan pointed the gun at Dan, who glared at him, breathing hard.

'Seven, six, five.'

'Put it down,' Dan screamed, trying to lunge at him. Solomon prevented it.

'Four, three, two.'

'No,' Naomi tried to come between Dan and the gun, but Dan pushed her to one side.

'One. Time's up.'

Nathan switched direction and aimed the gun at Naomi's head.

'No,' Dan yelled, trying to break free of Solomon's grip.

'Love you, Dan,' Naomi breathed just as Nathan squeezed the trigger.

30

There was muffled gunfire. Naomi recoiled, wondering why the pain was delayed. Nathan pulled the trigger again frantically until Solomon stepped forward and took the gun off him.

Naomi flew into Dan's arms and stayed there. Solomon pushed Nathan to the floor. 'Rule number three. Avoid deception. And rule one, always remember this. Never cross Vincent Solomon.' Nathan said nothing. 'A round of blanks, Nathan. An experiment, call it a character profile.' He picked up the money off the floor and stashed it in the bag with the papers and handed it to Dan. 'Yours.'

Carter dragged Nathan and Lorie away across the grass.

Solomon turned to weigh up Dan and Naomi glued together.

'I think we're done here.'

Dan followed Vincent Solomon with his eyes, but kept protective arms right around Naomi. 'That was a pretty sick way of solving a problem.'

'Good enough for King Solomon, good enough for me.'

'What?' Dan asked.

'Naomi's a Bible basher. I'm sure she'll fill you in.' He wiped his polished shoes on the grass. 'You had to believe I was going to do it. And now you know where you stand. Now you can send him down without losing sleep.'

'I planned to anyway.'

Solomon walked right up to Dan, who was clinging to Naomi almost cheek-to-cheek. 'I read eyes all the time,' he said, searching Dan's. 'Your eyes are the type that sit in front of a lot of deep thinking; the type that can't see an old lady struggling without offering a hand. They're the type that can't turn a blind eye when something's wrong. I spared you a truckload of wasted guilt, Solomon's way. And that part was for free.' He half smiled but it didn't reach his eyes. 'In my line of business, I don't look into eyes like yours very often.'

'Change your line of business,' Dan suggested.

'I never said I enjoyed looking into eyes like yours,' Solomon said. 'No money there.'

'Nathan wouldn't be in the mess he's in if it weren't for you,' Dan said back.

Solomon's eyes narrowed. 'Yes he would. I read it in his eyes the first minute I met him. He doesn't have eyes like yours.'

Naomi watched him from the safety of Dan's chest. She didn't even try to understand this man who was turning to collect his spade like a man collects a briefcase after work.

Solomon switched his attention to Naomi and handed her a single car key. 'The police are about to get an anonymous call about a stolen car spotted near a cemetery north of the city. Same car that disappeared after a wedding two weeks ago. Keep the call anonymous, yes?' He waited, staring. Naomi nodded. 'I bought this back at a financial loss. So we're even now, you understand?' He eyed her more intently than anyone ever had. Naomi looked down at the key to her dad's Rolls-Royce and nodded gently again. 'Good. I'll leave you with the business of resurrecting yourself. You were buried just here,' he flicked his head toward the grave, 'so it's a good place to start. You won't need to look over your shoulder either of you, at least not for me.'

'Nathan's going down,' Dan said. 'If he lands you in it, we're not responsible.'

Solomon smiled. 'Nathan's small fry. He can't touch me. If he ever thought he could, it's only because I allowed it, so I could manipulate him.'

Another hard stare later, as if he wanted to imprint a silent message upon them, Vincent Solomon disappeared into the darkness.

Dan held Naomi as if he couldn't bear to let go. 'Don't ever do that to me again.'

'What?' Naomi whispered.

'Place yourself at the mercy of a lunatic.'

'Nathan?'

Dan released some tension and laughed. 'Him too.'

'No more danger, Dan,' Naomi said. 'I just want to go home – safe, boring, uneventful, blissful home.'

Dan looked at her for a long moment. 'Then what will you do?'

She sighed and thought. 'Take a rest, get to know my family again, rebuild my life.'

'Will you go back to music college?'

She shook her head. 'Only to see my good friend, Siobhan. I owe her an apology. Long story.' Dan rubbed her back. 'I can finally admit that music's not what I want to do. I can thank Nathan for that much.'

Dan looked at her some more. They held each other in silence for a long time. Eventually, Dan released his grip a little. 'What do you want?' he asked, uncertainly.

'All day today, I sat in the tree house in our front garden, waiting for someone to come out of the house so I could watch them. No one came. I knew Nathan wouldn't follow me there. I sat for hours, churning over all my old memories and trying to imagine the future.'

Dan kissed her forehead. 'So right now? I just want to hug my sister and my cat, and I want to tell my mum and dad for the first time in my life that I love them.'

Dan nodded and pulled away. 'OK.'

'I haven't finished.' Naomi dragged him back and secured her arms around his neck and studied his eyes, picturing the blueness in the dim light. 'But first, I want you to kiss me again.'

'Here?' Dan hesitated. 'In a cemetery?'

Naomi nodded. 'The dead are less scary than the living.'

Dan removed the loose strands of hair from across her eyes. The palm of his hand was warm and smooth as he took hold of her face on one side and closed his eyes. Her eyelids dropped as Dan pulled her to him and leaned forward.

'Are you sure about this?' he whispered.

She could feel his breath on her face and the pulse in his wrist fluttering against her cheek. 'Certain.'

The cemetery disappeared as Dan's lips, cool and soft, connected with hers. Slowly, tenderly, he kissed her.

Eventually, they pulled back. 'So how did this future of yours look?' Dan's voice was low.

'I couldn't picture it,' she said. 'I couldn't get beyond today and how things might work out.' Naomi withdrew something from her pocket and held out her hand. Dan looked down. Her gold necklace with the cross sat in her palm.

'I found this in Lorie's flat along with my wedding necklace.'

'Shall I put it on for you?'

'No.'

'No? I hope this doesn't mean you've lost your faith.'

'I haven't. But the necklace didn't save me, Dan.'

She tipped it into Dan's palm. 'You did. I want you to have it.'

'OK.' Dan put it into his pocket and met her eyes again. 'Did you mean it when you said you loved me?'

'It was instinct. I thought I was about to die. In a moment like that, there was no time to plan words.'

Dan tried to smile. 'I get it.'

'You don't. Look, Dan, I'm a mess. It's going to take me a while to sort through my feelings, OK?'

'Yeah. I understand. I just need to know that you don't still love Nathan.'

She shook her head. 'I loved who I thought Nathan was, which wasn't real.' She fingered his face. 'I'd have put my life on the line for anyone tonight, even Lorie.'

'They didn't deserve it.'

'Maybe, but I couldn't have lived with myself if anyone had got hurt, Dan. I don't even know the Nathan I saw tonight.'

'OK,' Dan nodded, satisfied. 'So, what was that all about, Solomon's way?'

'Solomon was a king, Old Testament, known for his wisdom. Two women came to him with a baby. Both claimed to be the mother. Solomon thought about it and offered to cut the child in half so they could share it. The fake mother told him to go ahead. The real mother begged him not to hurt the child, but to give it to the other woman. Guess who got the baby?'

'Cruel to be kind, hey? Find out which mother's the real deal?'

'Correct.'

Another silence. A breeze worked through Dan's hair. 'Does that mean I've passed the test and get the girl?'

Naomi smiled. 'Maybe. Look, you'll have to be patient with me.'

'It's my speciality.'

'Good. The way I feel at the moment, I can't promise anything long term. It's going to take a while for me to trust again. But I do have feelings for you, Dan. I can't think about facing the future without you.'

'You won't have to,' he kissed her forehead. They stood, breathing against each other in silence a few moments.

'I think I must be the only married virgin in this country right now. How messed up is that?'

Dan laughed and held her tight and loaded in her ear, 'Listen, any time you need help with that . . .' Naomi giggled. 'Ready to go home?'

She pulled back and looked into his eyes. 'Definitely.'

Hand in hand, they retraced their steps through the grass, along the narrow path, along the wider path, through the bushes, slipped through the railings. When they found the road, they also found Nathan and Lorie tied to the gates, pulling and tugging to be free, hurling abuse. The Rolls-Royce was parked close by them with papers trapped beneath the windscreen wipers.

Dan strolled up to the car and looked at the papers. It was directions and diagrams of the Hamiltons' house in Lorie's handwriting, with a number code to the garage and photocopies of the documents. It was all the proof the police would ever need that she'd betrayed the Hamiltons' trust. And it was only the beginning.

Dan replaced the papers and turned to Naomi and Nathan.

'Police are on their way. It'll go better at the trial if you tell the truth for once in your lives,' he said. 'Naomi's going home now, but tomorrow, she'll be going public. One hell of a story. I advise you to make sure your side of it matches hers.'

They were yelling by now, both of them. Dan turned away and took Naomi to his car and placed her in the passenger seat like she was made of china, and closed the door. Two minutes later down a lonely country lane, a police car passed them, acting on a tipoff.

It was way past one in the morning when they got to Alderley Edge and turned into the Hamiltons' driveway. Dan switched the headlights off and rolled to the front of the house as quietly as possible and cut the engine. Nothing moved downstairs. A light was on upstairs. Annabel's room.

'We don't want to shock them,' he told Naomi.

'It's inevitable.'

Dan took his phone out of his pocket and asked for the number. Naomi sat, thinking her heart might explode, trying to draw it to mind. She gave him the digits. He pressed them with his forefinger and held the phone to his ear.

It rang six times. Naomi could hear it clearly from Dan's left side. Annabel picked up. Her voice was low and lifeless.

'Hello?'

'Annabel?'

'Yes. Who is this?'

'Sorry for ringing at this hour, but I have something important to tell you.'

A pause. 'Who is this?'

'It's Dan Stone. I'm Nathan's brother and I've come with some very good news for you. I'm sitting outside the house right now. Please don't be startled.'

Naomi looked up and saw the curtain twitch upstairs.

'OK. What news?' Annabel said, without enthusiasm.

'Are you sitting down?'

Another short wait. 'I am now.'

'I have someone with me who wants to talk to you.'

Dan leant over the gearstick and soundlessly kissed Naomi's cheek. There were tears in his eyes when he straightened up. He handed her the phone and Naomi held it to her ear and found it hard to speak. Her throat ached.

'Hello?' Annabel said, dazed.

Dan nodded once, encouraging Naomi to find her voice.

She did, with tears sliding down her face. 'Annie?' she said in a gush, clutching Dan's fingers for support. 'Annie, it's me. I'm home.'

The End

Thank you for reading Either Side of Midnight. I hope you enjoyed reading it as much as I enjoyed writing it. As yet, I'm an independent author and I rely on readers to talk about my books and review them. This is how the word spreads. Please review Either Side of Midnight. Thank you so much.

Please visit my website <u>www.torideclare.com</u> where you can sign up for my newsletter and hear about my current projects and other books.

Book 2

The Darkness Visible

Prologue

On a bitter late-October morning at nine forty-two GMT, with strangled light feeding through the venetian blinds at a large bay window overlooking an impeccably-kept garden, a person pulled back an office chair and sat down at a light oak desk. He deposited his mug of Brazilian filtered coffee onto an aluminium coaster and rolled up the sleeves of a new shirt that was as crisp and white as the frosted lawn beyond the window.

He dragged a laptop towards him, booted it up while he consulted his watch and noiselessly sipped his coffee, then added a carefully selected password and logged on to the internet. His Apple Mac took just over a second to obey the instruction, after which he positioned both hands over the keypad and suppressed a smile. The world had shrunk to a screen fourteen inches by eight. Everything was within reach. There was barely a pocket of the planet that couldn't be picked.

He highlighted the toolbar and added a website address one deliberate letter at a time: www.Flightradar24.com. The screen threw up a one-dimensional map of the world with small diagrams of yellow planes dotting the earth, with huge clusters smothering the major cities. He was watching all the world's flights. As they happened. Right then. On the top left of the screen, two tiny boxes stacked up. One showed a negative sign, the other a positive. He lined up the cursor and clicked the positive sign until the globe expanded and the USA and Russia vanished either side, leaving Europe centre screen with a hundred little planes swarming the UK, and a thousand others choking the continent.

He pinned the left button down and dragged the planet right to left, moving east and down, across Europe, through Turkey and the Middle East, and out into the Arabian Sea. He slowed now and plunged into the Indian Ocean where a solitary plane was flying solo across a watery chasm of apparent nothingness.

'Hello.'

He returned to the tiny box and clicked the positive sign and the area blew up to uncover the Seychelles, and further north, the Maldives, with the line of the equator scoring the bottom ring of the islands. Upon the latter, he focussed his attention. One more click and the capital, Male, revealed itself by way of a red splodge, indicating the position of the only airport in the region. The yellow plane shifted economically every few seconds, eating the small gap. He clicked on the plane itself and it turned red and threw up some information. Emirates flight EK0020 from Manchester to Male with a one-hour stop in Dubai. Aircraft: Boeing 777. Flight time: thirteen hours forty-five minutes plus an additional hour to refuel in Dubai. Expected landing time: 14.55 local time. Status: on time.

He checked his watch through habit, though clocking the time would only have needed a flash glance to a corner of the screen. The Maldives were five hours ahead. 14.55 translated to 09.55 GMT. It was 09.44. Ten minutes of flight time remaining. There was the option of tracing the journey so far, which he clicked to fill time. A perfect green arc plotted the line of the flight path from North West England to the west side of the Maldives where the plane now hovered above countless square miles of ocean.

Another click and he got a view of the cockpit. Out of interest he checked the speed, the altitude, the view from the aircraft. He opened another window and looked at average temperatures for the Maldives in October – the wet season. It typically enjoyed eight hours of sunshine a day, punctuated with rain, which didn't pull down the temperature at all. Highs pushed twenty-eight degrees with a difference of only three degrees at night.

'Nice,' he muttered, returning to the flight while he drew deep gulps of coffee and pushed back in his chair and watched the plane plummet another couple of hundred feet.

He finished the last half inch of coffee and returned the mug to the aluminium coaster, positioning it exactly centre. Then he linked his fingers behind his head and stretched out his legs and decided that the house needed some heat. The plane dipped further. Six minutes to landing.

'Showtime.'

PART ONE

1

Naomi Hamilton had her cheek squashed against the window as the plane descended through swirls of cloud towards a cluster of islands that looked like scattered pebbles in the sea. The plane clunked and slowed as the wheels rolled down and the final layer of mist cleared. The view from the air was an exotic display of dazzling shades of pale blue and turquoise amid a wider picture of deep indigo.

The islands took shape and gained detail. Each one was unique in size and shape – some perfect spheres, others small strips of land painted in vibrant oil colours in the middle of a very blue sea.

Dan Stone lifted the armrest and leaned over Naomi as the islands unfolded beneath them in all their glory and the plane descended and the water gained froth and yachts, then life and motion. Dan took her hand, knitted his fingers inside hers and placed his free hand on the top of her leg. Out of earshot of the middle-aged man who was dozing, mouth open, on the aisle-seat next to Dan, he leaned into her hair. His fringe tickled her cheek. His breath was warm against the air-conditioned cabin and smelled of the mint he was sucking to relieve the pressure in his ears.

'I want you so badly,' he whispered, depositing a noiseless, lingering kiss beneath her ear.

Naomi smiled and Dan squeezed her hand. 'Ditto.' They fell into silence for a few moments, until Naomi said, 'I can't believe we're actually here.'

'Me neither.'

'Have you ever seen anything so stunning?'

'Never.'

It was the way his voice hung on the word that made her glance over her shoulder to find that Dan was looking directly at her through those crystal blue eyes of his, set in an intense expression. His hair was dark and straight. He wore it long on top and short around the back and sides and was always pushing it out of his eyes. A smile played on his lips.

Naomi turned her back on the islands and twisted her body to face him. She tipped the side of her head against her seat and Dan shifted back and mirrored her position on his seat. Dan was never certain how tall he was, but he reckoned around, six one, six-two. He had broad shoulders, big hands and long fingers. Naomi reached out with one hand and touched the tips of Dan's fingers with the tips of hers. They sat gazing at each other, lips a few centimetres apart, legs shoved uncomfortably together.

'Soon,' she quietly told Dan.

'Not soon enough.'

'Would you two get a room,' came an ungentle voice from behind them. Annabel Hamilton, Naomi's non-identical twin, was standing and grinning down from the seat behind, her luscious blonde hair tied up in a high pony. It was Annabel's birthday. She wore a yellow badge which said, *birthday girl*. Naomi's birthday was the next day. They were born either side of midnight.

'Keep your voice down,' Naomi said, tilting her head up, feeling a flush of colour in her cheeks. The man next to Dan was beginning to stir.

Annabel's face was pale, her eyes a little bloodshot. She'd slept for half the journey. 'Get a room,' she repeated more gently, before dropping out of view.

Dan said quietly, 'We intend to.'

Annabel shot up again. 'About time.'

She was pulled down sharply this time by Joel Martin, her long-term boyfriend. Naomi could see him through the gap in the seats, his long, fair hair flopping about in his eyes.

Joel said, 'You're supposed to have your seatbelt on, you naughty girl.'

An air steward appeared and echoed Joel's words, 'Could you put your seatbelt on please? Armrest down, sir.' He was glaring at Dan now.

Annabel giggled again and Naomi grinned at Dan as he pulled the barrier between them. Naomi turned and looked through the window to monitor progress.

The captain said, 'Cabin crew, seats for landing.'

The water was fast approaching. The horizon – two almost identical shades of blue – was a line across the window now and Naomi couldn't see how the plane was going to land safely. Dan's hand was warm and made tiny sweeping movements across the top of her leg. He rested his chin on Naomi's shoulder and they held hands and watched the rest of the descent in silence.

The sea was rising to meet the undercarriage of the plane, which was unnerving when scattered islands dotted the sea and none were equipped for a landing. Finally, Dan pointed out a cluttered island that was in view right ahead and had buildings instead of palm trees. It was the capital, Male. The plane wasn't lining up with it. A hundred yachts and boats zipped along the coastline trailing lashings of cream.

The city was level in the window now. Dan squeezed

Naomi's hand firmly as the plane touched down gracefully on a slice of land adjacent to Male that was nothing more than a runway and a few airport buildings.

They collected their luggage and exited the building to be met by brilliant sunlight. To leave a chilled country one day and step into summer the next, seemed miraculous – like rising from the dead and being reborn. There was a short walk to a wooden jetty that had a floating plane at the end of it. The sun was radiating pleasant heat in an azure sky, fanned by a warm wind. The seaplane's engine chugged while it waited; the whole patch of water between the two islands was an artery of passing traffic as the capital collected and scattered holidaymakers all over the Maldives.

Reluctant to part with Joel's hand, Annabel climbed aboard the plane first, and Dan followed with Naomi. A handful of people filed in behind them and fastened seatbelts, and the plane skimmed the water and took off in search of the final destination, which was reached exactly thirty-four minutes later.

Conrad Maldives Rengali Island was actually a pair of idyllic islands about six-hundred metres apart, joined at one end by a narrow wooden bridge. Annabel and Joel's choice of accommodation was a beach villa on the bigger island with a private tropical garden and a shower room that merged with the house but had no roof. Naomi and Dan's place was across the water on the slimmer finger of land over the long wooden bridge that clung on to the bigger island like an umbilical cord. At the furthest tip in a secluded corner, overlooked by nothing at all, sat two luxury water villas a pleasing distance apart. The furthest one, theirs, was out on a long wooden limb and was suspended over the ocean on white stilts, with panoramic views of the lagoon and coral reef.

The plane touched down on water and was tied to the

jetty by a man who'd climbed out of the plane while it was still skiing. A small welcome committee was waiting on the beach, dressed in white, playing primitive music. Having stepped into a kind of heavenly paradise filled with exotic scents and the kind of colours seen only in Disney films, they made their way to Conrad reception area where a small, smiling man held an arm out to lead them outside again.

Having made plans to meet up with Annabel and Joel for dinner later on, Dan and Naomi said a temporary farewell and followed the man while he loaded their luggage onto a strange-looking open car and drove them to a jetty where they caught a ferry across to the quieter island. They emerged onto a wooden deck which sat on powder-white sands. A small man in a blue tunic was waiting for them. He greeted them warmly and pulled their cases a short distance across the sand, until they picked up a wooden path.

Dan and Naomi followed hand in hand as their luggage clattered across the bridge in front of them. A warm wind gently pushed them from behind. They were shown to a glass front door on the deserted edge of the island. The man stood the two cases side by side and unlocked the front door and invited them to enter first.

Naomi pressed cautiously forward onto slabs of marble tiles with Dan close behind. Beyond a small hallway was an open-plan sitting area with a huge glass panel in the centre of the floor, surrounded by padded seating. Glass doors on the outside wall had been thrown open. Sunshine flooded in, inviting them outside. They could see the bedroom, parallel to the sitting room through a big open archway. In the bedroom were matching glass doors on the same outside wall, opening onto the same wooden deck. There were no internal doors in the place so far.

'Wow,' Dan uttered into the room.

Naomi added, 'It's stunning.'

The small man couldn't have looked more proud if he'd designed and built the place himself. Dan slid an arm around Naomi's waist as they wandered, speechless, into the main bedroom where the beaming man had moved ahead to demonstrate the capabilities of a huge circular bed which could electronically rotate to watch the sun rise and set. That done, the man headed outside onto the private wooden deck to point out the sun loungers, a table, a whirlpool and a swimming pool that teetered on the very brink of the deck above the ocean. A wooden staircase beside the pool plunged into the ocean, which shifted smoothly around the second rung, and rose, he told them, to the fourth rung when the tide was in.

Naomi stood, aware of Dan's hand in the small of her back, the sea breeze rousing her hair. The water was pristine; the air clean. The water gurgled like a baby. It was possible to filter it out and listen to absolutely nothing. The sun was unrestrained. A few clouds were pinned into the sky, unmoving, and there was an unimpeded view of miles of empty shallow water, with a tide bubbling a fringe of froth onto the reef in the distance.

They had a brief tour of the rest of the place, which had another bedroom and bathroom. The man told them about the butler service and the famous people who'd stayed there, wished them a happy visit, bowed once, then left them alone. Dan locked the door. Naomi was looking out to sea from the sitting room, feeling strangely tearful when Dan returned in silence. He took her hand and they strolled through the bedroom and into the bathroom just off it, which had no wall or door, and had a round Jacuzzi bath in front of a clear-glass window with another spectacular open view.

Dan pulled her in front of him. The peace and seclusion of the place was a powerful presence. He cupped her face in his hands.

'So.'

She looked directly into his eyes and smiled. 'So,' she replied in a breathy whisper.

'The Darkness Visible' is available now from outlets or from my website www.torideclare.com

Printed in Great Britain
by Amazon

45664052R00267